Praise for *The Err*

"Kate Innes's glorious ... ... with the best of Pat Bracew ... ... itter immersion in an intric: ...
Manda Scott – autho

"The Errant Hours is a beautifully crafted epic tale of adventure, love and courage, worthy of the greatest Medieval Minstrels. A perfect read around a crackling fire."
Karen Maitland – author of *Company of Liars*

"A skilful mix of stories and an intricate and very gripping narrative. I enjoyed it immensely."
Dr Henrietta Leyser –author of *Medieval Women*

"An utterly delightful novel that kept me reading into the small hours. Very Enjoyable."
Helen Hollick – Historical Novel Society

Praise for *All the Winding World*

Rich, intricate and full of ordinary women finding power in a society that seeks always to rob them of autonomy. A fantastic testament to the power of love."
Manda Scott

"A brilliant sequel to *The Errant Hours*. The resourceful and ingenious Illesa has become one of my favourite fictional characters. A skilfully woven tapestry of historical fact and captivating story-telling that leaves the reader begging for more adventures."
Karen Maitland

"This is such a gripping tale that I read it almost in one sitting, and yet the story is well grounded in the realities of medieval life. 'All the Winding World' is a great achievement."
Dr Henrietta Leyser

"This skillful crafting of and immersion in a brutal, beautiful, breathing world rife with treachery, disease, and dangers unseen will enchant readers new to the period and delight those who know it well."
Misty Urban – Historical Novel Society

Having lived and worked on three continents, Kate Innes has settled with her family near Wenlock Edge in England, and it is this landscape which inspires much of her writing.

Trained as an archaeologist, teacher and museologist, Kate now writes fiction and poetry for children and adults, as well as performing, undertaking commissions and leading workshops.

www.kateinneswriter.com

Medieval Arrowsmith Trilogy:

The Errant Hours
All the Winding World
Wild Labyrinth

Children's Fiction:

Greencoats

Poetry:

Flocks of Words

Wild Labyrinth

KATE INNES

Kate Innes

Mindforest Press

Published in Great Britain by Mindforest Press
www.kateinneswriter.com

Copyright © Kate Innes 2021

ISBN 978-0-9934837-8-3
A catalogue record for this book is available from the British
Library.

Set in Garamond
Cover design by MA Creative http://www.macreative.co.uk
Maps by James Wade https://www.stclairwade.com

Printed and bound in Great Britain by Biddles Books

Cover image: British Library Arundel MS 98 f. 85v –
Map of Jericho in 14th Century Farhi Bible by Elisha ben
Avraham Crescas from Wikimedia Commons – both in the
public domain
Back cover monkey image: British Library Add MS 36684 f.125r
– a public domain image

For Carrie

and

For Claire

*"To see a candle's light,
one must take it into a dark place."*

Ursula K. LeGuin – The Farthest Shore

And as the house is crinkled to and fro
And has such complex ways to go –
For it is shaped as a maze is wrought –
I've a remedy for that in my thought,
That with a clew of twine the way he's gone
The same way he may return anon,
Following ever the thread till out he'll come.

'The Legend of Ariadne' from
The Legend of Good Women by Geoffrey Chaucer

Some events within the Burnel family and the English Court between *All the Winding World* **and** *Wild Labyrinth*

August 1297: Sir Richard Burnel sailed to Flanders with King Edward I, having been threatened, as were many other knights, with the confiscation of all his lands and property if he refused to serve with the King overseas alongside his Flemish allies in his continuing war with Philip IV of France. Impoverished by wars in Gascony and Scotland, as well as many years of high taxation, the barons of England rebelled against the King's demand for service. The force that arrived in Flanders was too little, too late. Sir Richard returned with the King on the 14th March, 1298, the expedition having achieved very little except the waste of vast amounts of money.

January 1299: Illesa suffered a late miscarriage, losing a daughter – Margaret. While she was recovering, Christopher was sent to the household of Thomas Corbet, son of the Baron of Caus, to be trained as a squire.*

June 1299: A peace agreement was reached between England and France, and the English King duly married Margaret of France in September 1299, but King Philip still would not hand over Gascony.

After 1302: Edward Burnel (1286 – 1315) heir of Sir Philip Burnel (who squandered all of Chancellor Robert's wealth and property) was married to Aline, daughter of Sir Hugh le Despenser. He became the Lord of the Barony of Holdgate, well-known for his costly, elaborate displays of heraldry on the battlefield in Scotland.

April-May 1303: a disgruntled ex-soldier and several Westminster monks tunnelled into and robbed King Edward's treasure house under Westminster Abbey whilst the King was engaged in battles in Scotland. Priceless relics and jewels were smuggled out. Many were never recovered.

20th May, 1303: After his devastating defeat by Flemings at the Battle of Courtrai in 1302, and the revolt against him by the citizens of Bordeaux, Philip IV eventually signed a treaty to return Gascony to English rule.

August 1305: Sir William Wallace was executed at Smithfield, near the site of Saint Bartholomew's Hospital

10th February, 1306:   Robert the Bruce participated in the killing of John Comyn III before the high altar of Greyfriars Church in Dumfries. Comyn had been a Guardian of Scotland and a contender for the throne. His murder and the desecration of the holy site enraged King Edward I, who began to prepare his army to destroy Robert the Bruce.

* indicates fictional event

The Hours

Matins	one or two hours before dawn
Prime (first hour)	daybreak
Tierce (third hour)	approximately 9:00 am
Sext (sixth hour)	approximately midday
Nones (ninth hour)	approximately 3:00 pm
Vespers	early evening, approximately 6:00 pm
Compline	darkness/sleep, approximately 9:00 pm

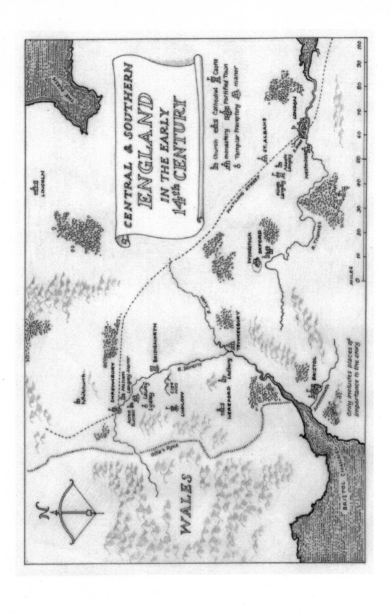

CENTRAL & SOUTHERN
ENGLAND
IN THE EARLY
14th CENTURY

☩ Church ⛪ Cathedral 🏰 Castle
🏛 monastery 🏘 Fortified Town
☩ Templar Meeting 🏠 manor

Only includes places of
importance to the story

WALES

N

MILES
0   10   20   30   40   50   60   70   80   90   100

LINCOLN

SHREWSBURY
BRIDGNORTH
The Priory
Legacy Manor
LUDLOW
R. Severn
HEREFORD
Ledbury

TEWKESBURY
BRISTOL

BRISTOL CHANNEL
Offa's Dyke

WOODSTOCK
OXFORD

WATLING STREET

ST. ALBANS

LONDON

Nottingham

R. Thames

Part One

Prologue

Sunday the 13th September, 1299
27th year of the reign of King Edward I
Hereford Cathedral

This day I finished charting the continents, and, to show my skill, I drew the centre of the world – Jerusalem's wall encompassing the dome of the Holy Sepulchre. I did not make much of it. All its magnificence is under that flattened roof. The limner will come at the end and add the touches of paint. 'From this navel the whole world will spring,' said Bishop Swinfield as he inspected my work. It is not so, I wanted to say. It does not spring, it is sweated out, squeezed out like blood by thorns. This world is not a clear spring, rather the tortured, redeeming blood of Christ that flowed down in that very spot under the cross, filling the skull of Adam below and spreading out into the wide world through the surging rivers and the terrible savage races.

But I said nothing. He would not understand. He is merely viewing this map as an attraction, to bring more pilgrims. The donations are down. He is a man of numbers and columns – a man who knows you have to spend to gain. To him it is only necessary there is a bright marvel above the altar by the new shrine. It need not be true. Perhaps it is my fear of this that makes me so angry when he sweeps his arm, pointing here and there on the expanse of whitest calf skin. 'Where,' he wants to know, 'will Hereford be?'

I pointed to the lower left-hand corner, and he looked disappointed, as if he thought it should be placed just below Jerusalem. Hereford as great as Calvary! I tried not to laugh. I think he does little study. The Bishop thinks only of his See, only of his dear, nearly canonised Bishop Thomas Cantilupe. It will be more than a year before I reach England on the map, and of all the places on this island, I will be drawing my own home first, exile that I am.

Before then, I must plot all the wanderings of the Jews – and they are many. The great cities and islands of the middle sea, the rivers that come from Paradise, the Pharos lighthouse

3

made by giants and the grain stores of Joseph. I must show the mountains of Horeb, of Ararat and Sinai. 'Do not forget to draw Clee Hill,' he said in parting. And I nodded, yes, of course, the great Clee Hill must be included. But as the Bishop turned to go, his deacon saw my expression, and now he will be watching me all the time. This is what happened in Lincoln. As soon as they had the slightest suspicion of my disobedience, they never stopped pursuing me until they flayed my soul and whipped me out of town, all the way to this other side of England, where I was to do 'a great work' as penance. I will make it so, but these simple clerics do not understand what that demands. This work will keep me here; I would not abandon it like a mewling infant for someone else to abuse. When it's done, I can leave and find her, if she still lives.

But I mustn't let these thoughts turn into words, as I did today. It was to no one of significance fortunately: an injured country knight and his wife, come to beg a miracle from the yet to be sainted Thomas. His wife was so engrossed in looking at the display of offerings, she walked straight into me as I was leaving the scriptorium. She promised to say a special prayer for me as compensation, despite my insistence that I did not need the big toe on my left foot for my work.

But she persisted, and, as she made her appeals, I saw that her eyes were the same hue as those of my beloved. I found myself telling her my name, and she claimed it was the same as that of her husband. He had but one eye, like the Agriophagi that live near Mount Hesperus, but he was shrewd. That eye seemed to share my consternation at his wife's eager belief. She asked if I'd witnessed any miracles, and I had to admit I'd seen none, having only arrived two months before and being busy directing the preparation of the great cloth of the world. I could see both disappointment and intrigue in her face, and that I would not get away from her questioning unless I fell down dead. But her husband put a stop to it: 'We will go and ask the saint in all good faith, wife; that is all we can do.'

Then she began worrying about the poverty of their offering. It was her eyes that opened my hoard of memories. To distract myself, I stood by the shrine and recounted some of the stories I'd been told when I arrived. I was careful not to look at the woman, but only at the knight, who, as well as lacking an eye, was cursed with one useless leg and a scar that pulled at his reticent mouth. I explained where the altar would stand and what the map would show – how the entire world would be there to glorify the faith and service of Bishop Thomas – much as everyone on earth visited the shrine of Saint Thomas the Martyr in Canterbury. I wanted to justify the hope in her eyes.

And I think in all this rambling speech of glory and miracles, I spoke of the hanged man brought back to life, and of the possibility that all those things we have lost might be restored to us. For a moment I believed. Then I bowed to them and left, feeling like a simpleton. Days in silence and then it rushes out – rubbish and foolishness flowing like the Styx.

My beloved is lost to me. At least half of me knows this.

Chapter I

Sunday the 22nd May, 1306
The 34th year of the reign of King Edward I
Westminster Abbey
Tierce

Illesa turned to stare at the young woman who had just jabbed her in the small of the back. The woman was wearing more jewels than was wise in a crowd. She didn't meet Illesa's gaze but turned to the prosperous man at her side, possibly her husband, and whispered in his ear.

It wasn't what the overdressed, spoiled girl expected. She'd probably been promised the ceremony would take place with full pageantry and solemnity, much earlier, and that many rich nobles would admire her. But as it was, Westminster Abbey Church was crammed to bursting with an impatient crowd, and there continued to be no sign of the King or the Prince of Wales – nor of the hundreds of men yet to be consecrated to God and the King and then given their spurs. Richard had suspected as much and spared Joyce the ordeal. Thankfully she was safe at their lodgings in the Prior's guest house, eating a good meal.

To knight nearly three hundred at once was a farce. It was impossible to see anything, and, when the young men arrived, the pushing would be even worse. Illesa turned to William. He was keeping her from being trampled by the crowd behind, his mouth set in disapproval.

"Let's go back to Richard," she shouted above the din.

He barely nodded and began pushing people out of the way. She moved in his wake, trying not to touch him. The aisle benches were crowded. Sir Richard was squeezed between a large sweating man, whose belly had escaped from the confines of an ornate belt, and an ancient nun.

He looked up glumly.

"Shall we go?"

"How ridiculous." Illesa bent towards him. "We just can't see anything from there so —"

A great door groaned open on disused hinges. Trumpets blared and the crowd surged towards the west end. The fat man launched himself off the bench and barreled past, knocking Illesa off balance. William's hand gripped her shoulder — pulled her upright. She clung briefly to his arm, then squeezed in next to Richard on the bench.

"Someone will be crushed and killed," she muttered. But Richard hadn't noticed. He was trying to stretch out a cramp in his leg. Another sound floated above the din — chanting. The monks of Westminster Abbey had filed into the choir. The crowd quietened a little.

"We'll never see what's going on in this mêlée," Richard said, leaning forward, hands on his knees.

Illesa rose to her feet.

"Not sitting down, certainly. Surely it will become more ordered when the King arrives?"

He snorted in derision.

Someone near the door was shouting:

"The Prince, the Prince of Wales!"

All Illesa could see was a standard of gold and red lions moving jerkily above the heads of the people, down the nave. She went nearer, joining the back of the crowd.

"The King will arrive last," a man beside her grumbled. "We'll have all the nobles first. And maybe a few bishops."

Illesa looked down at her hands involuntarily. The first bishop she'd met had been the Bishop of Bath and Wells — Robert Burnel. She'd kissed his sapphire ring before discovering that he was her father. She'd lied to him so that she could marry Richard. But he had lied more, and for longer, about her. He'd been a master of schemes and strategy. Perhaps the new Bishop or the new Chancellor were here. They might succeed at doing half of what her father had done — and do it badly.

Whoever was processing in was taking a long time about it.

A wave of noise, like some raucous flock of birds, came from the great west door, and despite Illesa's misgivings, the hair stood up on her arms at the blast of trumpets. Presumably the knights were moving down the nave. It was more like a tournament than a solemn ritual, and Christopher would be hating it. He'd want silence and prayer to express his dedication and devotion, not a riot. And his squire would be gaping like a trout, as he always did.

Illesa pushed between the two people in front of her. She could see the helmet of one of the guards holding back the crowds but nothing more. A woman in an embroidered surcoat stepped back on her toes. Illesa turned sideways and tried to edge in front as a long line of extravagant banners floated towards the chancel. It was no use. The woman stood on her foot again, this time harder.

William caught her sleeve. Somehow he had found her.

"Come." He had to shout in her ear. "There's a vantage point."

Illesa followed him again, the crowd closing in on their space like the teeth of a trap. She stopped to take a breath by the bench.

"Where is Richard? We'll miss the start of the ceremony."

William raised his eyebrows at her.

"My life wouldn't be worth living should that happen. I'm taking you to Richard. You'll be able to see more than the angels above." He headed towards the south transept, staying close to the wall, moving in his characteristic subtle way, like a shadow filling each area of dark between the light shafts. Wafts of incense drifted across the bright space. She stumbled after him towards a small door at the far end of the transept. He held it open for her. "Up there."

"Are we allowed? Isn't it only for the monks of Westminster?" She looked around. No one was watching them – all attention on the overwhelming display of pageantry.

"This doesn't link to the cloister. It's a closed passage. Come." He stepped into the stairwell, and when she followed, he leant across her and closed the door. For a moment they were almost touching, their breath mingling in the cold dark space, then he started up the narrow spiral.

Small windows gave enough light to see how steep it was – and William's legs above her. She hitched up her skirts and started climbing.

"How did you get Richard up these stairs?"

William's footsteps didn't slow.

"Stick and sweetmeat. But mainly stick."

The close stones echoed her harsh breathing. Sweat dripped down her back. They must be as high as the roof by now. She paused and looked up. William had stopped in a doorway a few steps further on.

"Crouch down here in case they think you're a Scot wanting to shoot an arrow through the King's heart."

He went ahead of her, crawling along like a hedgehog.

"William!" she hissed.

But he didn't turn or slow down. Her gown was not designed for this. It was a pale green silk kirtle, bought specially for the occasion. She gathered it up in one hand. The passage was narrow; the only protection from a long drop to the tiled floor a low parapet wall and colonnade of arches. She couldn't see anything ahead except the soles of William's shoes and the roll of his buttocks under his hose.

He always got her into undignified situations. Nonetheless she couldn't stop the terrible imaginings. The desire for him had come on like a sudden disease, an illness of the soul, in the years after Margaret had been born dead. As if the Devil had heard her prayers for one more child and had chosen to corrupt even this holy wish. The thought of him made her hot, brought blood to her cheeks. No matter how often she prayed for the temptation to leave her, it remained. Herbs and amulets were useless. She daren't be alone with him.

William had stopped. He was on his knees, looking over the parapet.

"You can stand up now. Stay with Richard by the column, and you'll see the whole ceremony." His voice was flat, as it had been whenever he addressed her since the Feast of the Resurrection. As if he were speaking to a wall.

The narrow passage had opened up into a wide gallery. Servants and retainers were hanging from the columns, peering down like boys secretly climbing apple trees. A short man picking his teeth under a stained, felt cap greeted William familiarly. Probably a groom. It was not the company they ought to be keeping, but Richard cared less and less about such things. Or anything. His strength was sapped by constant pain, his mind by worry. And instead of being his support, his wife was unfaithful to him in her mind, goaded by unclean thoughts day and night.

9

William was already laughing with the groom, sharing some easy jest, his expression open and good humoured. Soon he would have whatever information about the army Richard had required him to get. He was irresistible.

She turned her back on him and crossed herself.

A strong voice intoned the prayer to Saint Edward the Confessor. She leant carefully over the wall, searching the men and their heraldry.

"There he is," Richard said, pointing to the far end of the group.

She squinted at the distant assembly of men, dressed in loose tunics, waiting to be belted and equipped. It was hard to hear the prayer above the prattle. Illesa thought she could distinguish Christopher's bare, brown head from the angle of his body, the hunch of his shoulders.

She reached out for Richard's arm, looking into his eye. The sadness there was even deeper than usual. He knew too much about the brutality Christopher would face – knew also that if he hadn't agreed to send his son to Scotland, the King would once again have seized their manor. She cast her eyes down to find something to distract him in the pageant below.

"Look!" She tapped his shoulder and pointed. The floor of the chancel seemed to be made of the heavens, worked in radiant stone. Spheres of brightness whirling below, rather than above.

"That'll have cost more than the wealth of everyone gathered here today," Richard muttered, but he looked at it with attention.

It was hard to make out the full pattern, as several monks and a bishop were standing on it. The centre was a deep red orb with golden bands that shimmered like glass and rippled like a pond. A ribbon of light embedded with blue stars surrounded it, and swirling around that, in a line of perpetual motion, were four smaller orbs embedded in deep green and red, as elaborate as any embroidery.

Something touched her arm, and Illesa jolted back.

"You're not an angel." William released her sleeve. "So don't try to fly."

She'd been leaning out too far, had almost lost her balance. Her face burned; she leant back against the column and stared at the window tracery above, just to avoid his eyes. Beside her, Richard looked blankly down at the crowd, oblivious. William had already returned to his new friend, head tilted to hear him better.

Yet another fanfare, and a company of royalty processed in from the transept – the King wearing his iron crown, followed by the Prince and several retainers, including a very gaudily dressed courtier holding the royal cape.

"Just look at Gaveston; he dishonours the King by his display." Richard pointed at the overdressed retainer. "He looks more like a tapestry than a man." He peered over a bit further. "Thank God the Earl of Lincoln is here. I need to speak to him after all this madness."

The Queen and several court ladies arrived next. They were all placed on the swirling pavement, making a scene of such varied and intense colour, it was almost overwhelming. The King sat on the gilt throne – the Prince at his right hand. Beside the Abbot, a cantor began to lead the assembly in the words of the Psalm:

Hear my cry, O God, listen to my prayer.
From the ends of the earth I call to you,
I call as my heart grows faint;
lead me to the rock that is higher than I.
I long to dwell in your tent for ever and take refuge in the shelter of your
wings.
For you have heard my vows, O God –

The knights suddenly shouted the last line before continuing in the stunned silence of the assembly.

You have given me the heritage of those who fear your name.
Increase the days of the king's life, his years for many generations –

They roared out the last line again.

Richard's mouth twisted in a smile.

"The Earl of Lincoln must have planned that," he whispered. "Always one for the rousing psalm."

May he be enthroned in God's presence for ever, appoint your love and faithfulness to protect him.

"The King loves a bit of arse-licking," William hissed behind them.

"Shhhh!"

Then will I ever sing praise to your name and fulfil my vows day after day. *

The knights finished, their exultant faces raised to the roof – and Illesa could finally see Christopher's face, as joyful as the rest. She gripped Richard's hand.

"He is glad to be with his fellows," she said. "Perhaps he will make some allies at last."

Richard put his gloved hand over hers on the parapet.

"Perhaps. He will certainly need them."

Chapter II

Westminster Hall
Nones

Westminster Hall was almost bursting. It was impossible to find Richard and William in the midst of the loud, sweating crowd. A gust of fresh air cooled Illesa's face. At least someone had had the sense to throw open the large doors. She pulled Joyce towards the east wall.

"We'll wait here until William finds us." Joyce was flushed. In her new tunic and kirtle with her hair oiled into long waves, this pulsing, indifferent crowd was not what she'd been looking forward to. "It'll be better once they bring in the food and the entertainment begins." She gave Joyce's hand a squeeze.

Joyce scowled and pulled it free.

"We should have stayed with Christopher. He'd know where to get the best view," she muttered, turning away.

"I told you – we aren't allowed to be with him. He's in the company of the Corbets, and they will be seated separately, alongside the FitzAlans and maybe the Despensers."

She ought to feel proud that her son had achieved knighthood at the age of twenty-one – when many were so much older. But the reason why the knights were being dubbed so quickly, and in such numbers, was clear. They were fodder for the Scottish battlefields. If Christopher made it out alive, she'd be grateful – even if he had not achieved the glory he sought. Christopher longed for a return of fortune, of status and pride for the Burnels. It was impossible to reason with him about the benefits of a quiet life away from the court.

"Look! Something's happening."

Joyce was shaking Illesa's arm and pointing at the dais half-way up the wide stairway. A horn sounded, and Joyce gripped her very hard.

"It's the herald, darling. The nobles will start arriving now."

"I can't see anything," Joyce moaned.

"You'll be able to see them come in at the top of the stairs. Look at the banners – that will tell you who's arrived. I should

13

think it will be the King first with the Queen. They will stand up there so you can admire them."

"But we're so far away! Can't we get any closer?" She pulled Illesa's arm. "There's space over there."

"No, Joyce. We'll stay here. We don't want to be trapped in the crowd." She hadn't told Joyce about the death of the knight in the Abbey that morning. He'd fallen during the pandemonium when the warhorses had been brought in to control the crowd surging into the band of newly-made knights. Perhaps he'd had an injury and wasn't able to move out of the way. From the triforium, Illesa had seen him collapse, watched the monks check his breath and lift him away. "Crowds are like elephants, they barely notice the things they crush."

"You've never even seen an elephant," Joyce retorted under her breath. She stood as tall as she could, still not the same height as her mother, another source of irritation.

Illesa took a deep breath.

"There – the King and the Queen have arrived. You can see them perfectly." Joyce was already staring raptly at the brightly arrayed figures. Even though he was sixty paces away, Illesa could see how old the King had become, not bent, but haggard and thin, unsteady on his long legs. Queen Margaret was covered in red and gold drapery so dazzling it was difficult to make out her face.

"Curtsey as I've shown you," Illesa reminded Joyce, lowering her eyes.

When they stood up, the Prince was arriving and they both had to curtsey again, while he and Gaveston played at bowing to each other, overemphasising their obsequious gestures. They'd obviously already had a skinful.

The arrival of all the new knights and nobility became tedious very quickly, especially as the smell of roasting meat became stronger.

"There you are," Richard's voice said behind her. "I've been scouring the crowd. Come on, let's sit down before the young drunkards eat everything in sight."

"Where's William?" Illesa said, taking his arm. Richard was pale. Too much walking on his bad leg.

"He's in the endless queue to get us a flagon of wine." Richard waved his arm towards the yard. "It will probably arrive in time for the final blessing and departure."

"Father, where's Christopher? He didn't come down the stairs."

"Second rank," Richard said out of the corner of his mouth. "Haven't come in yet. He was overseeing the squires stabling the horses when I saw him last. Should be done soon."

Everyone in the hall was pushing somewhere, except for the higher nobility. The dukes and earls had been seated by liveried servants on covered tables below the royal dais. They'd already been served their wine.

"Over here. De Braose has saved space for us." They slid into place on the second-to-last row of tables from the back of the hall, next to an old knight with a burn scar across his cheek. The man paid them no heed, continuing his drunken conversation with the man opposite.

"Where will Christopher sit?" Joyce asked. "There's no room here."

"Over there." Richard waved towards the front. "He'll join the Corbets. He's a knight now and can take his food on the tip of his sword if he needs to." Richard's tone was bitter. He pulled a cloth bag out from his jerkin and handed it to Joyce. "Here, you'll want these. It will take a long time for us to be served any food. I got them from a huckster on Fleet Street – but they're good and clean."

The flat cakes looked fresh. Illesa gave hers a sniff before taking a bite. Joyce had already finished hers and was picking up a second.

"You eat like that, you'll never find a husband," William said from behind Illesa's ear. "They'll think their wealth not enough to keep you in bread." He placed a small flagon in front of them, while Joyce stuck her tongue out at him.

"Joyce!" Illesa snapped. "You are in polite company; keep hold of your manners. William, you must not provoke her."

"Yes, Lady Burnel." His tone was mocking. "Of course one must not ruin her chances amongst all this fine stock." He straightened up. "The food is being served to the dukes, so yours should be ready in an hour." He poured the wine into three goblets. "The ale is not bad, but I doubt they've brewed enough."

"What have you heard?" Richard sipped the wine.

"Nothing of any use beyond what you already know. The army will ride north if there's enough coin left to feed it after the useless Prince has finished emptying the treasury of cloth and jewels for his favourite." William looked around. "They probably won't leave for Scotland until the Prince and his retinue have finished the hundred butts of wine they have stored. That's what they were attempting last night, I believe."

"And this is the commander of the army," muttered Richard.

"The King insists upon it." William leant over the trestle to look in the cloth bag. Finding nothing there he shook his fist at Joyce, who grinned back. "He's determined that his son will win the north before he dies. Seems unlikely with a cavalcade of feathered hats and velvet hose." William sniffed dismissively.

"What's the word on the Corbet camp? Any useful men?" Richard emptied his goblet in one gulp.

"Besides Christopher? Possibly. I haven't found Sir Thomas Corbet's squire yet, but I will before the end of the day."

Richard looked up at him with his one eye.

"Yes, he may give away more than his own weaknesses. But don't forget our food, and this wine won't last us long."

"One flagon at a time, they said. Finish it, and I'll join the queue again if you cannot wait for me to have my ale," William said pointedly.

"I'd like ale instead, Father," said Joyce, smiling at William.

"Very well, get ale and wine, William. It'll be worth your while, no doubt, as you'll hear all the more. Joyce – keep on the right side of your courtesy."

William had already left the cramped aisle.

It was a late hour to start gathering information in advance of the ride north, but Richard had not been at court for years. There'd been little chance to find out the extent of the mess his son was riding into. What could he put in place now that would protect his son so far away? Only William. Illesa's heart hammered at the thought. William could replace Christopher's fourteen-year-old squire, and keep Christopher safe with the experience he'd gained in Gascony and Flanders. The way he'd protected Richard. They might both make it back.

16

They might not.

Illesa took a sip of wine to moisten her dry lips. The goblet trembled in her hand. There should be no question in her heart between protecting Christopher and sacrificing William.

But William was indispensable to the running of the manor. And William cheered up Joyce, who otherwise moped in her chamber too much. He'd made it clear he never wanted to go to war again. And Richard would not send him, surely. What would they do if both were killed?

Illesa put the goblet down carefully and turned to Joyce. She was looking better. Not as pale, a little happier. Her purgation was due soon, but not today, God willing, amongst this throng. It had been foolish to bring her, but how could they deny her the chance to see all the nobility of England in one place?

Illesa glanced up the aisle between the tables to see if the jongleurs had arrived. A large, red-faced man was coming towards her. His features wore an expression of habitual cruelty, his proud stride displayed his new belt and spurs.

Fear pricked the back of her hands – a cold spasm down her neck and spine. But who was he?

The man stopped in the aisle, gripped by a paroxysm of coughing. He bent over, gasping. A young knight came up behind him and whacked him on the back. The old man straightened up and gripped the knight's arm hard, swearing. And that grip brought back the memory – his face over her as she lay recovering from the collapse of the platform at Neigull, all those years before. The man who'd danced with her and then dragged her away to give her to Sir L'Estrange. He had been stopped, not by her pleas, but by Balthazar and his club.

Roger Mortimer of Chirk, kept alive by the Devil to do his work. Surely there would be some sign of judgement on him, some suffering for his depravity. But his cloth was soft and rich, trimmed with squirrel, and the belt he wore was gilt with silver and gems. He'd recovered, was coming nearer, walking stiffly, wiping his mouth and his forehead with a napkin, followed by the young knight.

Joyce turned round to see why she was staring just as he walked past them. The young knight's eyes raked her, his mouth twisted into the beginning of a leer.

"Sir Mortimer," Richard called. "I congratulate you on your knighthood. Is Lord Chirk well?" He pushed himself upright and cocked his head towards the retreating man.

"Ah, Sir – ?" the knight said, his voice cool. "He merely choked on a small nut, I believe. He is perfectly well now, regretting his habit of stuffing them into his mouth whilst speaking. Forgive me, your name –"

"Sir Richard Burnel. I've fought alongside your uncle many times. This is my wife, Lady Burnel, and my daughter." They all rose, Joyce's cheeks bright red.

Sir Roger Mortimer the younger inclined his head slightly, amusement around his mouth.

"Ah yes, I've heard. Your son is knighted as well. We will be riding north in the same company."

"Indeed, and we wish you God's protection. Would you –"

"Forgive me, I must rejoin my uncle. Enjoy the spectacle. The fabulatori and the jongleurs are assembling!" He winked at Joyce and strode away.

Richard twisted his napkin in his hand and looked after him crossly.

Joyce sank back down onto the bench, her eyes on her still empty platter.

"Bloody Mortimers," Richard muttered.

"You have fought alongside that man?" Illesa croaked, her throat still tight.

"Yes, many a time." He gave her a curious look. "You seem to know him only too well. How so?" He took her hand.

"If you don't remember, I will tell you in private." She slid her hand out from his. "Joyce, look. The food at last."

It all came at once to their table, not course by course as it should have, so there was barely space for all the dishes. William spooned some eel onto their plates and whispered into Richard's ear.

"Give me the full story later," Richard said, smiling. "Just keep our flagon full."

William bowed rather sardonically and left with it.

"What did he say?" Illesa asked, but Richard's answer was cut off by a blast of the crumphorn. The jongleurs had arrived.

"He said," Richard shouted in her ear, "Christopher is being entertained at the table of the Fitzalans and has had so much to drink he is telling them the story about when our dear young cousin, Sir Edward Burnel, rode into battle and tripped over his own livery, landing face first in a pile of horse shit. He elaborated on the subject for several minutes. Unfortunately Sir Edward was also at the table."

Illesa covered her mouth.

"He didn't!" she groaned.

"Look, they are beginning with the jugglers. Don't worry, Sir Edward is even more drunk – has been since yesterday. He won't remember. The only danger is if he knifes him in the meantime. Sit down, Illesa! You won't help by drawing attention to him. He will soon become aware of his place in this court."

"Mother, look! How are they not burnt by it?" Joyce was half-standing, craning her neck, her face rapt with amazement.

The fire breathers and jugglers of flaming brands were performing on a platform well away from the long gowns of the royal table, accompanied by musicians – drum, hurdy gurdy and horn. They were beginning with the rustic music and performers. Perhaps later the skilled players would arrive, but a drunken crowd would give them short shrift.

"I hope they have some large butts of water nearby. Would be a shame to have to douse a fire with this decent wine," William said, clanging the flagon on the table and turning to look at the spectacle. The fire breather in the middle was dressed like a dragon. "That lady in the front row should be careful of her veil with those sparks." He glanced around the hall with its timber beams. "This place would go up like tinder."

The song finished with a blast of flame so large, people screamed and fell off their benches. The Prince of Wales roared with laughter and got to his feet. The performers sank the burning torches into sockets around the platform, bowed deeply and ran up the stairs.

"More! Piers, get them to come back." The Prince pushed his friend towards the stage.

The herald bowed with a flourish at the King and then the Prince.

"For your Royal pleasure they will return, but first from the land of Charybdis, the Sphynx and the Sirens – the man-beast who says nothing but the truth – Reginald the Liar!"

The herald moved aside as a strange creature came pawing down the stairs, pausing to shake his head as if tearing off a bridle. It was hard to see his costume from such a distance, but Joyce with her young eyes could.

"A Minotaur!"

He clattered on to the platform, and they could all see his shaggy brown costume, a hood bearing two curved and bloody horns, his face marked with black and red paint. He pranced between the bright torches and blew red powder out of his nose, making the whole hall gasp.

"Behold! I am the Minotaur, and I will take tribute of seven youths and seven maids to my labyrinth lair! Despair!"

"The size of you! You pygmy mite!" someone called from behind the platform. "You couldn't tweak the balls of the smallest knight!"

"Oh behold, how I grow," Reginald the Liar said, and two figures lurched up from the shadow at the back of the platform, bowed down behind him and then lifted him high. He grew half as much again in height. The figures backed away, but the Minotaur did not shrink or fall.

"See and feel my might!"

"Stilts tied and folded onto the back of his legs, unfolded and locked in place," Richard muttered next to her. "Very clever."

Illesa was not looking at his miraculously elongated legs, but at his face. As the crowd had gasped at the trick, Reginald the Liar had smiled, and she knew that smile. It could be no other.

It must be Gaspar.

Chapter III

Westminster Hall

Reginald the Liar was already in full flow. Illesa pulled on Richard's sleeve.

"It's Gaspar! Look!"

Richard shook his head.

"Not possible. But I see his mouth is similar. Just someone who resembles him."

"We haven't heard from Gaspar for two years," Illesa said. "Perhaps he's been cured!"

"Shhhhh, I'm trying to hear," the small woman sitting behind her hissed. "If I can't see because you're so tall, let me hear him at least."

"He's covered with paint. You can't tell what he looks like," Richard whispered in her ear. "Just enjoy it and stop imagining things."

Ha ha! We'll have a glorious rout!
We will stamp the traitors out,
once I've had my fill of maids and men!
No one may depart till then.
I am the Minotaur
and I do not permit you leave
until I have taken all my ease.

He thrust his pelvis out.

My lustiness must be appeased!

There were high-pitched squeals around the hall. Illesa glanced at Joyce. She was sitting with both hands over her mouth, eyes wide.

Let me come and choose my feast,
I am a very hungry beast,
but I am loyal to my liege.

21

It's in Scotland that I'll lay siege.
Only Scots will make my bread,
and I will fill their hearts with dread!

He grabbed one of the torches and swung it before him.

Let them run and let them hide,
my labyrinth is where I'll bide.
I know its corners – its high walls,
the pile of corpses that appalls.

He stared out at the hall with a look of twisted glee, pointing to several lords.

They will pay for his treachery;
they will die for villainy.
Our Prince, so valiant, and his knights
will put the devilish Bruce to flight.
And into my lair they will him lead
and there I'll do the righteous deed:
I'll pull his arms from his traitorous chest,
and for this deed I will be blessed.

He crossed himself.

But he, Robert Bruce, will be damned to Hell,
and our brave Prince will ring his knell!

He shouted pointing to the grinning Prince of Wales.
"I pray you lie not, Reginald," he cried.
The Minotaur scraped his paw on the platform, and the sound of the stilt echoed across the hall.

I never lie about my lord.

He shook his head, and the bloody horns waggled as if they were about to fall off.

For I know the length of his fine sword!

Before anyone could respond to his swift gesture, he continued:

And the Prince is lord of all we know.
I am just Prince of the land below.
You see I am the Devil now –

A small black-clad figure raced forward to hand him a long-handled pitchfork.

Before me every knee shall bow!!

The crowd erupted into loud boos and happy shrieks of fear.

"That can't be Gaspar," Richard whispered, "but he *is* very like him. I'm feeling quite sick with the anxiety of what he will do next, which is exactly how I felt every time Gaspar performed." The Devil that looked like Gaspar was leaping out at people in the front row, waving his pitchfork and cackling. "I'll never understand how they do that in stilts."

I'm here to torture any knight
too frightened to take on Bruce's might.
Anyone who will not revenge the death
of Comyn in the church is mine, by right,
and I will chill their blood and fire their breath.

From behind his back another figure appeared. A young man dressed as a woman with enormous breasts, near bursting out of a bright green tunic cinched tight at the waist with a golden belt. He had a yellow wig and large red lips.

But dearest Devil you're no match for me,
all you have is enmity.
I have lust and life and love.
I will make those knights to move.

His gesture at this point was illustrative. He then sank into a deep curtsey, and there was a blast on the horn as the herald announced:

"Matilda Makejoy has come for your pleasure, and to take the victory from Monsieur Hell."

The Devil poked the man's large buttocks with his pitchfork, and he squeaked and jumped out of the way, lifting his skirts to show high red boots.

Whatever it is that you love best
I'll give you, knights, at your behest.
But stay with me and do not fight,
rest on my bosoms through the night.
John Comyn in purgatory will stay.
Revenge can wait another day.

He minced along the platform, winking at the knights sitting below and shaking his bosoms suggestively.

The Devil had returned to his smaller stature while all this was going on, and the two began to perform an acrobatic battle on the platform, jumping over one another, tumbling through each other's legs, the Devil throwing his pitchfork and Matilda Makejoy catching it mid-air.

"He's very good. Better than Gaspar, I'd say. Gaspar was always more of a musician than an acrobat," Richard remarked in Illesa's ear.

The resemblance was uncanny, but Gaspar had never played such a convincing Devil. Illesa fingered her paternoster beads. He should be in a Lazar house in Gascony, using the money Richard sent him each year to ease his sufferings, but he seemed to have forgotten them entirely.

The Devil and the lecherous lady finished their display, wrestling each other off the stage to loud heckling and a blast from the crumphorn. The herald stood forward again.

Let Hell and Lust be gone from us!
Now come to the King, those who faithfully serve,
and pledge to give Bruce what he deserves.
Come before your lord and liege,
his son, our Prince, will lay the siege
upon the traitors who Comyn killed
and our demesne expand and build.

New musicians came onto the stage and began to play the crwth and the citole. The King rose from his seat, taking the Queen by the hand, and walked to the platform at the centre of the stairs. Behind him the Prince rose too, Piers Gaveston at his side, and waited behind his father, whispering in his friend's ear and bursting into laughter. All the assembled knights got to their feet. For several moments it was impossible to hear the music with the clattering of goblets and plates, and the benches scraping on the floor. It resolved into a widespread and unhappy muttering.

"The earls and dukes hate Gaveston," Richard whispered. "He's twice as good as them in tournaments. The Prince is never far from him, like a pup. If he wants his army's loyalty, he should leave Gaveston in London to polish the silver plate."

"Do you think the Minotaur will come back?" Illesa asked, craning her neck to see the stage, as all the knights moved forwards.

"Oh no doubt. They'll get their money's worth out of him. He'll be back to sing or tell a tale. The feast will be hours yet."

"Why are they going forward now?" Joyce asked, standing up to see. "Is that Christopher?"

"Pray silence for the King!" the herald demanded.

"Yes, there he is," Richard pointed to the back of that group. "They're going up to pledge their lives to his service, and to vow to regain Scotland for the crown or die in the attempt. It's standard on these occasions, before a war. That, however, is a more unusual addition to the proceedings," he said, staring at the aisle between the long trestles.

Two men were pulling a large flat cart, draped in the King's livery. In the centre two swans stood, side by side, silent and immobile, held with golden chains. Alongside them lay a sword in an ornate scabbard, a shield and belt – all gilt and bejewelled.

"Are the swans alive?" Joyce asked. "They look it, but –" Her voice trailed off as the cart went past. "No, they must be dead and stuffed."

The cart was wheeled up to the base of the King's dais, silencing all as it passed.

The King spread his arms wide.

"On this *solemn* occasion," the King declared, "it is time to make our vows in this sacred duty to return Scotland to its rightful ruler."

The Prince took a step towards his father and bowed his head. Gaveston did the same.

"I call upon you all to fulfil your knightly oaths in my service and to pledge your fidelity to my son and heir, the Prince of Wales, Edward Caernarfon. He is the leader and commander of the army, and will now be armed to take your allegiance."

The King's gaze swung across the crowd of new knights.

"As I feed you, arm you, and horse you, so you will follow the orders and example of your commander in battle."

"That's going to go well," Richard muttered.

The King gestured Edward forward to kneel at his feet. They'd obviously practised this part, although the Prince looked rather unsteady. Gaveston stood behind him, a half-smile playing on his lips as if he were watching a young page doing his exercises. Two earls from the high table went forward, one taking the belt and sword, the other the shield.

"That's the Earl of Surrey next to de Lacy," Richard explained in her ear. They stood holding the arms, head bowed before the King. "He'd never ask a Marcher Lord to do that; they wouldn't agree."

"You are to take my place in Scotland. To seek the traitor Bruce and to bring him to justice. To restore Scotland to our rule, and to take reparations for their treachery," the King intoned as he raised his son to stand in front of him.

"Won't the King ride north?" Illesa whispered, as the presentation of the regalia dragged on. "Is he to leave it all to the Prince?"

"Perhaps he's sending him ahead to get him out of London, where he's been spending too much time and coin," Richard said. "There, see that part is done. Now to the simple task of hundreds of knights doing the same." The knights gathered before the dais had all dropped to one knee. "Ah, he's doing it en masse."

The Prince led them in the oath, but Illesa had stopped listening. Behind the ranks of knights, the musicians were moving about, and with them there was the familiar figure, now without fur, horns or paint, in a parti-coloured tunic, bare-headed, bare-faced, moving the burning torches, and preparing the stage. She went forward a few paces to see better. If it wasn't Gaspar it was the spit of him.

Something darted past her down the aisle and scuttled under the trestle at Joyce's feet.

"Oh! What's that?" Joyce jolted backwards.

"Take care, Joyce! Come away!" Illesa pulled her off the bench and out of reach of the monkey's arm.

"Look!" Joyce crouched down, trying to see. "It was grabbing at my skirt, trying to climb onto my lap."

"Have you got your beads? It will snatch them from you if you're not careful." Illesa pulled Joyce a bit further away and clutched at the amulet hanging from her own waist.

"I've never seen one so close."

The white-breasted monkey was sitting on its haunches, chattering, its head moving to and fro, looking at them.

"Don't reach out to it. They bite!"

Joyce looked at her crossly.

"I'm not touching it. I just want to see its tail."

The tail curled and twitched behind the animal, as one paw patted the stone floor feeling for treats in the cracks, and the other pulled at a narrow iron collar around its neck.

"Leave it, darling. Come a little nearer the stage so you can see Christopher. The monkey's mistress or master will find it soon enough." It was a wonder it was allowed in the hall when dogs had been expressly forbidden in the abbey precinct. Joyce straightened up reluctantly.

"It's not fair that they were allowed to bring their monkey, and I had to leave little Pearl at home!"

"She would not have enjoyed the journey or the feast. It would have frightened her."

"She would have been content because I would have carried her everywhere!"

The monkey lolloped out from the shelter of the table, swung up onto the bench and reached out for the bread.

"Leave it to its feast. Your father is over there, speaking to Christopher." The communal oath was finished, and all the new knights were milling about below the stage.

"Look, the monkey is trying to take that lady's bracelet!"

"Keep all your trinkets out of reach," Illesa said, taking her hand and heading for the crowd of knights. She'd lost sight of Christopher and Richard. "It's possible that a thief has trained that monkey and set it loose into this crowd of wealthy nobles for just that reason."

"Illesa! He's here. Come and see him before he is dragged off by these ruffians."

Richard held Christopher's arm. He looked both younger and older than he had the day before. His face, slackened by drink, had lost its anxious lines. But his garb was that of a soldier about to leave the tavern for the battlefield – his new gambeson already stained, his free hand fingering his sword pommel. There was a cut on his cheek, just healing, where he'd been badly shaved. He waved his hands wildly at the stage.

"Did you see the swans, Joyce? They were made of sugar! I thought they were as real as real, but one of the bearers hit one with a silver hammer, and the coating broke off, and he presented it to the Queen!"

Illesa managed to squeeze next to him.

"Sugar?" Joyce shook her head and smiled. "That can't be."

"No expense has been spared." Christopher lifted his tankard to his lips, but it was empty. He frowned. "But very few of these men are worthy of being knighted. They desecrated the Temple last night with their revelry. Trumpets and shouting." Christopher lifted his tankard again and looked inside disappointedly. "The few of us trying to prepare our souls for service guided by the Templar priest were scorned."

Joyce had edged away, perhaps aware that his complaint might be a long one.

"Didn't the Templar Knights bring them to order? I thought they were very strict inside their precincts."

Christopher grimaced, looking over Illesa's head.

"It's a dangerous thing to scold the heir to the throne. Especially when he's drunk. But the Master of the Templars in England was there. I spoke to him –"

Christopher's voice petered out. He was staring into the middle distance.

"William de la More? That was very fortunate. What did you speak of?"

He turned back to her with a look of irritation.

"Nothing that can be revealed to a woman. The Templars are true knights, pure and holy in the service of Christ. Their wisdom and mysteries are not to be shared with outsiders."

Illesa drew breath.

"You speak as though you are part of the Order."

But her reply had been drowned out by a horn fanfare.

"Make space! The players will lead you in the first carole."

Trestles and benches were dragged away from below the stage and folding stools brought in for the most important of the earls. The hall was a sea of moving people, and Christopher had vanished into it. Richard was leaning against the wall, speaking closely with Henry de Lacy, William at his side. She would not interrupt them. She knew how important that conversation was.

The musicians began quietly and slowly. Reginald the Liar was not among them. Richly dressed women were gathering, beckoning to their partners. The sky beyond the windows had turned golden in the evening sun. It would soon be dark, and they needed to be back at their lodgings before the Priory gate was bolted. Illesa backed away from the dancing. There was no sign of Joyce. A young girl shouldn't be alone amongst all these drunken men.

The crowd had thinned. The cruel Mortimer – Lord Chirk – might still be here, waiting for an opportunity. Illesa shivered, wanting the strong presence of William by her side. But there wasn't going to be a disaster this evening with all the gentry of the kingdom assembled. That was long ago. And she must put William out of her mind, or everything would be ruined.

At the back of the hall, boys were lighting the lamp sconces. The music was getting faster; she could feel the beat of the dance steps through her soles. Joyce had been warned not to go off by herself in the great city, even to find a privy. But had Illesa reminded her today – at the feast?

Illesa slipped out of the open door into the yard and walked amongst the tents, past groups of servants at tables, stacking and scraping. As she turned back to the doors, she caught sight of Joyce by the west corner of the building, her back to the wall, facing a man bending over her, gesturing wildly.

Illesa ran forwards, shouting – realising only as she came within ten paces that it was Reginald the Liar keeping her daughter pinned to the wall, helpless with laughter.

Chapter IV

Westminster Hall

Reginald turned and backed away from Joyce, twisting his face into an expression similar to a young pup that wants food.

Joyce straightened up, smiling.

"Mother, he's not hurting me! This is Reginald the Liar – one of the players."

Illesa took Joyce's outstretched hand. She stared. The man had both his ears. It was not Gaspar.

"Ah, Mistress, the way you are looking at me, it's as if I am a book and you are a monk! What spicy spirits do you find in my visage?"

His voice had the same accent but was deeper than Gaspar's. He winked, his arms folded on his chest, waiting for her to speak.

"Good evening, Master." Illesa cleared her throat, still watching the way his mouth smiled, wrinkling his cheeks. "Forgive me for staring. You resemble a friend of mine, and the likeness is startling."

His smile wavered and then widened even further.

"Why, you must mean the man known as Gaspar the player!"

"Yes, Gaspar!"

Joyce was staring at each of them in turn, uncertainly.

"Gaspar who saved Father's life?"

Reginald the Liar made a deep bow, both elaborate and lengthy.

"Please, get up, tell me how you know Gaspar!"

"Can you not guess, my Lady?" He had composed his face into a serious expression. "He is my brother; we shared the same womb. We are Gemini." He put an arm out as if holding a fellow around the shoulders. "His real name is not Gaspar, and he is certainly neither kingly nor wise, despite the name of his old troupe of players. Like myself, he is full of antic humours. As this beautiful young lady, your daughter I believe, must testify!"

"I didn't know he had a brother. He told me he was abandoned on the street in St Albans," Illesa said, without thinking.

Reginald blinked twice and then made the gesture of weeping.

"Indeed 'twas so. When we were born, our mother was accused of fornication because we came out at the same hour, and so she must have loved two men, as they reasoned. Rather than live with the shame, she left us. Or so we were told."

Joyce was staring at Reginald, open-mouthed. Illesa fingered her amulet.

"Master, the resemblance is so extraordinary that I have forgotten my manners. Forgive me. I am Lady Burnel, and this is Joyce. We both enjoyed your play and are glad to meet you." She bobbed her head, and Joyce did the same. "Gaspar is very dear to our family, and I would be so grateful to know if you have any news of him at all."

"Lady Burnel, I am *honoured* by your words." He didn't sound as sarcastic as Gaspar, but it was impossible to take his words seriously. "Gaspar, or more properly Castor, my dear brother, loves me so much that he has abandoned me yet again, until we've both grown old." He hunched his back, and doddered on the spot. "But I have heard that he's still alive, despite his leprous condition, and for this I thank God and all the saints." Reginald did a fair imitation of pious devotion. "What is your news of the old devil?"

Reginald put his head on one side and smiled at them, looking so much like Gaspar that Illesa's stomach jumped.

"Yes, I can imitate him well enough," Reginald said, "and he could mimic my voice, but he could never match me for my agility. He had the better of me in music. So, where is he now?"

An edge to his question made Illesa hesitate.

"We've had no word either. For two years or more. Before that, he was comfortable in a Lazar house in Gascony."

"That much I knew," he said, staring over her head towards the disappearing sun, twisting a silver ring on his left hand. He cocked his head towards the hall. "The first dances have finished, and I must sing for the magnificent King," he said twirling the last words into notes. "But where do you stay? I will come to meet you afterwards so that we may share more news of him."

"Yes, my husband, Sir Richard Burnel, should meet you and hear your history," Illesa said. "We stay at Saint Bartholomew the Great, in the Prior's guesthouse near the hospital, and Joyce and I must go now, before we are locked out."

"I vow I will meet you there tomorrow after I have collected my coin!" Reginald smiled beatifically. "So we will meet again, gentle Joyce. I see from where you have drawn your beauty – Lady Burnel." Again he bowed with a flourish and ran lightly down the length of the hall's north side to a small door that would take him behind the stage, no doubt.

"Let's go and hear him sing!" Joyce tugged at Illesa's kirtle sleeve as she watched him go.

"Just one song, then we must go to the Priory with William. We may already be too late."

Joyce raced into the glowing hall, changed by twilight and torchlight. Reginald was already singing – a very worthy song about Charlemagne and the amazing horse Tencendur, who ran down the enemy like skittles. His voice relished the bloody details.

William was not listening to it, however. He and Richard were in close conversation with a young lad, probably one of the Corbets' squires.

Richard gestured them to come closer.

Illesa nodded at the youth and stood next to Richard.

"We must go; it's growing dark."

"But I would hear the song!" Joyce pointed plaintively to the stage.

"We shall do both," Richard said. "I have Alan's word," he tipped his head at the lad, "that he will get a rouncey for me so that I won't slow you down, and the guestmaster has told the doorkeeper to wait for us. We will not be the last to find our way at a late hour. Let Joyce hear the song; it's no common voice."

"He is no common singer," Illesa whispered in his ear, "but Gaspar's twin brother."

Richard's head snapped around.

"You've spoken to him? And that's what he claimed?"

"That's what he is," Illesa insisted. "When you meet him you will see."

"When did you speak?"

"I found him with Joyce outside, while you were speaking to Henry de Lacy. He was telling her tales." Had her trapped against the wall. But Joyce had been laughing, happy. It was rare enough these days and should be welcomed when it happened.

"And?" Richard took her hand in his. "What's his history? Does he have word of Gaspar?"

Illesa shook her head.

"He comes to meet us tomorrow. Let me tell you more when we are away from here; I need to mind Joyce." She was out of sight again. Illesa picked her way through the crowd towards the stage and found Joyce standing against the wall where they'd started this long feast. Her face in profile was intent, absorbed, but her skirts moved, as if her feet were dancing.

As lily white she goes
Complexioned like the rose
She robs me of my rest.
Of girls discreet and wise
She proudly bears the prize
As loveliest and best.
This lady lives to the west,
The fairest of a noble kind;
And heaven a man would find
*At night-time as her guest!**

Illesa waited for the end of the song then tapped Joyce's shoulder.

"Come. We must go back now while the roads are still safe."

Joyce frowned and looked back at the stage.

"When will we see a diversion like this again?"

"Reginald has promised to visit us tomorrow, in our lodgings. Perhaps he will tell us a tale then before we leave."

She took Joyce's hand and pulled her away. Richard and William were at the hall door. The squire, Alan, stood beside a ragged, brown rouncey. Illesa looked back into the thinning crowd.

"Have you made an arrangement with Christopher? I haven't said farewell."

"He promised to meet us tomorrow. But for now, leave him to his festivities. There'll be little enough of that in the weeks ahead." William and the squire heaved Richard on to the saddle. He sat for a moment, pain wracking his features.

Joyce was looking around on the ground, patting her belt.

"My coral paternoster beads!" She looked at Illesa, stricken.

Illesa bent down and felt all around Joyce's waist. The belt loop they had been attached to was intact, but the beads were truly gone. Illesa took both of Joyce's hands in hers.

"Do you remember when you last had them?"

"I don't know," wailed Joyce.

Illesa shivered, remembering how much it had cost to buy that protection. The merchant in beneficial stones had had much to say about their amazing powers, especially when combined with a crucifix in silver.

"The monkey!" Joyce cried. "It must have stolen them."

"Don't be foolish, Joyce; they will have fallen off somewhere." Richard made to get off the horse.

"No, don't. We must go now. Look how late it is!" Illesa insisted. The moon had risen, and the stars of Orion rode high in the other half of the sky. "William, will you look for the beads while this squire escorts us to the Priory?"

William sucked his teeth.

"I have a fair idea of where to start." He darted into the hall.

"Joyce, pray that he finds them. Pray to Our Lady, who lost so much, that this protection of children would be returned to you."

Joyce closed her eyes and tears traced down her cheeks. She bowed her head.

"If anyone can find them, William aided by the Holy Virgin can," Richard said grimly, giving the nod to the squire. He clicked his tongue and led them to the tall gate that would take them onto the Strand, and then Smithfield.

By the time they'd arrived at the Prior's door, all were exhausted, and William had not caught up.

"If you see him on the road," Richard put another coin in the squire's palm, "tell him he needn't break in. The doorkeeper expects him."

"Yes, Sir Burnel."

"And make sure Sir Christopher Burnel remembers his duty to see us tomorrow, no matter what his condition. Find Thurstan and tell him too. We will stay only one more day. We can ill afford any more," he muttered.

"Will we have enough to get home, or must we borrow against our donations to the Templars?" Illesa whispered, walking close beside him. Joyce was a few paces behind, nearly asleep on her feet.

"We have enough, just. But not to replace fine prayer beads."

"God have mercy, it will be found." Illesa touched her own amulet, which was good for health but not for lost valuables.

"Don't hope for that too much. These thieves are well organised. William will not find it on the floor – and I think he has enough wit not to take on a gang of London cut-purses."

It was a relief to reach their dorter, a private room they'd been allowed after a sizeable donation to the Priory church. One lamp had been lit; a jug of water and one of ale stood on the small table near the three beds. Joyce sat down hard on hers and covered her head in her hands.

Illesa touched her hair softly.

"Don't worry, my darling. William will come soon with news."

Joyce shook her head and lay down, keeping her feet off the sheet of rough linen.

"Leave her," Richard said, lowering himself onto the bigger bed. "Pour some ale and let's sleep away these cares."

Illesa knelt and began to unlace Joyce's shoes. Joyce held still as she took each one off.

"I'm sorry I lost them, Father," Joyce cried, her shoulders heaving.

Richard pushed himself up onto his elbow.

"It's unlikely to have been your carelessness. We know how much you treasured them. There are thieves everywhere in London, even under the King's nose. Especially there in fact! Did you know that pounds and pounds of gold gems, relics and silver were stolen right out of the Westminster treasure house only three years ago? Not even the King and all his deadly knights can protect against the thieves of this place. So be comforted. You've only lost a small string of coral beads. Not your life or your honour."

"And the cross of silver," Joyce whispered.

"But not Our Lady's care," Illesa said getting up. "We will pray in the chapel tomorrow for her mercy and protection."

"Go to sleep, my girl." Richard stretched his legs, wincing. "Things will seem better after rest."

Illesa poured two cups of ale and sat down on the thin straw mattress next to him. They listened as Joyce's breathing slowed – waited until they heard it deepen into sleep.

"When do you think they were lost?" Richard asked, draining the last of his ale.

"I think the monkey took them while Joyce heard the last song."

"In truth?" His look was sceptical. "I've never seen a monkey turned thief."

"I've heard of one. In a tale Gaspar told. It took a poison ring and killed its own master. But he told it comically."

"That's just a fable. The monkey in the hall was a pet of one of the nobles, surely?"

"It was running about loose. *And* it tried to take the beads from Joyce when we first saw it."

Richard sank back on the bed and shut his eye.

"William will discover what has happened, no doubt. But I cannot wait for him to return. Do you have some draught to give me for the night?"

"In my pack. It will mix with the ale well enough, though it won't be warmed." It was soon done, and Richard was asleep, flat on his back, snoring.

Illesa had intended to watch for William. She thought she'd be sleepless, thinking of the strangely familiar Reginald, but she woke to the matins bell, and William rolled in a cape on the narrow bed by the door. Tied to the bed leg, a cinched cloth bag was jumping up and down, chattering angrily. One tooth was visible, biting through it.

Chapter V

Monday the 23rd May, 1306
Priory of Saint Bartholomew the Great
Matins

Illesa scrambled out of the bed clothes.

"Why have you brought that thing here!" she cried, watching the bag jumping even more wildly at the sound of her voice.

William opened his eyes slowly and yawned.

"Your thanks are most welcome," he said, "for my night chasing it all over Westminster."

Illesa went to the window and opened the shutters.

"But we didn't want the monkey, just the paternoster beads!"

Joyce sat up in alarm. Richard grunted and turned over. It took more than a monkey in his bedroom to rouse him at this hour.

"For the love of God, bring me a cup of ale at least before you begin berating me." William pushed his hair off his face and sighed loudly. "Whoever owns this lout," he poked the bag with his toe, "will be along shortly to reclaim it. At that point, I would expect we can exchange it for the beads. That was the message I left last night, before I walked back here with this little devil, to a cold welcome."

"How did you catch it, William?" Joyce was inching towards the bag on her hands and knees.

"I set a trap for it, of course." William got to his feet and stretched his arms until they popped in his shoulders. His hands were red and bleeding with several deep scratches.

"I should tend to your hands," Illesa said, pulling Joyce up to her feet. "Leave that creature for now. Look what it did to William. You don't want it scratching your face and making a scar, do you?"

Joyce scowled.

"It was cross because it was thrown in a sack. I'm sure it's been tamed."

"I'm not." William drank a cup of ale in one gulp and grimaced. "I'll need some more of that."

"Tell us what happened, William, and I'll fetch you some bread and ale," Illesa said, putting the empty pitcher down on the table. "There must be some in the refectory by now."

"At last," he muttered. "Go and get it while I dunk my head and relieve myself. And you, young mistress, can find the apples in my sack and cut them into little pieces with your knife. Then we will see if she is tame or not."

"It's a girl?" Joyce ran to get William's small leather pack. "I thought it was a male."

"Definitely a female," he said. "Much more deceitful and dangerous."

When Illesa arrived back from her excursion to the refectory through the early dawn, her hands full, the scene that met her was almost comical.

Somehow, William had managed to attach a cord around the monkey's collar and had tied this to the bed frame. The monkey had one hand on the cord, as if it was testing its strength, and the other long clawed hand stretched out to accept a morsel of apple from the tips of Joyce's fingers.

"It eats from my hand!" Joyce's face was transformed by this instant happiness.

"They would only give me enough for an invalid. Everyone else is supposed to wait to eat until after prime."

Illesa set down the small loaf and the heavy jug. Joyce laughed every time the monkey took a bit of apple and put it in its large mouth. It chewed thoughtfully and regarded the girl with something between suspicion and speculation.

"How on earth did you capture it?" Illesa passed William a cup and a hunk of bread and sat down to watch the show.

"The monkey had eaten so much from the feast it was sleeping on a tunic behind the stage. I knew it was no nobleman's pet."

Illesa leant over the snoring Richard.

"Wake up!" She shook his shoulder. "You should hear this. William won't want to explain it all again."

Richard groaned. His eye opened and shut again.

"I'll listen from here."

"Don't go back to sleep. There's a monkey eating apple from your daughter's hand, and a thief likely to come knocking any minute."

"This is one of my more unusual dreams," Richard muttered, turning towards the others and opening his eye again.

The monkey showed its teeth at Illesa as she went to sit on the floor next to Joyce. Its fur was thick, olive grey with a white bib below its cunning face. There was a bad smell coming from the sack and the fur was matted with waste.

"The sooner they come to take it away the better. Don't become fond of it, Joyce."

William swallowed a large mouthful of bread.

"It won't get attached to her; it's only interested in the food. Monkeys are loyal to their tribe, and I think I know which one this belongs to." William went to the south-facing window. "Its owner will be along soon, once he's collected his coin."

"What do you mean?" Joyce sat back and stared at him crossly.

"What would you rather have, this messy monkey or your beads back, young mistress? Because it can't be both. I told the Steward that if the monkey's owner wanted it back, they were to bring your beads here by tierce, or it would be drowned in the Fleet."

"No! You mustn't!" Joyce cried, and the monkey scuttled backwards waving its tail, shrieking and showing its long teeth.

"Stop upsetting it, you dolt," William said. "I'm not going to have to drown it because they will come with coin or beads. And this is the best place to do the exchange."

"William, I'm not sure it's worth it for all the uproar." Richard had sat up and was gingerly moving his bad leg off the bed.

"You are always so grateful for my help," William said, turning back to the window. "Ah, here they are, earlier than I thought. Put on your shoes and boots, my fine ladies."

Illesa rushed to the window. The street was still quiet, but there were a few boys carrying trays of meat and women lugging buckets back from the well. In the midst of them, two figures were walking up the street, in close conversation.

"Are you sure?" They didn't look distinctive to her.

"Yes. Look at their hose."

She peered out, squinting.

"My eyes are not as strong as yours."

"They are the players from last night. You can see their colours in bands on their hose. And one of them has a leather pouch over his shoulder."

As they drew closer, the man under a worn cap became Reginald, and at his side was Matilda Makejoy.

"Do you really think they own the monkey and trained it to steal?"

"Why else would they be here?"

"Reginald said he would visit us today. He's Gaspar's twin brother."

William whistled through his teeth.

"Two of them. What was God thinking?"

"It can't have been *Reginald* who taught it to thieve," Joyce said. "He was so jovial!"

"I hope it wasn't, but in any case, he has kept his word and come to visit us." Illesa brushed her crumpled tunic. Her teeth felt mossy, but there was no time to improve matters.

"We should all meet them," Richard said, getting up. "There's strength in numbers – and in the appeal of a young lady's entreaties, even to hardened players."

"We can't take that monkey into the Prior's parlour. What if it shat on the floor?" Illesa said. It was fortunate that the Prior himself was on the way to Rome, not in residence and likely to be insulted by it. The monkey had the rope in its mouth and was chewing enthusiastically.

William calmly stepped round the monkey, collected the bag and emptied the foul contents out of the window onto the street.

"It didn't hit them," he remarked, "although it would only be what they deserve. Now we'll get the monkey in the bag and greet our visitors. Joyce – put all the rest of the apple half-way in the bag and go and stand by your father."

She did so reluctantly.

"I want to pet it, it's so pretty."

"It wants to scratch you, you're so silly," William said, imitating her voice. "I'll put the bag where it can see and smell the fruit, and make it come nearer and nearer. Get that blanket, Lady Burnel, and be ready to throw it over the monkey."

In the end it was a simple exercise, although it can't have felt that way to the monkey. It reached in the sack for the apple,

William grabbed its tail and lifted it in one hand, the bag in the other, and dropped it in.

"Give me that thong to tie it and let's be going." He held the wriggling, shrieking bag at arm's length.

"It takes me longer than that to stand up," Richard complained. "It won't harm them to be kept waiting, visiting at such an early hour. Illesa, help me." His leg would no longer bend, and he couldn't reach to put on his boots.

She pulled them on quickly, lacing them tight.

"Have a cup of ale, Richard. You will need your full voice."

"That and a better night's sleep to cope with thieving players and shitting monkeys." He gulped it down, and she passed him his walking-stick. "I doubt this priory has seen anything to match this for amusement in many a year."

When they opened the door, a novice was on the threshold. He'd probably been listening at the keyhole.

"Visitors should not be admitted at this hour," he complained. "They say they're on the King's business. Is this so?"

"Indeed," Richard said. Luckily he was blocking the monk's view of William. "I believe it concerns the ceremony yesterday. Forgive us this disturbance, Brother."

The monk nodded and preceded them down the stair.

"I thought them odd messengers from the court, but then times are changing, and the discipline and traditions of courtesy are dying out, the Brother Doorkeeper says." He mournfully opened the parlour door. "The Sub Prior also says that you have missed the office of matins and will miss prime due to these visitors, but you must attend tierce," he admonished as they filed into the gloomy chamber. William had his cape slung over the bag, but it could not muffle the sound of chattering. "Pets are not allowed in the chapel." The novice glared at William and closed the door behind him.

"Are all London novices so emboldened that they order knights thither and yon?" Reginald the Liar mused, bowing elaborately to them.

"Are all players so opposed to sleep that they do their business before daybreak?" Richard glanced over both men and began the process of sitting down carefully on the largest stool, laying his stick on the floor. The room was cool in the early morning. Illesa held Joyce's hand and sat on the bench by the wall. Joyce was glancing at the players through lowered lashes.

"I believe you have met my wife and daughter already, Reginald. William, my constable. And your companion? I presume you are not, in truth, called Matilda?"

The other player was not as young as he'd looked on stage. Possibly in his mid-twenties, with a bruise on his cheek and a small cut above his eyebrow.

"Ramón," he said, bowing even more elaborately than Reginald. At his voice the monkey made an entirely new noise – a hooting call. "And you have already met my charming companion, *Mullida*." He said the last word in a high-pitched voice, like a sung note. The monkey replied with a loud hoot. The man's voice had a soft, foreign inflection. "Unfortunately Mullida managed to chew through her rope and went about. I could not stop my performance to find her." He shrugged. "Well – I thank you for keeping her for me."

"William deserves your thanks. And we deserve what the monkey has taken from us." Richard bent forward, pointing at Joyce. "Restore the paternoster beads, and the monkey will be yours again."

Reginald smiled the smile that was Gaspar's and put his hand on his companion's shoulder to stop his unsaid words.

"It is occasionally Mullida's habit to snatch bright objects. She's so curious. You may not be familiar with monkeys but this is an unfortunate aspect of their fallen condition." Reginald's voice had become tender and persuasive. "She brings them back to her sleeping place, like a trophy of war. Usually it's bright confits she believes to be fruit, or beads that look like berries." He drew the string of coral and silver from the bag slung over Ramón's shoulder. "These must have seemed like hard seeds or berries to her. It may be wise to wash them."

Joyce stood up with a small cry.

Reginald held the beads out to her and dropped them in her outstretched hand.

"I am sorry," Ramón said, smiling sadly. "She has bad habits, but she also is very good. Give her to me, and we will show you a trick."

William looked at Richard, who nodded. He placed the wriggling bag on the worn floor in front the players.

"It is not unusual for Mullida to perform in our smaller plays, but this one had to be so large." He spread his hands wide. "For such a crowd we couldn't do the scenes with her – the Garden of Eden, Noah's Ark. She was bored, I believe," Ramón said as he untied the thong looped around the mouth of the sack.

"Just one trick, Ramón, and then I must have conversation with this family about our mutual friend." Reginald bowed to Richard.

"Just one, Mullida," Ramón crooned as the monkey climbed out of the sack and clambered up his body to his shoulder, holding onto his head. She sat there, opened her wide mouth, looked at William and screamed.

"She doesn't like you very much," Ramón concluded. He took something out of his pack and held it up to her. The monkey took it carefully and chewed it in a thoughtful way. "Usually she would wear a skirt for this, but –" he shrugged. "Come, we will do Noah and his nagging wife!"

He clicked his fingers twice and rounded his mouth, making a low note. The monkey climbed down and sat on her haunches looking at him, before standing up on her hind legs. Ramón went to the back of the room, clicked his fingers again, and the monkey walked on her hind legs over to him, swaying, hooting loudly and wagging one of her arms at its master.

"Enough! You will bring the doorkeeper here with that noise," Richard said.

"But –" Joyce began.

"Enough. We have business today. And a monkey pretending to be Noah's wife was not part of it. We thank you for returning our property, Ramón. It would be best if you waited for Reginald in the street. The creature is a distraction for us all."

The monkey, now full of confidence, had climbed back up Ramón and was grooming his short head of hair.

"You can see why I'm covered in scratches." He bowed as well as he could considering the burden on his head. "Sir Burnel, Lady Burnel, Mistress Joyce – Mullida and I thank you for your hospitality." Illesa saw him give another click signal, and the monkey made a sound very similar to a burp. He grinned, darted up the step and shut the door behind them.

A gasp of laughter burst from Joyce, but Richard looked like thunder.

"I pray your mercy for him." Reginald brought his hands together. "He is from Castile and has rough manners. But as you may have seen, he is the best at tumbling, so we must put up with him."

"It is no matter," Richard said, pushing himself up straighter. "The beads are returned, and, at last, we are rid of the creature. Now tell us of Gaspar. What was your history? My wife says you were born twins. I never heard him speak of you, but the evidence is before our eyes."

"It's a long, sad tale, which must be shortened." Reginald gave them an apologetic smile. "I must race to the Prince's court to collect our payment. If we don't arrive in time, we are punished with less coin." He produced an expression of pure misery. "Castor and I were born to a poor woman, whose peddler husband, upon finding us twins, accused her of fornication. She was shamed, and because she would not confess to it, was abandoned by her husband and left to fend for herself. She gave us to a company of players when we were four years old. They played from town to town, for a pittance, but we learnt the trade. My brother excelled in music, I in dance and tumbling."

Reginald was acting out the gestures of his tale, as if his hands were quite unconnected to himself.

"We both looked for a better company, but, tragically, we could not find one together. He went to the Three Kings, taking on the character of Gaspar, and I to the household players for the young Prince Edward – Daniel and the Lions. The Prince still remembers all our ancient jokes," he said fondly.

"The last time we saw each other must have been fourteen years ago or more. He gave me this." He pulled a silver ring off his longest finger. "A ring to prevent my sudden death," he laughed. "I think he was afraid I would fall and break my neck. It is inscribed *Caspar, Melchior, Balthazar – Ananyzapta!*" He proclaimed, putting the ring back on with a flourish. "It has been remarkably effective thus far." He looked around at their astonished faces. "But now poor Castor is leprous, and what's more, in Gascony. I don't know which condition is worse!"

Richard coughed slightly.

"Has he sent you any messages?"

"From time to time, through other players. But not since he ended up in Gascony. And I understand you are to thank for that, Lady Burnel?" Reginald's eyes fixed on her for a brief moment, before he smiled again in the way that employed every muscle in his face. "You led him on a rescue attempt against the whole of the French army! If it was not so unbelievable, it would make a good tale for Reginald the Liar! My name at birth was Pollux, I should tell you, but I took on an old player's role as Reginald the Liar. People know what they like, and the venerable characters are always the best," he said in a country accent. "It guarantees they will be able to follow the jokes, even when blind drunk."

Reginald winked at Joyce, who hid a smile behind her hand.

"How do we know that you are speaking the truth now?" Richard asked mildly. "It is your habit to tell tales."

Reginald's face remained fixed in the animated smile, but his cheeks flushed a little.

"That is my role on stage, not before friends," he said, his head to one side. "You have been friends to my brother, and in return I shall be a friend to you. Name your pleasure, and I shall tell you the tale."

"It is enough for now," Richard said, holding his hand up to still Joyce's half-voiced objection. "If you are staying nearby perhaps you will join us at the table this evening, and we will hear more of your fables then. We must bid our son farewell, and until that is done, it is not seemly to be thinking of frivolities. Come to the door after the hour of nones; Christopher will have tired of our company long before then. But do not bring your friend unless he leaves his monkey elsewhere. Our daughter is already too fond of it."

"And it of her beauty, no doubt," Reginald agreed, bowing extravagantly and moving towards the door.

"Reginald," Illesa said, standing up. "Who was born first?"

The question caught him off guard, and he hesitated before turning to face her.

"Castor was. He always looked after me as if he were my elder of ten years." There was a studied sadness in his expression. "But now others care for him, and a wide sea separates us."

"We shall share our tales of him soon," Richard concluded. "I pray you good fortune collecting your coin. It's not an easy task from the Prince's coffers."

"That is a certain and eternal truth," Reginald said with feeling and shut the door behind him.

Chapter VI

Sunday the 28th August, 1300
The Feast of Saint Augustine of Hippo
Hereford Cathedral

From the City of God – Jerusalem, I have reached the writer of *The City of God* on his Feast Day, and the Bishop is content with me for once. He has been at my throat all these months – complaining at my slowness or that I put too many fantastical animals in the Holy Land. On this day perhaps he will understand that I have this entirely in my control, and there is no way to do it otherwise. The skin needs my skill, and if I listened to his every suggestion I would soon be adding an extra city, named Hereford, in all the regions of the world.

'When will I reach the shores of England,' he asks. 'In how many weeks?'

In how many years? He has no conception of the scale of the task. He saw a map on the wall of the King's Chamber at Westminster and thought that such a marvel would bring the world to kneel here, beside the tomb of the still un-sainted Thomas. His hope and faith give him the future glory, while I must struggle with the present labour.

But he could finally see my intent, that to draw Saint Augustine in his church today is auspicious, as was drawing Bethlehem on Christmas Day, and the towns of the Acts of the Apostles on the Feast day of Peter and Paul on the 29th June. I am not a novice, attacking the map one region at a time, like those of no understanding.

And so, following a calendar he knows nothing of, I drew the route of the Israelites as they wandered in the wilderness, on the same day that, years before, Chera left England to wander through lands far from me. Though she was no longer a Jew, had not been for five years, I could not be with her. She crossed her Red Sea on the 4th of May, while I was venerating the thorn in the Cathedral, knowing nothing.

It's my thorn now, my torture. Every night burrowing deep into my brain, sending me dreams, sometimes as hot as a salamander in its nest. In the daytime, I plot the placement of Alexander the Great's camp, sketch the tents and halls. When I have finished, I see the deacon standing in the scriptorium doorway, like a wolf, to escort me to my cell. I may have no freedom in my body, but this work will be done in the way I dictate. It is a spiral – a seven-coiled path around the Sepulchre – so nothing will be ruined or smudged.

One day I felt the Armarius's hot breath on my neck. The Dean reproached me for my outburst, but what should I do when there are people ruining my concentration? The Armarius must not make comment and suggestions over my choice of ink. This is no simple copying of psalms or feast days in red, that he would understand. The scribe will come at the end and write out the descriptions from his scraps of parchment, needing my direction in every detail, for he doesn't know his basilisk from his bonnacon.

Tomorrow I will finish the south coast of the middle sea – Mauritania and the seven mountains, the rocks of Gibraltar. Then I will rest. Much is done, but there is far more to do. This eastern half of the map is but a quarter done, and there are all the farther shores. When I rest, Gervase the limner will bring out his paints. I do long to see how he colours the great cities and the throne of the most high Almighty God most of all. Blue and gold. But he does not wish to hear my instructions any more than I long for his. He is a thin, tall man, with bulging eyes and no warmth. It's wrong that he has so much power to liven a calf skin, when his own skin is so cold, full of lizardous phlegm. I am sorry for my harsh judgement from time to time, but then, God should not tempt me by providing such impossible men to work with.

My own shriven mind works against me in sleep. The dream last night was the worst yet. I followed her through a dark gateway. I said we should not go on, desperate for the light of the sun. But she had already turned down one of the many passages, and I could hear her singing a song from the streets of Lincoln, calling me on, so I followed and followed. Into the dark, my hand tracing the walls, my ears listening for her voice and my heart pounding with fear. I woke before I found her.

All this day Saint Augustine has helped me. He lived with a woman for many years until he later became a monk. Now I wish to reverse this pattern – leave the brotherhood where I have spent more than half my life, and live with a woman I know to be a true convert.

Perhaps Saint Augustine will help me if I continue to draw the world and its lessons well. This work, piously done, may earn me the reward of her.

Chapter VII

Monday the 23rd May, 1306
Priory of Saint Bartholomew the Great

Illesa bit through the green silk thread and held the needle up to the sunlight. The tear in the kirtle was not long, but it would take many tiny stitches to repair. Caught on a splinter of wood from a bench, no doubt. Like everything else beautiful and delicate, she'd not looked after it well enough. The thread finally went through the eye, and she licked the end of the silk, twisting it into a knot.

There'd been no point attending the Office of Tierce. She may as well have been a heathen, for all the prayer she'd managed. And Joyce was no better, looking up and down, fidgeting like a hen on the corn. They'd argued again afterwards, and Joyce had stormed off to find William. She'd rather be with anyone other than her mother. Perhaps Illesa's thoughts were breaking through, and people could see her sins like the monstrous hybrids cavorting in the margins of a Psalter. Taking William's hand, leading him into the wood where they would couple like animals. Woodwose and wife.

Illesa stuck the needle into her bared arm and watched a pearl of blood grow, pain erasing the images in her mind. How had she strayed so far from herself? This desire must not be allowed to take hold of her. It was absurd. She was old – a dry, stony field, the lusty years over, her body unable to bear any more children. She'd nearly died along with Margaret. Richard had insisted they stop trying to conceive. And he could barely stand, never mind fulfil his marital debt in the prescribed ways at the proper times. She should be grateful for food, for their manor, her living son and daughter.

But how long would Christopher live, now that he had taken the King's vow?

Illesa took her napkin, wiped the blood off her arm and pulled down her sleeve. She made a stitch in the silk, and two more, like tiny leaves growing on a vine.

If William had married, she would not have been goaded by this lust. But her efforts to match him had only made matters worse. And here he was, like she'd conjured him out of her desires, walking into the courtyard, unhurried, self-contained, with Joyce skipping to keep up with his strides.

Richard hobbled behind him, leaning on his stick, Christopher at his side.

Illesa dropped her kirtle on the bench, stood up and held her arms out to Christopher. He was pale and unshaven.

"Our son is not feeling his best, so don't mither him, Illesa," Richard said, slapping Christopher firmly on the shoulder.

She kissed him tentatively on both cheeks and stepped away.

"How was the night?"

"It passed, eventually. Not many of the knights chose to sleep." He was attempting a lighthearted tone.

"I hope that wasn't thanks to the ladies of London town," William said, clapping him on the other shoulder. Christopher turned red.

"Drink was their mistress, and I spent my evening on the privy. The fish did not agree with me."

"How are matters with Sir Edward?" Richard asked innocently.

"All's well." Christopher looked at him blankly. "Should they not be?" He took a cloth from inside his sleeve and mopped his sweating forehead.

"Have some ale." Joyce gave him a cup. "You have to sit down and receive the things we bought for you." She pushed him down onto the stone ledge. "Don't groan; you have to wear this all the time because it's going to protect you from sudden death." She pulled the amulet she'd chosen from the merchant in Saint Paul's out of her little pouch and slapped it into his hand. "It's best if you wear it on your chest, that way it will make sure your heart will keep beating if you lose an arm or a leg. It's agate."

Christopher held it up to the light.

"It's got the cross on one side and the sign to ward off devils on the other, so –" Joyce looked at the sky. "It should help you. God willing," she concluded and kissed him suddenly on the cheek.

Christopher gave her a rare smile. He held the orange-brown stone in his hand for a moment and then put it in his pouch.

"I'll have Thurstan sew it into my tunic so it's in the right place," he promised.

"This will help you if you are in close fighting." Richard held out a dagger the length of his hand. "Stand up and we'll strap it on with your belt. William chose it, so it will be strong enough to go through mail."

The dagger was hafted in bone, riveted in bronze, with an iron blade.

"Sharpen it yourself; don't let that squire of yours anywhere near it yet. His skill is not up to it," William said, helping Richard push the tight leather strap onto Christopher's already burdened belt.

Christopher drew the dagger out of the sheath.

"It's a good blade," he said, turning it in the sunshine. "I'll keep it close. My thanks, Father – William," he bowed his head.

"Here, son, among these small things there is one that may help you feel better." Illesa handed him a small pouch.

Christopher weighed it in his hand, opened it and tipped the contents into his palm. The small green amulet dropped out first.

"Mother, you have already given me seven assorted small crosses and stones, which will make me as invincible as Achilles if they all work."

"I know. But this one is particularly important. It's green jasper which has the property of protection against troubles of the stomach. And that's what kills off half the army because of bad food. If the royal court can't even keep the fish fresh right by the river, I can only imagine what they will feed you on the road and in the north. Keep it close. It will protect you from dysentery."

"Well, I thank you. I hope it begins to work very soon." He felt inside the pouch and brought out the ampulla.

"It was the first thing I gave your father, the last thing my brother gave me. And the Sacrist has had it filled with holy oil, in case of dire need."

Christopher turned the battered lead container over in his hand. Then he looked straight at her, and she had to glance away to hide sudden tears.

"It saved my life." Richard reached out, took the ampulla from Christopher's palm and kissed it. "May it not need to do the same for you." He held it out by its leather thong and lowered it gently onto Christopher's palm again.

Joyce was looking unimpressed.

"It's not nearly as shiny as the amulet I gave you. Mine is well polished."

"I'll look after it. I will bring it back," Christopher said, looking at his father.

"Bring yourself back. With all your limbs, if possible." Richard put both hands on Christopher's shoulders and kissed him on each cheek. "Stay with the Earl of Lincoln. He has promised me to keep you in sight. And if the Prince can receive his opinion without knowing it, he will be wisely advised. You might make a go-between and save many lives. We would be displeased to lose you because of foolish risks taken by the inexperienced."

Christopher said nothing about his father's interference, but his lips were thin and his jaw set.

"There is another small thing in the pouch. You can look at it later," Illesa said to distract him. Would he remember the single page from the *Roman de Troie* that he'd given Richard before his journey to Gascony, when he was but nine years old? A wooden horse wheeled into the city containing hope of escape – or inspiration for stratagems. Christopher stowed the pouch on his belt with just a nod.

After that there was little else to be said. Christopher was glancing towards the gate. Joyce kissed him and whispered something in his ear that took some of the tension out of his face. Illesa didn't trust her voice. She embraced him until he stiffened and watched him walk to the Priory door with Richard and William, talking about horses or whetstones or –

"Mother, you irritate him by crying all the time." Joyce hopped from one flagstone to another, hoping perhaps that Illesa would scold her and stop weeping. "If you have as much faith in God as you say you do, why are you always thinking Christopher's going to die? Shouldn't you be sure of his safe return after all the candles you've bought and the amulets and everything?" She started back along the path.

"Joyce, stop! The canons will scold you if I do not."

"I want to know." Joyce hopped one more time and stopped in front of her. "You are always telling me to have faith that Pearl will be well after she has puppies. You always say that if I pray, God willing, she'll stop bleeding and the puppies will all breathe and suck."

Illesa wiped her eyes and sniffed.

"God does not always agree with us. His ways are broader, deeper, greater. We must remind him of our small concerns. If we keep praying, keep appealing, he will listen and grant our prayers, if it is right to do so."

"What if it isn't right and you've spent all those hours praying and crying for nothing?"

"Joyce, enough!" Illesa snapped. A canon walking towards the Prior's door turned round and stared at her. "Your father will return soon. Don't let him find you arguing again. It's unseemly now you are a young woman."

"But you and he argue about such things all the time." Joyce's whisper was barely audible as she stomped off.

And here was the serpent with his long, forked tongue again – William striding across the courtyard, the breeze lifting the hair from his forehead. She lowered her eyes.

"What's upset her now?" He held out a scrap of parchment. "Not her brother's departure, I warrant." Illesa took it without looking at him and turned the stained message over in her hands.

"Who's this from? And where is Richard? It's addressed to him."

"Lord Burnel said for you to open it. He's with the Brother Guestmaster – settling our wine account." William used the same icy tone that she had. She turned the scrap over again, examining the red marks.

"But who delivered it, William? There's blood on it."

He looked down at the parchment, his jaw working.

"A small boy. One of the players' apprentices, I think. There was blood dripping down his ear. I gave him some water and a farthing. Told him to spend it on a big pie." He twisted his cap tight in his hand. "If I find the man who beat him, he'll be the one bleeding."

For all his gruffness, William was soft when it came to children, especially poor ones on the street. Illesa opened the grubby scrap of parchment. It was written in English in a strange sloping hand. She had to read it three times before she could make out some of the letters. She looked up. Joyce was bending over her, being nosy.

"Reginald says he'll come after vespers to bid us farewell but is not able to eat with us."

Joyce kicked a stone and stalked down the path.

"I would be content to never see him again," William said, under his breath. "His resemblance to Gaspar is devilish."

Illesa shook off the impulse to agree, her eyes still lowered.

"He's been kind to us. I'm sure that Ramón trained that monkey to steal, and Reginald convinced him to give back those beads." She squinted at the parchment again. It was a scrap reused from some old account roll – the smears of blood fresh. "Besides, he must know more about Gaspar. I'd like to hear about their early years." Gaspar would never talk of his youth. He always had an appearance of great jollity and openness, but any query about his origins brought on a tale of Reynard or Howleglass, and so much laughter that you forgot your original question.

William's feet turned away from her.

"I doubt it was kindness behind the return of the beads. And if you want to know about Gaspar, remember Reginald will be able to lie just as sweetly as he did. They've had the same masters, after all."

Illesa folded the bloodstained parchment in her hand. Had Gaspar and Reginald suffered the same rough treatment when they were boy apprentices?

She tucked it away, deep in her pouch.

Chapter VIII

Vespers

Vespers in the Priory was also wasted. Illesa's mind wandered, full of the last moments with Gaspar. They should have moved him to England not left him alone in a foreign land, especially after Azalais had died. In one of his last messages, he'd recounted that her funeral procession was so long and noisy it rivalled that of a bishop. And they both knew how much that would have pleased her.

Richard had little patience for her concerns. To him, their donations to the Saint Nicolas house for Gaspar's sustenance were more than generous. Visiting him was out of the question. Richard never wanted to cross the sea again. So it was now eleven years since she'd seen Gaspar, and the messages had entirely stopped. The Lazar house would surely have sent word if he'd died. Her queries, however, remained unanswered.

The cantor was chanting the final prayer. Soon they would all file out. Joyce had her head bowed, eyes closed, mouth a little open. The strange food, the miles of walking, the late hours, had all made her more difficult. But she wouldn't sleep until she'd seen Reginald again. It was pointless insisting.

The congregation rose from their knees.

William had gone to find Thomas and Ralph, two young men from Bridgnorth who'd been in their company on the way south and would be returning with them. They were somewhere in Smithfield, he thought. Even in such a city, William seemed unconcerned at losing anyone or being lost himself, yet he never wanted to leave Langley and longed to return whenever he was away. He seemed to have no need of women, yet could have his choice of them. He gave away his coin without qualm. His indifference to the temptations of the world obviously provoked the Devil, who was doing his best to corrupt William through her.

They stepped out into the Prior's courtyard below a clear, twilit sky and sat down on one of the benches. Joyce was trying not to lean against Richard. If she did, she'd be asleep in a

moment. Illesa resisted the urge to stroke her chestnut hair –
Richard's colour not hers. At least everyone acknowledged that
Joyce had Illesa's eyes.

Richard tapped her shoulder.

"Get a flagon of wine for us to share. It will ease the time
and my pains."

Illesa got slowly to her feet and went to the guest hall door.

"Lady Burnel –"

A voice stopped her on the threshold. A canon in the
shadow of the eaves put his hand out to stop her from going
further.

"Brother Guestmaster. You surprised me!"

"You require something?" His full, round face wrinkled with
disapproval.

"A flagon of wine, if it please you. We have a visitor arriving
shortly."

The monk looked over her head towards the wide doorway.

"Guests should not come after vespers. The cellarer has
gone to his cell. The gates will be closed soon, and it is not right
for Brother Gatekeeper to be kept from his prayers." He
breathed in noisily. "It's not the joculators you entertained this
morning? That kind are a corrupting influence on our house –
and on the guests here. This is not a tavern."

He was breathing as loudly as someone running uphill after
his little sermon.

"Brother, these players have entertained the King – and
Prince Edward. They are not rough travelling jongleurs but
skilled servants of our sovereign – as was the founder of your
Priory. It will be a very short meeting, I assure you. Did Sir
Richard not tell you of it when he paid our donation today?"

"He did not."

"Let me settle with you for the trouble," Illesa said, feeling
for her purse. "I understand it's a disturbance. A gift for Our
Lady's chapel, for candles to restore the right worshipful peace
to this place."

The monk regarded her – hostility and greed battling for
ascendancy.

"There should be no loud noise, no laughter or singing. This
is a solemn house." He held his palm at his waist so no one else
would be able to see him take the coin.

58

"I understand, Brother." Illesa dropped the coin so she wouldn't have to touch his sweaty palm. "Sir Burnel has asked for wine."

"Bernard the novice will place it in the Prior's parlour, and he will wait on you briefly. Then he will eject your guest and lock the door before compline."

Illesa nodded curtly and turned her back on the self-righteous hypocrite. Every priory and abbey had at least one, in her experience, and he was usually the monk charged with giving alms or serving guests.

Richard and Joyce had left the courtyard, and must already be in the parlour. In every religious house, players were despised, and those who told stories in the market place were jeered at by nobles and merchants alike. Yet when there was a feast, they were applauded, their stories repeated, but paid little. She twisted the garnet ring on her finger. Those living comfortably had no understanding of the painful life on the road.

The room was in deep shadow – the novice going from one lamp to another with a taper, his young pitted face thrown into stark relief.

"No sign of Reginald yet." Richard said, looking up at her. He was on the stool, Joyce standing at his side. "Any wine?"

"I'm told that Bernard the novice will bring it," Illesa said. The novice stared at her, hollow-eyed, and wordlessly left the chamber.

"We are allowed only a short time, and the guestmaster wanted a bribe for allowing Reginald in. He claims that players bring temptation into the religious house."

"And coin washes that away. Was that the direction of his thought? We have little enough left. I'd rather not spend it on Reginald the Liar." Richard put his hands on his knees and stretched his back. "We need our beds. If he doesn't come soon, I'll have the gatekeeper send him away myself."

"Father, please!" Joyce turned from her pacing of the room. "I want to hear one of his stories."

"And so you shall," a figure said from the doorway, "by your leave, Sir Richard."

Reginald came down the step into the parlour and made a sweeping bow. Behind him the novice looked on dolefully, holding a tray.

"My apologies for being unable to join you earlier. The Prince insisted that we entertain the court during their meal in order to be paid for our first performance. I'd much rather have been here in this *hospitable* house," he grinned. Bernard the novice made no sign of hearing the jibe as he set down the tray and poured the wine into four cups. His sandals slapped on the steps as he left, but the edge of his habit showed where he stood listening outside the open door.

"We thank you for coming, Master Reginald." Richard indicated that he should sit on the opposite side of the room and took a cup from the tray that Illesa was holding.

"Oh, how welcome wine is!" Reginald sang, taking the cup she offered.

"No singing allowed, says the Brother Guestmaster," Illesa cautioned, sitting down next to Joyce and giving her the last cup.

Reginald glanced at the door.

"Ah, he knows me of old. Didn't like my characterization of greedy monks at Corpus Christi. I promise to be quiet." He winked at Joyce and took a sip of the wine.

"We give thanks to God for the wine and for finding Gaspar's brother," Illesa said, bowing her head,

"We have but a few minutes," Richard said, waving his hand at Illesa's piety. "As you know, Reginald, your brother did me a great service. Tell us more about your history. Your face is the only testimony we have of your shared parentage."

"And I have no such assurance," Reginald said, "but of course I know you to be an honest knight, spoken of with respect by sundry earls and kings." He made the sign of subservience with his palm. "Your manservant perhaps follows a different code. And I can believe how useful that is. Although, it's a shame he injured the monkey's foot, and Mullida will not walk thanks to his rough handling."

"No!" Joyce began, but Richard held up his hand for silence.

"She walked well enough when she took a turn as Noah's wife."

Reginald laughed.

"I'm teasing you. The creature is perfectly well. My Castilian friend is less so, but that is no matter. He will mend, and we will all be great friends. Just as Gaspar has been to you! Of course he told me of you, after that disastrous Round Table when his ear was sliced off. He stopped to see me on his way to the Earl of Lincoln's castle. Entertained me royally, particularly regarding your exploits, Lady Burnel."

He looked at Illesa knowingly.

"What happened there?" Joyce asked. "You haven't told me about a Round Table."

"Perhaps that is a tale for another place and time," Reginald whispered, "not a reverend religious house with ears sprouting from every stone. And then years later – he sent me a message revealing that he would not be sharing the stage with me at Christmas in Kings Langley because he was to be with you in another Langley in distant Shropshire, and how it was a very long ride but worth it to see a small lady no higher than a cat, called Joyce!"

"He did?" Joyce looked delighted.

"He did, and I almost forgave him for rejecting me, because he described how beautiful and sweet you were."

"That must have been when you were in Bordeaux, Richard." The Christmas when Azalais and her John had joined them. Both gone to the Lord now.

"Evidently, as I've never seen Gaspar at our Nativity feast." He was looking at Reginald appraisingly.

"So you and he performed together? It is interesting that I've never seen you before to my knowledge, although as you can tell, I can see but half of what others do." It was Richard's favourite witticism, and Reginald paid it homage very civilly.

"He and I trained together as children, but then we parted ways. We were too similar. Companies needed different-looking performers. He was happy to leave – he has a restless nature, as I'm sure you know, and his proclivities were unsatisfied in the small towns we worked. I was blessed to be sponsored in a company that entertained the royal children. Prince Edward soon became rather dependent on my stories to help him sleep, and he still keeps me nearby."

"But you will not be going north with him? They don't take players on campaigns, do they?"

"Few go to such inhospitable climes. We're waiting to see which noble guest might invite us to their hall to entertain them before we return to St Albans for his feast day in June."

"Come and entertain us," cried Joyce. "They could come to Langley, couldn't they, Father? It will be so quiet and boring without Christopher. I'll have no one to talk to."

Reginald clapped his hands just like a young child and pretended to run around in circles with delight.

"It's too far for these players to travel and have only us as audience, Joyce!" Illesa patted her knee. "It would be a strange thing to have a company of players to stay merely to keep you from boredom when you should be practising your needlework and writing."

Joyce scowled at her.

"Perhaps we might invite them another time – when we have something to celebrate," Richard mused. "Although they will find the Welsh March rougher than Kings Langley."

Reginald was mirroring Joyce's expression exactly, and she was trying not to laugh.

"It would be a great honour to visit your manor when you are in a merry humour, but perhaps it would be best if we did not bring the monkey." Reginald acted out it stealing Joyce's beads and she giggled.

"I would keep all my things locked up!"

"Clever girl," he said. "But don't lock up your self in a nunnery like this where you will live in perpetual gloom."

"Reginald –"

Illesa put up a hand to still his next joke.

"We have so little time. You say Gaspar sent you word when he came to us, but have you seen and heard anything from him since?"

Reginald straightened his face.

"I have not heard from him since his message of travel to Gascony, on secret business. I thought he must have died until the Earl of Lincoln told me he was a leper and would stay in Gascony, thanks to his patron." He brought his hands together as if in prayer and bowed to Richard. "I suppose he must have been ashamed, as he never wrote to tell me. He always wanted to be the strongest. I imagine you are just the same with your brother, Joyce?"

Illesa interrupted Joyce's reply.

"Gaspar hasn't written the Lazar house in two years. Do you have any idea where he might be?"

"I'd say it's a surprise he stayed there for so long."

Richard leant forward.

"So you think he has left – gone to live somewhere else?"

"If he's well enough to walk, I think he will be seeking out new friends in new places," Reginald said, with a leer.

"Maybe he's gone on a pilgrimage to seek healing," Illesa suggested.

Reginald shrugged.

The novice had moved so that half of his body was now visible in the doorway. The distant curfew bell was ringing inside the city walls. Richard stretched his legs out in front of him.

"Reginald does not know, Illesa. Only God does. Let it be. He must go now or risk having to sleep in a ditch."

Reginald nodded at this.

"I see the good brothers here are not in favour of housing a joculator for the night." He bent towards Joyce's ear. "They would never be able to forget the rude stories." He straightened up and made a smart bow. "Perhaps we might meet tomorrow and have good cheer in one of the city inns?"

Joyce jumped a little on her bench with excitement, but Richard held up his palm.

"We must leave tomorrow, at first light. But we know where we can find you again. Wherever the Prince is, you will not be far away. Thank you for your time, Master Reginald." Richard pushed himself up on his stick.

"Which road do you take? I am not familiar with the western routes." Reginald got to his feet and made them face opposite directions.

"Woodstock, then Tewkesbury where we will go by barge to Bridgnorth in company with some young merchants. But Illesa would have us go overland to Hereford from Tewkesbury to appeal to Thomas Cantilupe again, rather than be home a week earlier by river. Unless she has now decided she might be content to see all the saints between here and Tewkesbury instead?" Richard rolled his one eye.

"You should come with me," Illesa insisted. "It is for your health, and Christopher's safety, that I go to appeal to Thomas!"

"I've been before. My body will not bear so much road travel. We have discussed this already, at length."

Illesa shook her head and turned to the player. He was grinning at each of them in turn as if at a puppet show.

"I'm glad to have met you, Reginald," Illesa said. "I will pray for Gaspar at Thomas's shrine and hope we might both see him again."

"I pray so, lady. He is blessed to have such friends. Especially you," he said, turning to Joyce. "Perhaps we may meet on the road one day. Isn't it always the rule that you meet once then twice in quick succession and not again for a generation?" They filed into the open air. Bright stars had pricked through the blue twilight.

The gatekeeper beckoned from the Priory door. William was waiting beside him in the shadow, hands hanging at his sides, eyes fixed on the player.

"I'll speak with you for a moment," he said to Reginald, and nodded him through the gate. Reginald managed a twist of a smile, bowed to them all and stepped through the door into the dark street.

Chapter IX

Tuesday the 24th May, 1306
Watling Street
Tierce

"What did you talk to Reginald about?"

William did not turn to look at her, and she couldn't see his expression under the deep shade of his hat.

"I was inquiring about a few things."

"What things?"

"The apprentice that'd brought the message, the one who'd been bleeding all over it, was hanging around the Priory last evening. He didn't want to go back to the players. So I sat him down for a bit, and asked him this and that."

"William –"

"You asked me, and I'm telling you, unless you don't really want to know?"

"I do, but you can't save all the children you come across. You've said as much to me before."

"Are you my mother, Lady Burnel? Don't you think you've meddled enough in my affairs?"

Illesa looked away. He'd every right to be angry with her. But she couldn't explain to him why she'd encouraged Phylis, the saddlemaker's daughter, to think he loved her. It had only gone wrong because he continued to be completely indifferent to her, despite her comely willingness. Illesa should have spent more time assessing her character before trying the match. Now Phylis wouldn't leave him alone. Messages arrived from her every week. And on feast days, the distance from Shrewsbury to Langley was of no consequence to her on her costly mare and fine saddle.

"Please tell me about the boy, William."

William rode on silently for a few moments.

"I hope you haven't hidden him in your saddle bag." Illesa said, attempting a light tone.

"He would've been better off."

"What do you mean?"

"What I said."

"William, countless boys in London will be beaten when they're caught skiving. They'll all complain."

"That's not what I meant." He gave her an angry look. "And you know it."

"I know that you were treated cruelly as a boy, and you hate seeing it happen to others."

"And my sister had an even worse time with those horse thieves and that's what is happening to that lad. It has nothing to do with misbehaviour."

"I don't know what happened to your sister, William. You've never spoken of it since you came to live with us."

"I'll not pollute your ears with it if you haven't the experience to know what I mean. And we don't want Joyce overhearing." William glanced back at Joyce, who was talking to one of the merchants. The younger, more handsome brother.

Illesa turned back to William.

"Do you know who was mistreating the boy?"

"He could not say. He was so terrified as to what would happen if he did, he wet himself just thinking about telling me."

"Is that what you were asking Reginald about?"

"Yes." William slapped a fly on his arm.

William would never become a father at this rate, but his sympathy for children had no bounds. He was the same with horses.

"What did Reginald say?"

"He claimed the boy had only been with the company a few months but had been caught stealing and lying on several occasions since then."

"Did you ask him about the injury?"

"He said he knew nothing about it but would find out what had happened." William's tone was scathing. "He said the boy often played with the street dogs and one of them probably bit him."

"And you don't believe him."

"Would you believe someone called Reginald the Liar? Any road, I'd already given the boy a shilling and told him to run to the nuns at the Abbey of Saint Clare. They will take him in if he's not too scared to go and makes it that far. He can be the sisters' scullion. Work the kitchen spits. He doesn't eat much."

"And if he doesn't go? If the boy is a liar? He's tricked you into paying him a whole shilling!"

"*You* didn't see him, Lady Burnel." William said coldly. "The boy was not capable of that sort of game. Too young and too scared. The only thing he could do was keep silent. Besides, if he takes the shilling for himself, at least it will do him some good."

William touched his horse lightly with his heels.

"Who is the master of the players?" Illesa called after him. "Surely that's the man to ask!"

But they were trotting past an old man on a fat pony led by a retainer, and William did not answer. When they reassembled further down the road, Joyce was riding closest to her.

"How far is it until we stop? I'm so hot and hungry."

"Abbots Langley, not far away, I hope. Perhaps we should stop for water?"

"We don't have to climb that hill do we?" Joyce pointed to the round hill on their right – steep-sided, close-grazed.

"No, remember, the road goes around it."

"I don't remember anything about the ride down. It was so tedious."

"Don't you like seeing the different houses and towns? You seem to like talking to Ralph."

"They are just buildings, and he's only interested in trade. He talks about nothing but pack horses and how many he's going to need for his next journey with all their mountains of wool."

"Take this." Illesa pulled her waterskin off her shoulder. "It might help." She kicked Lady's sides, hoping to catch up with William.

But William stayed out of reach all the way to the next bridge and watering place. And by the time they eventually reached the inn, she'd decided to leave him alone. A hot day in the saddle after little sleep had made them all irritable.

The next two days were cooler. It was good to have the close, threatening crowds behind them. Despite the pain he felt, Richard was more cheerful the further they went. He spent plenty of coin at The Bear Inn in Woodstock on a good meal and a fine room. He even opened their board to Thomas and Ralph. After drinking more than usual, he insisted on telling the merchants of his escape from Gascony and how Illesa had fooled the assassin. They thought he must be lying, and Illesa had to confirm the tale.

"It is true, but I can hardly believe it myself. I wouldn't dare do anything like it now. But we should discuss the plan for the next part of the journey while we are all sitting together. Don't you think so, husband?"

Richard leant back against the wall, wincing.

"I haven't changed my mind and talking about it isn't going to make me do so. You should be the one to agree to come on the barge with the rest of us, rather than bending the ear of yet another saint at more expense. Haven't you spent enough in candles across all of London and every church on the way?"

"Can there ever be enough? You know what happens in war. Do you want Christopher to end up in constant pain, like you? Or dead?"

"The saints won't stop that happening. You should know that by now."

"They can – sometimes they do." The rest of the party were watching them. Joyce had her hands over her ears. Illesa lowered her voice. "It isn't much out of the way. William, you said you wanted to see the great cloth of the world, didn't you?" William shrugged and looked into his ale. "It wasn't finished when we were last in Hereford, Richard. And Joyce should see it. We don't know when we'll be travelling so far from home again."

"Next month, if I know you." Richard drained the last of his wine. "I'm going upriver from Tewkesbury, and if you must go to Hereford, William may go with you to keep you safe on the road, but he will be needed soon. We have already missed too much work in the weeks we've been away."

"We will go with you by river, Sir Burnel." Thomas the merchant stood up, and his brother followed. "The bargeman is already paid and expecting us this week, and we have business to conduct with him regarding the new fleeces. We cannot make an extra journey to Hereford at this time of year, even for the good of our souls! You travel with us, Sir, and when we arrive in Bridgnorth, we will see you safe on the road to Langley."

The men had decided on their plan, leaving her with William for a week. Exactly what she'd been trying to avoid.

"That must be that. My old body will not survive another week on horseback." Richard put up his hand to stop Illesa's argument. "Yes, I'm aware that Thomas Cantilupe cured an injured knight twenty years ago, wife. We have asked and not received. It would be churlish to keep asking. William, are you content to go with them?" Richard pushed himself to his feet.

William splayed his hands on the table, his face unreadable.

"I'll do my best to keep them away from the temptations of any more saints and be home soon after the nones of June."

Illesa lay next to Richard in the sagging bed in The Bear, listening to the snoring of William on a pallet nearby and the deep breathing of Joyce on the other side of her. Richard was wriggling on the uncomfortable mattress. Even wine and tincture of Saint John's wort could not ease the pain and cramp once it took hold.

"Shall I knead the muscles for you?"

"No." He sat up a little and sucked air in through his teeth. "I'll wake the others when I groan."

"Let me try. Those two will sleep through almost anything." She climbed out of the bed and stood over him, pressing the knotted muscles with the heel of her palm.

"What did you think of Reginald, husband?"

His breathing was harsh with the pain.

"Strange. Like Gaspar, but not."

"Yes, I know that. But what did you think of his character? Did you trust his words?"

"No. But why say the truth to people he didn't know who'd taken a monkey hostage? I think he said exactly what he needed to in order to get the monkey back and stop us from reporting him to the Westminster guards or the London aldermen."

"He seemed to want to be in our company, but he'd seen so little of Gaspar, and he didn't seem to want to know more about his welfare. Why was he so uninterested?"

"He might be tired of being recognised as him, or of being beaten up by Gaspar's many discarded paramours. I would guess that being Gaspar's brother was rather punishing at times. Especially if he moves among the noble members of the court with the Prince."

"He has both his ears, so there is no danger of him being mistaken for him."

Richard sighed as the muscles began to loosen.

"True, except from a distance, as you showed during the performance."

"Did William tell you what he asked Reginald as he was leaving?"

"No. I thought he was simply reiterating his desire never to see the monkey again. William's hand is quite swollen with those scratches. You should put salve on it again. The journey has made it worse."

Trust William to leave it to fester rather than ask her for help. She could use the last of the honey and valerian.

"I'll look at it in the morning. William was asking Reginald about the messenger boy. He thinks someone in the company of players was beating him cruelly. And maybe worse."

"Not again." Richard turned his head to look at her, his eye shining in the light of one candle. "I think the memories are more vivid now than when he was just a boy and first came to us. He never used to talk about his life at that inn in Clun, but now every time we go to a town and he sees the urchins, he has to find out what they've suffered."

"He gave the messenger boy a shilling and sent him to the nuns."

"He's doing nothing but stirring up trouble by that," Richard said, sitting up more easily. "I'll talk to him about it in the morning. I give him fair wages to buy good clothes and equipment, and he gives it away to the street children at the first chance. Then he looks like the retainer of a landless vagrant, and —"

"I know." Illesa smoothed the blanket over his legs and lay down next to him again. "I told him the boy was probably lying, but he didn't care."

"He mustn't spend any more of the coin on the poor boys in Hereford. You may need it if there is trouble on the way home. And you aren't to spend any more than for one candle either, Illesa. Let your prayers be enough, as they should be. The monks and clergy enjoy taking the offerings to make their churches rich. I'll put my faith in the sacraments, not in badges and effigies." He lay down and put his hand on hers on the blanket.

"Please try to believe that the saint will help you – and Christopher. If you don't, my prayers will be of little use. And I hate seeing you suffer."

"I try, for your sake." He saw her expression and winced. "I will. You know I'll pray for him in our chapel morning and night, and that is the place that knows him best."

Chapter X

Sunday the 29th May, 1306
Tewkesbury
Vespers

The road from Stow was rutted and full of holes. A cart had tipped over on a hill and the driver lay in the road, insensible. The cart wheel had only stopped when it lodged against his head. Illesa hadn't been able to revive him. They'd had to carry him to the nearest manor, where he was unlikely to recover. So it was nearly dark when they approached the tower of Tewkesbury Abbey, although they'd been able to see it for miles.

William had gone ahead to hire a room and prepare the stable to receive their horses. But when they arrived in the unlit yard of The Black Bear, he was nowhere to be seen. A boy came out from the stable, taking their reins wordlessly.

"Are you expecting us?" Richard asked. Ralph was already off his horse and helping Richard dismount.

The boy nodded.

"Your constable will be back soon. There's a room for you all." He stared at Illesa's muddy cloak and kirtle as she dismounted. "There's water over there by that door."

Joyce looked around morosely.

"I wish we were home now. Can't we go by barge with the others? We've been riding for so long!"

"No. You'll feel better after food and rest. And a wash. We're here for two days, so your saddle sores will get better. Come. We'll look at the room and make you a comfortable bed."

The inside of the inn was better than the outside, and their room overlooking the river was clean. One wide bed was already made up. The pallets piled up against the wall were well aired. The blankets had no holes. Joyce sat down on the edge of the bed and groaned.

"Lie down. I'll ask for food."

The hall was loud with bargemen and merchants drinking. It was the most costly inn in a costly town on the confluence of the Avon and Severn. They could really only afford one night here. Tomorrow, once Richard and the merchants had gone, they might need to find a cheaper room. But The Lamb, where they'd stayed on the way down, had been disgusting. And the Abbey was rebuilding its guesthouse and could accommodate no one. The choices were poor. On the other side of the hall, Richard and William were in conversation with the innkeeper. William caught her eye and pushed through to intercept her.

"We've already seen the bargemaster." He indicated the massive figure of Simon, who was drinking with a group of younger men. "Now Richard is negotiating for a reduced fee for tomorrow night, in a smaller room. There's one over the stable that will cost little. And yes, he has asked for bread and cheese immediately, before Mistress Joyce dies of her temper. And ale for those of us who've done more than sit on a horse and complain."

"Good. I'm glad we can stay here," Illesa said, checking her pouch.

William was looking over her head towards the front door to the inn.

"Are you expecting someone?"

"Saint Joseph and the Virgin, you mean? No. I hope not." He squeezed his cap in his hand. "Did you see the river? They will need a strong team to tow the barge up. Some ill wind has blown it."

"Perhaps it will have calmed by tomorrow." He made to move away, but she stopped him by nearly touching his arm. "Do you know the road to Hereford? I've heard that Saint Michael's at Ledbury is a favourable church to visit, but I've never been that way."

William shook his head.

"Finding the right inn is more important if you don't want to be robbed, as you should know by now."

"We will make sure we reach the town in time for you to find good lodging. Joyce and I will visit the Abbey Church tomorrow. The horses can rest. You too."

"I thank you," he said mockingly. "But it would be best if you two did not go anywhere alone. Besides there are things I may wish to see in the church myself. I'm not such a heathen as you think."

"I know you're not; I just thought you would be weary after all you've had to do."

"I'll rest when we reach home. Not before."

"What are you two doing blocking the aisle?" Richard limped between them. "Help me up the stairs, one of you, instead of arguing."

"We weren't arguing," Illesa insisted, taking his arm.

"Go and fetch the ale, man." Richard waved William towards the inn bar. "We will at least have some in the chamber if the food takes as long as I think it will."

William threaded his way towards the bar. Illesa put her shoulder under Richard's and began supporting him up the stairs.

"What's wrong with him? He looks like a trapped fox."

"I don't know. You interrupted me when I was trying to find out."

Richard grunted. They reached the top step, and Illesa wiped the sweat off her forehead.

"He's probably worried about our safety on the road."

Richard opened the chamber door.

"Or he's cross because he wants to go straight home to check on the new foal."

Joyce was lying on her side on the bed, eyes closed, but she didn't look asleep.

"At what hour does your barge leave tomorrow?" Illesa asked, sitting down next to Joyce.

"The bargemaster said tierce, but he didn't seem in any great hurry." Richard sank noisily onto the other side of the bed. "And they will have to gather the bowhauliers. I'm sure most of them are downstairs drinking. And Thomas and Ralph have yet to sell their horses. I'll be surprised if we leave before sext. We may reach Worcester tomorrow, or sleep on board, which would be cheaper for us all."

William opened the door, holding a jug of ale and cups on a tray.

Joyce opened her eyes.

"Any bread?"

Quite a while later, they'd all eaten a fish pie and frumenty in the hall, and William was on the other side of the table watching the merchants dicing with a bowyer from Stratford. They were losing, and when they'd handed over yet another coin, he tapped them on each shoulder and pointed to the stairs.

"Go to bed before you lose all the coin you gained for your father. It's time to go in and shut the door. You're being fleeced."

"We would've won the next throw." Thomas pulled at his brother's tunic. "Come along. Brother William has given us his wise advice, and we ignore it at our peril," he said with false reverence. They staggered a little as they went to relieve themselves in the yard.

William stood waiting for them to return. He'd remained watchful all evening, especially since Richard had retired to the chamber, worn out from the pain of riding all day.

"Go up to your father, Joyce, and make sure he is comfortable. He might need help. I'll be there in a moment."

Illesa watched Joyce drag her feet up the stairs and went to stand next to William.

"What is worrying you, William? It's not late but you are like a mouse on the granary stair."

"It's late enough. Those lads are already too drunk to be of any use if their strength is needed."

He moved towards the stairs.

"Are you expecting us to be robbed in our beds?"

"It's possible. There are plenty down here armed enough, poor enough and drunk enough."

"You weren't so worried on the way to London."

"We weren't being followed then."

Illesa's heart began to thump.

"What? Followed by whom?"

Thomas and Ralph came back through the door, singing an old sailor's song. William got them by the shoulders and pushed them towards the stairs.

"I don't know. I saw him at a distance."

She watched the merchants stumble up towards the chamber.

"Are you sure you are not imagining this, William? Why would anyone follow us?"

William rolled his eyes.

"In a lightly armed group of nobles and merchants like us, there will be coin at least. And there is a young woman to be taken hostage. She is worth something to gangs of outlaws. Then there are her jewels – and yours."

Illesa put her hand to her brooch.

"How many have you seen? Have you told Richard?"

"Just one. But he could be a scout for a large group."

"One? That's not likely is it? Why do you suspect him?"

"I just recognise the signs." William adjusted his dagger on his belt. "Richard can do nothing about it except worry, so I haven't told him. I'll sleep against the door tonight. The windows have good shutters. Those lads are merry but won't be insensible."

But there would only be William tomorrow. No extra swords in case of trouble.

"Maybe we should all go on the barge," she admitted. It would be a relief.

"No room for us now. I heard the bow hauliers complain. It's too heavy already. They're loading up half of the hold with wine barrels in the morning." William looked at her grumpily, shrugged and went up the stairs.

Illesa started climbing slowly after him.

In the chamber, the merchants were already on their pallets, grunting and pulling off their boots. Joyce was sitting on the bed next to a motionless Richard. The shutter was closed. Illesa pulled the door behind her and put the pin in the latch, shaking it to see how strong it was.

William took the last of the pallets and pushed it up against the door.

"I'll have my back to it all night. If anyone comes, I'll feel it."

"Thank you, William, but I'm sure it will be a peaceful night." She didn't want to alarm Joyce.

"Not if *he* starts snoring," Thomas said, pointing at Ralph.

Illesa picked her way between the pallets to the other side of the bed. Richard was half-asleep. He opened his eye a crack as she sat down.

"Will you make some tincture in the morning?"

"Yes, I've got some vervain left. It should be enough."

"How long will it take you to get home? I'll need to eke it out. Unless Cecily has some stored away."

"We will only spend one night in Hereford. As William said, we will be back as soon as we can. Maybe only three days later than you."

"That's unlikely," he grumbled.

"It's possible." She smoothed his hair off his forehead.

"I hope you're not going to make me visit all the small churches on the way home as well, Mother." Joyce tucked her boots under the bed. "We've seen hundreds already!"

"We will go straight home from Hereford. I promise both of you."

Joyce pulled up the coverlet and turned her back on her parents.

"I can't wait to see Cecily again. She'll make the fig pudding with the spices when I arrive because she knows it's my favourite."

"And she does everything you say," Illesa sighed, "sparing no expense."

"You are always talking about expense. Why can't we just enjoy things without worrying about how much they cost?"

"When you are married and the mistress of your own manor, perhaps you'll understand. Until then, the cinnamon and mace will remain under lock and key."

Chapter XI

Monday the 30th May, 1306
Tewkesbury

Illesa and Joyce walked down the muddy street towards the Abbey Church, William a few paces behind them. It was an hour after prime, and the street was already busy with carts and donkeys. The shops were opening their shutters, setting out their boards and wares. Perhaps they really would leave when the bargeman said. There was a feeling of rushing through the town, as if the wind could make everyone move faster.

"We must be sure to be back in time to bid them farewell."

Joyce did not look up. The prospect of a day without travel was fine, but losing the company of the handsome merchants had made her morose, even though she'd claimed to find them boring.

The night had been quiet. After waking at midnight, Illesa had checked everyone was still in the room and fallen back into a deep sleep. As she'd woken the second time, she'd been dreaming of the monkey, running around her feet, scratching her with sharp claws. It caught a ring that fell from her hand and ran off with it. She'd chased after it, shouting, but it only ran faster and got bigger and bigger.

A disturbing dream. But here in this church, bright with new paint, she had a chance to put things right. It had an impressive nave, with massive columns. High above, there was an arcade and triforium, smaller than the one at Westminster Abbey, but beautiful. A monk was pacing its length. When he had walked the whole length of the nave, he turned and started back again. A penance perhaps. In a quiet moment, Illesa thought she could hear his chanted words.

"Can we go to the chapels now?" Joyce was already ahead, hurrying her along by pulling on her arm. She loved the wall paintings; they were like a giant book where she could entertain herself for hours finding the saints by their attributes. Her favourite had always been Saint Veronica with her cloth impression of Christ's face. She was rare – so even more special.

"You go; I'm going to pray here," Illesa said, kneeling in sight of the high altar. Having missed Mass the day before, she wanted to go through it in her mind and make her confession. That would take long enough. Then she would try to imagine the river that flowed from the City of God as this River Severn that would take Richard safely home. And the City of God as London, where the angelic host would ride out to defeat God's enemies, alongside Christopher and the army. And the road ahead of them as the road to Emmaus when Christ came to walk with his disciples and broke bread with them in a simple home. Which for them would be their own home at Langley, eventually.

It seemed no time at all before her shoulder was being shaken.

"Time to leave. Where's Joyce?" William was looking around, a deep line of worry across his forehead. "I was standing by the painting of Saint Christopher by the door, praying for our journey. She hasn't gone past me, so she must be in the church somewhere."

Illesa got stiffly to her feet, looking around.

"She said she wanted to see the chapels. I should have gone with her."

They started down the south aisle. The monk in the triforium was gone. The sun no longer shone through the windows.

"It's so late! William, you find her and bring her quickly. I mustn't miss them leaving in the barge. I'll be at the quayside."

The blazing sunshine outside made her squint. It was not seemly to run, so she walked as fast as she could onto the street and then down towards the river.

There were several barges already underway, but the one farthest was the old blue and red barge they'd arrived in weeks before, and the master, huge Simon, was still ordering the barrels in the hold, shouting loud enough to wake the dead. Illesa slowed to a normal walk. Richard was leaning against the wall separating the quay from the town.

"No Joyce? Doesn't she want to bid her father farewell?"

"She's coming. William went to find her. You know how much she loves looking at all the wall paintings of the saints."

"There they are, I think." Richard squinted down the walkway. His eye had been getting worse and worse. That was the other reason he didn't like riding. Half the time he couldn't see what was in front of him. The figures were actually Thomas and Ralph.

"No. And neither will be happy to know you mistook them for the other. But there's no hurry. The barge isn't going anywhere for a while."

Thomas and Ralph bowed to them and settled a little way off, comparing their luck selling their horses, taking the coins from their purses and examining them closely.

Illesa felt for her own purse. It was very light.

"Have you settled the bill for both nights?"

Richard nodded.

"Yes. And paid for the meal tonight, so don't let him charge you any more. Did you find out what was bothering William?"

"Just one of his strange ideas. He thought we were being followed by a scout for a gang of robbers."

Richard sighed.

"The sooner he gets rid of that Phylis the better. The whole situation has set him on edge."

"Phylis might have been good for him if he'd given her a chance."

Richard raised his eyebrows at her.

"Don't start that again. Ah, here they are now."

William and Joyce were just a few paces away, both looking hot and cross. Joyce stopped at Illesa's side and began smoothing down her hair.

"Here you are at last." Richard got to his feet and adjusted his belt. Master Simon had started shouting the all aboard. "We'll be on our way."

Illesa kissed his cheek and he her hand.

The merchant brothers slung in their packs and turned, as one man, towards Illesa and Joyce.

"We will ensure Sir Richard reaches home safely, if it is in our power." Ralph smiled, as if at a small child. He held out two pennies. "Give this to the Blessed Thomas for us, and pray for our endeavours."

Illesa took the coins and tilted her head at the proud young man.

"I got Richard out of captivity in Bordeaux; all you need do is keep him company on the river."

The merchants glanced at one another uncertainly. Behind them, Richard looked amused. He opened his arms to Joyce, and she embraced him tightly – the way she'd used to hold Illesa.

"God speed." William took Richard's arm and helped him into the barge.

The four hauliers grabbed the ropes and began unwinding them from their stays. Joyce came to stand near Illesa.

"How long will it take him to get home?"

They began to haul it against the broad flow of the river. The barge was soon underway.

"It could take four days if there's no further rain. It depends on how strong it flows in the narrow parts."

They watched for a bit longer as the barge passed the moorings of the Black Bear Inn and onto the wide pasture of the river meadows. Illesa shivered in a sudden gust of wind. The world seemed empty and indifferent.

Two ducks flew up from their hiding place in the reeds on the far bank, quacking loudly.

"If only I had my sling." William threw a stone instead. "We must move our packs to our new chamber, then I'm going to care for the horses, so you two need to stay together." He looked at Joyce fiercely. She scowled back and marched ahead along the muddy track towards the inn. William started after her.

"Where did you find her?" Illesa asked William's back.

"In Saint Catherine's chapel. Alone – but it looked as if she'd been speaking to someone. Her cheeks were bright red."

"But – who could it have been? Were Thomas or Ralph there? I think she may have admired Ralph, after all."

"No, they were at the horse market." He kept on striding after Joyce.

"She has just become a woman. Perhaps she was praying for help and guidance."

"Is it that frightening?" William muttered, stopping but not turning round.

"It is."

"Then maybe it wasn't right to bring her on this journey."

He was voicing her own concerns.

"She needs to see the world. She will be going into it before long, without our council. We must help her to understand it," Illesa countered.

"We need to protect her from it. She is too trusting."

"And you too suspicious."

"I know what goes on in men's minds. You might see the saints in Heaven, but I can see the devils on earth." He set off again.

"William –"

Illesa pulled on his arm, and he stopped. His broad chest rose and fell under his tunic, a bead of sweat pooling in the hollow at the base of his throat. She looked away. They had reached the mooring at The Black Bear. A small craft was unloading a basket of fish. The kitchen boy was looking it over, arguing with the fisherman. Illesa let go of William's arm and took a deep breath.

"Please, keep your imaginings from Joyce. I don't want her to be afraid of leaving home. We should enjoy these new places and holy sites. I know you don't like being away from the manor, but she is young. Let her enjoy it."

He stared at her, stony-faced, hands in fists by his sides.

"As you wish."

"Don't be cross with me, William. I'm just trying to keep everyone safe and happy."

"You can't. Your prayers won't stop danger or make men content. The world is as it is – a place of sin and pain."

"And grace. When we get to the shrine in Hereford, you will see how God works through his saints, how many blessings –"

"How much corruption and avarice," he began, but stopped. He must have seen her dismay. "You may be right," he conceded. "Perhaps we will find special grace there."

"I hope so, William."

He might forgive her, and God might take away the thorn of temptation from her side.

Chapter XII

Illesa and Joyce were sitting in the hall after their evening meal when Reginald walked past. Illesa thought at first that she'd imagined it, that it was Gaspar again or some other man with the same up-turned nose, but as he came closer he stopped and bowed with his distinctive flourish. Despite the ordinary travelling clothes, it was certainly him. Joyce stood up smiling.

"Look, Mother, it's Reginald!"

"It is, my lady," he said, putting the cap back on his head and smiling broadly.

"What are you doing here?" Illesa stood up belatedly. "Sit with us, if you will. Tell us why you are in Tewkesbury."

"I will, certainly, join you." He slid adroitly onto the bench opposite them, looking around. "Are you alone?" He looked at them, concern creasing his forehead. "Where are the others?"

Joyce was grinning. There was something smug about her expression that Illesa didn't like.

"William is with us. He's seeing to the horses for the night. The others have gone ahead of us by river."

"Ah yes, of course. Now I remember, you mentioned that was the plan." He pushed his pack under the table with his foot. "I hope I didn't startle you arriving like this. It was just that I discovered that I was not needed for several weeks, and I was filled with the desire to see the shrine at Hereford that you spoke of." He looked over their heads through the window, as if he could see the tower of the cathedral in the distance. "My appeal there might help my poor son, who suffers from a palsied arm. He stays in St Albans with my wife and misses many joys of life. They say, Thomas of Hereford has cured hundreds of cripples. More than every saint except the Blessed Thomas of Canterbury!"

"I didn't know you had a family in St Albans." It had seemed more likely he would be in the local stew than with a wife. Illesa shook the thought away. "Would it not be better to bring your son with you to the shrine? It's more likely to be effective."

"Regretfully, there wasn't time to go all the way to St Albans and then to Hereford at his slow pace before the great feast and celebration there on the 20th of June," Reginald said. "But I

83

hope to see the difference in his body and spirit on my return. And in addition, I may spend more time with you and share more stories that were so rudely interrupted by the monks." He winked at Joyce. "May I?"

He took his tankard from his belt and poured out ale from the jug, topping them all up, before taking a gulp.

"I've been thirsty for this all day, walking so quickly, hoping to catch up with you and reach the town before curfew."

"So you've been on foot? Not following us on horseback at a distance?"

Reginald looked at her, and raised his eyebrows.

"Why do you ask that?"

Illesa shook her head.

"Just something William thought he saw yesterday. He may have been mistaken."

"William is *very* attentive." Reginald imitated William's most severe and anxious expression, making Joyce break out in fits of laughter.

"You look exactly like him! Oh, *please* sing us a song or tell us a tale. I've been so bored. It's been such a tedious journey!"

"Give Master Reginald time to drink and eat. There is some bread. The pottage is quite good. We have already supped, but I'm sure they have more in the kitchen."

"I would be delighted to sing you a song, but look, here is William." Reginald got up and made a neat bow. William's face became blank. He stood completely still.

"William – Reginald is coming with us to Hereford, to appeal to the saint for his son. He's been walking fast for days to catch up with us. Joyce is pestering him to sing. Would you go and ask for a bowl of pottage and bread?"

William stared at her, then he turned without a word and went towards the back room.

"A man of few words! Unlike me," Reginald said merrily. "I hope you are not worried by my sudden appearance. If I'd been able to speak to Sir Richard about it first, that would have been preferable, but the road was long, and I didn't reach you in time to catch him."

Joyce was playing with her cup, not drinking. The ale was too bitter for her.

"I'll ask William to get some milk for you, Joyce. No, it is good to have you accompany us," Illesa said, turning to the player and willing some warmth into her voice. "There is safety in numbers, and Joyce is delighted to have someone with new stories to tell. William and I have exhausted our supply, and these towns don't seem to have many travelling players at this time of year."

William was heading back towards them, his face set in a deep frown, fingers twitching on his belt.

"Most companies of players are keeping to the large towns and cities now. Not enough people with coin in these small places. It's all been taken in tax." Reginald took another large gulp of ale.

William was standing beside Reginald, waiting for him to finish speaking.

"Lady Burnel –"

Illesa didn't look up at him. She felt her cheeks burning.

"William, get Joyce milk or water to drink, please. This ale does not agree with her." Joyce was leaning over the table, whispering something to Reginald. "Joyce, tell William what you would prefer."

She looked up crossly.

"Milk."

"When I return, I must have a word with you in the stables, my lady," William said through his teeth.

"I do hope that your horses are not lame?" Reginald said, looking after William, who'd already gone off on his errand. He turned back to Joyce. "Would you like to hear the tale of Alexander the Great's horse, Xanthus? It's full of daring escapes and rides of bravery."

Joyce put her head on one side and pretended to consider.

"I'd rather have a funny tale or song, if you please."

"A fine choice," Reginald declared, standing up and clearing his throat.

His song revolved around the infidelities of the young wife of an old man. In the middle, William arrived with the pitcher of milk, met Illesa's eye and went out through the door to the yard, evidently not in the mood for comedy.

Joyce clapped with the rest of the drinkers in the hall when Reginald finished and drained his tankard.

"I must relieve myself." Reginald sprang to his feet. "Then I'll return and your beautiful mother may choose what song or tale she will have."

"It's getting late. I should find William," Illesa said. Outside the sky was dark blue. "We have a long way to go tomorrow."

"Just one more, Mother! *Please*. It's not very late, and I promise I'll get up as soon as you wake me."

"I'll be brief. The tale will be as short as an ant's arse!" Reginald bowed and almost ran out the door to the yard.

Joyce was finishing her milk.

"What a surprise to see him again. Isn't it, Joyce?" Illesa looked at her severely.

Joyce nodded.

"Yes. Why are you looking at me like that?"

"I think you knew he was coming. Did you see him at the church this morning?"

"No! Why do you think that? I'm just as surprised as you are, but happier. You didn't look welcoming at all. You always told me it was rude to show that you're unhappy to see someone."

"I'm not unhappy to see him. I'm surprised." She glanced at the empty doorway. "William said he wanted to speak to me." Illesa got to her feet. "Come Joyce, I think we've had enough entertainment for the day. If he's travelling with us, we will have a chance to hear all his many tales."

"I want to hear one more. You *said* we could." Joyce stayed in her seat and crossed her arms over her chest.

The hall was still full of loud, drunk men. She could not leave Joyce alone here at the table. If only she'd managed to convince Richard to come with them to Hereford, all this would have been so much easier. She was pulled in two directions by Joyce and William, and she was always wrong with someone.

Illesa sat down again with a sigh.

"Reginald is taking a long time to come back. I wonder where he's staying tonight?" Joyce was fiddling with her beads which she'd kept out of sight in her pouch for the journey. "Do you think there will be badges for sale at Hereford? Or do they only make them when the saint is canonised?"

"Maybe. I don't know. They will certainly be selling things to the gullible, claiming they will give you more chance of a miracle or a blessing. But we can only buy one candle. We must rely on the fervour of our prayers not our purses."

Joyce sighed, put her elbows on the trestle and rested her chin in her hands.

"I'm going to ask him for a story about dogs. I miss little Pearl so much."

Illesa stroked her shoulder.

"A week and you will be with her again. And then we will see how much the lambs have grown, and the wheat and barley. The piglets will be getting big too."

"Here he is!"

Joyce sat up straight and smiled. Reginald was coming in through the door, smoothing his hair back from his face. He looked flushed.

"I have kept you waiting. I was just trying to convince the innkeeper to fit me in somewhere, but he said there was no room. So I'll have to go to the other inn and see if they have a bed for me."

"Don't leave now! There's space for another pallet in our room, isn't there Mother? There are only three of us."

Reginald bowed his head, gratefully.

"I should not impose on you. But if you do have room for me, I'll pay you what I would have given the innkeeper." Reginald quickly put a silver penny on the board in front of Illesa. "Also, I saw William by the stable. He asked me to tell you that one of the horses needs a new shoe, and he must get word to the farrier. He's gone to ask him to come first thing in the morning."

Illesa looked at the penny and then at Reginald whose eyes were the same colour as Gaspar's but not as wide.

"You are welcome to share our room. I will use the penny to buy another candle and pray for your son." She held his gaze as she put it in her purse.

"Your generosity is abundant!" Reginald cried. "You have no doubt saved me from a night at the roadside. Now, what was the tale or song you wanted?"

"A tale about a dog, please!"

"Aah, a soft and loving pet," Reginald said, sitting down opposite her. "Then we shall have the tale of the 'Weeping Bitch', or in other quarters 'Dame Sirith'."

"No! That is not a suitable tale for someone of her age, Reginald. And it is a long tale. Choose something more honourable and shorter."

Reginald made an exaggerated face of sadness. Joyce began to object.

Illesa put her hand firmly on hers.

"No. I will not have it, so don't even begin to argue."

"Very well. May I suggest a tale told to me by my friend from Castile, all about a parrot? They are such amusing birds. You do know that they can speak?"

Joyce's eyes were wide.

"Please tell me that tale."

"It is all about the cunningness of women too, so you will like it, Lady Burnel, as I know you are not one that can be easily fooled."

Illesa opened her mouth, but he had already begun.

"There was once a man, Sancho, who had a beautiful wife – not quite as beautiful as you two ladies, but still, wondrously lovely. He was convinced that she was not true to him, because of her exquisite beauty, and because he worked away from home. So he went out and bought a parrot, and told it that it must report to him everything his wife did when he was not there."

He imitated the parrot's voice repeating the instructions of Sancho with a very comic accent. Reginald had many expressions to liven his tale, and his gestures were uncannily similar to Gaspar's.

"The man went away for a few days to trade his spices. So the wife was visited by her lover, and the parrot saw all that they did together, all the ins and outs. When poor Sancho came home, he quietly took the parrot aside and asked him what had happened while he was away. The parrot explained it all.

'They were at it all night long,'" Reginald said in his parrot voice.

"Well, poor Sancho was very upset and refused to speak to or touch his wife, he was so angry. His wife, who was shrewd as I have said, as well as being beautiful and lewd, thought her maid must have told her master what she knew.

'I would never betray you, mistress,'" Reginald declared in a high and common voice. "'But you should know, as I do, that the parrot told your husband all he saw.'

So the wife waited for nightfall and quietly put the parrot on the floor in its cage. Then she sprinkled water over the parrot, as if it were raining. Then, the clever lady took a mirror and attached it to the parrot's cage, and she lit a candle, making it flash in the mirror so that the parrot thought it was lightning. And then she began to turn a grindstone, so the parrot thought there was thunder."

Reginald could do very good sound effects as well, with all parts of his body. He breathed out long and loud when he finished.

"And the wife kept this up almost all night. The next day poor Sancho went to speak to his parrot. 'What did you see last night? Did my wife sneak her lover in through the window?'

'Bwaaak! I couldn't see anything last night, because of all the heavy rain, and the lightning and the thunder!'" Reginald said in his parrot voice.

"'Well, if that's what you saw, I cannot trust what you say!' Sancho cried. 'There was not a drop of rain last night! You have lied to me about my wife! I should have you killed for saying such slander against her!' And he threw the parrot out of the window."

Reginald made a loud parrot-like shriek, and everyone in the hall fell silent.

"And Sancho went back to his wife and made peace with her. None the wiser."

Reginald bowed his head as the people who'd gathered around clapped. When he looked up again he brought his hands together.

"And the moral of this tale is what – beautiful and clever Joyce?" he said, leaning towards her and speaking in an undertone.

Joyce put a hand over her mouth to stop the giggles.

"Don't trust an animal to do the job of a person?"

"Very good! They also say, never trust a woman, especially not a clever one," Reginald said, with a wink.

"And you could also say that the one who speaks the unpopular truth always suffers in the end," Illesa put in. "It's time for sleep. William should be back by now. Reginald, go and tell the innkeeper that you are in our room. It's above the stable, on the outside stair."

Joyce stood up slowly. Illesa took their lantern and lit it from the wall sconce.

The hall crowd was thinning out. Several people who'd overheard Reginald's tale were talking to him, asking for more.

Maybe William was already back with the horses. Illesa guided Joyce out of the door into the yard. Just an occasional star shone through, and the half moon was blurred in cloud.

"Can you see? Hold my hand. Let's look in the stable."

But the stable door was shut and bolted. No one replied to their knock.

"Maybe he's already asleep upstairs," Joyce said yawning.

They climbed the crooked steps carefully. The room was empty except for the pallets, a pile of blankets, two stools and a bucket. Illesa put the lantern down on one of the stools, looking around for the hook to hang it from.

"Where has he gone?" Joyce asked plaintively.

"I don't know. He should have sent the stable boy on the errand. It's not like him to be away so long. I hope he's not been attacked on the way."

"Should we go and look?"

"No." That would be even more dangerous. "I will go and ask in the inn if anyone has seen him or can search."

She turned to see Reginald in the doorway, his face deeply shadowed in the lamp light.

"Is William not back? Do you want me to go and speak to the innkeeper? I was just with him. I'll raise your concerns. Perhaps there is a simple explanation."

"No, I'll go –" Illesa started, but Reginald was already down the stairs and running across the courtyard.

She turned back to the room. William's small neat pack was on one of the pallets against the wall. He would not leave it behind, so he'd not run away. Not that she thought he ever would. But there was the person he'd seen following them. Yet another one, as well as the surprise of Reginald. Perhaps William had been attacked on his way to the farrier. But why?

Joyce was standing by the small window which looked out on the river.

"I can see men drinking in that barge. Do you think William went to join them?"

"No, that's not the sort of thing he would do. He'll be back soon, I'm sure." Illesa closed the single shutter. "Time to sleep, my darling. We'll put our pallets together here." She started dragging them to the far side of the small room. "Choose the blanket that looks best. I'll comb your hair quickly and plait it for the night. Sit here."

Joyce sat on the stool, and Illesa started teasing out the knots from the long day. Joyce's hair was thick – a strong chestnut rope like a horse's mane. Illesa did the simplest plait and tied it tight with a ribbon.

"There. You use the pot quickly before Reginald gets back. I'll watch the door."

Illesa examined the bolt and latch on the door in the dim light. It seemed strong enough. She did not like the thought of locking William out, but he could rouse them when he came back.

There was a light knock. Reginald stood on the highest step. She moved out of the way to let him in.

"The innkeeper says that it's possible the farrier was drinking, and perhaps William is having to visit every tavern in the town to find him. He said he would be awake for an hour yet. And the boy on guard at the yard gate will let him in if he arrives back after then. Perhaps he's had a few drinks himself. He had the look of a man in need of a night off."

Illesa slid the bolt across the door and went over to Joyce on her pallet.

"My thanks for asking the innkeeper on our behalf. William would not go drinking when he is meant to be guarding us. I fear something has happened to him, but until matins we may as well get some rest."

"Indeed. It has been a long day, and I'm more than ready for sleep." Reginald pulled a pallet and a blanket to the other side of the room.

Illesa tucked a rolled blanket under Joyce's head and put her pack by her side. She lay down on the pallet next to her, pulling a rough wool blanket up to her chest.

"What if William doesn't come back?" Joyce whispered.

"He will. Don't worry. It's William, not some ordinary peasant. He gets out of trouble more often than he gets out of his jerkin."

There was already the sound of snoring coming from Reginald's pallet.

"We should have brought Ajax or Pearl. They would have protected us," Joyce said, under her breath. She turned on her side and brought her legs up to her chest.

Illesa lay flat on her back and took a deep breath, staring at the roof beams. If they'd all gone together on the barge she would be lying next to Richard, with William close by, all safe and sound.

'Saint Christopher help Richard and Christopher safely home. Holy Thomas bless our journey to your shrine,' she prayed silently – and closed her eyes.

Chapter XIII

There was an owl calling from across the river, but that was not what had woken Illesa. It was a gurgling, choking cry coming from the other side of the room. She sat up, her heart thumping. The lantern was dim, guttering on its last trace of oil. There was something wrong with her left hand; it was numb and cold. She felt for Joyce with her right, patting the flat pallet and the empty blanket.

"Joyce!" she screamed. She lurched to her feet and lunged towards the noise, but her left arm was tethered to the beam overhead, the leather thong tightening around her wrist as she pulled against it.

There was a curse and a smack.

"Why did you have to wake up now?" A dark shadow that had been crouching on the other side of the room rose and came towards her. She kicked out at it with a strangled shout, but it dodged away.

She only had a few feet of movement. The figure stood, hands on hips, just out of reach. The choked crying was coming from a prostrate form. It was kicking on the pallet where, not long ago, Reginald had pretended to fall asleep.

"You must learn to be patient." Reginald's voice was low and angry. "You will be next, after I have enjoyed the fresher meat – and taken my time about it. Meanwhile, let's stop your tongue. I can't bear the shrill sounds you make." He stretched out his hands, a length of cloth tight between them. Illesa tried to cry out. He was coming nearer. She darted left.

"I'll shut your mouth, and it will never open again." Reginald said. "That's what your stupidity deserves." He approached her more slowly, arms wide to trap her against the wall. "You are tethered like a sheep. There is no point fighting. I will make it more painful if you do. But lie back and let me tie your hands behind you, like your whoring daughter, and I will make you enjoy it."

"Don't hurt her," she pleaded. "Don't hurt her!"

"You take with one hand, and you give with the other," he said, weaving side to side in front of her. "You took my boy away, but you open your room to me so I can take what I will."

He was trying to keep her talking, distracting her so she would not scream. So he could trap her. He had seen to William, somehow. Taken him by surprise.

With her free hand she felt for the small sheath under her wide belt, and eased out her mother's old iron knife. Sharp enough to skin a goat. She kept it behind her, out of his sight.

"Good girl, Joyce, run to the door!" Illesa shouted suddenly, staring at the struggling form of Joyce's body.

As he turned round to see if Joyce really was escaping, Illesa pulled down on the leather thong and cut through it with one strong slice.

He was already upon her, whip fast, shoving her against the wall, his body tightly muscled under his thin tunic, strong as an ape.

"She's trussed like a chicken," Reginald grunted. "You think I'd be so negligent. Don't take me for a fool." He pushed her face, slamming the back of her head against the wall, grabbed her around her throat, then shoved the cloth half into her mouth, sloppy in his anger. He was grabbing at her arm, his knee in her chest. She went limp against the wall, and, as he bent down to tie her, she reached around his back and drove the knife in, up to the hilt as high as she could, and slid out under his body.

The gasp was more shock than pain. The knife was between the ribs, not high enough. Reginald put a hand to the wall and dropped to his knees, his other arm reaching back to grab the knife, teeth bared.

Illesa had slaughtered enough pigs to know where to strike the next blow. She stepped around him, kicked his back, pulled out the knife and shoved it into the top of the spine until it would go no further.

That did it. His gasps were gurgling, filled with blood. His breath would stop soon. His body would twitch for a while, but he was as good as dead. She left the knife where it was and ran to Joyce.

She was on her side, her arms tied together behind her, a cloth in her mouth, tied tight round the back of her head so her mouth was pulled wide.

Illesa sat down and pulled her onto her lap, working at the knotted cloth. It came free quickly and she threw it away.

94

Joyce gagged and spat out a wad of wet wool. She took a ragged breath, coughed and started to sob while Illesa pulled on the knots tying her wrists. But they were tight, and it was a leather thong, like an animal snare. She stroked Joyce's cheek and rose to get the knife from Reginald's neck. Taking it out would release all the blood onto the floor. She jerked it quickly, put a blanket over the wound and rolled his body onto its back to soak up the flow, wiping the knife on the blanket.

His eyes were open, shining in the lamplight. Looking at her. Illesa scrambled backwards. His foot jerked and subsided. She could not bring herself to feel for his breath.

She crawled back to Joyce, who was kneeling, bent over, her forehead pressed into the floor. Illesa quickly cut the thong between her hands and lifted her under the shoulders.

"Come here, sit here with me. He's dead. He's gone."

She took her child onto her lap and held her tight to her chest. After a while Joyce's sobs slowed, and Illesa began to try to unwind the leather from her wrists. They were swollen, bleeding, and one looked as if it might be broken. Joyce held it against her chest, tears falling from her cheeks.

"Did he hurt you anywhere else?"

Joyce pointed to her head.

"Did he hit you?"

She felt across the scalp for a lump, but Joyce pulled away breathing harshly with pain. Illesa's fingers were wet with blood. Reginald had pulled her plait so hard it had torn her scalp.

Illesa pulled her pallet near and laid Joyce down on it, kissing her face.

"Stay there, don't move. I'm going to make some medicine for you."

The powder would help her sleep, take away the pain for a while, so that Illesa could deal with the body and the blood. There was water in her skin. Illesa jiggled the lamp. It flared a little. Her hands on the pack were shaking, but her mind felt clear and cold. There were things she must do – and things she must not think about until they were far away from here. She wiped the knife again and sheathed it, then mixed the pinch of powdered henbane with the valerian and water in her tankard and took it to Joyce, propping her against her side.

"Drink it all; it will help. I promise, darling."

Joyce had trouble swallowing it; her tongue had been hurt by the gag and the wool, but most of it went in, and she lay down again, like a limp rag.

Illesa waited long moments of precious darkness until Joyce's breathing became deeper, then she went to the door. She had to find William. He might be injured or dead, but he could not be far away. Reginald had only had those few minutes when he said he was relieving himself. That was when he'd done it. Not enough time to drag William to the river, so he must be hidden somewhere in the inn buildings around the courtyard.

The moon was clear in the sky, showing the steps and the shining cobbles of the yard. She darted down the stair, tried the stable door, but it was still locked. The stable boy inside was evidently a sound sleeper to have remained undisturbed. Or perhaps Reginald had bribed him.

To the right of the stable was the cart shed. A small wagon loaded with horse manure and straw took up most of the space. She walked the length of it to the deep shadow at the back. On the ground was a lumpy shape between the cart wheels and the wall – a long form covered in coarse sacks.

Illesa knelt by it and started pulling off the hessian. The figure twitched. She flung the rest of the sacking off. William lay there – gagged, legs and arms tied, smelling of urine and horse shit. But with open, desperate eyes. He was alive, trapped behind the wheels.

Illesa quickly moved the wedges that stopped the wheels and pushed the cart a few inches out of the shelter. When she ran back to him, he was already sitting up. She ungagged him, putting a finger to her lips to stop him speaking.

"I'll untie you," she whispered. "Do you think you can walk?"

William nodded, bending over so she could cut the bond holding his hands. She quickly released the thong between his ankles, and he knelt for a moment, balanced on his hands, before trying to stand.

The blood rushing back into his hands and feet was obviously painful. He bit his lip and reached for the arm she offered, limped across the yard and crawled up the stairs. Illesa opened the door, and he sat against the wall, feet out in front of him, looking at Joyce and Reginald.

"What happened? What happened to Joyce?" His voice was choked, harsh.

"Shhhh. She's alive, just sleeping. I've given her henbane. Let me look at your hands."

"Did that devil hurt her?" He lurched forward as if he would punch Reginald's slack face.

"Peace, William." She pushed his chest back to rest against the wall and squinted at the welts across his wrists. "You'll wake her up. What did he do to you? Do you think you'll be able to walk further?"

William was still staring at the body of Reginald. He took a moment to answer.

"He asked me to help him with a thorn in his foot, and, when I bent over, the pig knocked me out. He must have been holding a hammer – or a stone." He felt the back of his head gingerly. Illesa did too. There was a large lump.

"You were lucky he didn't crack your skull and kill you."

"I'm sure he wanted to. He must have tied me up to be on the safe side and then dragged me to the shed. Is he dead, or have you just injured him?"

"Dead."

Illesa shivered, suddenly aware of her shaking hands and the hammering of her heart.

"Good. Let him rot in Hell."

"Why follow us all this way to –" Illesa felt a catch in her voice and stopped. She must not start crying now.

"It was because of the boy I warned off. He was using him. I told him if he pursued the boy, I'd have him arrested by the alderman." William flexed his wrists and winced. "He wasn't used to anyone seeing through him or telling him what to do."

"How could he be Gaspar's brother?" Illesa breathed.

William shook his head, stopped and screwed his eyes shut against the pain.

"No time for that. We need to decide what to do with him." He bent his knees, pushed forward with his hands, grimaced and stood up, swaying a little, one hand on the wall. "I can feel my toes again. Is Joyce injured?"

"Like you. Hopefully no worse. I haven't had a chance to look properly." The thought of it made her feel sick. "Thank God we're all still alive."

"But his death might condemn us, Illesa. Reginald the Liar is a favourite of the Prince of Wales. He is a well-loved player in court. His death here – who would believe what he was doing? They will not take your word of his intentions. They will not want to believe us. We will be the ones accused."

The Prince would be furious to be deprived of one of his best joculators. Joyce would have to be examined by the Bailiff and the Sheriff, to show what he'd done. They would be tried by the courts, kept in prison until the justices-in-eyre came to dispense their verdict, and then they might be convicted of murder and hanged. People had seen them together with him, talking and laughing. She'd let him sleep in their room.

"What can we do, William? If we leave him here and ride off, they will just raise the hue and cry."

"No, we can't leave him here to be found." William went slowly over to the body and knelt by its side. "You've stopped the bleeding nicely with that blanket. He's not going to stiffen for a few hours. And luckily he's not large. We must put him in the river, weighed down. It's high and fast at the moment. He won't be found for many days. I could skin his face to be on the safe side; he would never be recognised then."

"No! We can't desecrate his corpse. He is Gaspar's brother."

William swore under his breath.

"He is a devil in human garments. But very well. We'll need some heavy stones to weigh him down, and we need to get to a deep channel. Let me think."

Illesa knelt down on the other side of the body.

"We should take anything that could give away who he is." She picked up his hand – calloused, still warm. There was the silver ring, the one Gaspar had given him. She pulled it over the swollen knuckle and held it tight in her fist. The trembling was spreading through her body now that William was here. She could not allow herself to become useless. Illesa put the ring in her small pouch and opened Reginald's tunic, averting her gaze from his face, but he had no other pendants or beads. His clothing was simple travelling weeds, nothing distinguishing. She felt for a purse, but he'd taken off his belt, in preparation. She found it in a neat pile by the wall, with a knife, unsheathed next to it. Near where he'd been about to rape Joyce. A wave of revulsion came over Illesa, and she had to swallow the bile rising in her throat.

"What do we do with his pack?" she whispered.

"If we are pursued and it's found on us, we will be convicted immediately. It must go in the river too, but separately." William was getting blankets spread out, preparing to move the body. "If we throw him in clothed, with stones loaded in his hose, they may think he took his own life." He rolled the body onto its side.

Reginald's slack mouth opened wide, and dark blood covered his teeth. His eyes seemed to be fixed on her. The face that had once resembled Gaspar now looked like a demon.

"Close his eyes, William, or cover his face. Please!"

Illesa pulled the leather strap out of the loop and opened his pack. He had little enough. Four shillings in his purse, some odd pennies. His tankard, another pair of hose and tunic, a pair of thin-soled leather shoes, a wide-brimmed hat. And several more coils of leather. He'd been prepared to tie up all their party if that's what he'd found. At the bottom, scraps of parchment tied with a thin ribbon of silk. She couldn't see the words in the bad light. Perhaps they were letters or messages. She put them on one side and shoved everything else back in the pack, leaving the coin until last.

"Should we give the coin to the shrine at Hereford?"

"No, leave it in the pack. Then they will know we didn't rob him, if they catch us."

She pushed it down the side and strapped it up again.

Joyce rolled onto her back, breathing fast. Illesa knelt down beside her, but her eyes were closed. Henbane could give bad dreams.

"I'm going to find some stones," William said. "It will get light soon. We'll have to make do with what I can find." He struggled to his feet and limped out of the door, closing it behind him.

Illesa went to the window and opened the shutter. She needed the fresh air. The smell of blood and urine was making her feel sick. How would she clean the floor, the blankets? How would they remove all the signs of what she'd done? She looked out of the window onto the dark water, breathing the night air. Tell the innkeeper that they'd been ill in the night with vomiting, and she needed to rinse the blankets. A low raft was floating past the inn's jetty, pulling in traps or nets. They would need to be very careful that the fishermen didn't notice a large splash off the bridge.

William opened the door and slid back inside.

"Change of plan," he said. "Too many people. I'll leave at first light, him on the horse in front of me. Ride out of town quickly to a desolate place and toss him in there. There are no stones here, anyway. He'd come bobbing up soon as we'd turned our backs. I'll meet you at the next town tonight. Ledbury?" William looked around the room. "You take the pack and drop it on your way. At dawn I'll knock up the stable boy. You keep him distracted while I load Reginald on the front of Sorrel, with his hat well down over his face. They don't look at those leaving the town gate." He strode over to the body. "We must put his clothes and boots on properly. Get his hat and jerkin."

The jerkin covered the wound and the large blood stain on his back; the hat shadowed his staring eyes. Illesa found the wool he'd used to gag Joyce, and William pushed it into his red mouth, holding it closed. Reginald had voided his bladder, but that could not be helped. William would have to ride with him and his stink. When the body was ready, they pulled it towards the door.

"Make sure you keep the stable boy out of sight of the horse until I've got him mounted."

"I'll send him to get a bucket of water from the river." She took a breath and straightened up looking at William in the early light coming through the door. He was haggard, his fingers bloodstained, his eyes fierce. "You will need to wash, William. You smell terrible. People will wonder."

"Too late. I'll wash when I'm putting him in the river." William went to the door. "Wait a little while, then come down." He closed it behind him.

Illesa listened at the door until she heard hooves on the cobbles and muttered voices.

She came down the stairs as William was inspecting Sorrel's girth. The chestnut mare whinnied at her, but she did not have time for strokes.

The stable boy was rubbing his eyes with one hand, holding a rake in the other.

"Here, boy. Go and get me two buckets of river water. We've had sickness in the night, and there's mess on the blankets and our pallets."

The boy looked scared, then rather disgusted.

"Quickly, or you'll have to clean it yourself!"

He shot across the yard to the gate leading onto the jetty.

As soon as he'd gone, Illesa held Sorrel, and William went up the stairs. Illesa glanced at the shuttered inn. There was some noise from the kitchen at the back, and a dog was growling behind one of the upstairs doors, but there was no one on the gallery.

William came back down with his arm under Reginald's shoulder, holding him upright. His feet were dragging on the steps. His head lolled forward, but the hat stayed in place.

William took Reginald to the mounting step and heaved the body up as high as he could reach.

"Help me with his leg," he hissed, "and hold him steady." Illesa got her shoulder near the body, lifted the leg high and pushed it over the horse's back, her eye on the inn's watergate.

William mounted behind him, clasping Reginald's upper torso with one arm.

"It will have to do," he muttered. "Pray for me."

She ran to the gate and pulled the bolts at the top and bottom. The chamber shutters were starting to open, but the guests would only be able to see William's back and Reginald's feet, hanging limply, as she swung the doors wide and they rode out.

"God speed you." Beneath the bright morning star, William walked the mare out and onto the bridge over the Severn, slow and steady, as if he weren't running for his life with a dead body.

Chapter XIV

Monday the 3rd October, 1300
Hereford Cathedral

Now that I have come back from the dead and have the strength, we are going to go up and down that middle sea. I must explore where all have sailed or drowned in the terrors of the ancient world. I spent days drowning in my own dread – the dark pit. I was as weak as a newborn lamb for weeks, barely able to relieve myself, at the mercy of the monks' servants, who are only there to prepare you for the world to come. Cold water, cold beds, cold beans and sops. No meat allowed – they said the fast will cool my humours. They said I was too full of passion, blood and bile.

Despite them, I recovered. They were disappointed. They think me strange, proud and stupid because I refuse to argue with them about theology. I've had enough of it from all those years in Lincoln. And there is no one worth discussing the ancient mysteries of God with, but her. My Chera.

I am back in the scriptorium – so disrupted by my massive board, which irritates the old scribes working on the same bible for ten years, not to mention the scurrying Armarius. My work threatens them. So I examined it minutely on my return, checking there weren't additions beyond my hand. There were none. The end of the continent, the Pillars of Hercules, still mark the end of our world. I finished them when I began to feel the melancholy. But still my hand was firm and steady, and the pillars are straight.

Now I must go back to make the islands and the whirlpools, the sailing paths. The places we know from all the ancient tales. But I can only trace the great ocean as a border, beyond which we dare not speculate.

I will begin with the great island of Crete, land of Minos and his bull, where Daedalus built his labyrinth. With my compass I build it again – whorl after whorl – so small that you cannot see the monster within. I am skilled enough to inherit his fame. Isn't this world I am making just the same, a house of monsters, a place of winding paths and traps, but also wonders?

With all this land, the sea is squeezed tight. I will have to draw carefully where the rivers come and go, the tracks that snake into the deserts and plains. But now, I must put these islands in order. The mermaid and her mirror, representing the dangers of looking into the swallowing waters for your desires. Every island I draw will be a sanctuary for my beloved. In my world she will not be shipped off as a sacrifice to some monstrous creature. Instead she will travel the path to peace.

The Bishop is busy and will not visit the map for many days, I'm sure of it. Everyone is rushing to make the most of the new shrine. The monks are lining up the pilgrims, standing waiting with their quills already dipped in the ink to record the new miracles. Yesterday, a blind girl was healed, but Thomas was only warming up. Today the Bishop expects a resurrection. The Dean feels it too. He and all the canons are on hot coals, so there is no peace in the scriptorium at all. I've told them I need to concentrate, but they have not listened. It is the clamour of the crowds they want, the fervour and the fever of devotion.

But this is also devotion.

The slow mapping out of Creation and the depiction of Judgement. The ink shining bright and wet on the middle sea.

Chapter XV

Tuesday the 31st May, 1306
Tewkesbury

The stable boy was waiting when she walked back from the gate. He placed the two buckets of water at the base of the stairs and backed away. Illesa nodded, looking at him hard.

"Have our two palfreys made ready. And I'll need a brush and a cloth. Also milk and bread." She bent down to the buckets. "Knock and leave it all on the step." Illesa went up the stairs, a bucket in each hand, without a backward glance. Let the boy think her rude. It was important that she was not disturbed.

The light from the small window illuminated Joyce, still asleep, on the pallet. The corners of the room were in shadow, but she could see the dishevelled piles of blankets and smell the blood. She peered out of the window, but William was not visible on any of the paths. He would find a shadowed, lonely place. There would be somewhere quiet enough at this early hour, although it would have been easier in the dark.

Illesa bent down and felt Joyce's cheek. Her hands were shaking again. She stood up abruptly. While Joyce slept, all the evidence of what had happened must be removed, and then Joyce must be taken away from the terror of the room as quickly as possible.

She started with the lengths of leather and the gags, stowing them in her pack. Luckily the pallets were not stained, although when Joyce woke, hers might be. She started rinsing the blankets in one of the buckets and, with the brush, cleaning the blood stain from the floor. As she dipped the brush in the water, she glanced at Joyce. Her eyes were open, but she didn't move at all.

Illesa put the brush down and went to kneel beside her.

"How are you, my love?"

Joyce opened her cracked lips. No words came out.

"You'll be thirsty. Sit up a little, and I'll give you some milk."

Tears were falling down Joyce's nose onto the pallet.

"Come, my love. William is well, he has gone ahead to the next town. We will see him there tonight. We'll leave in a few minutes when I've finished packing."

Joyce stared at her, as if she could not tell if it had been real or a dream.

"We must be quick. You drink that up and then relieve yourself." There was a sudden wrench in her gut. What if he had violated her, and she was injured below? "Do you want me to help you?"

Joyce, ignoring the cup of milk, pulled at her sleeve and stared at her wrists. They were marked with red welts – her fingers puffy and purple.

Illesa sat down in front of her, taking each hand in turn. Luckily she still had a little of the salve, and some bandages could be made easily out of her spare tunic. When Joyce's wrists were anointed and wrapped, the sun was fully up. She would not eat the bread but finished the milk. Relieving herself on the pot made her wince, but when Illesa looked, there was no blood in her urine.

Illesa pulled the soaked blankets out of one bucket and pushed them into the other, throwing the red-stained water out of the window. She looked around the room. The pallets were stacked, there was nothing hanging from the beams, no marks on the walls. She examined the floor. It was made of old beams, dark with dirt. A bit of blood would not show.

She helped Joyce up and got her into her travelling kirtle, belting it at her waist. Joyce submitted to it all silently, holding her hands stiffly at her sides. Illesa put her travelling cap gently on her head. It would take a while for the scalp to heal. To get the clotted blood out now would be too painful. It would have to wait. She stowed the bread in her pack, shouldered Joyce's and Reginald's as well and took her arm.

"Can you walk, darling?"

Joyce got to the door slowly but without a limp, her eyes wide and staring. Outside their two palfreys were tethered and waiting. Joyce was looking all around the yard, her grip on Illesa's arm tight.

"He's gone, darling," Illesa whispered in her ear. "He'll never hurt you again. Will you be able to mount the horse, or would you rather walk?"

But Joyce would not let go of Illesa's arm.

"Can you mount the horse, my love?" Illesa asked, holding Joyce's shoulders. Her mouth opened, but still no words came out.

"Come, we'll just walk the horses out of the gate," Illesa whispered. "Boy!" The stable boy emerged instantly from the shadow of the doorway. She fished out a penny and a half. "Give this to the innkeeper for the food and drink. The half is for you. Open the gate for us, and point out the road to Ledbury."

He held his hand out for the coins gingerly, his eyes darting to Joyce's shocked, pale face, then ran to the gate. Behind them, a man in the stable shouted for him, and Joyce startled like a deer in the wood.

"Hold on to me." Illesa took both lead reins and pulled the horses along. By God's grace they were good mares, who liked each other well enough and didn't mind walking side by side. She got them through the yard gate and onto the street. The boy pointed to the bridge, just a few feet away, the direction William had gone.

"Go by there and head west by north along the road." He turned to shut the gate and see to the shouting man.

They joined a line of loaded carts heading down to the island quays across the bridge. It was good that they were leading the horses and not trying to ride alongside all the cart horses whinnying against the whips. But Joyce would not mount her horse even after the carts and crowds had left them behind, when they were alone on the road with nothing on either side but scrub and grazing. The unfamiliar countryside was making Illesa uneasy. They were vulnerable alone on foot.

"Joyce, sit with me on Lady," Illesa said after a mile of slow walking. "Look, we can both sit astride if I take off the saddle." Illesa strapped both saddles and all the packs on Stampie and tied the reins with hers. Joyce sat sideways in front of her, holding on around her waist, but they could go no faster than a walk. If she tried a trot, Joyce whimpered and Illesa couldn't bear it.

Every person that trotted or galloped past made Joyce hide her face on Illesa's shoulder, making it hard to control the horses. They only stopped once to water the mares and drown

Reginald's pack. Joyce still would not let go of Illesa's arm. It was as though she were an infant again, hanging on to her skirts. They had to stoop together to cup the water and drink. Illesa got her skin, filled it, took out the bread. Joyce looked at the piece in her hand, but did not even try to eat it.

More hours of small hamlets, farms, hills, scrub and fear. What if William still had Reginald's body on his horse, or had been caught with it? What if the Sheriff was riding up behind them?

Illesa shivered and peered ahead into the low western sun.

There was a tower; it must be a town. She crossed herself with the hand holding the reins and thanked God for Lady – still plodding along despite carrying double the weight. It was nearly another mile before they reached the gate. Illesa dismounted and showed the guard her sealed testimonial allowing travel.

"Has a stranger come, with a large bay mare, name of William. Light hair, green cap?"

The guard said nothing, looking around. He was waiting for a coin before answering.

"I'm here, by Christ's love, long awaiting you," came a voice from the other side of the wall.

The guard smirked. Illesa glared at him and went through to find William unharmed and almost smiling to see them.

"Poor Lady horse, I hope you haven't ruined her," he said, lifting Joyce off around the waist. She clung to his arm, tearfully.

"Come now, come. I've found us a place in the best of the inns. Not a private room, but it's not full." With one hand, he led both horses up the dirty cobbled street, the other supported Joyce. Illesa followed them, head down, too exhausted to ask what she wanted to know. They passed the market square, avoiding the fresh slops in the gutters.

The Oak was an inn near the church. It had a new gallery, and the stable boy looked bright, not beaten. William handed the reins to him without a word, arrangements presumably already made, and turned to Illesa.

"There are only two other travellers staying the night, both pilgrims. Do you need food first or sleep?" They both looked at Joyce, but her head was bowed, and she did not respond.

"Sleep I think. We can bring her food later if she feels hungry." Illesa watched the innkeeper walk across the yard in alarm.

"Here are the other two guests. You can see they've had a hard journey," William said putting his arm protectively around Joyce, "and need to recover in peace. Would you kindly give us leave to eat and drink in the dormitory?"

"You poor creatures. My wife will bring it up herself. Harassment from outlaws is more and more common these days since the taxes came down hard on us all. Where did you say they attacked you?"

"They came down from Ragged Stone Hill," William said. "Gave the women a terrible fright. I wounded one, at least."

"You should travel in a larger group. That deters them. They wanted your horses, I warrant. You did well to keep them at bay. I think the other pilgrims also travel to Hereford tomorrow. You should go together."

"We'll speak to them about it. Our party split in Tewkesbury, which was unwise." William slapped his folded cap hard against his thigh. "I thank you for your help."

"No trouble. If you need anything at all, call for me. Or the boy, Jack. He's good at finding what people need." Jack had come out of the stable and grinned at them. He looked like a happier, healthier William at that age.

"I've noticed that," William agreed. "Good with the horses as well." He nodded at the lad. "I'll come and help you bed them down for the night."

"Master," Illesa said, "may I trouble you for a jug of vinegar and some hot wine?"

The innkeeper nodded.

"Your man said you might need the makings of simples. Up the stairs there, first door you come to. All that you've asked for will be brought."

Illesa helped Joyce up the stairs behind William, who carried all the packs. Joyce looked up and around, suddenly aware of where she was, eyes red and swollen. Illesa pulled her arm to get her up the last step.

"We're nearly there."

William was holding the door. Joyce stopped at the top, looking back and forth along the gallery.

"It's safe. William is here – no one else." She took one arm, William the other and they pulled her into the room.

Two windows looked onto the church. William led them to the far end where there were two low, wide beds with straw mattresses draped with blankets. He dropped the packs on the bench beneath the window. They both helped Joyce lie down, and Illesa began to undo her boots.

After the innkeeper's wife had come with a full tray and gone again, Illesa opened her pack, and rummaged for the fabric bag of herbs. She poured the wine out into a bowl. Her mind was seething with questions, but until Joyce was asleep and resting she would not ask. William was pacing the length of the room. As she stirred in the valerian, he stopped suddenly and went to kneel by Joyce's bed.

"Joyce, Reginald is dead," he whispered, his mouth close to her ear, his hand stroking her cheek. "He is gone. Gone to Hell. You will never see or hear him again. I myself drowned his body in the river."

Joyce's body was shaking with sobs.

"William, stop!"

"She must know. If she doesn't know, she will always wonder and fear. I learned that as a child, and I don't want it for her. You saw her when she arrived. She thinks he could be around any corner or door. She must understand the truth of what happened."

"Not now, William. You are making her more upset." Illesa went to the other side of the bed and held Joyce's clenched fist, trying to relax it. William shook his head, still stroking Joyce's wet cheek with the back of his calloused hand.

"It will pass, once she has heard it and understood it, it will pass. Make her the infusion. The best thing now will be sleep."

They didn't even try to make her eat. Took off her cap, spotted with blood, washed her face with a wet cloth, held the cup for her to drink and covered her with two blankets. She was shivering despite the warm evening.

After a while, she started drawing deep breaths. They looked at one another across the bed and stood up. It was nearly dark. William went to light the lamps with a taper, hanging them on either side of the beds before joining Illesa by the window. Bats were looping above the young trees in the churchyard as the bells sounded vespers.

"We should talk before the other guests come upstairs."

Illesa nodded and sat on the stool. William shuttered the window, brought the tray and sat down opposite her.

"Where did you leave his body?" she whispered, shivering in the night breeze. She took a gulp of the warm wine.

"It's best if you don't know. But I found a place – downstream from Tewkesbury." He stopped, looked down at his clenched hands. "I had to tie him under the water. But it was deep enough. He won't be seen. The water was rough. God willing, he will lie there for ever."

Illesa put her hand on his – spread out his swollen fingers. They were warm, but there was no fire in her blood, no immodest thought. She looked at his unruly, golden hair, his dark brown eyes. Nothing. He was the child she'd met at Clun, grown to a man. Her servant and friend. Nothing more. Thank God. She felt light-headed. Perhaps that temptation was finally gone. Burnt away by the terror of the night, and Joyce's overwhelming need for her.

But a worse devil had invaded their family.

She looked down at her left wrist, red and swollen from the snare.

"How could I have slept through him tying her up and tethering my hand to the beam? I don't understand it."

Illesa filled her mouth with bread, to stop the shaking of her voice.

"That's who he was. Agile, nimble, light on his feet. He trained all his life to be so skilled." William took a gulp of wine, his eyes closed. "These are the methods he would use to do acrobatic tricks, swinging from beams, using sling-snares on other players' limbs. He fooled people, charmed them and put them in his power. You saw how he flattered Joyce, how he paid her attention and made her feel special. He would have woken her, asked her to get up quietly and help him do something. Then he would have tied her hands behind her back and gagged her before she could scream. He thought he had plenty of time." William drank the rest of the wine in his cup to the dregs and tipped them on the floor.

"He will have done this many times to many people. But he made a mistake this time because he was angry. He didn't attack one unguarded child. In his pride he thought he could better all three of us. It was my fault to step in his way by trying to save the boy, and now he has hurt Joyce."

William's voice harshened. He was trying not to cry. She didn't look. The wine was gone, but there was a full jug of ale. She poured it out for both of them.

He took a long gulp and wiped his mouth on the back of his hand.

"Joyce needs to be at home," he said, looking at her curled-up form. "If she can't ride, we will have to borrow a cart."

They had no coin for extras like that.

"Tomorrow, early, we will see if she can mount Lady. She's the lowest and most steady. Even if she sits with you on Sorrel, we might make better progress." Illesa got up and her head swam. She put her hand on William's shoulder. "We should go to Hereford. It is the best way home from here, and we can ask for healing at the shrine – and for forgiveness."

"We need no forgiveness for killing a devil!" William glowered at her as she shushed him. "He should not have been on this earth for one more day. God should have taken him earlier!"

"We must pray that our deed stays hidden then. That we are not convicted of it," Illesa whispered. "We need the saint's help to protect us."

Chapter XVI

Wednesday the 1st June, 1306
The Dragon Inn
Hereford
Compline

After their long slow ride to Hereford and an indifferent meal, Illesa had been able get a basin of water in their private chamber and help Joyce wash. When she finally fell asleep clutching a blanket, Illesa met William on the gallery overlooking the inn courtyard. Voices and songs rose up from the hall.

"Have you found out what he did?" William's hands gripped the railing, his eyes fixed on the men drinking below.

"I don't think he violated her. But there are bruises and scratches where he grabbed her legs."

Illesa's throat contracted, and she couldn't say any more.

"Thank God, if that is true."

They were probably both imagining the same terrible consequence if it wasn't.

"Will you do something for me, William?"

He half-turned to her, his glance apprehensive.

"Get rid of this for me." She held out the old iron knife in the palm of her hand.

He took it quickly and slid it under his belt.

There was silence between them for a while.

It was better that he do it. She couldn't throw away the last reminder of her mother, but neither could she continue to carry it. She would never eat from it again. Reginald had tainted it forever.

"William, where should we stop tomorrow? I was wondering about a Templar preceptory. Isn't there one north of here?"

"No, I think it's west. And we don't want to make this journey any longer than it need be. There is a town on the stone road, Leintwardine. I'll ask the innkeeper about it." He went down the stairs, eager to get away, to return to the everyday conversation of working men. It was not something he should have to know about. But he was good at keeping secrets. Illesa would have to decide how much to say to Richard. He would be angry with them all, and that would make it harder for Joyce.

She went back into the room and started taking off her boots. The knighting, the feast, the pilgrimage, the journey – none of it had been as she'd hoped. One disaster after another. Perhaps Richard was right. They should stay at Langley and never travel any further than Shrewsbury again. Christopher was far away, and she'd forgotten to pray for him. Tomorrow, she would make her appeals before the shrine.

Illesa lay down beside Joyce, her hand on her arm, determined to stay awake until William returned and the door was locked. But she fell asleep as quickly as a dog.

The following morning was very wet, and Illesa was glad the cathedral precinct was nearby. Joyce was able to walk through the streets just holding Illesa's hand, not clinging as hard as before, but she still looked at them mutely, on the verge of tears, when they asked her anything. It made them all silent.

The pilgrim entrance was through the north porch. Beggars had lined up along the path, shaking their little bowls. One was a leper; he pointed to his scarred, mutilated feet. Illesa could not stop for them with Joyce on her arm. She kept her eyes averted. They came into the north transept's rising columns, stretching up like stone trees, the arches above carved into swirls and filigree.

On her last visit, she'd been desperate to find help for Richard's pain, and now there was new pain on top of the old. Joyce was looking up, noticing the painted scenes, the coiled decoration on the capitals. They were being ushered along, almost pushed by the crowd behind them. It was the only place to come on a wet day. The shrine was as brilliant as a jewel, and above it, on the wall of the transept was the map of the world, flanked by angels.

Behind her, William let out a mild oath.

"That's bigger than I imagined." William pushed forward and they all stood in front of the map, peering up at the small writing. "Here, come and tell me what these places are, Joyce. You can read these letters better than I. Where is England?"

Joyce looked, but made no sound. She pointed to a lumpy island in the bottom left, the north west corner of the map. He peered at it.

"Is that where we are? Look at the castles! What's that city?"

"Lincoln," Illesa said. "That's where the mapmaker came from."

"Well, look how big he's made it. Bigger than London almost!"

"Look, it's Clee Hill," Illesa said, "and there is Hereford, where we are standing. Tomorrow we might see Clee Hill, Joyce, and know we are less than two days from home." Near the first home she could remember – Holdgate. In the mornings she'd watch the sun rise behind the hill as she let out the hens and scattered the crumbs. The light drawing the line of the summit –

"No, we don't go that way. We travel due north from Hereford," William corrected her.

Joyce was looking up absorbed in the map, her face happier and less frightened.

"What's that?" William pointed to the middle of the map where waves of green were spotted with islands. On one, there was a circle of paths, like the rings of a felled tree.

"Look Joyce, it must be the labyrinth where the Minotaur lives! And look there's a mermaid!" Illesa realised her mistake as soon as she glanced at Joyce. She was frozen, staring blankly, remembering Reginald in his costume.

William had not noticed; his eyes were still on the map.

"I think this is Aquitaine." He pointed to the fortified city of Bordeaux. Below it along the coast was the much smaller Bayonne, which she and Richard had never reached. "No monsters in France," he remarked, "except the French king. Look, here are the real monsters." He pulled Joyce over to the other side of the map, the south, where the monstrous races described by Pliny were drawn. She was following his pointing finger, jolted out of the memory.

There was too much to look at. Illesa craned her neck. Above the Holy Sepulchre at the centre of the world, above the crucified Christ, was the Lord enthroned in glory, his mother Mary bare-breasted, pleading for mercy at his feet, the blessed and the damned on either side. The devils and fallen angels dragging the condemned into the door of Hell while the beast waited, open-mouthed, for sinners to devour. Illesa's skin crawled. The images squirmed, distorted before her straining eyes. She put her hand out for support and backed up against a pillar.

Reginald in the shadowy room, the guttering lamplight, his familiar and wicked face. She'd killed him like an animal – deprived him of his chance to shrive his soul. Condemned him to eternal torment. Would she be taken from her family on the Day of Judgement and sent to Hell, where Reginald would be waiting for her?

"Madam? Madam? Are you well?" A man was tapping her shoulder, looking at her with concern – a priest and scribe by his attire and ink-stained hand.

Illesa pushed herself upright and tried to smile at him.

"I was just overwhelmed for a moment. But forgive me, aren't you –?"

"I am Richard of Sleaford, but you may call me Orosius now. That is who I've become. We met before, years ago. I would never forget your eyes."

He was much aged, but his height, staring eyes and full lips were vivid in her memory.

"I was here with my husband, Richard. You told him about the cyclops you would be putting on the map."

"Indeed. There are the Agriophagi – strange creatures! You have come back to see the work? And what do you think of it?" he asked, both pride and embarrassment in his voice.

"It is a true marvel," Illesa said. "A work for which God must have endowed you with great strength. When did you finish it?"

A young clerk was standing at Richard of Sleaford's elbow looking impatient, and Joyce and William were still absorbed in the wonders of the world – Babylon, the great tower of Babel, the bright red sea, elephants, giants, Bethlehem.

"Two years ago. For nearly a year after that, I was so ill I thought I would die. Again." He swallowed and looked lost for a moment. Then he gave his head a shake. "But the work lives. The great Creation of God from the beginning of time," he declared, sweeping his arm to indicate the expanse of it. "And the young Orosius riding away, surveying the earth, about to describe it and all its travail, commissioned by the great Saint Augustine."

He stopped and blinked twice. He was looking over her shoulder.

"Is this your daughter?"

Joyce was standing just behind Illesa, her eyes wary, questioning.

"Joyce, this is Richard of Sleaford, also known as Orosius, for he has mapped and described the whole world."

Joyce lowered her eyes and hid behind Illesa. She tried to pull her round, but Joyce turned away, covering her face.

William came to hold her other arm, whispering in her ear.

"Joyce is not well at the moment," Illesa said, letting go. "We hope Blessed Thomas will be of help," she said smiling apologetically and pointing unnecessarily at the shrine.

"We had a mute woman claim she was cured two months ago," the priest said. "But these things are hard to authenticate." He stared at Joyce. She was now facing them at least, her head bowed, holding William's hand.

"We shall pray for his mercy," Illesa said, "but we are taking you away from your guest and shouldn't detain you any longer."

Richard Orosius looked across at the clerk, who'd gone towards the shrine and was staring morosely at it. He bent over conspiratorially.

"I'll not be long with that one. He has no real interest. The Bishop of Carlisle wants a cloth of the world of his own to put in his poor cathedral. He sent that dullard to gather information." The clerk in question glared at Richard, evidently of good hearing. Richard nodded, indicating the man should precede him to the map. "If you are still here when I've finished with him, I'll give you a more complete explanation of it."

He'd already walked off before Illesa could say anything.

Joyce was already kneeling at the shrine, William standing behind her.

"Have you made your offering, Madam?" A large priest was at her shoulder, light blue eyes in his pudgy red face. She didn't have time to reply. "Do you wish to buy a figure in wax to donate. Or silver?" He looked at her doubtfully. The past days had not been kind to her clothes, and she felt poor and ragged.

"Whatever your ailment or prayer, there will be an offering that is best for it. If you care to look at the selection?"

"No thank you, Father." He was certainly not a priest to whom one could confess anything more than a cross word.

"If it is a complaint of the mind, we also have several suitable effigies, or the internal organs. The eyes, ears, legs, heart," he went on with his patter, fixing her with his small pupils. "Even the tongue. Or if it is for a journey, we have ships, both small and large. Come with me –"

"I do not require an effigy, Father, nor can I afford one."

"But can you afford not to have one?"

William was at her shoulder.

"All I require is a candle, if it please you," she said, a hand forestalling William, who was about to let his tongue go. "One of an arm's length will do."

The priest looked at them both with disappointment.

"That way." He pointed to the aisle and went on to the next pair of pilgrims.

"You go and buy it, William," she said, reaching into her purse. Her fingers closed over Reginald's ring, and she dropped the purse as if she'd been burnt. The coins rolled and spun on the tiles. William gave her a look and bent over to collect them. He kept one silver penny and gave her back the rest.

"I'd rather spend it on the beggars on the porch. Not these fat priests."

Illesa tied the purse securely to her belt, her heart still racing.

"It doesn't go to them. It goes to glorify God's house." There was plenty of noisy building work going on to prove her point.

William raised an eyebrow at her and went to find the chandler.

When Illesa reached the shrine, Joyce opened her eyes. She looked around warily. Illesa put a hand on her shoulder and knelt down, squeezing into a small gap. William returned and they saw their tall candle lit amongst the many others. Illesa tried to pray in the way she used to, but it felt as if her unconfessed sins had formed a net that would not let her prayers rise to Heaven. She was a dog under the table, too ashamed even to look for crumbs.

William eventually tapped her on the shoulder.

"We have many miles to go, and if the pace is slow –" He looked towards Joyce meaningfully. Her eyes were shut, hands hanging at her sides, mouth closed. It was hard to know if she prayed or relived her attack.

"Very well." Illesa got up, looking one last time at their candle.

"There's that priest again," William said. "Why is he following you? What does he want?"

Illesa held Joyce's hand as she got up, looking dazed.

"He is a kind and holy man. He remembers me from when Richard and I visited years ago. That's why he wants to show it to us."

"It's not natural," William muttered, stopping as Richard Orosius swept up to them.

Joyce was hiding behind her again.

"There you are," the priest commented trying to see round Illesa's back. "Any help from Thomas Cantilupe? No. Ah well, maybe once he's been canonised the miracles will start again. I've managed to rid myself of that boring clerk from the north. Now I can show you the details of the map you may have missed."

William glared at Illesa.

"That will be fascinating," she said to Richard's back as he strode ahead, "but we are due to leave shortly."

Richard Orosius didn't turn or show any sign of having heard her. He was waiting for them in front of the huge parchment.

Joyce came out of hiding once he began to talk about the salamanders, bonnacons, elephants and other bizarre creatures inhabiting the far reaches of Asia and Africa. The cunning lynx and sharp scorpions that the unwary might come across in Europe. At one point Illesa thought Joyce would interject her own knowledge from her hours spent pouring over their Bestiary, when Richard got the information about the cirenus bird wrong. But she just squeezed Illesa's hand and frowned.

"The people of Norway ride around on skis," Richard Orosius was saying, "and the Hyperboreans and Essedenes are very warlike cannibals, so even in the frozen lands, there is terrible sinful passion."

William tore his gaze from the map.

"We must go." He took Joyce's hand. "She needs to eat before the long journey. We'll collect the horses and meet you at the precinct gate."

Illesa nodded and turned back to Richard Orosius, who had barely noticed. He was pointing to the string of islands along the coast of the middle sea.

"Why are the Minotaurs in the northeast, so far away from the labyrinth?" Illesa asked. "Surely they should be in Daedalus's house in Crete?"

Richard Orosius smiled.

"Yes, that is a good question. That Minotaur had offspring, and they fled into the Caspian range, I believe, before Theseus could kill them all."

"Did this occur after Noah brought all the animals on the ark, or before? Would we still find such creatures there?"

"A noble question. I see you think deeply about these phenomena. I believe they are still in the world, but driven by the virtue of man into the distant fiery and cold places. One day I hope to be able to travel, like Orosius, and find the nest of the phoenix and the pelican, the Skiapods near Samarkand, and the Troglodytes in their caves." He was speaking very quickly, his fingers tracing the air, as if he drew the creatures again.

"Have you been to many of these countries?" Illesa asked, admiring the great city of Paris, the shrine of Santiago, the many edifices.

"No." Richard Orosius shut his eyes. "In dreams I've gone to find my exiled friend. That journey would be just this distance, but almost impossible." He moved his finger from Hereford to Toulouse. "I *will* go, when the Bishop allows me. But these monks are all against me. They report lies to him, even though I have created this wonder for their cathedral." His voice was rising in volume, his hands waving agitatedly.

"It is a great offering," Illesa said, taking a step away. "I pray one day you will see those places, perhaps even the Holy City of Jerusalem that you have drawn with such skill. Forgive me, I must be going now. Thank you for your time and work."

Richard Orosius grasped her hand.

"Yes, I will. A pilgrimage to the distant shrines, far from these provinces. But in you I see this same fire to discover. The same intelligence that makes it worthwhile. Many go, but all they see is how it is different from home, and all they come back with is complaint. But you will find the wisdom, the meaning of the world hidden in its material." His words were coming so quickly, they almost tripped over each other on their way out of his mouth. "I recognise this, even in women, because I have found it there before. They are not all of Eve's gullibility. You are much wiser than these lazy clerics who are only interested in this small place and their big tower."

Luckily there were no clerics nearby to hear him.

"If we ever cross the seas, you would be the best guide," Illesa said, placatingly.

Richard Orosius was walking alongside her towards the north door.

"I was new to these parts when we first met, and I did not recognise where you came from, if you told me."

"Langley in Shropshire. It is very small, much smaller even than Hereford." She squinted up at him.

Richard Orosius barked a laugh.

"I know my sin is pride! I was sent here to receive a punishment, and I have endured it. But if I ever travel, I pray my companions have half your wit."

Illesa was trying to push her way through the pilgrims and beggars crowding in the porch, with him in her wake.

"But you must be going. What a bore I am. They often accuse me of it!" he concluded.

They emerged into the rain. Illesa turned to him and bowed her head.

"You are a master mapmaker, the creator of a miracle. We thank you for your precious work."

"Farewell – I've forgotten your name."

"Lady Burnel. Farewell, Richard Orosius. I will pray for you, as your map requests."

He stood for a moment looking up at the rain with a comical expression of surprise, then turned without another word, disappearing inside the wet stones of the cathedral.

He was touched by holy genius. Not surprising after delving so far into God's mind. Illesa pulled her cape hood up and looked around the cathedral close, half expecting to see one of the strange beasts. Or an officer of the King come to gaol her.

But instead there was William, exactly where he'd said he would be, Joyce on Stampie by his side.

Chapter XVII

Saturday the 4th June, 1306
Langley Manor

They had pushed on all day determined to get home, despite Lady going lame and needing to be walked from Rushbury. Despite the heat and the terrible inn they'd had in Ludlow where the beds were riddled with lice. Despite ending up on the floor next to a snoring fuller from Droitwich. Illesa only fully believed they would reach Langley when she heard the familiar bells of Cardington, having gone the length of the Lawley, skirting the Templar's lands.

How to explain her irresponsible behaviour to Richard? How to explain the muteness of his daughter and why they'd hidden the body and run? It was too much to imagine. William had said very little all day, probably thinking the same. If anyone was going to be punished for the disasters – but Richard had never been vindictive. Why was she thinking that he would be now? The change in him had been gradual with the realisation that he would never be free of the pain. He had grown short-tempered, with long weeks of black moods. He struggled to free himself from it but was impatient with her attempts to use new medicines or amulets.

Here was the end of the wood and the start of the their fields, the old chapel, just turning pink and gold against the northern sky. Their beautiful home. Joyce was urging Stampie to walk faster. Illesa allowed herself to fall behind with Lady. Her feet ached. Perhaps when she saw her father, Joyce would find her voice and let the horror of that night out. A dreadful thing for Richard to hear, but anything was better than her silence.

The drawbridge was down. Stampie pranced across it, and Joyce dismounted. Her little white dog, Pearl, came racing across the cobbles and jumped up on her stumpy legs, trying to lick Joyce's face.

"Hail! Is anyone there?" William called.

Little Stephen ran out of the stable and took hold of Stampie, who was trotting around the yard. Joyce was at the kitchen door already, the dog in her arms, looking for Cecily. Richard came limping out of the hall with his stick, Christopher's dog Ajax at his heel.

"Here you are! What a sight! You all look as though you've been dragged from Tewkesbury." Illesa went to him. "What's this? You're home, you're all here. Why are you crying? And there is Joyce, crying too." Joyce had found Cecily and was wrapped inside her arms. She had her face buried in the woman's large chest, but they could still hear her sobs.

Illesa wiped her face, looking round for William. He was explaining the treatment of Lady's foot to Stephen. Keeping a distance. Ajax sloped away, worried by it all. Illesa squeezed Richard's hand.

"Let me speak to you quickly, inside, before you greet Joyce."

He held her at arm's length, nodded and followed her into the hall.

Illesa sat down at the table where Richard had been taking his dinner and tried to take deep breaths.

"Here, you need to drink." Richard poured wine into his own goblet and gave it to her. His face was drained of colour, the scars of all his injuries showing as red weals.

"I'm sorry, I should not have taken Joyce and William on such a fool's errand," she whispered, and took a gulp of the wine.

"Is that all it is? There was no blessing at the shrine, and you see I'm just as crippled? Don't be sad for me. This is my purgatory on earth, perhaps I'll rise straight into Heaven. I am no worse for your prayers." He held his arms out to show her they still worked.

"No," she said, pulling his hand down to hold hers. "Something terrible happened to Joyce the night you went on the barge. And it was my fault, not William's. I must tell you now, quickly, before you see Joyce." She took a deep breath and another gulp of wine.

"Reginald the Liar followed us from London. He wanted revenge for William sending his boy away. He knocked William out with a stone."

"Where? When did this happen?"

"In the Black Bear, that evening. Reginald told me William had gone to find the farrier to see to Sorrel's shoe, and I believed him! Even when William did not come back at compline, he said it was because he'd had to hunt down the farrier round all the taverns. Then he told me there was no room for him in the inn, and could he share our chamber, and I still thought William would be back soon so I agreed."

Richard looked up at the roof and swore.

"He's called Reginald the Liar for good reason."

Illesa bowed her head, staring at her hands on the table. She managed to get through the rest of the tale in one breath, swallowing the sob in her throat. She picked up the goblet, but it was empty.

"Joyce was so frightened she couldn't speak. She can't seem to say a word. We prayed at Hereford for her voice to return, but –" Illesa took a deep breath. "I know you will be angry, but this was only *my* fault. Not William, not Joyce. I should not have been so foolish as to trust that man. I just could not believe that Gaspar's brother would harm us."

Richard was staring at the table, not looking at her. He'd refilled the goblet. She drank again, but it was making her lightheaded on her empty stomach.

"Very well," he said. "I will not punish William, as I see that you are determined to take all the guilt of this and spare none for anyone else. You've not even left any for the man who insisted on going home, leaving you at Reginald's mercy."

She looked at him, the tears spilling from her eyes.

"There is always another side to a story," he said, carefully getting to his feet. "I will find Joyce and see if she will speak to me. Cecily will bring you food. Rest now. Killing a man can be a noble act, but it's a wound to the soul. Rest." He put his hand on her shoulder and limped away.

She waited until Richard had reached the kitchen before she left the hall and crossed the yard to the stable.

The horses were whickering, shaking their manes, glad to be home. They preferred the taste of their own grass. William was helping Stephen clean out their hooves. It was not his job, but it was obviously a good way to avoid Richard.

"Stephen, take Sorrel and Stampie to the pasture," Illesa croaked. "I'll help William with Lady."

He looked surprised, but untied both from their stalls and led the excited horses out without a word.

Illesa picked up another brush and began on Lady's tail.

"I have told him everything. He's not angry with you."

"He should be," William said. He was on his knees, examining Lady's swollen ankle. She put her head down and pushed at William's head. He got up. "She wants to be out with the others. Not for a day or two, Lady. Eat your hay." He glanced up at Illesa – and away. "I expect you told him about the body?"

"Yes."

William turned to look out of the stable door.

"It would've been better if you'd waited so we could tell him together. I would have taken responsibility for killing him, and then if they came to arrest the culprit, Richard wouldn't know any better."

"Don't be ridiculous!" Illesa dropped the brush. "You know that I would be treated with more mercy. You'd be hanged. No question. And what would I do to atone for another life lost because of me?"

"It won't come to that, anyway," William said, picking up the brush and handing it to her. "It would just have given Richard more peace of mind."

"He wouldn't have much peace knowing his constable was likely to be executed."

"Shhh. The boy is coming back. Only Richard and Cecily should know. No one else. Maybe it is a good thing Joyce is silent for now. She never could keep a secret."

Illesa held the horse hair and pulled out a burr. Stephen was at the door, waiting to see if he was allowed to come in.

"Here, finish this off." She beckoned him and gave him the brush. "William, leave the mare and eat. Lady can wait." She marched across the yard, feeling a huge wave of anger that their homecoming, which should have been joyful, was so full of fear and hurt. And it might never be the same. Reginald's lust and pride could have ruined Joyce, could ruin them all.

Illesa shut her eyes and leant her head against the wall of the manor, trying to calm her breathing. They were all alive, had made it home. The fires were lit. The pots were full of food. The smell of Cecily's good frumenty was filling even the courtyard. If anything could make Joyce feel safe, it was that. And if Illesa was going to face Cecily she must eat first.

The kitchen was silent. Only Alfred, the kitchen boy, was there, scouring a pot. Joyce and Cecily must have gone to her chamber. The lad spooned warm porridge into a bowl for her wordlessly. By the time she'd finished it, Cecily had come down the stairs. She stood, face set, hands folded across her chest, eyes red.

"There you are. You can't avoid me any longer. I've just put Joyce to bed and tried to brush her hair, poor lamb! Had to leave the coif on to protect it overnight! William has told me only the bare bones, so now I need to know what actually happened from you."

Illesa took Cecily's hands in hers and led her through to the small larder amongst the jars and bowls. It was the only private place. Alfred was still cleaning – and listening.

"She won't say a word. Barely eats. Can't look me in the eye. So changed –" Cecily only just stopped herself from wailing. "Do you think that man –?"

Illesa stroked Cecily's sleeve.

"No, I don't think so. I think she was so frightened, the Devil took away all her words. It will be good for her to sleep next to you. She may cry out in the night or talk in her dreams – that might break the spell. We'll bathe her in the morning."

Cecily sniffed.

"She let me look at her poor wrists! I will take up that infusion you made for the girl in Plaish." She pointed to the upper shelf where the stoppered jars were kept. "There's still some that I can mix with warm wine. Being home will chase away his evil." She bent forward, whispering although the door was shut. "When is her next purgation coming?"

"Soon." In fact it should have already happened. "Keep a close eye on her, Cecily."

Before going to her chamber, Illesa looked in on Joyce and Cecily. They were asleep with a single lamp by the head of the old bed. Cecily had brought in more blankets and pillows so that it looked like a giant bird's nest, and she slept with one hand on Joyce's arm as if she were sheltering her under her wing. Cecily and Joyce had been inseparable since Illesa had gone to France to help Richard escape from the French army. Joyce's feelings had stayed fixed on Cecily, even when Illesa came back. She slept better with Cecily, she confided more in her, gave her more embraces.

Illesa shut the door. She was blessed to have such a hard-working woman with a heart as big as the whole world. And jealousy was a trap set by the Devil himself.

In their chamber, Richard was sitting on the edge of the bed trying to stretch out his leg. Illesa knelt on the floor and began to knead his muscles.

"Didn't you ask Cecily to help you? It's all seized up again."

"I don't want her hands on my old legs. She thinks I'm dough. I end up covered in bruises and ten times worse off. That's getting better," he hissed through clenched teeth.

"Did Joyce say anything to you?"

"No. She would barely look at me. I told her that I wasn't angry with her, but she just started crying."

"We need to give her more time," Illesa said without conviction, sitting back on her heels. "Cecily will work her magic. Once her wrists and head have healed, she will begin to feel more herself."

"What? What happened to her head?" Richard made as if to rise.

"Don't go in there! She's asleep with her coif on. He pulled some of her hair and her skin was torn." Illesa couldn't say anymore.

"That disgusting beast! Damn him to Hell!" Richard lifted his hand as if to strike. Tears fell from his eyes. Illesa pulled him to sit down next to her on the bed and held his head against hers.

"He is there – suffering in the torturing fires. He died like an animal."

"You did well." Richard whispered.

"But I gave him no chance to repent."

"He deserved none. As our Lord said, if a man causes a child to sin, it would be better that he had a millstone tied round his neck and was thrown into the sea. That is what he deserved and that is what you and William have given him. The Lord's judgement. Pray to all the saints that he stays there."

Chapter XVIII

Monday the 13th June, 1306
Langley Manor

Illesa had run up to her chamber to find the book that Joyce wanted to read when she saw it. Having opened the chest, taken out the *Bestiary*, and carefully replaced the lid, she was walking to the door, when her eye was caught by an object shining on the coverlet in the light from the open window. Thinking Cecily must have left something there when she shook out the sheets, Illesa went to collect it.

But it was Reginald's ring, lying in the place where Illesa had been sleeping a few hours before. Heavy and cold, engraved with the names of the Three Kings. Who had found it in her purse in the locked family chest and thought to put it on her bed? William would know it would frighten her. Joyce did not even know she had it. Perhaps Richard had found it and put it there, on her side of the bed, to question her tonight. Illesa stood facing the door, the book in one hand, the ring on the palm of the other. If he'd left it there, it would be better to replace it. He would talk when he was ready. If she confronted him, it might make him more angry.

Illesa put it back on the warm cloth and shivered. It was glinting like an eye. She walked out and shut the door behind her.

Joyce was sitting by the window in the hall on the stool in front of the small book table, her back straight, Pearl curled up on her lap. Her chestnut hair was flowing down over her shoulders. They had not plaited it since she came home. Her scalp was still raw in places.

"Here we are." Illesa forced some cheerfulness into her voice and drew her own stool up to the table, putting the book in front of Joyce. "Where would you like to start?"

Joyce pulled the book nearer and opened the cover carefully. She turned a few pages, going past the lion, the tiger and panther, and stopped at the bonnacon, pointing to its curved horns and its sad, startled expression as it was speared by the man to the left.

"Do you remember seeing the bonnacon on the great map?" Illesa asked, looking at the illustration carefully. "I don't think we've read this one before."

Joyce smiled – a rare, sly sort of smile.

"You read it then, Joyce." But she just shook her head.

"Very well, I'll read it, but you must try to read the next one." Illesa pulled the book closer and squinted at the small letters.

"In Asia there is an animal called the bonnacon which has a bull's head and body, except for the mane of a horse. But its horns wind back on themselves in such a way that anyone who falls on them is not wounded. The protection which is denied to this monster through its horns is provided by its belly. When it flees, the excrement from the stomach of the beast produces such a stench over an area of two acres that its heat singes everything it touches. By this poisonous dung it keeps all pursuers at bay."

Joyce had covered her mouth, but she was certainly trying not to laugh. Thank Christ.

"Joyce, did Christopher show you that one? It is just like him to remember the rude descriptions." She shook her head to hide her smile.

Joyce lowered her hands. She pointed at the subtle spray of excrement coming out of the bonnacon's arse and hitting its green-faced pursuers. She turned the page and stopped, her face stiffening. Her eyes darted across the pictures and words. It was an ape or monkey, carrying two babies, climbing in the trees, while a trio of boys prepared to shoot arrows at it. Joyce pointed at the words. Pointed at Illesa.

Illesa felt nauseous. Just when they had found some joy, the shadow of evil fell again. Joyce was jabbing at the page. Illesa pulled the book away and put her arm around her daughter.

"It's only a picture. We will put it away. Find another story instead."

But Joyce wouldn't stop. She pulled the book back on the stand, found the page and looked at Illesa, jabbing at the letters until she started to read.

"Apes are so called because they ape the behaviour of rational human beings. They are very conscious of the elements and are cheerful when the moon is new, and sad when it wanes. Apes have no tails. The devil has the same form, with a head but no tail. If the whole of the ape is hateful, his backside is even more horrible and disgusting. Monkeys have tails but that is the only difference between them and apes."

Illesa stopped, her throat closing with her own tears. She shut the book and put both arms around Joyce. Pearl was trying to lick her face.

"He's gone. He's dead, my darling. I promise you," she chanted, her lips on Joyce's thick hair. Joyce had started her bleed two days before, to Illesa and Cecily's overwhelming relief, but there had been no change to her silence.

She'd hoped that reading together would help Joyce to start speaking again, but with Illesa's choice of the *Bestiary*, thinking to reflect Joyce's interest in animals, she'd upset her again. Illesa stroked Joyce's back, feeling her ribs beneath her soft linen shift. She was becoming gaunt. That was the first thing to solve. More food would give her strength to speak. She pulled Joyce up from the stool, and took her to the pantry. Cecily would have made a custard or some soft bread. And Cecily could make Joyce eat with her persistent cajoling.

In the evening, Joyce sat at the table and played with the tiny pieces of meat that William had cut specially for her. Pearl kept running between the stairs and the table, yapping. Richard threatened to kick her, so Cecily took the dog into the kitchen and gave her a bowl of milk. After a few moments, Ajax began whining, his long muzzle pointed to the landing, making a heartbreaking sound.

"What do you think he wants?"

"Nothing. Our attention. He should be in the stable. Get William to take him out."

"You don't think something has happened to Christopher?" Illesa whispered hoping Joyce would not hear.

"And he knows about it before we do? Don't be foolish, woman."

Illesa turned away from him.

"What do you think is wrong with the dogs tonight, Joyce?"

Joyce looked up from her plate with glazed eyes. Shook her head. She wasn't even trying. It was easier for her to not speak, get sympathy that way. Illesa felt immediately guilty for the thought.

"Come, I think we are all too tired for this. We must pray and go to bed." Illesa got up quickly and went down the passage leading to the pantry and the larder.

"Cecily, Alfred, come and clear away," she called. "William?"

William appeared from the other side of the back door, wiping his hands on his tunic.

"Take Ajax to the stable. He's unsettled. Is there a storm coming?"

"Yes. I think so. The wind is getting up." He whistled, and, when there was no response, went into the hall to grab Ajax.

"Have you moved the horses?" she asked, as he came back towards her pulling Ajax by the collar. The dog tried to lick his arm. William just nodded. Of course he had. It was always the horses first.

"You didn't take Reginald's ring out of the chest, did you?" she said in an undertone.

"What?" William shook his head, trying to think. "The silver one? No."

He looked at her oddly.

"Why?"

"It was on my bed."

He shook his head knowingly.

"It will be Joyce. She's playing tricks on us all now."

"That's not so," Illesa said. "I don't want you saying that to anyone. She's still upset."

William shrugged and turned to go, holding on to Ajax's collar with one finger.

"William –"

He stopped, half-turned.

"Can you find her a new pet? A weasel or something?"

He rolled his eyes. Illesa folded her arms on her chest.

"It might help."

"If I have time," he grunted and opened the door. The wind banged it against the outside wall. He slammed it shut after him.

Illesa helped Richard slowly mount the stairs, a lantern in her other hand, dreading the next conversation she'd have to have. She went into the chamber ahead of him and hung the lantern from the hook. He came in and sat down heavily on the bed, just where the ring had lain.

She rushed over, looking behind him.

"What are you looking for?" he grumbled. "Here, give me a hand with this boot; it's shrunk onto my foot." By the end of the day his bad leg was so swollen it was hard to remove any of his shoes. She gave the mattress another pat. There was nothing there.

"The ring," she said, kneeling down next to him and starting to tug off the boot bit by bit. "I thought you wanted to ask me about it."

"A ring?" he said, through gritted teeth. The boot came off, and Illesa sat back hard on the floor. He moaned a little as he tried to stretch the swollen limb. "What ring?"

She frowned at him as she got up and set his boot down deliberately next to the other one by the bed.

"Didn't you put the silver ring on the bed?"

"I have no idea what you are talking about, wife. You have several rings. Which one needs repair? We will ask the silversmith when we next go to town."

Illesa crawled onto the bed and started looking in earnest.

"No, it's not my ring. It was here earlier today, sitting in the middle of my side of the bed, and I thought you found it in my purse and put it here to question me."

"I'll question you indeed! Did you buy a new ring in Hereford?" Richard pulled off his supertunic and glared at her. "I told you not to spend more than necessary."

"No. I didn't buy it. I had to take it – from Reginald's finger," she whispered urgently, close to his face. "Gaspar gave it to him. It had the names of the Three Kings on it, and a charm against sudden death. It could have been used to identify him." Her chest felt tight. She sat down on the edge of the bed next to him. It was nowhere to be found.

"Well, that didn't work, did it?" Richard said, with satisfaction.

"What?"

"The charm against sudden death. Failed spectacularly."

132

"Richard, I put that ring in my purse, and my purse was in the chest. You have the key to it, but you didn't take the ring out?"

Richard held up his empty hands.

"I didn't. Look for it in the morning." He yawned wide.

Illesa got up and started looking on the floor and under the bed. Richard hobbled round to his preferred side. There were deep shadows under the bed and even a shiny silver ring would be able to hide. She went to check the shutters were latched, listened at the door. There was no sound other than the wind.

She could still see her own hand, stained with his blood, drawing the ring off his finger in that room in the inn, while the warmth drained out of his staring corpse. Surely he was now half-eaten by fishes. No longer recognisable.

She climbed into bed and felt for Richard, burrowing into his chest to try to remove the pictures in her mind.

He put his hand on the back of her head and kissed her.

"It takes a woman of particular strength to counteract a charm against sudden death," he whispered.

Chapter XIX

Tuesday the 14th June, 1306
Langley Manor

In the morning, Illesa stripped everything off the bed and shook the sheets and pillows out in the bright sun coming through the open window. She crawled under the bed, through the whorls of dust, and looked behind the bed legs. She searched the rest of the room, thinking it might have rolled across the floor. She checked all the gaps between the floorboards. Hot and cross, she went downstairs to find Richard. He was sitting at the table in the hall, reading an inventory or some other red-scribed parchment.

"May I have the key to the chest?" she asked, holding out her hand. He looked up at her.

"No sign of the ring then?" He reached for the chain at his waist where the key hung near his knife.

"No," she said shortly. "I'll ask Cecily to clean the room thoroughly."

He placed it in her outstretched hand.

"Bring it straight back to me. If things are leaving our chest, we need to be sure of the location of the keys at all times."

"Where is the other key?" Illesa asked. It was odd that she had never thought of there being another key to that chest, but of course there should be, despite its age.

Richard got up and stretched.

"I'll show you one day. I'm going out to see the herdsmen."

He was walking a little better since she'd come home and given him regular treatment. He was right about travel being bad for him. She must not insist on it again.

The chest was in the buttery. The room itself was locked at night, including the shutters, but it had already been opened so that Cecily could begin cleaning. Illesa knelt down in front of the chest and pushed the key into the hole. The wood was warped, and there was a method to making it open. She turned the key in the padlock, pulled it out and set it next to her on the floor, then she pushed down on the lid of the chest so the latch would align and pulled the bar of the lock through the ring.

The chest was not as full as it used to be. Yet more taxes had been demanded the year before, and they'd had to pay using their citole and the candlesticks of gilt silver, and the dishes of the same. It was easy to see that everything was in place. Her purse was on top of Richard's, which was above the pile of embroidered table linen. She picked it up. There were only two pennies left – and no ring.

She opened Richard's purse, but it wasn't there either. She began taking everything out of the chest, piling it on the bench by the wall.

"What are you doing?" Cecily was standing in the doorway with a basket. She put it down on the floor and stared at the precarious pile of linen.

"Looking for a ring. It's silver, a thick band with an inscription. Have you seen it?"

"No." Cecily wrinkled her brow. "That doesn't sound like any of your rings. Is it new?" She bent down to look in the chest.

"It's not mine. I found it on our journey. It was on my bed last night. Now it's nowhere. Leave those things, Cecily," Illesa said pointing to the basket of newly dried herbs, "and go up to my chamber. Give it a good clean and look for the ring. There's lots of dust under the bed."

Cecily squinted at her and then at the pile of cloth.

"You'll put all those back, right and proper?"

"Of course. I'm no slattern. I'll put the herbs in as well. Now get on with the chamber."

Cecily left, muttering. After a few minutes Illesa could hear her huffing and puffing up the stairs with her broom and bucket. The last things were out of the chest. She felt all around the darkest corners and shook out all the cloths. The ring was certainly not in the chest. She layered the dried strands of mugwort, sweet woodruff, bedstraw and rosemary among the linen, taking care to fold them in the way Cecily always did. She must ask her to keep an eye on Joyce. Joyce must know about the second key. Perhaps she was trying to tell Illesa something by putting the ring on her bed. Joyce couldn't know how much it disturbed her.

Illesa pushed herself off her sore knees. Joyce was not in the kitchen, the hall, nor any of the back rooms. She started up the stairs, hearing the hour of sext sounding from the church, carried on the wind. She'd spent the entire morning looking unsuccessfully. Cecily was just coming out of the chamber, her face red and wet with sweat.

"All done? Did you find it?"

Cecily put the bucket down and fished in her pouch.

"No, but I found that toggle that was missing from your winter cape." She put the small horn clasp on Illesa's palm.

Illesa moved out of the way as Cecily went past to the stairs.

"Do you know where Joyce has gone?"

"It's a lovely day. I told her to go and see the horses in the meadow. It might give her more of an appetite."

"Thank you, Cecily. If you see that ring anywhere, bring it straight to me."

She waited until Cecily was at the bottom of the stairs before going into Joyce's room. She either had the ring on her person or had hidden it somewhere amongst her things.

Illesa spent more fruitless time looking through Joyce's bed, her chest of clothes, her small basket of dolls and toys – which she would not yet give away. Even shook the covers off the pillows. She straightened up at a sound by the door. Joyce was standing there, her hair loose and tangled under her cap.

"Darling, I was just seeing if your pillows needed washing, to prevent lice." Illesa got to her feet and took a step towards her. The kitchen bell was ringing, calling the men in for their dinner. "Have you been to see the horses? How is Lady's leg now?"

But Joyce was staring at the bed. She gave it a quizzical look, took a step closer and pointed. The silver ring was lying on the plain sheet that covered the bolster. It had not been there a moment before.

Illesa snatched it up.

"Ah there it is. I must have dropped it," she muttered. "Wash your hands, and come to the table; you must be hungry," she said, racing out of the room. The ring was ice cold in her fist. She went into her own chamber and closed the door, sitting down hard on the edge of the bed. It could not be Joyce moving the ring. She'd looked unsure of what it was. God willing, she'd been standing too far away to recognise where it came from.

136

It must be all in her mind. She had simply missed it, or it had been inside the sheet and had rolled onto the bolster when she smoothed out the linen. In that case, Joyce had been playing with it. Illesa cautiously opened her hand. It was just ordinary silver, worn on the inside where it had rubbed against Reginald's skin. The thought made her shudder. She traced the inscription's dark grooved lines.

"Caspar, Melchior, Balthazar, Ananyzapta," she whispered.

Illesa closed her fingers over it and went to the small table by the window, feeling for the key hanging on the chatelaine at her waist. Inside the casket were her combs, her four brooches and five rings, and her crucifix pendant. She placed the ring on top of the ornate cross and pressed the lid back down, locking it before hanging the key back on her belt.

This was the only key. The ring would be safe inside. She wiped her face with shaking hands and went down to eat.

Illesa could not settle to reading with Joyce that afternoon. She felt like a leaf driven by the wind – but there was no wind; it was a hot summer's day. She put the Psalter down on the table. Joyce was not paying attention; she stared out of the window towards the wood. Pearl had fallen asleep on her shoe.

"Let's go to the chapel. It will be vespers soon, and we can bring the Book of Hours to read, even if Father Thomas does not bother to come today."

Joyce sighed. She would have complained. That was the only good to come out of her silence. She could frown – but not moan as she used to.

"Have a cup of clarea water before we leave, it will give you strength."

Joyce rolled her eyes and stomped into the pantry where Cecily would be making pastry, Pearl tapping along at her heels.

Illesa felt suddenly lighter – here was the remedy to all that disturbed her. Kneel in the quiet of the little chapel under the painted saints, and then stand by Little Robert's grave and remember him. It would help her pray and be thankful. She went upstairs to find the Book of Hours but hesitated on the threshold of her chamber. From there she could see the casket on the table, exactly where she had left it. She peered around the door frame. There was nothing on the bed. Cecily had folded the sheets on the bolster next to the embroidered cushions. Nothing was out of place. She shook her head in annoyance with herself and crossed to the cabinet.

"Lady!" Cecily called from below. "Lady Illesa!"

Illesa took the Book of Hours and hurried down the stairs. Cecily and Joyce were waiting in the hall, Cecily's arm protectively around Joyce's shoulder.

"She's not well, not well at all. Feel her forehead; it's all clammy." Cecily shook her head as Joyce did a good impression of a dead fish. "I don't think she should be walking anywhere. I'll mind her in the kitchen and feed her up. There's a posset I've made that's just ready."

Illesa felt Joyce's forehead.

"She just doesn't want to pray. You know that's when you need it most, Joyce." But she had to stop herself laughing at the sick expression Joyce was able to conjure up. If it meant that Joyce was returning to her amusing nature, that was to be encouraged.

Illesa set off alone along the lane. The vespers bell was ringing, so at least the sexton was there, even if the lazy priest did not arrive. Someone leading a horse was coming along the track towards her. It was surely William. Even at this distance she could tell he was angry. Phylis had sent a message this morning – full of queries and demands. She would have to say something to the woman – tell her that regretfully she'd made a mistake about William's feelings. It had been so foolish of her. It was hard to believe the lies she'd told, now that the temptation had gone. Illesa quickened her pace and put her head down to walk by, but William put his hand out to halt her.

"What is it? I'm going to be late."

"The priest isn't there, and I need a word with you." He looked behind him at the empty road. "We can't speak of this in the manor." He cleared his throat.

A cold finger traced Illesa's spine.

"What is it?" she whispered.

He bent close to her.

"What did you do with Reginald's pack?"

She stared at his angry face.

"I did exactly what you said to do. I sank it with some rocks in the river, in a place where no one could see."

"But you took something out, didn't you?" He held her shoulder. "What was it?"

Illesa opened her mouth, trying to remember.

"It was the lengths of leather, the snares and the gags." She felt sick at the thought of them. "You know we dropped them in the Wye. And I took the ring –"

"Not those." He shook her shoulder. "You brought something else of his here."

Her cold fingers inside his pack in the dark room, the smell of his blood. The scraps of parchment wrapped with a ribbon. She had taken them, had not thought about them since. Where had they gone?

"I took a packet of parchment but –" Illesa said, pushing his hand off her shoulder, "I don't remember what happened to it. I thought they were messages – or letters."

William looked up at the sky and swore.

"You left it in the bottom of *your* pack. After Cecily took all your clothes to wash, she left the pack for waxing by the stable. Stephen found the parchment when he started polishing today. Asked me what he should do with it. You're fortunate it was him, not someone with more experience of the world."

"Where is it now?" Illesa felt breathless, giddy.

He glared at her.

"Did you look at them? Full of the Devil's words. I've hidden it behind the casks in the buttery. You should burn it, tonight, so there is nothing left to find."

"But William, I had to take the ring and the parchment," Illesa said, catching his arm as he started walking away. "I couldn't leave them behind to help identify him."

He turned back to her.

"You should bury that ring far from the house. Take it to the wood and push it down deep. It's foolish to keep it near you."

Richard had needed her help with the manor accounts until their evening meal, and she'd had no chance to retrieve the parchment, never mind visit the wood. As Richard was readying himself for bed, she made an excuse and took a lamp downstairs.

Alfred would be on his pallet by the back door. William was in his chamber above the stable. An owl called outside, a second replied.

She opened the door carefully and put the lamp on the floor, ignoring the scuttling mice. It would be hidden behind the furthest cask from the door, in the darkest and most neglected corner – the agreed hiding place for any treasures when the tax men arrived. Reaching below the wide wooden belly of the barrel, along the wall, her fingers brushed the smooth parchment. She pulled the packet out carefully and knelt down by the lamp.

There were six scraps of parchment, all with writing on one side. She peered at the topmost sheet, but the words meant nothing to her. The letters or symbols were strangely shaped, slanted, with legs and feet. It was not Latin, or French or even English.

She flicked the other scraps open. They were all the same. Words, perhaps, that ran along the page with no stops, no pictures. No order or sense. Except one, which had letters in a square, evenly spaced back and forwards, up and down.

She shivered and dropped the parchment on the floor. It was some infernal language.

If she burnt it, there would be a foul smell. Maybe sulphur.

It would have to wait for tomorrow. She would take the scraps and the ring and go up the hill into the beech wood and dig it a grave.

The sooner it was safe under soil, the better.

Chapter XX

Saturday the 2nd July, 1306
Langley Manor

It was the thirteenth morning since Illesa had buried the ring and the scraps of parchment in the wood, and the twelfth nightmare to leave her covered in cold sweat. They were the same each night – earth covering her, entering her mouth and eyes. More than that – filling her up as if she were an empty, fleshless skeleton. And unable to scream her fear and rage or fend off the heavy, muffling earth. If the dreams stopped when she dug them up again, Reginald's ring and parchments were certainly cursed.

She'd already gathered wood sorrel, yarrow and meadowsweet as she climbed the hillside, to give an excuse for her journey. Ajax followed at her heel, sometimes nosing her free hand. It was good to have some protection. She'd thought of bringing William, but could not, in the end, picture explaining the events that had led to this need to revisit the wood. And he was still angry with her. There was no one she could confide in without having to explain the devilish things she'd experienced.

It was so hard to pray. Christopher also needed divine protection, but her petitions died on her lips without the usual lifting of her soul. They'd had no word since the letter sent the day before the army departed London. It would be months before he was allowed leave. The oaths they'd made bound them to the victory, not to the usual period of service, and Christopher was very particular about oaths.

There was the tall beech tree just below the crest of the hill, and, just behind it, the holly. From here she had a good view. She'd sit for a while, catch her breath and make sure she was unobserved. Ajax would bark if anyone came. She placed her basket near the base of the beech and sat next to it, while Ajax lowered himself to a sitting position, alert to all the movements of the wood. Illesa shut her eyes to listen.

A slight breeze caught the holly and its leaves cracked against one another. A crow was cawing as it flew across the wood from the south. From the valley, the sound of hammering was faint and intermittent.

She opened her eyes. Ajax had lain down. His muzzle was resting by her hand, his golden-brown eyes on hers. She must do it now, before she lost her nerve.

"Come on, boy."

At the base of the holly, there were no signs of where she'd buried the packet, but she remembered clearly enough and moved away the broken sticks and dead leaves to find the disturbed earth. Holly was meant to protect from evil, like the precious drops of Christ's blood. That power did not seem to extend to its roots. She took out her new knife and began loosening the soil, pulling it out in her cupped hand. Ajax was a few paces away, sniffing around the trees at the wood boundary, tracking a scent.

It was buried further down than she remembered, and, when her fingers finally felt the edge of the cerecloth, she jerked them away. Illesa sat back on her haunches and looked around. The fields would be filling up again with men and women weeding the crops after their food and drink, but here she was alone.

"O Christ, defend your servant from evil, and all foul spirits put to flight," she whispered.

Illesa reached in and freed the packet from the soil. The crossed red thread around the cloth was intact. The ring would still be inside, in its russet silk. She brushed off the remains of soil, moved the herbs to the side and put the packet in the bottom of the basket. First hide it with the plants, then refill the hole, then decide where to hide it next. Or how to destroy it. Her breath caught in her throat as she pushed the soil back amongst the roots.

Illesa picked up the basket, sweat crawling down her forehead. She whistled for Ajax. Thankfully, it was an easier walk back, downhill and past the chapel.

If the ring moved again when she brought it back to the manor, it was at least predictable and less terrifying than being buried alive in her dreams every night. Perhaps that was what Reginald was experiencing in Hell. Her punishment might be the same.

The chapel stood, lonely and small, below her in the long valley. She could not take Reginald's things there. The church

142

over the hill at Acton Burnel had many more hiding places, and she'd had to drag herself out of the most disgusting of them before. She would not go in there again. Not even for this. If Father Raymond were here, he'd know what to do. Instead all they had was Father Thomas, who worked for Sir Edward Burnel and would be glad to use her sin to dispossess them of Langley.

As she joined the lane, she nearly bumped into Harold of Hawksley, his sons on either side, heading for the barley field.

"Strange man gone to the manor," Harold said, squinting at her. "I'll walk back with you, Lady."

"Right odd he looked," the eldest son added. "We should all go with you, with likes of that on the road."

"It'll be the peddler. He's just arrived a bit earlier in the year," Illesa said with false brightness. "Go on to your work. William's at the manor, and I'll be safe enough."

"Not the peddler. I knows *him* well. This one's foreign looking," Harold said, running his hand over his cheeks and chin. "Dark."

Illesa pushed her hat back a little.

"You come with me then, Harold. Let your lads go ahead to the field."

Illesa saw him as soon as they crossed over the moat.

"There he is," Harold muttered, "at the stable door with William. I'll stay by you."

"No need, Harold." Illesa mustered her most authoritative voice. "I know the man. He's not dangerous. You may go, with my thanks."

"Oh aye?" Harold said, squinting at her again. "What part's he from?"

"London," she said and went to the hall door, slowly setting her basket down just inside, to give herself time to stop trembling – to think. First she needed to know what William was telling Ramón, so that she would not contradict him. And next if the lump on the Castilian's back, covered with an old blanket, was his monkey.

Harold was walking remarkably slowly away, wanting to hear their conversation no doubt. But William was whispering, and Ramón's voice, so loud in a play on stage, was now soft, indistinguishable. There were no signs of anger or accusation. Yet.

Illesa rubbed her sweaty, dirty hands on her apron and started across the yard, as William held up his hand to Ramón.

"You will wait here," he said. "We will bring you refreshment." Ramón turned to watch him walk away, saw Illesa, grinned and bowed, doffing his cap. A chattering sound objected to the sudden movement, and the monkey's hand reached out and clung to the player's tunic.

William intercepted Illesa.

"Come with me." He strode towards the kitchen. "Find Cecily, get her to put some food out for him, some ale. He can eat where the workmen do. We must make sure he has no chance to get his claws into us, or stir up Joyce's fear."

"Why is he here? What has he said?"

"He's looking for Reginald the Liar, who did not arrive at St Albans for the Feast as he said he would. They were meant to entertain the Sheriff and all the nobles of the town."

"But why is he here?" Illesa whispered. "How does he know?"

"Reginald told him he was going to follow us. That's how he knows. Boy! Get some ale in a jug. Cecily!" Cecily and the kitchen boy turned round from where they'd been grinding and stirring. "Bread, meat and cheese for our guest."

Cecily peered across the courtyard.

"What kind of guest is that?"

"One that must be fed." William spat on the ground. "And kept out of the house."

"Is he a new peddler? That's a strange-looking pack."

"No, Cecily. It's not a pack. It's a dangerous animal."

Cecily opened her mouth to ask the question, but Illesa interrupted her.

"Where's Joyce?"

"Inside, in her chamber reading the Bestiary, I think."

"Don't let her come out, Cecily." Illesa took Cecily's hand and pressed it hard. "It's important that you don't let her see him."

Cecily opened her mouth, but seeing the set of Illesa's face, she shut it and nodded.

"Here, Alfred. Cut some cheese in the larder, get a trencher. See to it the man sits out of the sun, and keep his ale topped up." She pushed the kitchen boy towards the door.

William bent close to Illesa's ear.

"I'll sit with him. You mustn't talk to him."

"But it looks suspicious if I don't greet him."

"He's already suspicious. That's why he's here with his sly mouth and that monkey."

"I'll see about that." Illesa marched back to where Ramón was standing in the shade. The monkey was out of its pack now and sitting on his shoulder.

Illesa stood at a safe distance. She had too many precious things hanging from her waist.

"Ramón the Player, welcome." She cleared her throat. "We've arranged for you to be fed and watered. You've come a very long way. William says all the way from St Albans?"

He nodded, grinning widely.

"My lady!" He made a gesture, and the monkey bobbed its head on his shoulder. "We are not yet too tired to greet you properly. We beg your generous hospitality." Another waggle of Ramón's finger, and the monkey bowed even lower.

Illesa forced a smile.

"Tell me how you come to be so far from the court. The last we saw of you was in the Prince's employ. Do you have engagements so far west?"

"My lady. You know why I've come." He winked at her. The monkey chattered excitedly and pulled at Ramón's cap. "But we talk later. I see there is food for us, and we are famished."

Cecily was lumbering across the yard.

"Come this way, Master." Cecily gestured for him to follow her. "We have some good food and ale for you."

"We eat outside in the yard," Ramón commented, going with her. "She beckons us like animals. For now, Mullida. Just for now." He smiled crookedly at Illesa and followed Cecily, trotting along behind her like a dog.

Chapter XXI

Illesa found Richard and William in close conversation in the threshing barn. William's cheeks were red, his jaw working furiously.

Richard put his hand on William's shoulder.

"Ramón doesn't know. He suspects. He guesses. He sees an opportunity for gain. We must not let fear cloud our thinking!"

William shook his head.

"I don't fear him! But if Joyce sees him it will remind her. He might even ask her about Reginald."

Richard put up his hand to silence him.

"This needs very careful handling. We must get Joyce away. And you should take her, William. He has particular enmity to you because you took his monkey. But where to go?" He looked around the barn.

Illesa touched his arm.

"To the Templars commandery at Lydley, on an errand. There is a holy well nearby; she should drink the water to bring back her voice. The Templars will allow you to stay the night because of our donations."

It was strange that she hadn't thought of it before. There was said to be healing power in that water by Holt Preen.

"Good. That's a sensible plan. William, go and sit with Ramón. We must keep him in sight at all times. Then you must take him to look round the gardens, Illesa. See if his monkey would like to climb in the orchard so that William can prepare the horses."

"Wait." William shook his head. "I can't leave you here with him. If Reginald was capable of rape and murder, this man is too. At the very least, he's a thief. You need to have him locked in gaol, not entertained!"

"And if he is locked in gaol, he can accuse us of the murder of his friend, and then we are there in gaol too, waiting for the justices to visit next year while the King takes our manor. No," Richard said. "We will handle this carefully. And we will not be endangered by him, because we will set a guard. I will speak to Aron the smith – and his sons. They are discreet. They can keep watch and sleep below tonight. There's new hay to fill the bags for mattresses. I'll send the stable boy to fetch them."

"Will that vagrant be sleeping in my chamber?" William asked.

"Where else?"

William took off his cap and angrily scratched his scalp.

"I don't like to think of the mess that monkey will gladly make all over my bed."

"I will make the necessary arrangements," Richard said, dismissing William with a jerk of his head. William stalked off towards the kitchen.

Illesa avoided Richard's eye and set off after him. She needed to hide the packet, still in the basket, before anyone found it. She ran up the stairs with it clutched to her chest. Cecily's voice came from behind the door to Joyce's chamber.

"It's a special treat. Today you can eat your dinner in your chamber with me." Her tone was wheedling, as if speaking to a very small child. Something clanked. "Come my angel, sit down again and eat your bread. It's soft, the way you like it."

The door thumped, but held. Illesa could not stop to help Cecily. Joyce couldn't stand to be refused anything by her nurse, but it would do her good to be thwarted. And if she wanted to complain, she'd have to speak.

Illesa closed the chamber door behind her and took a deep breath. For now, the only safe place was the casket. She untied the red twine and unfolded the cerecloth. The parchment was none the worse for its time underground. Illesa picked up the scrap of scarlet cloth that contained the ring, but she did not unwrap it. The parchment barely fit into the narrow casket. She placed the wrapped ring on top and laid the crucifix over both of them.

There was no sound from outside the door. She put her finger on the crucifix.

"Oh most mighty Angels of God, Michael and Gabriel, Raphael and Uriel, guard this place from the evil one, through the mercy of Christ Jesu, Amen."

She quickly shut the casket and locked it. That should stop both ring and monkey.

Her hands were filthy. How had it come to this? Dishevelled, frightened, pursued, and yet Reginald was the rapist.

Illesa straightened the pins holding her rough veil. There was no avoiding it. She must face the man who wanted to ruin them – and keep him away from the house while Joyce was bundled off to Lydley. She shut the chamber door carefully behind her. Downstairs, there was no one in the hall; no sound from the buttery or larder. Outside the glare blinded her for a moment. She walked slowly round the side of the manor towards the outer kitchen.

The monkey was sitting on the roof over the ovens, scratching itself. Below, William and Ramón sat on a bench at the trestle, their backs to Illesa. Ramón was delivering instructions and the monkey by turns patted its head, stood balancing on hind legs on the thatch, and then held its arms up and screeched.

"Shhhh!" Illesa said. The monkey hooted at her. Ramón knocked twice on the table, and it came leaping down, shot up his arm and sat on his shoulder.

Illesa glanced back. Joyce would certainly have heard it – and probably guessed what it was.

"Have you finished?" Illesa looked down at the player, who smiled his knowing smile. William was already half-way across the yard.

"Yes. My thanks."

"Come with me, we will look at the garden. I don't like your monkey near the kitchen. It can come and play in the orchard."

"Very well," Ramón said. "But your girl would like to see her, no?"

"No. She would be frightened. Come this way, please."

"Mullida is not frightening," he said, swinging his legs over the bench and following her. The monkey was sitting on his shoulder, holding onto his jerkin, her long tail stretched out behind.

Illesa kept walking past the sheds and the carts. Behind her she heard Cecily's voice, high with desperation. Joyce must be out of her chamber. William was able to ready horses faster than anyone, but even he needed longer than that.

"There is some trouble?" Ramón's soft voice asked behind her. "Should we go and see?"

"This way." Illesa opened the gate to the orchard, shooing one of the chickens. "Your monkey can climb here. That's what they like, isn't it? The bee skeps are at the far end, so don't let it go there or it will be stung." Illesa motioned him in and stood, barring the gate. "These are apple trees, the others are pears and plums. There are medlars on that side."

Ramón touched an apple tree and the monkey ran up his arm and into the branches. He turned to look at her.

"You are getting me out of the way." He nodded to himself, as if satisfied that he'd been right.

"I thought your pet would enjoy the trees. Especially when you have travelled so far. She's happy up there." Mullida was pulling the leaves and small swellings of apples from the branch where she sat, tasting them and throwing them to the ground.

"She is not a pet. She is a performer. Like me."

The monkey swung down to the ground and walked around the tree.

"She does this part in the play of Adam and Eve," Ramón said, pride in his voice. "But you think she is just a thief."

Illesa wiped the sweat from her brow.

"She is very clever. Did you train her yourself?"

"Of course. With some help," he said with a sly smile. "When will you let us out of the orchard? Are you the angel with a flaming sword at the gate?"

Illesa felt herself flush red.

"Where do you go next? Are you heading to Chester for the plays there?"

Ramón whistled and Mullida galloped towards him on all fours, standing at his side and reaching her arms up. He held out his arm. She grabbed his sleeve, swung around, tucked her legs in and ended up sitting on his shoulder again, smacking her lips.

"There! Now you smile!" He grinned at Illesa. "I could not bear to see your serious, sad face any more. But you see there is no more plays for me until I can find my partner. And only you know where is he."

"Do you mean Reginald the Liar? Gaspar's brother?"

Ramón nodded sardonically.

"You play with me now. Maybe you think I don't know about Reginald. But I do. I do." He shook his head. Mullida shook her head as well and regarded Illesa with her yellow-brown eyes.

"Know what?" Illesa whispered.

149

Ramón reached behind and stroked the monkey's back.

"I think we talk with the master. He must see me, and I must speak to him. Man to man. Not to his wife or his servant. It is not the information to share with a woman."

"You must think I'm very delicate." Illesa folded her arms across her chest. "Sir Richard is much engaged around the estate. He will see you at his convenience. Until then, you might tell me what has brought you all the way from St Albans, without your company, and caused you to seek us out."

But he said no more and wandered off around the orchard, singing an old tune, the monkey alternately stalking behind him or climbing up his body to ride on his head.

Illesa strained her ears for any other voices coming from the yard. Just the sound of bees and the song of a lark above the meadow. William should be riding off with Joyce by now. Perhaps it was safe to leave. Ramón was pacing the width of the orchard, stepping in time to his tune.

Behind her a small sound made her turn.

Joyce was at the end of the barn, staring, her mouth open, eyes wide. She took a step towards the orchard, but William grabbed her, and they both disappeared behind the barn wall. Illesa glanced back at the orchard. Ramón was looking at her, his head on one side.

"Someone wants to see us," he said, nodding.

Distinctive uneven footsteps came up behind her, and Richard was at the gate, staring balefully at the unwanted guest.

They led Ramón into the hall.

"The pretty girl is gone?" Ramón was looking all around, up at the gallery, as if Joyce might spring out from somewhere as in a play.

"Sit down, Master Player," Richard said. "Lady Burnel and I must hear your explanation. Here, the boy is bringing us refreshment for the hot day." The kitchen boy had come in with a tray, and laid out the cups, ale and wine. "You surprised us with your arrival, but we have ample to share. Even with your monkey." He was trying to sound friendly, but he couldn't stop glaring at the monkey, who was scampering along the floor, looking for scraps.

Ramón sat down and patted his legs. Mullida ran to him and sat on his lap.

"We are grateful." He looked up to Richard before drinking. "And I say, may your house be blessed by God for welcoming the stranger."

Richard raised his cup in response.

"You are not quite a stranger. Why did you come to find us here?"

"Ah well," Ramón said, putting down his cup of wine deliberately and tickling Mullida under her chin on the white ruff. "Now we get to the meat. Yes." He looked at Richard thoughtfully. "You want me to speak to you in straight lines, like a column. Your wife, in coiling spirals, like a path through the forest. Still, I speak as I know, a story."

Richard cleared his throat, but Ramón held up his hand.

"Please, it will not take long. I came to the company of players as a boy. You know, this high." He put his hand on top of the monkey. "Well, Reginald was in charge of my training, and he taught me many things. Many, many. But not all about the plays. You know what I mean." He glanced at Richard out of the corner of his eye. "Well, I grew up and that was that. He and I were a partnership on stage, no more in other ways. But I knew that man, in and out. Yes. And because I never complain, no, or tell anyone, he trusts me. He trusts me with his secrets. You know?"

Richard nodded carefully, his hands flat on the table.

"So he tells me what he does to remember his many lines, how he recalls the tales, how he makes sure that his voice stays strong, how to get the power over the audience. He shows me all this. It is good for me to know. I keep it secret from the other players. They don't like him. He don't like them. We are a partnership, he and I. We do all our plays together." Mullida hopped off his lap again. She was under the table by Illesa's feet.

"You said this wouldn't take long," Richard said.

"You are impatient. That tells me you are worried about something. If the story is not finding your heart, your heart is bound up with all kinds of troubles." He tapped rapidly on the table with his ragged fingernail. "So I will make it quicker. Reginald came back from seeing you alone, that night after the feast, and he was very angry. Very, very. He says to me that he is going to teach the servant a lesson. I ask him why, but really I know why. It was his boy that was gone. He'd been missing since the dinner, and it was your servant that sent him away."

Illesa felt the monkey's paws tugging on her skirts. She pushed it away with the tip of her toe. Her cheeks felt hot and her heart was pounding, loud and fast in her chest.

Ramón's head was bent, staring at his hands as he spoke.

"I said, no, he should let him go. There are many poor boys in London who need a home and will satisfy. But he would not listen. He says I should get revenge too, for him taking Mullida." Ramón shook his head. "I say no. But he's going to follow you; he's going to get revenge on that man. Maybe even more than that." He looked straight at Richard and leant back from the table. "He's going to find William the servant, beat him, and be back in St Albans in time for the play for the Sheriff, when we will be paid very well. The play of Adam and Eve in the Lost Paradise. And the play of Noah. He gets his pay from the Prince's wardrobe, then he leaves. I no see him again."

Ramón's fingers drummed, one by one, on the wooden board.

"He never arrives in St Albans. No one sees him. I wait for four more days. But I know." He looked around the room. "Yes, I know he is dead. Your servant killed him. The one that took your little girl away." He shook his head sadly. "I have no partner now."

Illesa opened her mouth, but Richard clamped his hand on hers.

"You are making a grave accusation, Ramón. Be very careful what you say."

Ramón drank from his cup and nodded.

"Yes." He looked morose, as he had not before. "I bring many truths that are heavy with me." He looked around and whistled.

Mullida did not come. She was not in the hall. Ramón stood up and whistled loudly. Illesa stood up too, her stomach twisting with fear. She started for the stairs, but then there was the sound of claws scraping on polished wood as the monkey came racing along the gallery and swung down the bannister, leapt across the floor and clambered up Ramón, screeching with excitement.

"What this? Eh?" Ramón looked at the monkey. He pulled at the thing she was clutching in her front paw. "What did you find?"

Chapter XXII

Ramón held up Illesa's casket key to the light. It was all she could do to stop herself snatching it from him.

"That's mine." She held out her hand. "That's the second thing she's stolen. Keep that monkey in sight, or I'll lock her in the tack room." Her hand was trembling as he laid the key solemnly on her palm.

She felt at her waist for the chatelaine. The other tools and amulets were there. Why had the monkey taken the key – the smallest and least shiny? And why had it gone upstairs with it?

"She is how you say, like a bird that collects things?" Ramón shrugged. "Magpie?"

"Control the monkey, or she will be locked up," Richard's tone was even, but Illesa saw his fury. "You have come many miles to make a grave accusation against William with only fantasies and inventions."

Ramón pursed his mouth.

"Well, I know what happened. So I come because I need some of his things. They are important. I said he showed me how he learnt things quickly, how he got the audience to pay attention so much? These things were written down. Also, I need some compensation in coin." He shrugged again. "You know, I have no partner now, I must train one. I will have not much coin for a long time. So I ask for you to pay me and give me these things and then I leave you alone." He drew a line on the table with the tip of his finger. "I know you don't want your servant to be put in gaol. He is hanged or worse. So you pay me to keep your servant alive and out of gaol. It is good for both of us." He smiled wearily. "I think you see this is the best way. Then we do not have to find the Bailiff or the Sheriff or any of these officials and –"

"You threaten me! And I have not seen Reginald since we bade him farewell in London, by my life and on the blood of Christ!" Richard was half out of his chair and stabbing his finger in Ramón's direction.

Ramón nodded.

"You are angry. It was not you who killed him. You sent the man who did it away. I know." He sighed sadly. "But he cannot

154

pay me, you must do that, otherwise I go to the officials, and they find out he was one of the players favoured by the Prince. It goes badly for him – and for you if you protect him. I don't want that." Ramón stared at his lined palms. "Reginald did not care for any life." He looked up at Illesa with his dark gleaming eyes. "It's truth. But now I must protect myself. I have suffered from his life, I don't want to suffer from his death." His head jerked up suddenly. "Mullida, ven aquí!"

She was walking along the upper gallery on three legs, her tail high in the air.

"I'm desolate. I forgot she will always go back if she finds something bright." His face was more proud than angry. He whistled. "Don't worry I give it straight back to you, lady."

But Illesa didn't want it back. The thing the monkey was holding was shiny, silver, clutched round its little fingers as it lolloped across the floor towards its master. It came to him, climbed up and chattered in his lap, showing its sharp teeth and whiskery lips.

Ramón held its paw out and with his long fingers began to remove the ring. He held it between his two fingers and turned it round, mouthing the words of the inscription. He looked up, stared at one then the other, and closed his fingers over the ring.

"That was a ring given to me by Gaspar," Illesa said quickly. "Reginald's brother." She held out her hand.

Ramón pressed his lips together. His head waggled from side to side.

"I don't think so." He was stroking Mullida with the other hand.

"What is it?" Richard asked. He peered towards Ramón. "Hold it out."

"You know it, husband," Illesa insisted. "It's the ring Gaspar gave us when he left. Remember?"

Richard sat back in his chair.

"Ah yes. Give it to Lady Burnel, Ramón, or your monkey will be locked away."

The player looked hard at Illesa.

"I did not expect that," he said, softly. "You know I have ten people will swear this ring belonged to Reginald, enough to convict you. Do you have anyone to swear against them?" He gestured around the hall. "Gaspar is not here." Ramón opened his hand.

She took the ring from his palm and held it tight in her fist by her thigh.

Ramón twisted the monkey's iron collar round and round.

"I try to do best thing for all of us, but still you lie to me. Give me the parchment and a pound of silver and all is forgotten. That is less than what the Prince gave his harpist for one night. And I will vanish!" Ramón snapped his fingers.

Richard pushed himself to his feet, both fists on the table.

"No, you have threatened us and stolen through your monkey. Now we've had enough. You will be locked in. Master Aron!"

The smith and his two large sons entered the hall from the door to the yard. They'd been waiting there. Probably listening.

"Take this man and lock him into the upper room of the stable. Stay guard there, outside his door." Richard looked at Ramón, who was draining his cup. "Food will be brought to you. We will not let you starve."

The men surrounded Ramón. He looked up at them sadly.

"It could all be finished. No need for this —" He waved his hand in the air like a butterfly's wing. "La antipatía, no need." He tapped his shoulder and the monkey hopped up. The men led him out, holding his upper arms in their large hands.

Illesa looked at Richard for an instant, and away.

"Is that the ring you mentioned?" He slapped the table, hard with the flat of his palm. "Why did you leave it out for anyone to find!"

Illesa shook her head, not trusting herself to speak.

"Now what? We can't keep him here for ever. We can't kill him. And if we pay him, he will just come back in a little while demanding more. Damn Reginald and all his kind to Hell. I've had enough of players! They can all go up in flames, as it pleases the Devil." Richard banged his stick on the floor with each step as he stalked out of the hall following the smith and his sons.

Illesa raced up the stairs. The door to her chamber was open. The casket was turned on its side on her table – the lid closed. The scarlet cloth was on the floor. She bent down for it. That cursed monkey had stolen twice, and she'd felt nothing. But could a monkey put a key in a lock and open a casket? She sat down on the stool and picked up the ornate box. The key was still in the lock.

She let out her breath, her whole body trembling. The monkey had either opened the casket, taken out the ring and locked it again, or the ring was already outside the box, in the chamber. Both were frightening. But it was clear what she must do. And it would need to be done soon. With or without Richard's knowledge – she was not yet sure.

Illesa looked down at the ring in the palm of her hand. She would have to keep it on her person. Tight and close, as she once kept a precious book. It was possessed with an evil spirit. Perhaps she could drop it into a holy well and leave it there, that surely would stop its unnatural movement. Until then, it had to be under her watch.

The smell in the upper stable room was foul. There were rags covered in filth in the far corner.

"Martin, get a bucket of water," she whispered to the older of the smith's sons. Illesa went back into the room and put the lamp down on the floor. Ramón, on William's bed, had propped himself up on his elbow. The monkey was curled up at his feet, asleep. Or pretending to be so.

"You know I am still here because I want to make an agreement," Ramón said hoarsely. "I could have left any time. Mullida can fit through the bars on the window. But I thought you would come." He sat up fully and folded his legs under him.

Martin put the bucket down behind her.

"There you are, my lady."

"Thank you, Martin. Close the door, but stay on the other side." She waited until the door was shut and leant her back against it, so Ramón wouldn't see how much she was trembling.

"Put the soiled rags in this bucket. Is your monkey not well?"

"Mullida ate too much bread. It's not good for her." He shrugged. "She recovers quickly, usually."

"How did you train her to use keys?"

Ramón shook his head.

"I didn't. She copies. She's always watching me. If I use key, she tries."

Inside her cote, Illesa put her hand on the shape of the ring, which she'd strung on a length of cord around her neck and strapped to her chest with a band of cloth.

"Does she lock things as well?"

Ramón laughed.

"She is not a housekeeper. So you want to know about the monkey; is that the only reason you came? I'll be gone by morning. Either to the Sheriff or not." He reached for his pack and took out a wineskin. "The end of the fire water," he commented and drained the last drops. The smell was like wine, but more powerful. "There is no more, so far from the sea." He wiped his mouth with the back of his hand and put on an amiable expression.

"I came to speak to you about the parchment," she said sternly. His eyes snapped to her face, the look of indolence gone. "You should know that Reginald tried to rape and kill Joyce. He would have killed me as well as William. He deserved his death. But what I have of his can be yours, if your word is true."

Ramón sucked air through his teeth.

"The pig. The Devil took his soul when he was playing him one day. That is why he did these things, no? The Devil would not let him stop. Your pretty girl, she is hurt?"

"Yes." Illesa crossed her arms over her chest. She had no wish to relive the night in that different upper stable room, in the dim lamplight, with this man, who, for all his sympathy, might be just as bad. "So we don't want his evil works here, nor do we want you reminding Joyce of what happened to her." She fixed her eyes on his, until he lowered them. "The parchment that was in Reginald's pack is written in strange figures. If these are charms summoning demons to help him in his performances, then I would counsel you to burn them, not read and cherish them."

"No, my lady. That is not what they are. You have them? I show you."

Illesa shook her head.

Ramón made patting gestures in the air.

"They look strange, but they come from the court of Alphonso el Sabio, the very learned king and his sister was the Queen of England, no? He was like Solomon. He gathered wisdom from all the world together and made it to be written in all the languages of God. Let me show you, please? The ancient knowledge of the stars, the planets and the stones of the earth bring strength and learning. And with the Mercury square the powers of memory are increased! You can see this gives no evil powers, otherwise why would I be on foot, dressed in rags, sleeping over a stable? Eh?"

Illesa pulled the packet of parchment out of her belt and placed it in the middle of the floor, backing up to the door again.

"I don't want to see or know any more about them. Or about you," she whispered, as he pushed himself forward onto his knees and took the packet. "I hope never to see you again. If we do, my husband has promised to have you killed. We have little coin, but this." She threw him a leather purse. He caught it in one hand. "Take it and go."

The monkey had woken at the sound of the coins in the purse. It sat looking at her, its tail curled over its master's knee. Ramón was stowing the purse and the parchment carefully in his pack.

"What about his ring?" He jutted his chin, in imitation of Richard. "The ring given you by Gaspar, eh?" He grimaced. "You don't want it, es claro."

"It is cursed. I will take it to a holy place. You should listen to what I said and burn those before they take you to the Devil too."

She turned away from him.

A loud hoot made her glance back as she was closing the door.

"Mullida says farewell, Lady Burnel," Ramón explained, as the monkey spun round on the spot on its back legs.

"May God find you and return you to the right path," she whispered, crossing herself and shutting the door.

Chapter XXIII

Thursday the 18th August, 1306
The Feast of Little Saint Hugh of Lincoln
Hereford Cathedral

It is best when there is still light, and the crowds have all been pushed out of the doors like the sheep they are. Bleating, noisy animals, following one another, putting their money in the dish, mouthing their prayers, like a herd following the farmer with fresh hay. God, give me patience when they come again, and lengthen this time when the north aisle is silent and empty.

I have brought my own offering, given to God for all time. And I know it is prideful to kneel and admire my own work, but is it not also God's? His creation – his noble, holy plan? I brought it all together in one mighty place, for his glory, not mine. And through this work, people pray for me, and I need their prayers, for I have not repented, nor forgotten. Especially not now, with the news from France the Dean was eager to tell me today.

'You should hear this, Father Richard.' In his supercilious voice. 'The Jews have been exiled from the French lands as well. They have no foothold except in Aragón and Castile now. Is that not good? God removes those that reject him.' He wanted to see my temper and gain another reason to punish me by further confinement.

I did not give him that satisfaction. For I had fortified myself against all his words. Whenever he speaks, I imagine he is a goat – that protruding chin, the buck teeth. But his words, when I recalled them later, did make me weep. I don't know where she has gone, and I cannot reach her until, God willing, she comes safely to rest.

My confessor insists that it will fade, with prayer and fasting, but it does not. He's another one of no imagination. Look, there on my map, the Garden of Paradise where Adam and Eve lived in unity before the Fall, and were they not also Hebrews? But we know them to be God's pure creation. So it was with Chera. She had already taken fruit from the Tree of Knowledge, that was evident. Her learning something inherent, inherited from her Rabbi father. She would use the stories of the prophets to refute me, until I was forced to stop her lips.

On this day every year in Lincoln, all the Jews would be made to stand on the street to hear the Dominicans preach against them and their murdering kind. The cross would be processed before them, and then the people would begin spitting on them, pushing them. Chera standing in black cloth, defiantly watching, while others hid their faces from the statue of Little Saint Hugh, being carried through the streets. People flocked after it, more sheep, running to the cathedral shrine to beg the poor boy to heal their piles.

'Someone killed him and hid his body in that well,' I told her. 'Why would any Christian kill a child?'

'Are there no Christians in Hell?' she replied. 'Does the Devil not inspire men to the most disgusting crimes? And if then this is blamed on a whole people, is the Devil not happy that so many die, are hanged, are imprisoned with no guilt? Then is God's plan foiled by the Devil when the innocent are executed instead of the wicked. But for us, we know our innocence and we go to God unafraid. Can you say the same?'

I told her that many believed all her kind were consigned to Hell. But she always had an answer:

'Even Moses? Even Samuel? Even Solomon?'

'Those who killed and denied Christ, God's son.'

'Those who never saw him and are not convinced by this Christian testimony? Is it not up to his followers to make it obvious that he is the Messiah by their love and power? And if his followers are brutal and ignore justice and mercy, then why should we believe they are right?'

I could say nothing convincing that she didn't have an answer for. She'd bitten through the apple to the core of knowledge. When I kissed her, I hoped to gain some, but all I found was torture.

Look again at my great work. Outside Eden, she and I have been exiled and ashamed, torn apart. She has been exiled again and again, on a journey like Moses and the Israelites, forced to wander through the wilderness for forty years for worshipping a false god. Did her worship of me make her an exile in this world?

But that is my sinful pride. She never worshipped me. Nor was her love half as strong as mine for her. She took on the garb of a Christian to save her life, with her father's permission, and left my faith again as soon as it was clear we could never be allowed to live in peace. And the Dean insists the Hebrews worshipping the golden calf on my map must be grotesque, and all the while he counts the rings and coins, the haul from the bleating crowds.

I will stay here until the light is completely gone. Here I can trace her journey in the physical and spiritual sphere. Lincoln, London, Bordeaux, Toulouse, and now over the mountains and into Aragón, places I draw but have never seen.

That will not always be so. I will be like Paulus Orosius, an obedient dog of great Saint Augustine, who, at his word, left Catalonia to describe the world and write of Christ's victory against Pagan time. I have drawn him leaving on his dappled Spanish horse, looking back on the world with all its victory and loss. He takes a bearing down the length of his hand. He has placed and fixed the world, as have I. He went before. One day, I will have gone before. One day I will go. *Passe Avant.*

I will see her again, in this world, because I will not see her in the next.

I will go on pilgrimage to find her. I know the way. Soon the door will be opened.

Pray for me.

Chapter XXIV

Thursday the 8th September, 1306
The Feast of the Birth of the Virgin
St Mary's Well, Outside the Walls
Shrewsbury

It had been a mistake to arrive at the well on the Feast of the Birth of the Virgin with every other woman in the whole of the Welsh March, many of them pregnant. The increased chance of blessing from the auspicious day could be counteracted by the large number of petitioners. And Joyce was unhappy in the crowd.

It was hot in the sun, packed together along Water Lane, but a black cloud was skirting to the west. If it started to rain, some of the weaker people might leave. Joyce sighed loudly and leant against Illesa's side, fingering her paternoster beads. She'd wanted to come, had even whispered the word, 'Yes.' But there was little excitement for her here. All the entertainment would be going on near St Mary's Church, and Illesa had insisted they visit the well first. At least they could see the small wellhouse now and the wellkeeper at the gate, collecting alms. Illesa clutched at the purse hanging from her waist, took out a penny.

The cries of the women inside the wellhouse echoed in a disquieting way. Just one pair of women remained in front of them: one very pregnant, the other with a bright red rash across her face and flaking, scaly skin. Illesa looked away when the pregnant woman caught her staring. When she'd come here last, a few months after Margaret was still-born, she'd begged the Virgin for another child. As if the Virgin could grant another immaculate conception. She'd had to force herself to attend other women's births – the jealousy yet another thing to confess.

Illesa felt for the cord around her neck and the ring, which today she wore loose, not strapped tight to her chest. Since she'd begun wearing it, it had not appeared anywhere else. The dreams of burial had also stopped. Instead she relived the killing

– except Reginald did not die when she stabbed him. He kept getting up from the floor and moving towards her.

They watched the pair of women walk up to the small stone chapel and kneel before entering.

"Alms, alms for the poor," the Franciscan wellkeeper said sing-song, holding out a clay pot. Illesa put the silver penny in the slot. By the sound, the pot was nearly full.

"Have there been any miracles today, Brother?"

"Yesterday, lady. Yesterday there was a girl cured of a squint in her eye. Came out proclaiming the power of our Holy Queen of Heaven."

Illesa crossed herself.

"Where did she come from?"

He waved his hand vaguely towards the west.

"Frankwell way. Just a mite she was. But I saw her on the way in, and she certainly had been healed. Praise our merciful Lady of Heaven. Her mother had given a gold ring." He nodded in approval at this lavish gift. "Look, they're out already. On you go."

He waved them through the gate.

Illesa took Joyce's arm and they started up the slope towards the narrow stone entrance.

There was too much in her mind and on her heart. She should have seen a confessor first, even if it meant waiting for hours. Joyce bobbed her head and went in. Illesa followed. Perhaps there would be mercy for Joyce, even if Illesa's prayers were useless.

The well chamber was bright with candle flame reflected off the pool, fed by a stone channel coming from the hillside. The steps into the pool disappeared into the murky, disturbed water. There had been too many people today polluting it with their illnesses. Joyce and Illesa knelt in front of the east-facing altar. Rain began falling through the window above it.

"Most Holy Lady, Mother of God, have mercy on us. Intercede for us with your son, Christ Jesus. Amen."

Illesa's heart felt empty. Joyce's eyes were closed, her mouth still moving. Illesa gripped the cord and pulled the ring out from between her breasts and over her head. She held it in her closed fist. If she left it here, would it pollute the spring with evil, or would it wash the curse away? She did not know. Nothing was clear.

Joyce was on her feet again. She knelt by the stone spout, put her hands under the water, lifted them to her lips. Illesa crouched beside her.

"Put your head right under, Joyce. Let the water touch your throat." She gripped her shoulders while Joyce held her head under the flow, her hands cupped underneath her mouth. The water was sparkling on her face and hands, golden in the flames.

"Merciful Mother of God, heal Joyce's tongue and take away the hurt she suffered –" Illesa began.

Joyce made a choking sound. She was trying to speak. Now was the time to make the offering. Illesa held her clenched hand over the pool. A gust of storm wind guttered the candles. The chapel darkened as the clouds rolled overhead. A clear sign that the ring was not the right offering.

Illesa tugged the red cord back over her neck and fumbled with her purse. She had no gold, but the small amethyst amulet, inscribed with a cross, was a noble offering worthy of the Queen of Heaven. She placed her hand in the water and let the gem fall into the bottom of the well. Illesa put her hand on Joyce's shoulder.

"Say the Hail Mary with me."

It was no good. Joyce knelt shivering next to the pool of water, water dripping from her nose, mingling with her tears. They tried until the wellkeeper came and said they'd taken too long. Didn't they know that others were waiting?

Joyce hid behind Illesa as they came out into the light rain. Already the worst of the storm was over.

"Go down there. You must record any divine help with the Brother Scrivener." The wellkeeper pointed to the other side of the enclosure where a small canvas shelter was set up. The monks had made sure they were prepared for crowds at the feast. Joyce was sniffing and trying to wipe her face and neck with her sleeve.

"Don't do that. I have a cloth here. Put this over your head, and tie it round your throat." Illesa passed her the linen she'd folded over her belt.

The monk under the canvas was staring at them with protuberant eyes. A length of parchment marked with red and black lines lay on a small sloping table in front of his stool.

"Nature of your ailment?" He had lowered his eyes to the parchment and was poised on a blank line. Illesa tried to read the previous entries upside down.

"My daughter was unable to speak."

He glanced up at Joyce.

"A mute," he said, dipping his quill in the small inkpot and scratching the words on the parchment. "And what blessing have you received today?"

"Joyce, can you speak? Tell the Brother." Illesa tried to pull Joyce closer to the desk, but Joyce shook her head and covered her mouth with the ends of the cloth.

The Brother raised his eyebrows and bent over the parchment again.

"No blessing." He finished the words and looked up, frowning. "What offering did you give to Our Lady?"

"An amythyst gemstone carved with a cross."

The monk was silent, marking it down. When he finished he laid down his quill, glanced up and made the sign of the cross.

"May the Virgin bless you and keep you from evil."

They walked back up the steep lane to the watergate. The tired guard barely glanced at them. Inside William was leaning against the stone wall, still looking cross. He'd not wanted to come for fear of running into Phylis.

"You've taken your time," he began, looked at the bedraggled, sniffing Joyce, and changed tone. "But Cecily is still at the market checking all the goods three times. So –"

"I'm not ready to leave yet, William. I still need to make my confession."

"I know. I know. You keep saying. I looked in at the Friary and there are only a few waiting. That's why I came to find you." He squinted at the sky. "I'll take Joyce to see the jugglers. They'll start up again now the rain has stopped. The last thing she needs is another church." He started off, Joyce walking eagerly behind him.

"Meet me outside the east gate then. And tell Cecily she only has the two saddle bags for the goods!" Cecily always bought too much. They often had to ride home with woodcocks hanging from their saddles, bouncing along uncomfortably.

Perhaps it was true that she took Joyce too often to church, but shouldn't that be a good thing? There was no help to be found elsewhere. And Joyce needed help – that was beyond doubt. She'd not stopped having nightmares either.

Illesa walked back down the hill. She had never said confession to the Dominicans before. They were useful to those who'd rather remain unknown to their confessor. There was only one man waiting by the Friary's public gate. He was staring at the cap he held in his hands. A stonemason, perhaps, by the dust he had on his hair and his cloth. What could his grave sin be? Throwing stones?

She pinched the skin on her wrist between her fingernails. She should not judge or be amused by him. Unlike her, he was surely not a killer. A man came out of the gate door, a bargeman, perhaps. He reminded Illesa of the Tewkesbury barge captain: long, muscled arms, a distinctive hat, overhanging at the front. He loped away towards the jetty. The stonemason went in, and she was alone, standing in the shade cast by the town's tall buildings, waiting to put down her sins at the feet of one who would know what to do with them. Her fingers worried at the cord around her neck. The skin was itchy, irritated. Could she ask him what to do with a cursed ring, or would he think her an evil-doer herself, harmed by her own attempts at magic?

Perhaps the stonemason took a long time to come to the point; the moments dragged by. Finally he came out, eyes firmly on the bit of earth just before his feet. She let him leave the porch and then stepped over the lintel into the parlour.

The Dominican friar was sitting in a stall along the far wall, a prie-dieu in front of him made of rough-hewn wood. He beckoned her forward.

"Kneel, lady." His voice was mild. She caught a hint of Gascony in it.

She approached and knelt down on the hard wood, clasping her hands together.

"When did you last confess your sins?"

She looked up at him. He was younger than her. Maybe thirty years old. Thin. His eyes bright and focused.

"In Lent, at the Feast of the Annunciation." She bowed her head. He reminded her of Father Raymond, the Templar. His face weathered and brown. Unhurried. Unlike Father Thomas, pale as a maggot, full of certainty and impatience.

"Very well. You have something important to confess. Please."

He was certainly Gascon. Illesa felt the tears begin to drip onto the wood support. He waited, silent, his head bowed, until she could speak.

"Father, I killed a man who attacked my daughter, intent on rape. He threatened to kill me. I know this is not sinful." Illesa rubbed her cheek against her sleeve. "But I did not give him time to confess. My servant hid his body in the river, to save us from imprisonment. The man was important to one of the members of the court. His body has been rotting for months. His spirit is goading me. Invading my dreams."

She took her cloth and wiped her nose.

"I am a God-fearing woman. I say my prayers every day. But my daughter will not speak since the attack, and I cannot pray!" She gasped for breath. "I say the words but they mean nothing. I cannot speak to the saints as I used to." It was impossible to look at the friar, so she rested her forehead on the prie-dieu.

Her heart was racing. Outside, a bird called by the river – a long chirruping song.

"Join me in prayer before I state your penance." The friar had knelt down on the flagstones. His black habit was too short, revealing thin ankles. They recited the Lord's Prayer and the Ten Commandments.

"You are not hiding any sins from me, lady? I am not speaking of small lapses of judgement, but perhaps some lechery with this man you have killed?"

"No, Father! I swear on the Virgin and her tears, although I have been sorely tested with temptations, I have never –" She could not continue.

There was a long silence.

"I believe you have acted to protect, but you have not acted in faith. Is not God more powerful than the rulers of this world? He protects those who do right. So your sin is one of fear of worldly pain, of lack of faith in your one true Father. You have not relied on him for your protection. So you must renew your faith, put yourself at the mercy of God. And as you have sworn your oath on the Virgin Mother of God, it is to her that you must go for salvation."

The Dominican got to his feet and raised his hand in the air.

"You must say your devotions twice a day, and within the year you must go on pilgrimage to the Virgin. Walsingham is not far enough. Rocamadour is a powerful site of healing. You will go on foot in penitence there and confess your sin at her shrine. Then your sins will be remitted, and you will find your prayer and inner joy again through the cardinal virtues. Keep the sacraments faithfully all your days. You have performed the contrition and the confession, but this remains – the satisfaction of your penance."

He made the sign of the cross in a large sweeping gesture in the air between them.

"By Almighty God, the Virgin Mary and all the Saints, I commit your soul to this pilgrimage, or face damnation."

Chapter XXV

Thursday the 18th October, 1306
The Feast of Saint Luke
Severn Bridge, Atcham

"I've already told you, countless times! It is ridiculous to make a journey like that. You certainly cannot go in the winter, you'll drown in a storm, and how will that help anyone? I can't see why a journey to Rocamadour, in the middle of nowhere, is any better than one to Canterbury. It's not as if you killed an innocent man and you have to go to Rome or Jerusalem."

Richard was leaning against his tethered horse at the jetty near the bridge. They'd not been waiting long but already he was in pain and regretting his decision to ride out to meet Christopher. And she'd made the mistake of mentioning her pilgrimage.

"I won't be going in winter, husband. The friar gave me a year to undertake the journey. But he was certain that I should go to Rocamadour, to submit myself to the Virgin. I would not risk going against the penance he assigned. It must now be satisfied, or I will never find the way out of purgatory."

"But you could go to Canterbury and then to Walsingham, all without leaving these shores!" He stared at the empty road. "It's putting the blame on you for defending your child."

Illesa glanced at the darkening sky. Christopher was coming overland from Chester. He was supposed to have left there the day before and spent the night in Whitchurch. It had been foolish to come to the bridge. He might take another whole day to reach them if his wound troubled him. And meanwhile Richard became more and more irritable.

"No, it was hiding the body that was the sin. We've talked about this already."

Richard struck the ground with his stick.

"But now the body is no longer hidden. It has been found and certainly been buried by now. So what is the need for you to do penance?"

Reginald's body had been exposed in early September, when the river level dropped after a month without rain. By then, the fish had eaten most of the flesh, leaving only sinews and bones. They only knew he was a man by the shreds of his clothes. But no one recognised him. There'd been no local Tewkesbury man who'd gone missing. No one came to claim the body. William had gathered all this from the crier in Ludlow when he went to sell one of last year's foals.

"We should have buried him," Illesa whispered. "His body and soul were unable to rest, that's why he is unquiet." Why his spirit would not leave her alone.

Richard shook his head.

"You imagine it. And you frighten Joyce with your nightmares and constant prayer. As if it isn't bad enough that she sits there like a statue, saying nothing." He looked away across the river.

"She spoke the words of the Lord's Prayer yesterday." Whispered, but words nonetheless.

"I mean a conversation! I ask her how she does, and she looks at me with wide eyes like a dog! How are we going to find a suitable husband when she will not say even a simple greeting?"

"She's too young, yet, Richard, for God's love! She's not yet thirteen. Besides I've heard many husbands claiming they'd like their wives to be mute."

Richard grunted.

"Joyce will also benefit from visiting the shrine of the Virgin," Illesa insisted. "And with holy help, she will come back with her voice, strong and well."

"And what if both of you die on the way, or on the way back? What good will that have done? You know what it is like travelling through Aquitaine. It's a bloody foolish plan."

Richard pushed himself upright and walked down the lane as fast as he could, leaning heavily on his stick. It did his leg no good to stand or sit for too long.

Illesa let him go alone. There was no point saying any more. If he'd been well and able to travel without pain, Richard might have gone with them. But that was impossible, unless he was pulled in a cart, and he would never submit to that humiliation again.

Stephen, the stable boy, was coming back from the hamlet, his cap cradled in his arms. It was full of apples. He'd grown broad in the last month. His tunic was too tight around his shoulders. She'd have to find him an old one of Christopher's.

"You found some, Stephen?"

He nodded and gave an apple to Sorrel. The horse crunched it in his big yellow teeth, foam around his lips. Illesa took three from the cap and gave one to Stampie. The palfrey wanted her to hold it while she snaffled it in her lips. Illesa started eating one, but there was that old shooting pain in her back tooth when she chewed. She gave the rest of it to the horse.

Stephen couldn't stand still for any length of time either; he was already inspecting the bank, looking at the rafts and barges tied up, wandering away up-river. Richard had turned around and was limping back towards her. He twisted his head to see if anyone stood within earshot.

"We haven't decided what we are going to tell Christopher. If he ever arrives."

She handed him the last apple. He squinted at it and took a bite.

"He has to know some of it, or how can we explain why Joyce is mute?"

Richard chewed quickly and swallowed his mouthful.

"Maybe she'll start to speak when she sees him. She's had little company of her own age or anything near it. She needs to be with young people, then she'll see the benefit of talking."

"Pray God it is so." Illesa crossed herself. "I think we should tell Christopher everything. It is not good to compound the sin by lying about it."

"Does that mean you're going straight to the Bailiff to confess to him?" He shook his head and looked away. "It's too late for honesty. And we have to think of how Christopher will take the news."

Christopher hated anything that was out of order, or against rules. Knowing what she and William had done would disturb him.

"We will have to see how bad his injury is. There's no point telling him anything if he's not well enough to hear it."

Richard pushed a bit of apple out of his teeth with his tongue and threw the core into the river. The bells in the church began to ring for nones.

"If he doesn't arrive soon, we'll be riding home in the dark."

They stood in morose silence. Leaves blew around them in a gust of wind. The mist rose from the river into the cold air. On the bank a figure began running towards them. It was Stephen.

"Have you seen him?"

"I think so," he nodded. "Two men on horseback and another leading a pony? They're on the road from the north, just approaching the church."

Illesa followed him to the bridge. It could be Christopher with Thurstan, his squire, and some other company to deter bandits on the road. Hopefully the stranger would not require a bed for the night. It had been so long since they'd had Christopher to themselves.

"Go back and hold the horses, Stephen."

The party was approaching the other side of the bridge. When they stopped to pay the toll, she'd be able to see if it was Christopher.

Richard arrived behind her.

"Well, is it him?"

"I can't see yet."

"Your eyes are getting as bad as mine."

"It's the curve of the bridge, I can only see their top halves. Do you think it's him?"

"I think so," he said, hesitantly. "It's hard to see below his hat. There's someone else with him –"

Illesa peered at the blurry figures. One of them was retrieving coins from his purse. His movements looked familiar. And that was certainly Thurstan with his bright blond hair poking out of the cap.

"Christopher!" Richard called.

A hand went up in greeting.

"Yes, it's him, and he's well enough to be on horseback. Saint Martin be praised. Oh –"

The third man had also raised his hand, and Illesa had seen his face clearly. All the hair stood up on her head.

"No! Richard, it's Ramón!"

The travellers were only twenty paces away.

"What?" His hand went to his belt, to his dagger. "By God, I'll throw him in the river!"

"Richard, listen, Christopher doesn't know about it, unless Ramón has told him," she whispered in his ear. "Don't say anything yet!"

Richard gripped her hand in his.

"How has he done this? How has he found our son?"

"Don't look angry!" Illesa squeezed his fingers. "We must seem glad."

They stood frozen watching the riders, the clop of hooves echoing on stone and water.

Christopher stopped his black mare in front of them and slid awkwardly off his saddle. His arm was strapped to his chest with an elaborate arrangement of bandages across his right shoulder. His complexion was pale and there were shadows under his swollen eyes.

Richard embraced him briefly.

"We are glad to see you, son. Not glad to see the hurt you've suffered. But you will tell your mother all of that." He waved her forward.

Illesa put her arms around him gingerly. Out of the corner of her eye she saw Ramón dismount. He waited by his dappled rouncey. He'd either spent all the coin she'd given him on the horse or exploited some other patron.

She held Christopher at arm's length.

"An arrow through your shoulder?"

"Into my shoulder and out my upper arm," Christopher said, without emotion. "A small enough arrow, but strong enough to worm its way through." He gestured to Ramón. "Do you remember Ramón of Cartagena, from the excellent entertainment at the feast? He joined us in Scotland and agreed to travel south with me."

"We remember Ramón," Illesa nodded. "Although I believe you were known as Matilda Makejoy?"

Ramón bowed.

"Indeed, my lady."

"And Thurstan, you survived your first war unscathed," Illesa said, turning quickly to the lad. His clothes had suffered much from the experience. "You need some new weeds to match your new length." She reached up to ruffle his thatch of unruly hair.

Ramón was back on his saddle.

"Where are you bound, Ramón?" It was strange that she now felt no fear of him, with his long arms, dark face and crooked smile. It was something about his looseness, as if every movement was a happy accident. "And where is your monkey?"

"I go back to London. To Westminster. More work making joy!" he declared. "Mullida has gone to the Lord." He crossed himself. "She became ill, and, although I prayed to every saint, none of them would help." Ramón wiped his cheeks with a sleeve in an exaggerated gesture, but his eyes were shining with real tears.

"Thank the saints for not listening to him," Richard muttered in Illesa's ear.

Ramón took on the visage of a poor beggar.

"And now I am truly alone, but for the good company of Sir Burnel." He bowed his head towards Christopher.

"He has proved excellent company for me – given cheer all these miles and kept me from feeling pain," Christopher said, turning to his parents. "He should stay with us, Father. For as long as he needs. His service to me was vital."

"But you had Thurstan, did you not?" Richard waved at the squire, who was adjusting the packs on the pony and talking to Stephen.

"He's not an equal companion," Christopher muttered. "Ramón has a store of the most amusing tales – and very godly ones too, Mother. He will make a merry guest. Joyce will be well entertained."

Illesa put her hand on Richard's twitching arm.

"You are welcome, Ramón of Castile," Illesa said. "For Christopher's sake. But you will find our home simple and plain compared with the Prince's court."

"No, no. I will be grateful for a room over a stable, if that is all you have. I am used to every kind of lodging," Ramón said with an innocent expression. "I am in your debt."

Illesa took Richard by the arm and walked him to their horses.

Christopher had remounted and was waiting for them, all the time smiling, his head tipped towards Ramón, listening to his soft words.

"That man has attached himself to Christopher like a leech," Richard said, adjusting Stampie's halter. "How are we going to keep him away from Joyce?"

There was a loud burst of laughter. Christopher was clutching his chest with his good arm.

"Oh, you must tell that one to William!" he managed. "Wait until you meet him. You'll get on so well."

Richard and Illesa looked at one another. It was the first time in years they'd heard Christopher laugh out loud.

"The sooner he hears the truth about that man, the better." Richard flicked the reins and set off down the lane.

Chapter XXVI

Friday the 19th October, 1306
Langley
Tierce

"How have you ridden all that way with such a wound?" Illesa straightened up and looked at Christopher sternly. "It's not been properly treated. I'm surprised you're not burning with a fever. See the swelling? Any longer and you would have been past my help."

Christopher touched the red skin around the wound in his shoulder and winced.

"The surgeons of the army are butchers. They took the arrow out, washed it in wine, wrapped it up, and sent me on my way. No use to them any more." He leant his other elbow on the table and rested his head in his hand. Taking off the bandage had been very painful.

"Well, you are plenty of use to your father and me. Although you are nothing but skin and bone. I expect you haven't eaten properly since the knighting feast." Illesa went to the brazier and stirred the pot that was heating the wine and mandrake. "You will need this for the pain as I pack your wound." She poured the hot wine into a clay cup.

"Have you seen Ramón this morning? I want to show him the place where the hawks nest."

"He went out with your father to help with the plough team."

"What?" Christopher jerked his head, and looked at her accusingly. "He's our guest, not a servant."

"He wanted to go. Drink this." She put the cup next to him on the table. It was going to take a long time before the stinking wound was clean enough to bind. Cecily came in with a pile of linen strips and a pot of honey.

"What's this, what's this?" She bent over to look at his shoulder and whistled through her gap teeth at the seeping hole in his arm. "What's the point of all that expensive mail, eh?

Look at you! You're worse than that dress I'm trying to mend for Joyce. Full of holes!"

Christopher looked up at her, making a grimace that was meant as a smile.

"We will need the vinegar that's been through the sieve as well, please Cecily. And that pot of yarrow ointment."

"I'll bring my needle and thread and sew you up!" She boxed Christopher's ear playfully and left.

Illesa moved the cup towards his hand.

"Are you drinking that? It takes a while to start working." He picked up the cup, took a gulp and pursed his lips against the taste.

"Bitter. Reminds me of when you set my broken arm."

"Yes, that was your other side." She took a step back. "We must move to the window for the best light." If the weather wasn't so foul, she would have done it outside.

He pushed himself off the bench and drained the cup in one, wiping his mouth on the back of his hand. Illesa dragged Richard's chair across the flagstones to the high open window. The wind was gusting the small feathers from the freshly plucked goose across the courtyard. But this window faced east and was protected. Cecily came through with the vinegar and put it on the floor near the chair.

Christopher sat down heavily. His eyes were already looking vague.

"Do you want me to stay, lady?" Cecily was wringing a cloth in her hands, looking concerned.

"I'll call if I need you. Christopher is used to this. He won't need to be held down."

His eyes flickered in alarm. She picked up the jug of vinegar.

"Here, hold this cloth so it doesn't ruin your hose." He clutched the linen to his chest, and she started pouring the vinegar into the shoulder wound in a slow trickle. Christopher screwed his eyes shut. "Tell me how you came to know Ramón so well."

He opened one eye.

"I will if you then tell me why you have been so cold towards him. I've never seen you behave this way with any guest before."

Illesa dabbed the dripping vinegar.

178

"Bend forward." She poured some into the wound in the back of his arm. The flesh around it was swollen and tight. "You may not like what you hear."

Christopher shook his head from his position bent forward.

"Even more reason to know."

Illesa straightened up. His eyes were shut, the pain severe. But he'd never shied away from what was hard or uncomfortable.

"Very well. But answer my question first."

Christopher rested his head on his hand, eyes still squeezed shut.

"We took Lochmaben from the Scots. The Prince wanted to hunt Bruce further north. He said we should raze the land on the way."

Illesa took the yarrow ointment and started dabbing it. He jerked away, then set his teeth and held still as she pushed the ointment inside and all around the mouth of the wound. It was a while before he could continue.

"I noticed Ramón with the Prince's servants when we moved on. In the evenings, he'd take our minds off what we'd seen. Terrible sights. Like the Apocalypse. Burnt bodies, burnt animals. Crops destroyed. But when we set up camp, Ramón would tell us tales, make us forget it all. Stories from around the world."

Illesa smeared the honey on both wounds and wiped her fingers on the cloth. Sweat was beading on his forehead. But the worst of the treatment was done.

"When I was shot at Kildrummy Castle, during the siege, he distracted me while the surgeons pulled out the arrow. After Fraser and the Earl of Atholl were executed, the Prince left the wounded there. We were no longer of any use. Like the captured ladies of Bruce's court in their cages." He looked up at her, dull-eyed. "Do you think I'll ever wield a sword again?"

He was sweating with the effort of staying still.

"Of course." Illesa began winding the cloth over his shoulder and around his arm. "But you must care for your wound and allow me to examine it, not go riding off in search of hawks and risk further injury. Stay quiet and at home for a week. Then we will see."

Ajax had wandered into the hall and put his muzzle on Christopher's knee.

"So why did Ramón not go with the Prince? He was not injured."

"Ramón was left behind to keep the wounded merry," Christopher said morosely, stroking Ajax's narrow head. "The army had the Prince's favourite musician."

"But he came even further with you, all the way here." Illesa finished the bandaging and stood back.

"He was going to London. There was a group of us, walking wounded, going south. Some stopped at Carlisle, but there was no one there skilled with herbs." Christopher glanced up at her, and quickly away. "I told them I'd be better off going home rather than die of an infection in the north."

"You can use your arm now, but only gently. If you'd kept it in that sling any longer, you'd have lost the use of it altogether." She held up his tunic and slipped it over his wobbly head. "You should go and sleep for a while."

Christopher fondled the dog's ears.

"First tell me why you are treating Ramón so coldly. And what's wrong with Joyce? She hasn't said a word to me yet."

Illesa placed the jugs and pots carefully on the table.

"First of all his monkey stole the prayer beads that we gave Joyce for her feast day."

"But he returned them! And that was his monkey, not him. Everyone knows how mischievous they are. And besides, the monkey died in Kildrummy. It's not here to anger you. Meanwhile he's been a great help to me." He looked up at her, his eyes vague, cheeks flushed. "I would probably have died without his company on the long journey home."

"We'll speak of this later, after you have slept. Sleep and good food is what you need. And regular cleaning. Go and lie down."

Illesa walked out into the drizzle of the courtyard. It was impossible to begin to explain to Christopher all that had happened. So much of it was intangible, except for the dead body pulled out of the Severn, now buried. Reginald's ring. Those parchments, which Ramón would have brought back into their midst. And Joyce's voice, which was conspicuous by its absence. The player had come back to get more coin, no doubt. They would be milked, again and again like this, for as long as he or they lived. If he told the Prince, they would be convicted for Reginald's murder. Without the evidence of the bindings and Joyce's injuries, there was nothing to say it had been done in self-defence. There wouldn't even be the possibility of Joyce testifying about his attack on her, as she couldn't speak. Why had she listened to William? This would blight the rest of their lives.

She went into the stables, hoping no one would be there. But Stephen was mucking out. She left before he saw her and went round the back to the barn. But Richard had returned from the fields and was discussing the right way to repair a broken plough with the smith.

Illesa walked back towards the hall. She would lock herself in her room and read the Psalter. That would still her mind. As she neared the door, Ramón's voice came through the window, speaking to someone. It could not be Christopher, who was sleeping off the mandrake in bed. She stopped beside the window, hard up by the wall, where he would not see her if he glanced out.

"I can teach you how to do it. It is easy to learn, very easy if you are eager. And I see you are. Look, this is the sound A. This is L. This is E. If you can read, you know that I need some ale! That is the case for me, so I will find the kitchen boy soon. Then you can say M. Y. T. H. and if the person knows the signs, as I do, and most players and monks would, we would know that you are giving your thanks."

There was a brief pause.

"That's good. Practise doing those signs quickly, and I will teach you some more. I tried to teach them to Mullida, but she was not able to move her fingers in that way. It is a shame because I would have valued her opinion at times, no?"

There was an unmistakable snort of laughter from Joyce.

"I am so sad without her. I'd had her from when she was a little monkey, taken from her mother. Like I was! She always knew what I was thinking. But she did not like the north. I should not have taken her there. Very, very cold. Wetter than the bottom of the ocean. I had to bury her there. My heart was broken."

He hummed a few notes of a dirge.

"But I will find another monkey. I know the best market where they sell them young. In Tarragona. They need to be young or you can't train them to do all the tricks, all the magic."

Another pause.

"You wonder how she stole your beads? These monkeys are very quick. In the wilderness they race to snatch something and are away before anyone sees. She saw the beads like berries on a bush. I will get another female, they are slighter and quicker than the males. Less dangerous. I have the special ways to make them learn. Mullida kept me free of lice, you know?"

Joyce giggled. A sound Illesa hadn't heard in months.

"Why don't you try singing with me? When we sing, we give our souls to the wind, and it gives them back again." He started a tune with a high voice, like a woman's but loud and strong.

I know of a beauty, a beryl most bright,
As gentle as jasper a-gleam in the light,
like onyx she is, esteemed in the height,
like coral her lustre, like Caesar or knight,
like emerald at morning, this maiden has might.
My precious red stone, with the power of pearl,
I picked for her prettiness, excellent girl!*

"We will sing it. You join me."

But the only singing came from Ramón. Joyce was sniffing, trying not to cry. Illesa moved to the door and then stopped as Ramón began to speak again.

"You mustn't cry for your voice. It will come back. It hides, like a bird at the very top of a tall, tall tree. You stand at the bottom looking up. You can see that pretty bird, its lovely feathers? Now can you hear it singing? That's your voice, it will fly down and sit on your shoulder soon, and you will sing again, Joyce. It's waiting for you to be ready. Maybe you will climb the tree and catch it?"

There was a long pause before the next sniff.

"You will find it. I did. The man who tried to hurt you did the same to me. But see, I am well. And he is gone. The Devil

182

has him now. But I miss his jests. He could conjure smiles out of stones." There was a brief silence.

"Come, I need ale and food. We go and find Cecily. Do you think she will have made it ready yet? I could eat that dog of yours!"

Chapter XXVII

Vespers

"Alfred, bring another flagon!"

Illesa returned from the doorway and sat down next to Richard.

There was a feeling of revelry in having Christopher at home, despite his injuries. They'd already drained two flagons of the Gascon wine. It made Christopher more talkative, and she wanted him to talk. At the moment, he was under the spell of Ramón, the centre of his attention. Christopher's colour was high, but she couldn't tell if it was fever or wine. She would tend him before he went to bed and find out how deep the infection ran. It was very clear how deeply Ramón had infected both of her children. They were looking at no one else.

Illesa reached for Richard's hand. His mouth was set in a deep frown. Down the table, nearest the door, William was staring at Ramón, who was in the middle of a remarkable imitation of the Prince. William's jaw was working, only just keeping his anger inside. None of them knew what to do with him, while Christopher, Thurstan and Joyce spluttered with laughter, their eyes watering. Ramón seemed to realise that the lord and lady were not joining in and turned to them.

"This good food reminds me that soon we will have meat again, not only fish. I saw a great fish in your moat today, Christopher, and it made me think of the tale of 'The Scrounger', and it's a tale the esteemed Lord and Lady Burnel will appreciate as they have one of those at their table this very minute."

"Not at all," Christopher said, looking at Illesa and Richard reproachfully. "We're all glad you're here. You kept me safe all the way —"

"Safe from bandits but not from scroungers — isn't that right, William? But I am willing to sing or speak for my supper — and for any room except those above stables." He winked so only Illesa and Richard could see him.

William got up, the bench screeching on the flagstones.

"I must see to the horses," he muttered, looking only at Richard, and stalked out.

Ramón raised his cup to William's disappearing back.

"A man of much work. He's not at all like the man in this tale. This man was so opposed to working for his meal, he was called 'The Sponge'. And one day he heard that his friend was having a feast –"

Illesa held up her hands.

"Ramón, you have a great store of tales. But we wish to know more about your plans. Where are you going next now you have left the Prince's army?"

Ramón took another gulp of wine and slapped the table.

"My story is not exciting. You would prefer the tale of the scrounger, certainly. But my lady, my lord, I have little to engage me, my partner having died, suddenly, and my monkey." He made an expression of deep grief. "Even our apprentice disappeared. God has plucked me, alive, out of the northern vale of death! I give thanks for his mercy, but I am left with no partner to enact my plays." He tilted his head and widened his eyes. "I must find someone with good skills and tricks. I start again from the beginning. This time I will be leader. But the leader of a troupe of players with no patron is a poor man."

Joyce was staring down at her hands on the table.

"How did your partner die? You didn't tell me about that," Christopher began.

Joyce sprang off the bench and bolted for the stairs. She clattered up, one hand over her mouth.

"What's wrong with Joyce?" Christopher turned round to stare as she dashed along the gallery and into her chamber. "I don't think I've heard a word out of her, and Christ knows that's unusual."

Ramón sat, looking innocently curious and staring at Illesa's neck. She put her hand to her throat and felt the cord that held the ring. She pushed it under the neck of her tunic. Richard put his goblet down, but Illesa spoke first.

"Poor Joyce, she was injured on the way home from London and finds it hard to speak now. But she is otherwise well. Cecily will tend to her."

"What? Why didn't you tell me? What happened? Who hurt her?"

Ramón leant forward, mirroring Christopher. He was daring her to say it.

"It was a brigand, a robber. He dragged her off her horse by the throat."

Christopher was standing up, staring at the gallery.

"But where?"

"On the road, near Tewkesbury," Illesa felt her cheeks burning. "After your father had gone by barge. They wanted to take her hostage and make me turn out my purse." She had opened her mouth without knowing what she would say. Now she would have to remember her lie.

"Wasn't William with you? Was he sleeping? How could he let this happen to her?"

"There were many of them. We had no chance against them." Illesa twisted round to look for Cecily but she must have gone out to the ovens.

"Did you raise the hue and cry? Have they been apprehended?" Christopher was nearly shouting. Ramón turned his head from one to another, his forehead creased with fake concern.

"Yes. But they are a large and powerful gang. There is little to be done against them without an army." Illesa reached out for Christopher's hand, but he pushed back from the table and started for the stairs. "Christopher, you don't look well, perhaps it would be best to –"

"It was my fault. I shouldn't have left them to travel alone," Richard said. "Sit down, Christopher. This is a matter best left to the women. Cecily!" he shouted in the direction of the kitchen. "Come and see to Joyce!" He slapped the table with the palm of his hand. "Christopher, sit down!"

Christopher walked slowly back to the table and sat down next to Ramón without looking at Richard. When he picked up his cup, his hand was shaking.

"Joyce will be well. Don't worry," Richard said, leaning towards his son. "As you can imagine, her mother is haranguing the saints five times a day to make her well. And she has improved. She speaks some prayers."

"It is interesting that she can speak for praying but not for conversation?" Ramón said still with the expression of sympathetic curiosity. "I wonder if singing might also be a way of helping her. I could –"

"I thank you, but we have the matter in hand," Illesa said abruptly. Cecily was climbing the stairs, looking down at Illesa with alarm. She shooed her on to Joyce's chamber. "We are going on pilgrimage to the shrine of the Virgin at Rocamadour for her healing. It is a most powerful statue, known to show special care for young girls."

Ramón nodded earnestly and put a hand on Christopher's good arm.

"Your lord father and lady mother are diligent in their care of all things. A blessing to be savoured!"

Christopher glanced at Illesa and nodded grudgingly. His eyes were glassy; his skin a yellowish colour with a sheen of sweat.

"You see, Christopher," continued Ramón, "that Lord Burnel would have prevented this attack if he had been with his family, but God put him elsewhere and therefore in some way this attack must be God's will, and, as God works for the good of his people in all things, in some way this attack must be for good." He smiled around the table.

Richard grunted and drank from his cup.

"I was in fear of pain, or I would have gone with them to see the Blessed Thomas, and that would have been a holier journey. Perhaps there would have been a miraculous cure for my broken body." Richard held Ramón's gaze. "I repent of my cowardice, my lack of faith. We can only hope for God's generous mercy for Joyce – and damnation for the one that hurt her."

Ramón nodded again and pressed his palms together, as if in prayer.

"But you mentioned that this terrible crime occurred near Tewkesbury, and I've heard some news from there, that a man was found in a river, just a body of bones and sinews in his clothes, because the fish had him for their supper, instead of the other way around. And that he was tethered there, in the water. Do you think this man could have also been attacked and murdered by the gang of bandits? They hid him to give them more time to escape? No?" He held his hands out, palms up. "Who knows this man? They have gone from town to town

187

looking for someone to claim him. What a terrible fate for a simple traveller! The sooner the gang is brought to justice, the easier we will sleep."

A wave of fear and rage came over Illesa so that she had to grip the goblet in front of her and press it down into the table to stop herself from throwing it at Ramón's open, eager face. Ajax rested his muzzle on her knee under the table, and she took a deep breath.

"You speak truth, master player," Richard said quietly. "Those that kill or harm the innocent deserve the most excruciating of deaths."

Ramón spent a moment picking something out of his teeth while they all watched him, wordlessly. When he'd thrown the toothpick behind him, he looked around the table.

"The body in the river reminded me of the tale of 'The Three Apples'! Do you know it? A casket is found at the bottom of a river and inside is the body of a most beautiful woman cut into pieces –"

"God preserve us from this tale!" Illesa said, standing up and folding her arms across her chest to stop them shaking. "I'm going to see to Joyce. She needs a warm infusion before sleep. Christopher, you look ill. I will bring you valerian. Alfred! Stoke the fire. Sir Christopher must not grow cold." She went to the windows and began to latch the shutters. "Ramón, I trust you are comfortable in the room with Christopher?" she said, her back still turned. "Or would you prefer your own chamber?"

"Lady, you are full of courtesy!" Ramón said. "I will stay with my dear friend and watch him through the night, although I am grateful for any accommodation you might find for me." He stood next to Christopher, an arm around his waist, almost holding him up.

"I'm not drunk. I just feel very tired," Christopher said, his voice fading.

"Get to your bed. We'll bring all you need to your room."

Illesa stomped into the kitchen. It was unusually empty as Cecily was upstairs and Alfred was seeing to the fires, but she didn't dare give vent to her fury. Ramón was more than capable of spying on her. She would not give him the satisfaction of knowing she was frightened.

She took a lamp and went to the larder. When she got back with the jug and pot, Richard was standing by the brazier.

"Where is he?" she hissed.

"In Christopher's chamber. I've instructed Thurstan to watch the stairs, and report to me if he sees Ramón go anywhere. He is sleeping by the fire tonight with Alfred."

"What are we going to do? He's goading us! Tomorrow he will ask for more coin. It will go on and on."

"We must consider carefully. He has befriended Christopher –"

"Why is God allowing Ramón to torment our family and turn our son into his lapdog?" She poured the wine out of the jug into the pot on the brazier, crushed the herbs and threw them in – sloppy in her anger.

Richard touched her shoulder.

"That is not how Christopher sees it. We must speak to Christopher alone, tomorrow."

She breathed out slowly, put a hand on his.

"I pray he is well enough to listen. The wound was not properly treated, and he looks ill."

Of all the remedies her mother, Ursula, had used, was there one that would be stronger? Powerful enough to clean out the entire wound, full of pus as it was? Perhaps she'd have to soak his arm and shoulder in a bath of hot water infused with mint and yarrow. And give him hot coriander water.

Richard had moved to the doorway and was looking out into the courtyard.

"I wish he'd died instead of his monkey."

Illesa sighed.

"Then our son might have died too. He is convinced Ramón saved him."

"Well that lump Thurstan isn't capable of much. I hope he grows in mind as well as body, or I will have to thrash some sense into him." Richard jutted his chin and spat into the yard. "Ramón didn't save Christopher's life, he's just made him dependent on him."

Illesa touched Richard's sleeve.

"I heard him tell Joyce that Reginald also attacked him. I don't know if he was trying to help or –"

Richard turned awkwardly on his bad leg.

"He might have the *same* urge. Might be waiting for an opportunity to attack Joyce just as Reginald did."

Illesa shook her head.

"I don't think so. He was trying to teach Joyce to sing and encouraging her to speak. And he had some gesture language that he was showing her. There's part of him that wants to do good. But he's determined to bleed us dry for killing his murdering partner."

She turned to the brazier and poured the hot wine back into the jug.

"Tomorrow," Richard said, pushing the hair back from his worried forehead, "we will confront him. It is better to have it all out in the open. I hate this game of cat and mouse! We must make it clear that if he stays here any longer, William will beat the life out of him."

And round and round it would go, hurt and violence and sin. Men seemed to have found no other way, despite the example of Christ.

"There must be a godly way to get rid of him. We cannot have any more blood on our hands." Illesa picked up the jug and met Richard's gaze. "We need to think it through."

"In the morning, wife. I need my bed." He limped away into the hall, and she helped him upstairs with her free arm.

But in the morning, when Illesa went in to see how Christopher was, Ramón and his pack were gone, Christopher was raving with fever and the ring had disappeared from round her neck.

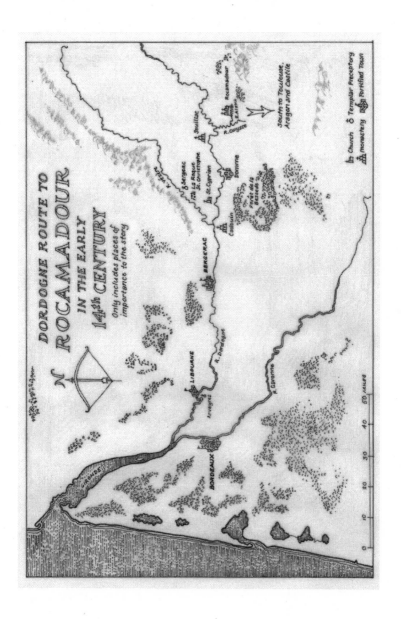

DORDOGNE ROUTE TO
ROCAMADOUR
IN THE EARLY
14th CENTURY

Only includes places of
importance to the story

N

GIRONDE

BORDEAUX

LIBOURNE

Arveyres

R. Dordogne

BERGERAC

Cadouin

Fruit de la
Rouge

R. Garonne

Beynac
Domme

La St. Cyprien

Bergerac
Côte la Coste
St. Christophe

Sarlat

Souillac

R. Ouysse

Rocamadour
St. Laurent

South to Toulouse,
Aragon and Castile

Church   Templar Preceptory

monastery   Fortified Town

0   10   20   30   40   50 Miles

Part Two

Chapter XXVIII

Tuesday the 15th August, 1307
The first year of the reign of Edward II
Feast of the Assumption of the Virgin Mary
The Church of St Mary, Acton Burnel

It had seemed an auspicious day. They'd been up since first light, and the sky had been clear, cloudless. Richard's face as he mounted Sorrel was the darkest aspect. It was only as they crested the hill between Langley and Acton that the wind got up. By the time they reached the church, the rain was lashing down. Illesa, Christopher and Joyce had worn their pilgrim cloaks, God be thanked, but Richard was wet through.

They stood dripping in the porch listening to the buzz of voices inside.

"Come on, let's get it over with," Richard grumbled. He opened the door.

Every man, woman and child in the crowded church became silent and stared at them as they walked up the nave to stand at the crossing in front of the rood screen. A deacon was lighting the altar candles with a taper. He finished and went into the vestry. The conversation started up again, mainly about the appearance of Joyce and Illesa. Christopher was looking straight ahead, his eyes on the altar. Richard had been accosted by the Steward, a man of many words, hardly any of them important.

There was a shuffling of feet as the deacon entered through the west door and began to sing the Ave Maria. The crowd moved to the sides of the nave and a novice carrying a cross led the singing deacon and the priest through the crowd and up to the chancel. Somewhere in the crowd was Kathryn, the fletcher's wife, who'd approached Illesa the week before and asked her to pray at Rocamadour for her infirm daughter – given her coins for the shrine. The year before, Kathryn had come to the manor, and Illesa had given her lungwort and wormwood in oil to rub into her daughter's legs. Nothing seemed to help. But she was a quick, practical woman, and Illesa had warmed to her at once.

They all knelt on the stone floor, except for Richard who couldn't. He bowed his head. The priest was rattling through the prayers; it was hard to keep up with his rapid flow of Latin. She stared at the cross. Underneath her pilgrim cape she was cold, trembling. What if Richard's fears came true and the dangers of the journey overwhelmed them? She'd had to beg him to let them go, once Christopher was fit and well, before the year was up. He'd finally relented, insisting that they join another band of travellers in Bristol with a pilgrim guide – a man who'd been to Saint James three times and Rome twice.

She reached out and took Joyce's hand. Ever since she'd been told to go on pilgrimage, she'd always imagined Joyce going with her. But the nearer the date, the less Joyce would eat. The last time she'd been on a long journey, and the first time, was when she was attacked. Perhaps she feared it would happen again. And Illesa could not say it wouldn't, although Christopher was with them, would be constantly on guard, and the smith's younger son, Hamo, was coming as far as Bristol.

The priest was calling them forward to kneel on the steps of the chancel.

Illesa held hands with her children, and they knelt together. Richard stood behind them.

"You must state the reason for your pilgrimage to this site, so far removed from your home," Father Thomas said. "The heir to the Burnel estate and Lady Burnel going abroad – there must be a burning sin behind your pilgrimage."

The church was silent except for a baby crying at the back.

"I was in the north with Prince Edward a year ago. I saw and did many things not in keeping with Christian virtue. I must atone for these, and seek mercy and a remission of time in Purgatory." Christopher's tone was far from humble, but his head was bowed.

The priest stared at him.

"A public confession is not necessary for knights. It is noble to fight in the Prince's service. You might be permitted to go on pilgrimage if you are not being cowardly and seeking to avoid the next battle."

Richard's breath hissed through his teeth. Father Thomas was in the pay of Edward Burnel, charged with weakening their authority in the area, and he did it through insinuations. The richer branch of the family were greedy to claw back all their previous demesne.

"I have faithfully served my King," Christopher said, his voice surprisingly calm. "But, as you know, there is no army in the north now. The new King Edward is preparing for the burial of his father. As you also know, I was wounded in my right arm and still cannot wield a sword. I will be little use to my liege until healing is complete, God willing."

The priest frowned and cleared his throat.

"You should be going to Rome or Saint James. Why do you visit the Virgin at Roc? It is a weaker shrine. Go further to make your penance count for greater benefit."

The priest had been suspicious ever since they'd told him of their intention. He could sniff out gossip like a dog that looks for a gobbet of meat under the table.

"If Saint Thomas of Canterbury and King Henry both appealed to the Virgin at Rocamadour, I see no reason why I may not ask for her intercession. On the way I intend to view the relics of Saint Martin at Tours, another soldier who preferred the way of Christ."

Illesa glanced at him out of the corner of her eye, could almost feel Richard stiffening behind her. Tours was not in their itinerary.

"A noble shrine. You will return before the Feast of the Nativity, with evidence of your travels." He turned to Illesa, ready for his next attack. "Lady Burnel, you have decided to go with your son. Is this not contrary to your duties to your husband?"

"My husband has given me leave for this appointed pilgrimage. Saint James or Rome would be too far, but we wish to appeal to the Virgin for an easing of our troubles. She has healed many."

"You have no sin to confess? Don't you seek mercy, like your son?"

"I have confessed, Father, as has Joyce. You heard our confession at the Feast of the Resurrection."

"Why doesn't she speak? A written confession is not natural and indicates a grave sin."

Behind them, the congregation had begun speculating out loud.

"Her silence is not due to sin, but to hurt. She was attacked by a bandit. We told you this already." Richard had raised his voice. "They go to seek healing, Father Thomas, as is right and proper. I trust God to protect them on their journey. They come to seek a blessing from you, who has the cure of their souls."

Father Thomas squeezed his red nose as if there'd been a bad smell.

"Let her come forward then, and I will anoint her with oil. On this the Feast of the Assumption of the Virgin – healing may occur in her mother church. There may be no need for this extravagant, reckless journey." The priest beckoned Joyce forward with a plump finger.

Richard put his hand out to forestall Christopher's outburst.

"Very well. We welcome your holy words."

Illesa stood and helped Joyce to her feet.

"You only need to pray – say the Lord's Prayer or Hail Mary, Joyce. I'll come with you." She started up the steps taking Joyce by the arm, but on the other side of the rood screen Father Thomas put his hand up to stop her.

"Only the girl."

Joyce glanced unhappily at Illesa and went up with tiny steps. She was sniffing back tears. Christopher had one foot on the chancel step, ready to follow.

Father Thomas pressed the top of Joyce's head, and she knelt before the altar, the soles of her new boots showing to the whole congregation. Father Thomas held up his other hand, and the church grew silent.

"We ask our Holy Virgin of Virgins to have mercy on this child and bring out the evil that stops her tongue, the sins that bind it, the demon that has lodged itself in her mouth." He tipped healing oil on his thumb from a lead chrismatory and began to make the sign of the cross on her forehead. "Oh Holy Mother of God, release her from these evils and let her praise you with her voice, confessing before us all the sin that she is being punished for."

Illesa squeezed Richard's hand tightly. The priest had no shame.

The crowd held their breath, listening for a demon emerging from her mouth.

And there was a voice. It came from above and around the chancel. A high strong voice, singing the *Magnificat*. Father Thomas looked from the deacon to the altar boy, but no sound came from their open mouths. He looked up to the roof. The voice echoed, swelled, faded and returned as if the angel were bouncing up and down in the air.

"Search the congregation. Make sure it's not one of the villagers!"

The deacon went down into the nave, but it was obvious the voice did not come from there. Uninterrupted it continued its pure, ethereal words.

"Look outside!" Father Thomas shouted. "If this be a miracle, we must have proof! And the Lord will bless us." The priest clutched the processional cross held by the novice. "This is a sign of her favour! Kneel!"

He didn't need to tell them. The congregation were already on their knees. Joyce was still shaking before the altar. Illesa ran forward, bowed, and guided her back to the nave. The song came to an end with the *Amen*, and the congregation groaned as the last note died away.

The deacon came rushing back through the west door.

"There is nothing outside! I saw no angels or men. No vision."

"It's clear that the Virgin blesses and approves our pilgrimage," Christopher said very gravely.

The priest was still looking up at the painted walls of the church, as if sure there was some hidden triforium where a man, or a woman, could hide and sing.

"It may be a trick of the Devil to distract us from our purpose!"

But the people were crowding around Joyce, trying to touch her, asking for her prayers for them at the shrine.

"Silence, silence!" the priest commanded, nearly knocking Joyce over as he pushed people away from her. "We will continue with the office of praise for the Virgin, and perhaps she will sing again. But always look for the lies of the Devil. If you see his smoke, or smell his odour, it could be the demon inside this young woman tricking us."

Illesa put her arm around Joyce and held her close. Her face was tear-stained, but there was a gleam in her eyes similar to the amusement in Christopher's. And Illesa thought she knew where she'd heard that voice before.

After another hour of listening to the priest's declarations, the congregation were sent away. The pilgrims filed into the vestry to receive their sealed testimonials. Illesa looked around the small, cluttered room. The last time she'd been in that room it had been in the company of the previous incumbent, no better than this one. He'd also made accusations and insinuations, some of which were justified. But this time she'd been told to go to Rocamadour by a friar. *He* had not thought it necessary for her to be gaoled for killing in self-defence, whereas Father Thomas would see them incarcerated for his own benefit and amusement.

He finally let them go when they'd paid coin for his trouble, as well as the cost of parchment.

"If I discover you've played out some trick here, you will all do penance publicly on your knees to Hereford!"

They said nothing as they filed out.

It had stopped raining and the sun was hot. Steam rose from the grasses. Birds were wheeling in the sky. Tiny angels. Illesa took a deep breath and turned to Joyce, kissing her on both cheeks.

"It's done. We have our leave to go."

But Joyce's attention was elsewhere – her eyes flitting around the churchyard.

"Here's that woman to speak to you," Richard said, tapping Illesa's shoulder. "Meet us by the road."

Illesa walked towards the lychgate where Goodwife Kathryn was waiting.

"Good day, Goodwife. I pray your child is well?" There was an elaborate cloth arrangement holding the sleeping girl on her mother's back. Perhaps she was three years old now or more.

"As ever, my lady! Did you hear that singing? It was like the great Archangel Gabriel had come back to say the Virgin was called to Paradise. But between you and me, I think it was a man. I could hear his breaths. I don't think angels sing like us, do you?"

"I don't know," Illesa smiled. "It's a mystery."

"It confused Father Thomas, which was worth watching. So high and mighty. It shocked him out of his little speech! Then he flapped around like a great big bird, trying to find out who it was," she said in a loud whisper.

The child she carried was very pretty, with bright hair and a sweet face, but her breaths were rapid and shallow, and she had no strength to walk or even to sit up. Illesa stroked the girl's back, but she didn't wake.

"What is your child's name? I've forgotten."

"Juliana – the saint bless and heal her." Goodwife Kathryn tipped her head back and stroked the child's pale cheek.

"I see why you can't travel yourself. She's a heavy burden."

"Not at all – she's light as a feather. But I mustn't leave my other children. My husband is always away with one army or another, and none of the children are old or wise enough to resist danger or temptation," she grinned. "But I wanted to ask you, when you reach the shrine, if it please you to look for a holy thing I've seen. My aunt brought one back from Rome. A mirror in a case." She held up her fingers in an oval. "Like this. You show the mirror to the statue of the Virgin and then shut the lid. Bring it back to me unopened, and the power of the Virgin is retained in the mirror. Or so they say." She took her purse from her belt. "If I hang it round Juliana's neck, the Virgin might help her breathe. I've collected a few more pennies." She held out three silver coins.

"I will try to bring such a mirror back for you, but keep your coin for now. You may need it to feed your children if the rain keeps ruining the harvest."

The woman took Illesa's hand, her eyes shining with some mischief.

"Now that we have a resident angel, I'm sure all will be well." She curtseyed. "Thank you for your kindness, and God bless your journey."

Richard was already mounted with Christopher and Joyce at his side, waiting in the lane. They walked quietly along behind

Sorrel until they'd passed the last of the dwellings and were nearly in the wood.

"Why did you say you were going to Tours, Christopher?"

Illesa had to trot to keep up as he lengthened his stride.

"It's important as a knight that I dedicate my pilgrimage to the right saint."

"But that takes us north-east. The Santiago pilgrims are going south from Bordeaux."

"Then we will find another group."

"No, it's too late to change the plan."

"Don't you think we should be wondering what happened in the church, or do you all know already?" Richard said crossly.

Christopher and Joyce smiled at each other.

"Is this something you have schemed together?"

Christopher looked behind him, shaking his head.

"No, Father. But we know how it happened."

They'd arrived at the wood, and, as they began down the track, a figure crept out from behind the trunk of an ash tree. Richard's horse shied and wheeled round.

"By the Devil's beard! I should run him through," Richard cried, pulling the horse straight. Christopher grabbed the reins.

"He just saved Joyce from being exorcised by that horrible priest. You should be grateful."

"I'd be grateful if I never saw him again. I'd be grateful if he would go and hang himself."

"Your thanks are noted," Ramón said, bowing deeply. "Perhaps you would have preferred if I'd told them the real reason for this pilgrimage? That was the other possibility. But for Joyce's sake, I chose to be an angel of God. In return, I will be accompanying you on your travels. You'll need assistance, even if it is not divine."

The oath that escaped from Illesa's mouth shocked everyone.

It wasn't until twilight, when all the packs had been tied and everything readied, that Illesa found Ramón alone, standing by the drawbridge, looking over the moat. He glanced up as she approached and made a gesture taking in the pink light of the setting sun reflected in the water, the sound of the last birds of the day, the stars appearing in the east.

"Why leave all this for such a long, hungry journey?"

"Why do you want to come with us? If it's more coin you're after, I'll provide it to rid me of your company."

Ramón grimaced, his head on one side.

"That is not kind, Lady Burnel."

"I'm tired of your games! What have you done with the ring?"

"It's safe. I don't want you to lose it, so I keep it, how do you say – as surety?" He smiled with just one side of his mouth.

"You're holding us to ransom. Why come with us all the way to Aquitaine? I'll give you compensation."

Ramón did not answer for a few moments. He looked up at the curl of smoke in the darkening sky.

"You don't know how precious *this* is – how rare," he said quietly. "No idea." He shook his head sadly. When he spoke again, it was with a different tone. "I am going south to buy a new monkey in the markets, maybe in Toulouse if I have luck. Until then, I am your servant. You might find me of use. As you have seen, I have some particular skills."

"Devilish tricks," Illesa said. "I don't want you teaching maleficium to Christopher or Joyce."

She turned away before she was tempted to push him in the moat. But his voice followed her.

"There is nothing to fear, my lady. Nothing at all, except what remains hidden. When all is brought into the light, we sing and dance. In this life or the next."

Chapter XXIX

Saturday the 19th August, 1307
Hereford Cathedral
Tierce

While they stood in the queue of people lined up to enter through the north door, Ramón entertained Christopher and the others with drolleries about monks. Joyce giggled as if they were watching a puppet show, not waiting to visit a holy shrine.

"Quiet now! We're nearly inside." Illesa glared at Ramón.

"Not you, Joyce, obviously. Only we need to be quiet. You say whatever you want," Ramón said archly. Joyce tried to hide her smile.

"This is not a play, Ramón. People know us by our pilgrim clothes, and if we are behaving in a loud or unseemly way, they will not treat us as pilgrims."

"I am no pilgrim. I am a companion – more like a mule than a man," he declared making large ears from his hands and shaking his head as if a fly had landed.

"Then stay outside if you don't want to behave."

Ramón removed his cap and looked like a penitent herdsman, full of woe.

"Stop pulling faces; this is God's house."

"Doesn't God love a fool as much as a saint?"

"Just be quiet. Your tongue is a cart running downhill!"

The monk at the door was watching them. She bowed and showed him their pilgrim testimonials.

"After the shrine of our Blessed Thomas and the Mappa Mundi, you may go on the path past the new effigies of the bishops," he intoned.

They shuffled forwards, finding their way through the mass of people.

"We come here as pilgrims this time, Joyce," she whispered in her ear. "So we must first pray at the shrine before we look at the map."

Illesa knelt down beside her and could just hear Joyce whispering the words of the pilgrim prayer. It should be some comfort that her voice still worked, but with Ramón in their company, the pilgrimage was becoming less holy with every step. He made it impossible to concentrate with his constant prattling.

Even now she was thinking of him when she should be praying to Thomas Cantilupe to heal and forgive them – to protect Richard. The list of requests was ash on her tongue. She no longer wanted to go to Rocamadour. She wanted to be at home sitting beside Richard, talking about the herds and the orchard. Or watching William lead the excited horses out of the stable and down to the meadow. When he called them in, they would canter over to him, tossing their manes and nosing his hand. It reminded her of their first meeting, when he was an orphaned boy only interested in horses – and food. He'd brought trouble in his wake but soon made up for it. And all had been well between them until her temptation – and her foolish scheme to get him a wife.

He was still very angry with her.

Phylis's claim that he'd promised to marry her had made the past year even worse. She'd accused him of breach of promise at the Hundred court, and the case would go to the Shire court in September. William had barely bid Illesa farewell when they'd left Langley. Although that could have been due to Ramón's presence.

Joyce had risen from her knees. If Illesa insisted she pray for longer, there would again be that feeling that she was in the wrong somehow, that Joyce should not be harangued as she could not answer. She never thought she'd be grateful for an argument. Illesa let her go to the map.

A loud voice cut through the murmur of the crowd.

"This is it! Haven't I prayed every day for just this thing? Her eyes staring at me! This is the day the Lord has blessed my endeavour; this is *His* call!"

Illesa got up and hurried to the crowd around the map.

The mapmaker was standing before Joyce, his face exultant. Christopher had a protective hand on Joyce's arm, his expression alarmed.

"Father!" Illesa said, standing in front of Joyce and breaking his intent stare. "We are pleased to see you and your great work again."

The mapmaker blinked and looked up at the roof of the cathedral.

"I know now that my plans are approved by Heaven itself." He sounded slightly less certain.

"What plans, Father?" Christopher said gruffly, pushing Joyce behind him. Ramón was at his shoulder, looking amused.

"This is the mapmaker, Christopher," Illesa said quickly. "He drew and created that whole world."

Christopher bowed his head very slightly.

"It's a wonder, a miracle."

"No miracle! I slaved over it for years, but God gave me the strength, until he took it away. Now you have given me the sign. My strength has returned."

A monk was approaching cautiously from the south transept, as if he had an escaped wild animal in his church.

"Tell us more, Richard Orosius, but come and speak with us privately, where we can listen without everyone else hearing," Illesa said, gesturing towards the quiet passage behind the choir.

Richard Orosius turned around and saw what she'd been looking at.

"They pursue me constantly! Always watching!" He started down the aisle, walking quickly on his long legs. They all jogged after him, and, a few paces behind them, the monk slapped along in his sandals.

Richard Orosius swept into the lady chapel and pushed the praying people out.

"Go and find another altar. Go. There are many."

He knelt in front of the altar.

"Mother of God, bless this journey. I have found fellow pilgrims, and we will travel together to find that treasure I know is waiting for me." He crossed himself and rose to his feet, turning to them with a wide smile. "The sign of her eyes – and your pilgrim weeds. This is what I have waited so many years for. Which shrine?"

Christopher and Joyce turned to Illesa, looking horrified.

"We go to Our Lady of Rocamadour, the Black Virgin," Illesa whispered.

"On the way, on the way!" he declared. "I will show you!"

He raced out of the chapel and back towards the map, pushing unwary pilgrims aside. They followed at a distance, Christopher with his arm still protectively around Joyce.

"See, I know where it is, although the Bishop did not wish it to be included. There below that river, the Garonne, there is another, the Dordogne. It is this small unwritten shrine here. And if you go south from there, look how near you are to the mountains, just south of Toulouse!"

"Where is Tours?" Christopher broke in, hoping to steer the conversation. "I wish to visit its shrine."

"Tours? You can see it with your own eyes – you're not blind are you? There." Richard Orosius stabbed his finger at it. "But we go to Rocamadour." He pointed to the little church at the end of the river. "And then –"

"Come away, Father Richard. You have upset these pilgrims enough." The monk had waded through the crowd and had hold of the mapmaker's robe.

"Brother, I am not upsetting them. They have been sent by God to take me out of your clutches." He yanked his robe free. "Go and tell the Bishop. I need leave to go on pilgrimage. God has sent me a sign, and I will go with these holy pilgrims. His Excellency will be rid of me for many weeks."

The monk opened his mouth, but Richard Orosius was not to be stopped.

"Tell him I will not be here to upset everyone when the inspectors come to hear the witnesses. Tell him, if he wishes, I will go to Poitiers and see the Pope himself, to speak to him about the long delayed canonisation of the blessed Thomas Cantilupe. I will tell him to read all those reports by the inquiry. Perhaps I'll be gone for ever, if all goes well."

Richard Orosius licked the spittle from his lips, his face quite red with excitement.

"I need pilgrim's weeds and the upkeep I would have cost him until the Feast of the Nativity. Go and tell him. He'll be pleased to be rid of me. Run away on your flat feet! Off you go!"

He turned to Illesa and Joyce.

"It is because of you I feel such joy! I know God has not forgotten me even in this place where I am tormented. I will return with my few belongings."

He strode off towards the west end and the cloister door.

Ramón was whispering something in Christopher's ear. Joyce gripped Illesa's arm tightly, her look questioning.

"That man is mad," Christopher said. "We cannot let him come with us."

"He is not mad. He is a genius, a scribe of extraordinary skill. Look at what he has made. Maybe a journey away from this place is exactly what he needs. He will be a good guide. He knows all the routes."

"No. He's rude and thinks there's something magical in Joyce's eyes. What if he has fallen in love with her?"

"Don't be silly," Illesa said, but a sense of misgiving came over her. She turned to speak to Joyce, but she wasn't there.

Joyce was standing in front of the map again. Her finger was in the air, tracing their journey past Clee Hill to Hereford, to Gloucester and out of the great river Severn into the sea, past the islands and the sea monster to the mouth of the coast of France and Aquitaine, and the great stone city of Bordeaux, and down the next river to the little figure of a shrine he had pointed to.

Ramón laughed.

"You have a new pilgrim who even casts me in a good light!"

"He is not coming with us." Christopher pulled off his pilgrim's hat and bunched it in his hand. "If he does, I'm going back. I'll not share the road with a madman."

"If God wants us to share the road with Richard Orosius, that is what we will do. He will calm down. You've had your choice of companion," Illesa tilted her head at Ramón. "Don't become troublesome if God provides his own."

Christopher rolled his eyes.

"If Father were here, he'd agree with me."

"He isn't here. And although you are heir, you are not master yet. If this man needs relief from his suffering, of whatever kind, we should help him."

"Good words, Lady Burnel!" Ramón applauded. "But good deeds often punish the doer. As do bad deeds, indeed." He looked over Illesa's shoulder. "How diverting! His gaoler returns looking joyous!"

The Bishop was indeed eager to get rid of Father Richard. A sealed testimonial was drafted within the hour. When Illesa and Joyce returned to the north transept after their meal, Richard Orosius had already been commissioned and provided with a staff, cloak and scrip. He was only lacking the hat.

"We will leave in the morning," Illesa said, half-hoping the mapmaker would have changed his mercurial mind by then. "It's too late to start on the road now."

Richard Orosius groaned and cast his eyes to Heaven.

"Now that I am going, I cannot bear the thought of another night in my cell."

"We will meet you at prime. Perhaps you can beg a hat from a pilgrim who has nearly reached home? There are so many, I'm sure you'll find a willing donor."

Richard Orosius slumped down on the bench by the wall, still holding his staff out straight in front of him.

"At least I'll have time to smoke the fleas and lice out of it. God bring tomorrow quickly!"

Chapter XXX

Saturday the 26th August, 1307
Temple Fee Preceptory
Bristol
Sext

Illesa stared over the courtyard from the upstairs window of the guesthouse dorter. Beyond the tiled roofs of the arcade, the river was sluggish and muddy, like her mind. Rain was pelting down. The longer they stayed here, the worse she felt, the more she wanted to turn around and go home, leaving Ramón and Richard Orosius to board a ship going to the other side of the world.

In her mind she wrote the letter she couldn't send to Richard.

> *My husband,*
> *I am sorry I kept secrets from you, that I didn't listen to you about the pilgrimage. I could have gone to Canterbury. Now we are at the mercy of not only the Castilian but also the bad weather. I thought God sent Richard Orosius to guide us, but he has disturbed our company with his outbursts of temper and his refusal to compromise. I wish I was still beside you. I want you here. I want to die next to you not drown in the sea far away.*

The risk of it being opened on the way – read, reported to Father Thomas, or simply lost – was too high. And she didn't have spare coin to pay messengers to go half-way across the country. They would wait for the weather to change, wait for the other group of pilgrims to arrive, while every lost day made it less likely they would accomplish their journey before winter set in.

'Go if you must, but return quickly,' Richard had insisted.

They should have left at Easter, caught the Templar ship that departed then. But Christopher had not healed well enough. And Richard had been weakened by a winter fever that took all his strength for months. She couldn't leave him in that state. Now, here they were, waiting, eating through their coin, arguing.

Joyce and Ramón were practising their gesture language on a bench in the arcade. She'd insisted they stay in the preceptory. But Christopher had disappeared that morning, determined to escape Richard Orosius for at least a few hours. She couldn't blame him. They were all impatient with his stories of how he had nearly become Chancellor at Lincoln, how all the chapter had blocked his election, the accusations against him that were exaggerated.

And there he was, coming into the yard like a ship in full sail. He'd resumed his black tunic and cappa clausa since it had become clear there was no chance of sailing soon, and was clearly enjoying the respect his habit conferred away from Hereford. Behind him seven or eight pilgrims trundled in, talking loudly and staring at the buildings, the Templar's evident wealth. The guestmaster ran out to meet them.

There were three pairs of pilgrims – and the guide. He looked too young to have visited St James so often, although his demeanour was confident. Perhaps her eyes were unreliable. One couple, a father and son, seemed more richly dressed than the others, but it was hard to tell beneath their dripping hats. Now that the last of the pilgrims had finally arrived, they would be able to leave, if the wind changed direction.

Joyce and Ramón were watching and laughing behind their hands at the newcomers' dripping noses. Joyce was always whispering to him, but what they spoke of was a mystery.

"Here you are." The voice at her elbow made her jump.

Richard Orosius was just sitting down on the bed behind her. He moved remarkably quietly when he wished to.

"You can see the herd of cattle that have just arrived. It's like market day. And the leader is just like a herdsman. No knowledge, just move here, move there." He gestured as if he held a whip.

"It is a large city. I suppose he doesn't want to lose any of them."

"This is *not* a large city!" He was about to begin on his list of better, bigger more impressive places. She cut him off.

"Perhaps it's larger than many of them are used to."

"The thought of travelling with this menagerie!" Richard Orosius got up and stood next to Illesa, pointing. "That one is a fishwife. And that man speaks just like a ploughman. I tried to impress on them the enormity of the world and journey, but they just spat on the ground and asked when they would have their bread and if there was anywhere to piss."

"People will be the same wherever you go."

He sniffed and wiped his nose with the back of his hand.

"On my first journey to the Outremer it is not right that I'm in the company of such peasants."

"Peasants are just as important to God as the nobility." Illesa said sternly. He would probably condemn her own mother for living in a cott. Not that she could tell him of that part of her life. Richard Orosius just sniffed and hid his hands inside his cape.

"To God certainly they are, but not to me. I require mental stimulation, otherwise I develop terrible melancholy."

"Did not Christ himself eat with the poor and Saint Martin share his cloak with a beggar?"

"Indeed, but Christ did not spend weeks walking and sailing amongst them. He chose his companions, the apostles, carefully."

"And they were fishermen!" Illesa said.

"You see this is what I need – companions who can argue and debate!"

Illesa sighed. He looked delighted – as if he'd seen the open door to Paradise.

"Ramón will keep you company," she said, moving away. "He is full of tales and moralities. I must speak to the guide."

"I am not travelling with them! I've decided. I will find the way for us, and then we will all see the wonders of the world and be saved their prattle."

She didn't turn back, not wanting to encourage him any further, and took the stairs two at a time.

The rain had stopped, but water continued to drip enthusiastically from the eaves. The pilgrims had gone to the refectory for ale and bread while their guide talked to the guestmaster in the east arcade. Coin was changing hands. Illesa waited for their conference to conclude.

The hoot of an owl made her look up in surprise. Out of the corner of her eye she saw Ramón lowering his cupped hands. She walked towards him reluctantly.

Joyce's eyes were shining.

"What do you think of our great gathering of pilgrims? Do you like the one with the hooked beak? And the one tasting the vinegar?" Ramón imitated the sour expression of one of the older men. "I can't see them all managing the journey over the mountains myself."

"Shhh. The mapmaker has already insulted them all, no doubt. Don't start *us* off on the wrong foot."

Joyce made some quick signs to Ramón, and he grinned. They were always having their private little jokes.

"What did you say, Joyce?"

Ramón leant towards her.

"She said that the short woman has the nose of a pig."

"Joyce! You should not be so rude! God hears what you say, even in gesture. This is a pilgrimage. We should behave as good Christians, with charity." Illesa straightened up and rubbed her forehead. It was beginning to throb.

Ramón looked down at his worn shoes with an exaggeratedly sad expression.

Illesa crossed her arms.

"Why don't you practise speaking with Ramón instead? That would be of more use."

Joyce frowned and turned her head away.

"Well, I'm going to talk to Master Ralph and see when we can finally leave this place."

Ramón was making matters worse. Joyce liked having her own secret language with him and not having to make conversation with others. Illesa should try to learn the signs herself, but they were so quick she couldn't distinguish them.

Master Ralph was waiting for her by the door to the refectory; obviously the guestmaster had pointed her out.

He removed his pilgrim hat, covered in badges, and bowed deliberately.

"Lady Burnel."

"Master Ralph of Exeter. We finally meet."

"There were many delays, but I see it is no matter as God's weather has made us all wait."

"Yes, indeed." Illesa held her hands up to the heavens. "Now that you have arrived, may the wind turn."

"I met the cleric travelling with you." Master Ralph looked up at the window where Richard Orosius had been standing. "An interesting and well-studied priest. I have the impression that he knows much of the world, from his books. I have not travelled to Rocamadour before, but I am very well versed on the routes to Compostella. You will be well guided, my lady. Do you have the coin I agreed with your husband?" His hands were gripped tight together.

"I will settle with you soon, Master. I've given my coin to the Templar sergeant for safe keeping until we leave. There will be little enough left after our passage and your fees come out."

He frowned.

"It will be worth a hundred times what you pay, my lady. You must imagine your soul being washed clean in the spring at the centre of Paradise. That is what it feels like to be in the presence of these relics."

"I understand it to be so. My rank forbids me from begging like the others, so I must be sure I have provision for the journey and return for us all. That is all my concern."

Master Ralph pressed his lips together in what was trying to be a smile.

"But of course I understand, my lady. It is your first time on pilgrimage and living with these deprivations. You'll get used to it very quickly, I assure you, and you will not want to return to your wasteful life at home when the purity of pilgrimage takes your heart."

"No doubt." Illesa eyed his shoes: new and thick-soled. "You have a vocation for pilgrimage, so we must wait to gain the same wisdom."

He nodded.

"God gives wisdom to those approaching his shrines with genuine penitence. He knows the ones travelling for the wrong reasons, and they are given what they deserve."

"I trust there are none such on our journey?"

"We will know them by the end," he said ominously. "For now, we wait on a dawn message from the shipmaster tomorrow. Have all your party ready, we need to act quickly to depart when the benign hand of God gives us favourable winds."

Illesa cocked her head at his officious tone. He was the one who'd kept *them* waiting for days on end. She turned to go, but he put a restraining hand on her sleeve.

"What is the nature of that man? Is he part of your company?"

He was pointing at Ramón.

"He is accompanying us."

"Is he a true pilgrim? Has he been given his staff and scrip, but chooses not to bear them?"

"No," Illesa looked towards Ramón and Joyce, who were sitting as before, watching their conference. He was looking guilty – had probably been pulling faces at Master Ralph. "But he is accompanying us, and the Templars have agreed to take him. He was a servant of the young King Edward, but fell from his position and seeks to mend his ways."

"I don't like the look of him. Resembles one of the thieving innkeepers in Castile. I'll keep a watch on him." Master Ralph glared at Ramón.

"Do as you see fit. But remember that he is part of our company, and you should come to me if you require redress."

Master Ralph widened his eyes.

"Do you put yourself at the head of the company, my lady? I thought it would be your son."

"My husband entrusted the purse to me, and it is not your place to question him."

"My lady," he bowed slightly. "I did not mean to insult your husband. It is just that I have seen how grievous it is for women on these journeys to be weighed down by responsibility, and they are often grateful for my help."

"Then I am blessed to have so many men to turn to, should that problem arise."

Illesa turned away from the greedy fox and walked back to Joyce and Ramón.

"Well?" They looked expectantly at her.

Illesa turned back to make sure Master Ralph was out of earshot.

"He thinks you are a thief and hopes that I am a mindless, helpless fool. It will be a long voyage."

Chapter XXXI

Tuesday the 5th September, 1307
Aboard *La Buzard*
Bay of Biscay

"Can't you understand how late we are? Disembarking here and going through Tours and Poitiers will mean we won't sail home until December – and may well die in a storm. Is that what you want?"

"Of course not." Christopher looked across her towards the stern, gripping the side of the ship as it pitched.

"I promised your father we would be back as soon as possible. You heard what he said about it. Besides if we disembark now, we'll have to stay in the company of Richard Orosius. Go to Tours another year. Or if you must, go on the way back, and Joyce and I will make our own way home from Bordeaux."

Christopher shook his head angrily.

"Father also made me promise not to leave you."

Illesa looked up at the flapping sails.

"You can't have it both ways. When we planned the pilgrimage it was to Rocamadour from Bordeaux. No mention of Tours. We would've left earlier in the year for such a journey."

"But I need the guidance of a saint that understands soldiers. I have decisions to make."

Illesa wiped the spray from her face with her veil.

"You have done your duty and spilt your blood in the service of the King. Your sword arm will never fully recover. You are needed at the manor. What is there to decide?"

Christopher looked down into the racing water. La Rochelle was a bright white blur on the shore.

"I think God may have other plans for me."

Illesa stopped herself from cursing. She must not fall out with Christopher before they'd even landed in Aquitaine.

"All young men want adventure. But now that you've experienced war, you must understand it's not good for the soul."

"The Templars wage war on evil, not on villeins trying to harvest their crops. They have a strict rule but work in the world."

Illesa bit her lip.

"You want to become a Templar Knight?"

"I don't know. Their life seems full of purpose." He looked beyond her at the grey sea. "They are guided by God himself."

"They are guided by their master – like any other monk! They've been encouraging you, haven't they?" She nodded towards the two young Templar knights guarding the ship. They would not speak to her, staring into the middle distance if she addressed them, but she'd seen Christopher in conference with them for hours. "If you join them, you leave your inheritance, leave your father to manage the demesne alone, leave me." She swallowed the grief rising in her throat. "No women! No visits from Joyce. But being an associate of the Temple supports their work just as much."

Christopher shook his head slowly.

"If no one makes sacrifices, the work of God is left undone."

Illesa rolled her eyes.

"There are all kinds of sacrifices, and your parents have made plenty to see you knighted. I can understand that the Templars seem preferable to the King's ill-disciplined army, but this is not something you can decide on your own."

"That is why I must go to Tours!"

Illesa turned away and shut her eyes. He was so desperate for a special calling – a way of living above the dust and sin of ordinary life. He didn't yet realise that sin was ever-present, lodged deep inside.

"If you want guidance about such a decision it would be better to speak to a wise Templar priest who understands the order as it is now, since the loss of the Holy Land. Father Raymond is in the preceptory at Sergeac, near Rocamadour. He will tell you the truth."

Christopher frowned.

"Why are you so eager for me to speak to him? Are you going to prepare his answers?"

"Why are you so suspicious? I have trusted him with my life and that of your father. He is a man of discernment. If you are meant to serve God as a Templar, he will be able to see it."

"Is that why you insist on going to Rocamadour? Because it's close to your friend?"

"You know why we're going there. Stop being so argumentative."

"It seems a harsh penance for simply not reporting a death and letting a man's body remain unburied."

Illesa looked at him through narrowed eyes.

"What did your father tell you about the attack on Joyce?"

"He told me what happened. Reginald followed and attacked Joyce, William stopped him, killed him and hid the body."

Illesa sighed.

"And what did he tell you about Ramón?"

Christopher turned instinctively to look for his friend. Ramón was leaning over the ship's port side with everyone else.

"He said that Ramón knew Reginald had followed us, and so, when he didn't return, he came to get compensation for the loss of his partner. Which is his right."

Richard evidently hadn't wanted to point out that Ramón had become friends with Christopher because he'd already found a weakness in the family that he could exploit. She didn't blame him. Friends, whatever their motives, had not been plentiful in Christopher's life.

"Have you talked to Ramón about it?"

"I've asked him about Reginald," Christopher said uncomfortably. "He told me what he'd done to that boy."

Illesa pushed her flapping veil back off her face.

"If we are travelling together on pilgrimage, you should know the truth, not what your father wishes had happened." Her voice had become hoarse. "I killed Reginald. William had been knocked out and tied up. After I found William, he hid the body in the river. Reginald's unshriven death is on my conscience, as well as his unburied body."

Christopher stared at her, then blinked.

"How did you kill him?" he whispered.

Illesa shook her head.

216

"No, I am not a soldier to talk about such things."

"But you killed him in self-defence, just as a soldier does. So the only sin is in hiding the deed."

"That is why we have to bear the company of your friend. Ramón has threatened to accuse us if we don't pay him. Compensation might have been awarded to him by the court, but compensation is not a payment without end. Talk to him. Convince him to give the ring back to me and put an end to his threats."

"What ring? And what are you talking about? He said you threatened him with imprisonment!"

Illesa looked over his shoulder; Ramón and Joyce were side by side watching the port come nearer. She leant close to Christopher's ear.

"We locked him in the room above the stable because his monkey was stealing our things, and he was threatening us. The ring belonged to Reginald, given to him by Gaspar." She touched her neck, where the cord used to be. "I took it from the body so that it could not give away his identity. To this day, the *only* other person who knows is Ramón. He has us tied up like a milk cow, especially now he has befriended you and taught Joyce a secret language only he knows."

Christopher wiped the sea spray from his scowling face.

"So you believe he only became my friend because of the opportunity to get coin from you?"

Illesa looked away.

"No. You are a true friend to him. Why should he not be to you? But I cannot rest until the ring is returned, and he is back in Castile, far away from the Royal court where he could accuse us. That is why I agreed to have him on this journey. Even to pay his voyage!"

She'd said more than she intended, and now Christopher was pale and angry. It was the sickness and lack of sleep that made her so irritable. That and Christopher's disregard of his family.

"I will speak to Ramón about the ring, if what you have told me is true."

"Do you doubt me in favour of a foreign man you've known only briefly?"

"You don't like him. You think his friendship is beneath me."

"Well, it's a pity that William is not here. He would tell you. Ramón is not innocent. He knew what Reginald did. It happened to him too. He lies to protect himself. How can we trust such a man?" Illesa put her hand on Christopher's forearm. "Joyce and I will carry on to Bordeaux with the other pilgrims. If you choose to disembark here and go with the priest, that's your decision to explain to your father, in this life or the next."

Christopher stared into the water.

"He should have entrusted the pilgrimage to me. I'm a knight, not a child."

"He knows I have more experience of such a journey. If it was left to you, we'd be away half a year or more, and all the time the risks of attack and illness mount. When we return, you will resume your authority in all its forms. Until then, give me the respect you owe and think on what I've said."

Christopher grunted dismissively.

The sailors were pulling down the sails. Soon they would be turning into the harbour. The oarsmen were mustering.

"If you are set against my visit to Tours, I suppose I must submit to your purse, despite my own convictions." He stomped away to join the other men preparing to row.

Illesa wiped away angry tears and watched the towers and walls of La Rochelle coming nearer. It would be pleasant to leave the ship, get a good night's sleep and escape the fear of drowning, the sickness and the foul smell of the hold. But Reginald's attack had happened when they'd separated. She would not be tempted to risk Joyce's safety again, even though Master Ralph was insufferable.

"This town would have been worthy of inclusion in the map!" Richard Orosius had crossed over to see the tower on the steerboard side. Priests, it seemed, were not required to row.

"It has been interesting to hear your tales, Father. I'm sorry that our ways part here."

The smile vanished from the priest's face.

"I thought you were all disembarking here to visit Tours? That's what your son said."

"Our plan was always to go to Rocamadour first. Christopher may visit Tours on his return," Illesa said firmly. "I'm sorry you will not have his company, but there will be many people journeying from here to Poitiers on church business. I'm certain of it."

Richard Orosius stared at her vacantly for a moment.

"Why then I'll come with you. That suits me well!"

Illesa's stomach lurched.

"Don't you have an important letter to deliver to the Pope? Isn't time of the essence?"

"No, it can wait. There will be an opportunity to speak to the Pope once I have submitted myself to the Holy Virgin. Much better," he muttered. "I might have been caught up there for many months."

He smiled as if an angel had delivered a shining star into his lap. But by the next day, he was unable to move or speak. A terrible melancholy had descended on him.

Chapter XXXII

Monday the 11th September, 1307
Saint Nicolas Lazar House
Bordeaux
Tierce

Illesa left the Lazar house and shook the dust off her feet outside their porch. She would not demand the coin returned, although it would have been useful, but she expected their donations to be recorded at least, and masses said. All possible prayers were needed.

Imagine forgetting to inform a donor that the man they supported had left this Lazar house for another one. And then having the temerity to suggest that they might have lost the letter, when they'd continued sending coin to the Lazar house via the Templars for two years with no message.

At least she knew now that Gaspar was not dead. Only the relief of that news had stopped her from shouting at the Lazarite Brother, with his red-rimmed eyes and frog-like lips. And from what he'd said, Gaspar was now lodged in a Lazar house near Sergeac. They would be able to see him and Father Raymond at the same time. It seemed ordained.

She crossed the street dodging a cart full of straw. The last few days had been exhausting, on top of the rough sea voyage. When she'd stood by the wall of the Cathédrale Saint André and read the short inscription it felt as if she'd just been told of Azalais's death – the grief that overcame her was so strong. Although it was wrong to weep. Azalais must surely be singing in Heaven by now, with all the masses the people of Bordeaux had paid for the washing of her soul. She'd brought back the old songs to them in a time of war, and they'd been grateful.

Meanwhile Richard Orosius lay like the dead in the Hôpital Saint Julien where, so many years before, she'd seen Azalais and Gaspar for the last time. None of the Brothers could say what ailed him, except that he appeared to have been struck down by God.

'It was his decision not to go to Poitiers, obviously,' Christopher had declared. 'He didn't do as his Bishop commanded, *and* he showed disrespect to the Pope. What did he expect?'

But the priest's eyes followed Illesa as she prepared his infusions or helped him to the pot. He looked as if he wanted to speak. The other pilgrims were leaving soon. Master Ralph was certain the illness was a sign that Richard Orosius was a bearer of a curse. He would only give back three shillings of the coin she'd paid him to lead them to the shrine. And she'd had to argue with Christopher again. He was not in favour of waiting in Bordeaux.

'Didn't you say you wanted to hurry and accomplish your pilgrimage quickly? And now you are insisting we wait for the most tiresome of men to get better. This is the sign from God that we should leave him to his judgement.'

She could not exactly say why she disagreed with his opinion, except that it was lacking in mercy. Let Master Ralph and his herd go on. Let them go and bleat their way east. Richard Orosius had been certain God had brought them together for a purpose. She should not be the one to abandon him when he was ill, leave him friendless in a strange city. She'd agreed with Christopher that they would wait a week, no more. If God could create the whole world in a week with a day off to rest, he could heal this man, if he meant to, and make him well enough to guide them to the shrine.

She passed a busy tavern, breathed in the smell of bread and ale.

The Lazarite brothers had offered her no refreshment, and she was parched. But it was not far to the hospital. She needed to speak to Christopher about this news. Seeing Gaspar was surely something they could all agree upon, and hopefully Father Raymond would set him right about his real duty. Perhaps things were finally falling into place – their plans and God's becoming aligned.

Ramón was waiting at the end of the street.

"The Oracle of Orosius speaks." He held his arms up as if seeing a glorious sight. "He asks for you. However, he neither rises nor walks."

He kept up with Illesa as she quickened her pace.

"Did he have anything to eat?"

"Yes. A piece of cheese. That was it. Cheese the divine elixir of Heaven gives speech to the stricken."

"For God's sake!" Illesa muttered. "What's his colour like?"

"Not unlike the cheese."

Ramón pulled his cheeks down to make a good imitation of Richard Orosius's long, doleful face. Illesa had to look away to hide her smile.

"And where is Christopher?"

"Waiting to have his tooth plucked from his gums. He prefers that to the smell of the infirmary. Surprising considering the smell of the army."

They had nearly reached the hospital. Illesa stopped and turned to face Ramón. He was looking more and more like a vagrant every day.

"Ramón, did you ever meet Reginald's brother, Gaspar?"

Ramón smiled in a conspiratorial way.

"I did. I was just a boy. To see the pair of them together! As if your eyes doubled after a blow to the head, no? They wore the same clothes for a tumbling routine, and the women fainted."

"Did they love each other? Were they close?"

Ramón stopped and did an elaborate pose indicating consideration.

"I don't think so. If I had a brother I loved I would not hit him on the side of the head until he was nearly dead. No. I wouldn't do that."

"Which one did that?" Illesa said, gripping his arm.

"I couldn't tell. They both looked so alike, and I was hiding in the fold of the tent."

"Are you being truthful or are you just trying to confuse me?"

"Truthful, Lady Burnel! When have I not been?"

"Always, as far as I can tell."

"I saw them fighting. That is very true. They were dressed the same, and I could not tell who prevailed. I fell asleep where I sat, and, when I woke they were both gone."

"How old were you then?"

"Maybe I was eight or nine years?"

"And now?"

"Perhaps I am twenty-three, but perhaps twenty-four. It is hard to keep track of this time that passes." He snatched at the air as if catching a fly.

So Gaspar would have been in between patrons. After the Earl of Lincoln went abroad.

"Is that when Gaspar gave Reginald the ring?"

"No. I think not. I don't remember." Ramón shook his head sadly. "But if you find this Gaspar, you may ask him yourself."

"He might be with the Sergeac Templars, where we were going anyway." She stopped walking abruptly and took his arm. "I need you to give me the ring back, Ramón. I'll return it to Gaspar, and then all will be forgotten."

Ramón hugged his chest.

"You would like to forget. So would I. But we cannot. It will always be there in our minds and dreams, no?" He looked down at his battered tunic and hose sadly. "I need new clothes. It is not seemly to keep your son company in rags."

She silently gave him three coins.

"Choose something inconspicuous."

"I will afford nothing else," he said pointedly, looking at the lonely coins in his palm. He left her by the hospital gate.

Richard Orosius was in the dormitory, Joyce at his bedside looked panicked. The priest had hold of her arm and was trying to pull her down to speak in her ear. A Brother Hospitaller was at the other end of the long room, well out of reach.

Illesa removed his grip from Joyce, and she sprang away. Illesa knelt down by the bed.

"Father, are you feeling better?"

His eyes flicked backwards and forwards over her face. He raised his head a little.

"I am not better. No," he slurred. "But I get better. Each time it happens I think I'm dying. But I never do. I suffer in this world."

"This has happened before?"

He lay back on the bed, sweat gathering in droplets on his forehead, and nodded.

"When? At the Cathedral?"

He held up a finger, then two more.

"Three times?"

He shut his eyes then opened them a slit.

"How long does it last?"

"I will get up soon." He murmured. "My body will rise again, but the black melancholy will stay for weeks. Maybe months or years."

"How did they treat it?"

"They bled me." He shut his eyes tight. "They pricked my toes with hot needles."

She squeezed his hand.

"I won't do that. I have herbs that will do you good."

"You are like her," he muttered. "But she frightened me, and you do not. I think you were sent to me by God."

"So you said." Illesa prised his fingers off her hand and got up.

"What's wrong with him?" Joyce mouthed at her.

Illesa walked with her into the middle of the room between the rows of beds.

"His humours are out of balance. Too much black bile. Perhaps he suffered from too much cold on the ship. But it is something that recurs. I don't know. He was so lively, so full of his own voice. Now he is empty. It's strange. The planet Saturn may be affecting him. I will see if they have an infusion of clary sage."

Joyce was pulling her sleeve, reaching up to whisper in her ear.

"He called me a strange name – Chera."

Illesa shrugged.

"I don't know that name. It's not an angel or a saint. Perhaps it is something from the map?"

Joyce shook her head.

"A woman. He tried to kiss me."

Illesa held her shoulders.

"Keep your distance from him, Joyce. He is not in his right mind. I will look after him for now. You go and wait for Christopher and Ramón in the courtyard."

Illesa found them later when Richard Orosius had once again fallen into a stupor. Christopher's back tooth had been pulled, and he and Ramón were drinking wine from a skin. They were already far gone. Ramón wore a new green tunic and a pair of brown hose. Joyce sat close enough to hear their conversation and far enough away not to be accused of doing so.

"How is the mad priest? What's his latest delusion?" Christopher wiped his mouth with the back of his hand, looking both drunk and surly.

"He's had an attack of melancholia. It's not easily cured."

"It is no match for My Dame Physician!" Ramón flourished a bow.

Illesa ignored him.

"We need to discuss our plans."

"Leave him. Leave him here." Christopher waved his hand around the hospital courtyard. "He's making Joyce unhappy, trying to kiss her. A priest!" Spittle flew from his lips.

"The Brother Hospitaller says there is a special mass for the sick next Sunday. We should wait and take him to the Cathedral for that – before we travel on to Rocamadour."

"What? More days wasted? I thought you said we needed to hurry. You didn't want to go to Saint Martin at Tours." Christopher stood up a little unsteadily. "Why are you willing to waste time on this priest and not on your own son?"

"Christopher – the wine has your tongue." She pointed at the red spill on the path. "The priest is part of our company. We should not abandon him in his condition. He's afraid of the treatments they will use on him."

"I'll use a treatment on him if he ever tries to kiss Joyce again. Disgusting old man." Christopher mimed strangling someone by the throat.

"I'll not speak to you until you are sober." Illesa beckoned Joyce. "We'll visit the Monadey family. They are also associates of the Templars and took many risks to hide Richard after he escaped from the French. They'll know if Father Raymond is at Sergeac. And, if he is, as you're such a fine, temperate, solemn knight, you can make plans to leave the temptations of this world behind and join the Order."

She took Joyce's arm and left, ignoring the snorts of laughter from Christopher and Ramón.

Chapter XXXIII

Monday the 18th September, 1307
Commandery of Arveyres on the Dordogne
Vespers

"A priest so stricken by melancholy? I've never seen it amongst the brethren." John of Primey was trying not to look shocked. It was hard to explain their various afflictions to this young Templar knight who was the same age as Christopher. Not a scratch on him. Fresh as a newly laid egg.

"It has plagued him for many years. But he has served God well, with his great skill."

It had seemed a sign of good fortune that Sir John was called to Sergeac and could take a message for them, begging Father Raymond and Gaspar to attend them there, so that they could visit after their pilgrimage to Rocamadour. He was also willing to delay his journey to accompany them as far as the fork in their paths, even though he would usually ride and make the journey in a third of the time. His horse was pleased of the rest, he said, and it was a clear blessing to Illesa, as Richard Orosius was unable to take any interest in their whereabouts or relate any part of the real world to his map.

But Illesa had not realised how much their strange company of people had formed its own society even in their short journey. Their behaviour seemed bizarre to Sir John, a young man whose experiences had not yet included mania, melancholy or muteness. He stared while Joyce made her quick signs to Ramón. Tried to speak to the silent and blank Richard Orosius, but soon gave up. Illesa felt embarrassed, and then shame for it. She tried to explain to Sir John the circumstances of Richard Orosius, his great work in Hereford, the vast scope of it. Sir John nodded politely, bemused.

"I trust he is a true Christian. And pilgrimage will surely do him good." Sir John looked dubious and uncomfortable, his Norman accent becoming more pronounced when he was covering his true thoughts.

"It will. And we are grateful for your protection." She was treated to a broad smile at that. At least he was not like the other Templar knights on the ship. They had refused to even converse with women.

"Protecting vulnerable pilgrims is a service to God and the Virgin. I thank them that I am strong enough to serve."

She could not argue with the strength of his body. He was tall and well built with a long stride. He forgot that they were not so quick, and their feet were unused to the terrain. When they fell behind he waited for them, almost able to hide his impatience.

Sir John had addressed them all happily enough by the east gate of Bordeaux that morning, full of enthusiasm, but he already seemed to doubt the benefit of their company. He'd only entered the Templar order five months before, and had no experience in battle as yet. A few brigands intent on robbery had fallen to him, but nothing to disturb the good temper of his mind nor his handsome face. Evil and good were unmixed in his experience. His smile was a blessing none of them felt they deserved. It even quieted Ramón.

"Where does your family come from?" she asked

"Chartres, the most beautiful place in all of France. Our Notre Dame Cathedral can be seen for days as you walk. You have surely visited?"

There was a shine in his eyes. The poor lad was homesick. Illesa turned away so as not to embarrass him.

"No, but I have heard of its greatness."

He walked on a few paces, obviously disappointed.

"Most pilgrims wish to visit. I expect you have not because of the war?"

Illesa only nodded. He would have been a young child when the war over Gascony had ripped their family apart. He would have no real understanding of her fear and loathing of the French King and his court, and she would not explain it to him. She would not travel in French territory if she could avoid it. Meanwhile he was still speaking of Notre Dame de Chartres and its magnificence.

"In that building, there is even the pilgrimage in miniature on the pavement – a great House of Daedalus. It takes many twists and reversals, but with devotions at every turn, you come to the centre and the fulfilment of the soul's journey. There we defeat sin as Theseus did the Minotaur."

If only it were that easy. Every night disturbed. Every day a struggle to know God's will, pulled in every direction by all the company. At least now they were all on the road and going the same way. But she would not disillusion him – he was young and full of certainty.

"We always receive great blessings when we travel the labyrinth on our knees, through the night, lit by candles. You might visit it on your way back to England? I could accompany you."

It was a plea more than a suggestion. Someone had sent him away from home too early, and all he wanted to do was return.

"My thanks. You have great devotion, but I believe we must travel on the Templar ship home again from Bordeaux. We have no coin for other shrines."

Sir John looked away into the distance, nodding. There was a long silence.

"I should converse with your son. He says that he is interested in the Order. My lady."

He bowed his head, pulled the lead rein of his pale grey rouncey and loped off to catch up with Christopher, who'd put as much distance between himself and Richard Orosius as possible.

Thanks be to Our Lady, who had given her blessing on the day of Sainte Croix and enabled the priest to gain enough strength to ride, if not walk. He'd made Illesa promise not to leave him to rot in Bordeaux. In his flat voice, Richard Orosius in turn had promised his condition would not last. Perhaps he'd been talking to himself.

They were struggling along a rocky path heading towards a high promontory with buildings and barns in the distance. Behind her, Ramón began to sing a sad little tune. He and Joyce caught up with Illesa as she stopped to look.

"Now the pilgrimage has truly begun! This is the life of players all over the world. Walking very far. Hoping the next town will want our skills and give us enough for bed and board. But we have no such worry with Sir John leading us. All will be well with him at the head of our company! Don't you think so, Joyce?" Ramón winked provocatively.

Joyce coloured and hid her mouth behind her free hand. Illesa rounded on him.

"What do you want, Ramón? We do not need your insinuations after a long day."

"Nothing harmful. Your chastisements are always a balm to my soul. I was thinking maybe I should sing and tell tales to Richard Orosius. It could bring him back from the dark places."

"Your tales are hardly suitable for priestly ears." Illesa took Joyce's arm as they climbed uphill.

"I have many tales and sermons." Ramón gave her an uncharacteristically hurt look. "Many have holy morals. But I believe that adventures are what he needs most. He is first a man, and after that a priest. It is his inner being that needs calling back. I knew a man with the same affliction."

"And it helped? Listening to tales and songs?"

"He was strong again within a fortnight."

"Why didn't you tell me before?"

Ramón shrugged.

"He enjoys your company most, and of course the angel, Joyce, who called him on this pilgrimage." He batted his eyelashes.

Joyce swatted at him, scowling. Ramón dodged her and pointed to his side.

"My lady could sit by me while I speak to him at first."

She could think of no way he could use this against her. Except one. She bent her head towards him.

"Help me keep watch over him then, Ramón. He has been threatening to take his own life, and I cannot mind him constantly." Ramón's head snapped towards Joyce, but Illesa waved her hand dismissively. "Joyce has heard him say it more than once. He has recognised that she is not the 'Chera' he mistook her for, and that sent him into an even worse state. We must watch him at night. He is often wakeful then – when I'm exhausted. But be careful that you only tell your tales, not any *other* information."

He looked affronted.

"My lady, your suspicions are most terrible."

She ignored him and paced ahead, desperate to sit or lie down. It would be good to have an extra person to share the burden of the priest's melancholy. Christopher was dismissive, impatient, perhaps afraid of what might have caused the attack. And it was bad for Joyce to constantly witness such delusion.

The company was coming to a halt outside the gate of the commandery. Sir John was standing as if about to lead an army into battle.

"Pilgrims, welcome! I must enquire of the Master here where you may be accommodated. I understand they have a generous guesthouse, much better than the hospital in Bordeaux. Wait here quietly while I make us known inside."

Illesa craved a good meal of roast meat. But this was penance. She would not taste it until she had satisfied the conditions of the pilgrimage. The commandery walls were of the marl grey stone they'd seen all along their walk in the Entre Deux Mers, softened by the evening light and the sound of doves settling to roost. As they waited two stars rose in the eastern sky. The western horizon was fading from gold to deep madder. To the north there was a thin line of darkening cloud.

In that direction, over the sleeve of sea, William would be settling the horses for the night. The bell in the chapel would be ringing, and Cecily would be preparing the vegetables. Richard might be sitting by the window, looking south towards her.

She turned away from the others. It was too far, impossibly distant, but a mere hand's width on the great map. They were not half-way through their journey yet. She rubbed her tired eyes. Christopher did not seem weary. He was at the end of the promontory, perhaps to look out over the Dordogne. And Richard Orosius was still slumped on the jennet they'd had to buy to bear him. She went over to help.

His eyes were shut, his arms crossed over his chest, as if he hoped to be dead and buried. The horse was a docile, amiable beast, which was just as well. It was cropping the tufts of grass and weeds within reach, ignoring its listless rider.

"Come, let's get you down," Illesa said, taking his hand and pulling on his tunic.

Ramón came alongside her, holding him by the torso. They slid him off the worn saddle. He stood looking around as if he'd landed in another world. There were dark shadows under his eyes, and his hands were shaking.

"Where are we?"

"Arveyres, Father Richard." Ramón said, taking his arm. "A house of Templars overlooking a wide river. As safe as the great Tower of London. I'll help you walk and tell you a tale about the Templars, if you wish?"

Sir John had returned, alongside a Templar sergeant. He beckoned them forward. Illesa watched Ramón patiently taking each step with Richard Orosius and sighed. Perhaps she would be able to sleep tonight. Perhaps it would be dreamless. She entered the porch arm in arm with Joyce, Christopher behind them, scraping his boots.

Chapter XXXIV

Friday the 22nd September, 1307
Forêt de la Bessède
Vespers

"I am not familiar with this place." Sir John was walking beside his horse very slowly down the track through the rain. "Cadouin is a large abbey, I've heard, so we should be able to see it soon. All these trees hide it from our gaze, but it can't be much further."

The dark forest stretched all around them. They'd been expecting to reach Cadouin and its relic, Le Saint-Suaire, the face shroud from the tomb of Christ, much earlier in the day. But Sir John was certain they were on the right path. Returning to the last village would take a long time, at night, and in thick fog.

"We may have gone wrong at the forked path. The old man was hard to understand." Sir John, they had learned, was confident with the Dordogne River on his left hand side, but away from that landmark he was at a loss.

"Isn't that a shelter?" Christopher pointed to the side of the cliff they'd been skirting. Where the scrub ended there was a shadow, a dark recess in the stone. "It might be best to stop here and light a fire. The women are cold, and the chance of ambush is high in these woods." As if to prove what he said, Joyce sneezed. Christopher's respect for the Templar had waned over the previous days as Sir John's inexperience had become apparent.

There was a cracking sound to their right, its cause invisible through the dense branches. Everyone strained their eyes in the gloom and haze.

"A deer or a boar, surely," Sir John said, sounding far from sure.

"Or a gang of robbers. Up to the shelter; we can use it as a stronghold," Christopher said. He pulled the reluctant jennet with its lumpy passenger after Sir John, who had mounted his horse. The Templar had not thought to ride as rear-guard.

Ramón was holding onto Richard Orosius in case he fell out of the saddle on the steep slope. Sir John dismounted under the shelter of the overhanging rock, bent over and disappeared into the recess.

Illesa didn't dare look behind her until she was under the shelter of the cliff. She could hear nothing over her own panting. With two knights they ought to be safe enough, but not if the brigands had bows and arrows. She pulled Joyce further back into the cave. Ramón was heaving Richard Orosius off the horse. Christopher had drawn his sword and was standing in the mouth of the cave.

"It's quite large," Sir John called. His voice echoed off the limestone. "Plenty of space to sleep."

"Shhhh!" Christopher hissed. He was listening for any sound of pursuit, fiercely concentrating. Ramón stood nearby, holding the horses and staring at the edge of the forest just below them. Richard Orosius leant against the cave wall, his eyes closed. Illesa pushed aside some fallen leaves with her foot. Underneath lay a scattering of animal bones and charcoal. Those using this cave might not be happy to share with strangers.

The mist thickened into another downpour of rain. They watched it drenching the last of the light. The jennet shook its mane and whinnied unhappily.

Nothing emerged from the wood.

"Let's make a fire." Sir John had a fistful of dry branches and was getting flint and steel out of his pouch.

"That will draw attention," Illesa said.

"We have nothing to fear here," Sir John insisted, sitting down on his haunches and laying out the sticks. "There's a perfect view. No one will take us by surprise. Attacking Templars is known to be unwise, even amongst the worst gangs of thieves."

Joyce was staring at him in the way she had begun to do, intently following his every move. It was good that he was going to be leaving them tomorrow, when he'd eventually led them to Cadouin. Joyce needed to fill her mind with the healing power of the shrine, not the smile of a Templar knight who could be manacled for consorting with a woman.

Christopher sheathed his sword.

"We will explore the cave once the fire is lit. Ramón, come with me."

They scurried along the cliff edge, looking underneath scrub and bushes for wood that was not drenched. It would be a smoky fire.

"Sit, Joyce. Sit and rest." Illesa pushed her down so she had her back against the cave wall. Richard Orosius was opposite, head in his hands, looking out into the gloom – the rolling banks of cloud.

The horses would want grazing, but she couldn't let them roam. She poured water from her skin into a cup and held it out to each in turn, watching them trying to drink with their big lips, dripping onto the pale, sandy ground.

Eventually a spark took in the bark, and Ramón nurtured the small flame. Joyce shuffled forward to sit near him. There was little to eat, but Illesa got out the maslin bread. Sir John found some dried fish. There was a round cheese as well, to cut into pieces. They sat in a semicircle around the small fire. The rain had eased, and there was only the sound of the sticks cracking in the fire and drops falling from the leaves.

"Tell us another of your stories, Ramón." The Templar pulled a strand of dried fish from between his teeth. "We should fend off the night with good Christian moral tales." Ramón's eyes were black and glittering in the firelight. He folded his legs underneath him.

"What of some payment for my trouble?"

"You've been given plenty. Do what you're asked," Illesa retorted.

"Here, drink." Christopher passed him the wineskin.

A bright thing flew out of the darkness and landed in Ramón's lap.

"Talk or sing. There is your coin." It was Richard Orosius, still against the cave wall but leaning forward, one hand on his purse.

Ramón had already tucked the penny in his pouch. He nodded at the priest.

"This will make you merry and please the other religious – the good Sir John. It is called 'The False Messiah'."

"That doesn't sound suitable." Illesa put another stick on the fire. "A false messiah – how could there be such a thing unless it is the end of days?"

"It is eminently suitable, I promise. But if it doesn't please you, share the coin I was given." He held it out as if to tempt her. "You may bite out your share." He looked around the company, with fire-lit eyes. "Does anyone know this tale?"

They all shook their heads.

Ramón rubbed his hands together.

"Good. Once in the ancient town of Selucia, there was an old Jew with a most beautiful daughter."

"Is that possible?" Christopher asked, grinning.

"Of course it is, idiot." Richard Orosius waved his hand in the air. "Don't interrupt him. Let him speak. He does so with my coin."

Ramón made a flourish with his hand and bowed to the priest.

"In the highest room at the back of the Jew's house was his daughter's chamber, and it had a good window at which she would sit to sew. She was not allowed out onto the streets but sat there day after day, singing strange words in a sweet voice. And the sill of her window was only a few feet from the back of a good Christian house, where there lodged a Christian student, who was reading all manner of theology. He was destined for the cloth and the altar. But the student soon became saddened by the Jewish girl's situation and inflamed by love! Not just love of her as-yet-unsaved-soul but full of passion for her dark comeliness, all locked away from the world. Of her part, I do not know, except that she spent hours pouting at his smooth cheeks and full lips. So he resolved to fix it for both of them, for what can stop a fire from roaring into life when the wind of passion blows?"

"A downpour of rain?" Christopher suggested, spluttering with laughter at himself.

Ramón tugged at his cap in pretend admiration and continued:

"One night he got a long board, I don't know where from, and laid it between the two windows, then he crept across on his bottom and took the Jewish girl into his arms." Ramón looked around the semicircle of faces, his expression one of innocent astonishment. Joyce's eyes were wide open, her cheeks crimson. Sir John was keeping his head down, picking at something on his boot.

"After many nights of this, it came as a great surprise to both of them when she found herself pregnant. 'Don't worry about it, my darling,' the student said. 'I will fix everything. Leave it to me.'"

Richard Orosius was staring at Ramón, his face completely still, as if dead.

"So the next night he brought with him a narrow reed that he'd cut. After he had enjoyed her thoroughly, he found a hole in the floorboard and pushed the reed through so it popped out the other side into the Jew's bedroom, where he was preparing to go to sleep alongside his wife.

"And when they were just nodding off, the student began to speak down the reed.

"'You, Abraham, and your wife, are highly favoured! I have chosen your daughter to be the bearer of the Messiah. This night she has conceived of the Holy Ghost. Treat her well, and give her all honour, for her son will be the saviour of the Jewish people.'

"Abraham was astonished and fell to his knees, grateful he had been selected for such an important role."

Richard Orosius suddenly lunged forward on his knees, his eyes fierce, pointing at Ramón.

"Why do you tell this tale? What do you know?"

Ramón put a hand up, palm out.

"It is a drollery, nothing more. It shows how gullible the Hebrew race is, and how quickly the Christian can get the better of him."

But the priest was already on his feet, bending over Ramón and pulling at his tunic until he'd lifted Ramón up by the neck.

"Why tell it to me? With my coin?"

"It is not pleasing to you? See they only know that she does not bear the Messiah when the baby is born a girl! But if that tale does not amuse you, let me tell you another one. Sit, master," Ramón wriggled out of Richard Orosius's grip and sat down on the other side of Christopher.

"This one will certainly be approved by all you good Christians as it is about a minstrel, even poorer than I, and the

236

great Saint Peter, may he bless us all!" He looked over at Richard Orosius and licked his lips. The priest still stood above him, fists clenched by his side. Ramón cleared his throat. "This vagrant of a minstrel would spend whatever coins he earned from his voice and harp, when he hadn't pawned it or lost it at dice, which I know is not right. He seldom had shoes, for he lacked patrons as kind as mine." He held out his worn boots to be admired before continuing.

"He was evidently soon dead, having lived long enough. In fact much too long, so his mother said, and the Devil came to take his soul."

"I should take yours," Richard Orosius muttered, backing away and sitting down.

"Drink, Father," Sir John said, passing him the wineskin. "It is permitted to listen to instructive tales. I'm sure this will show us what to avoid in our lives, as we laugh at the creature described."

"You don't need to tell me," Richard Orosius muttered. He was sounding more like his old self. Angry and bitter. "Forced to live in a cave like a Troglodyte because those leading us have lost their way. Useless."

"Let him continue, for Christ's sake," Christopher said. "Before he forgets the ending!"

He'd drunk more than anyone. If they were attacked, he'd be no help.

"Kind sir, I thank you. The ending is safe in my treasure box." Ramón knocked on the side of his head, making a hollow sound that echoed around the shelter. Joyce stifled a laugh. "As I was saying. This tale brings joy to all those who love songs and laughter and hate the Devil and all his demons."

The tale of how the minstrel outwitted and cheated Satan was long, involved, and seemed to placate the priest. Sir John laughed until he choked, but Illesa had become more and more aware of the great black mouth of the cave behind them, like the Hell's mouth on church walls.

"Has anyone found the back of the cave?" She had to ask three times, because Sir John, Christopher and Ramón were having a loud disagreement about which country had the best minstrels, watched by Joyce. Richard Orosius had turned his back on the company and was pretending to sleep.

"I went quite far," Sir John said. "It gets lower and narrower. Without a torch I could not see if there was a back wall or a passage."

Illesa pushed herself to her aching feet.

"We should know this before we settle down to sleep. What if it's a bear den? Or worse?"

"There would be fresh signs, claw marks, bones," Christopher said. But in the end he and Sir John found thick sticks and wound them with some waxed cloth and set them alight in the fire.

"Ramón, you stay here with the priest and keep watch. You too, Joyce."

But Joyce shook her head and followed Christopher into the swaying shadows.

Ramón was sitting with his arms wrapped round his knees on the opposite side to Richard Orosius. The fire was only embers.

"We won't go far. Call if you are in need," Illesa said.

"Always, we wait for your rescue," Ramón said, blinking devotedly.

Illesa turned away and hurried after the others. The cave roof lowered quickly as they went further back, their figures making grotesque, hunched shadows against the rough walls. In some places there were piles of shattered bone. Illesa's skin began to crawl.

"I don't like the look of this," she said pointing to the remains. But the men with their torches were already further on, and the dark was overtaking her. The cave was narrowing as well as lowering.

Christopher was down on all fours, holding his torch in front of him, crawling forward.

"There is a way through," he called.

"No, Christopher! You mustn't. If you disturb something it will attack you!"

He turned to look at her.

"Come and see, Mother. It's full of glittering pillars like a jewelled cathedral."

Joyce was kneeling beside him by a hole in the cave wall.

"Imagine if there is treasure inside," Sir John said, his guttering torch distorting his handsome, excited face.

Treasure meant thieves and guards. Trouble for them all. But that wasn't what was in the further chamber of the cave. It was glittering with some kind of stone accretion that covered strange shapes and forms, flowing from the ceiling and rising up from the floor, like a forest of flickering light. It was impossible to see what was lurking behind the glittering columns.

"Stay away from it," she said, pulling Joyce back. "It's the Devil's trap, to entice us in and drag us down to Hell. Take your torches out of there." Christopher took a step back, looking irritated.

"Don't be ridiculous, Mother. Why would the Devil put an entrance to Hell here in the middle of the woods? There are plenty of places to enter in every town and city."

Joyce was trying to push Illesa out of the way so she could see.

"Let *me* look in. We are trained to recognise the Devil's work." Sir John went forward awkwardly on his knees. He pushed his torch into the opening and carefully leant inside.

"It's beautiful!" His voice echoed back strangely. "So intricate – like God's handiwork in flowers and stars." He was climbing through into the chamber.

"Hold his feet, Christopher, in case he is grabbed by demons. They may try to pull him in!"

Christopher ignored her.

"Let me look again, Sir John," he insisted.

Illesa had to stand watching them while her heart hammered wildly inside her chest. But she wouldn't let Joyce look unless Christopher held her ankles.

"A wonder of Almighty God!" Sir John declared, bending again into the opening when Joyce had come out. "What a gracious sign of his love even in the darkest of places."

"Not a single demon, Mother." Christopher brushed the dust off his knees. "But as we don't know how far back that cavern extends and there may be wolves or bears, we need to have a watch on both sides of the camp. I will be on first watch; who will join me?" He looked around. "Sir John should do the second watch. It's best to have a trained soldier used to watches on each duty."

"I will." Illesa took Joyce's hand. "Come near the fire, Joyce, and we'll get out the blankets. I'll watch until the end of the first sleep."

At the mouth of the cave, Ramón had one eye open, his hand inside his tunic, stowing something away. Richard Orosius was lying on a cape on the cave floor, taking up much of one side of the fire. But he was not asleep. It looked as if they'd hurriedly broken apart when the others had returned.

Joyce began excitedly making signs to Ramón, watched by Sir John.

"We should know this language for our silent meal times in the commandery. But why doesn't she speak?" he asked the fire, as if it could solve the mystery that no one had bothered to explain to him.

Illesa crossed her legs under her damp skirts.

"With the Virgin's help, she will again. God protect us this night, from anything that may assail us."

Sir John nodded slowly and lay down under his cloak. Within seconds his mouth was open, droning with sleep. Joyce took much longer. Ramón was resting his head on one hand and gazing into the coals, his mouth moving silently as if he told himself a story, or a spell. Illesa put another branch on the fire and looked out into the black forest. There was a sliver of moon visible in the clearing sky. Behind her, Christopher guarded the back of the cave. Or he might be exploring it. She could not tell which, but would not be tempted to leave her post to look for him. Illesa knew the tricks of the Devil, and it was Joyce that needed her protection most now, against a whole world of dangers.

She kept herself awake by making designs in the fire ash and pinching the skin of her wrist between her fingernails, and trying not to think about the back of the cave. Sir John stirred when an owl hooted nearby. The others were too tired from walking to wake. He sat up and looked around. The fire was down to a few embers, but the night was far from over. Sir John got up, adjusted his sword belt and went to the cave mouth, looking out like a captain of a ship on the ocean.

"It's been quiet. I think a herd of deer went through, but I couldn't see anything." Illesa got up, stiffly. Her limbs did not like sitting on a cold stone floor. She placed the last stick on the fire. "I'll go and tell Christopher. You wake Ramón."

She went into the darkness at the back of the cave.

"Christopher!" Her whisper sounded loud and close. There was no sign of his torch. "Christopher!"

Nothing. She would have to look into the other chamber.

"Where's he gone?" Ramón was behind her holding a new torch. The light lurched over the receding walls. Christopher's pack, tied up tight, lay abandoned on the floor.

"He must have gone into the further chamber."

"The one full of jewels," Ramón said happily. "What a tale to tell!"

"It's a trap, Ramón. We must get him out before he's taken."

They bent down at the entrance, and Ramón pushed his torch into the chamber.

"Santa Madre de Dios!"

Chapter XXXV

"Can you see him? Is he injured?"

"No. Need to go further in, past the columns."

"No, Ramón! You might disappear too. Call out to him. Use your loudest voice."

"If you want me to use that, I need to be standing up. I go through. The roof is higher in there." He waved away her hand that tried to stop him.

"Stay where I can see you! Don't go any further."

His agile body slid through and the flames of the torch guttered in the new air.

"Coño!"

"What happened?"

"I nearly fell, the floor is covered in lumps."

Illesa leant further into the chamber. Scattered over the floor were little white piles of stone like the glittering white columns, as if sculpted out of marble.

"Stay close. Don't move around!" she whispered.

"Christopher! Eh Culo!" he called. The words reverberated, like answers from the blackness.

"What are you saying?"

"He knows me by this. It tells him I am not a demon but his little foreign friend. Listen for an answer.'

There was just a distant dripping. The torch guttered in a gust of cold air.

"Christopher! Cabrón!"

At the end of the echoes there was a knocking. Metal against stone. And another sound, perhaps a voice.

"Call again! He's there, somewhere!"

"Christopher!"

It was a voice – very distant. The word indistinct.

"He is there. Why he does not come back? Maybe his torch went out." Ramón turned to her. "I will sing a song, so he find the way back."

His accent had become more pronounced, his worried face made strange in the torch light.

"Wait. Listen, he said something."

There was silence. They waited.

"Call him again. Maybe he is hurt."

"Eh tarado! Are you injured?"

"Yes." The voice was faded, tired.

"Can you walk?"

"Yes."

"Follow my voice." He turned back to Illesa. "I sing a Castilian song. But it doesn't matter as long as he can follow the sound, so it's loud, no?"

Ramón began to sing a song, and Illesa was glad she did not know the words because they were no doubt extremely rude. He stopped after a verse.

"Call to me, Christopher!"

They waited.

"Here."

He didn't sound any nearer.

"Don't go in the wrong direction, idiota!"

There was someone leaning beside her. Joyce was trying to see in through the gap.

"What happened?" she whispered in Illesa's ear.

"He went in there and got lost. He is following Ramón's voice. He'll come out soon."

Joyce rubbed her eyes and stared into the chamber, the light reflecting on her gleaming eyes.

The song stopped again.

"Call out to me!"

"I'm here!" A bit louder.

"Good! You are not as estúpido as I thought. Come on this way!"

He sang another verse in a ribald tune that Illesa had heard set to a tavern song. In the silence at the end of that verse they heard a different sound. Knocking and a shuffling. Ramón held the torch high above his head.

"Can you see me, cabrón?"

"Yes, you bastard. I see you. Keep holding it up. These fucking little knobs on the ground want to trip me with every step."

He was coming past one of the glittering columns. Blood had dripped down his forehead and onto his cheek.

"Did you fight off demons with your bare hands?"

"Shut up, Ramón." Christopher was cradling his left arm in his right and watching his feet. "Just help me get out of here."

Illesa pulled Joyce away from the gap. Christopher shuffled through on his knees and one hand, holding the other off the ground. He turned himself over and sat against the cave wall, breathing hard. Illesa sat down next to him as Ramón thrust the torch out to Joyce and then followed on his hands and knees. Joyce held it over Christopher as Illesa began to examine his wrist.

Ramón put his back against the wall.

"What happened, eh? You went exploring on your own into the bowels of the earth?"

Christopher grimaced at him and wiped his bloody forehead carefully with the back of his uninjured hand.

"It's full of passages. Dead ends. Like a labyrinth."

"So why didn't you take a spool of thread with you, idiota?"

The cut on his head was not deep, but his wrist was swollen and useless. A broken bone.

"I didn't know I was going to trip over and put out the torch. And break my arm."

Illesa sat back on her haunches.

"It's your wrist, and you shouldn't have gone alone into the dark after you'd had a skinful."

He glared at her.

"Of course, you always know best! But how can you leave such a place without seeing it fully? It's like having a beautiful book but never opening it. I should have waited and gone with Ramón or Sir John, perhaps. But you would have us move on to see the face cloth of Christ," he said it mockingly, "and miss this creation of God!"

Illesa helped him up.

"Come. I'll bandage it by the fire."

"Imagine how much there is below our feet! Riches and caverns of glorious sights, hidden in darkness."

"And a skeleton of Sir Christopher Burnel, if you had not had your Ramón to guide you out, like Ariadne. My voice was so beautiful it brought you to safety."

Christopher smiled despite himself at Ramón's girlish wiggle.

Illesa found a skin of water and began treating Christopher's injuries. Richard Orosius sat up, and looked around crossly.

"It's not first light. Why have you woken me? What's happened to him?"

Ramón explained, with extra embellishments, and took Richard Orosius to see the cavern, while Sir John spoke of the various minor injuries he'd suffered over the years to an attentive Joyce. He stopped short of showing her his scars.

They were all haggard when it was time to set off in the clear dawn. Sir John had climbed to the top of the cliff and been able to see the distant spire of Cadouin to the north. He led them through the thinning trees. Richard Orosius was now talking incessantly – noticing the land, the types of buildings. But he still had no desire to walk, even to give the exhausted Joyce a turn on the jennet. In the end, Sir John let her ride on his rouncey the last miles to the Abbey Church.

They arrived at gates already thronged with pilgrims.

"This is where I should leave you. But with Sir Burnel injured you are without protection." Sir John looked from Christopher to Illesa, uncertainly. Christopher bowed his head, embarrassed.

"We will travel with these good pilgrims, many of whom will be going to Roc." Illesa gestured at the variety of people waiting to enter the shrine. "You have discharged your duty kindly."

Sir John smiled, relieved. He helped Joyce dismount and then remembered he was not supposed to touch women and backed away.

"May it be an easy road from here to Rocamadour, with many devout people alongside you. I will prepare the brethren at Sergeac for your coming."

"We thank you, Sir John." Illesa bowed her head. "Our Lord and Saint Christopher bless your journey." She stepped back to let the others bid him farewell.

Richard Orosius moved close to her. Too close.

"You may rely on my guidance from now on."

She backed away from his intense stare.

"I'm glad to see you are feeling better. Now that we can join a group of other pilgrims on a well-worn track, it will be easier for us all."

Sir John was urging his horse away. Some of the party waved. Joyce had pulled her veil across her face. Perhaps she was hiding tears.

"It is not the well-worn track we should rely on, but God's guidance for where he would take us." Richard Orosius crossed himself. "The two are not the same."

"For now they are, Father. We stop here, pray, eat, and, please God, sleep well. Then we will be in Rocamadour in only a few days if we take the pilgrim path."

"God's ways are not our ways," he muttered looking up at the impressive church tower. "There is more to his world than we can know or compass. I used to think I had drawn the whole world. What pride!" His eyes had become glazed, unseeing. "He has humbled me, and now I long to learn his will, his ways."

"But you are expected in Poitiers – to deliver the Bishop's letter. You do remember that?"

Richard Orosius stared blankly for a moment. Then looked accusingly at her.

"The Bishop only sent me there to get rid of me. He didn't want me in the cathedral while the Pope's investigators were in Hereford examining the miracles of Thomas Cantilupe. They thought I would say something shameful, or cast doubt on his sanctity. They never trusted me." He crossed himself and looked up to Heaven. "But now I am free of them all. Free to follow the path God has laid out for me."

The gate opened and the first pilgrims shuffled through. Illesa took his upper arm in a firm grip and pushed him forwards.

"First we are going into this church, Father. Then to eat. That is the only path we have today."

Chapter XXXVI

Friday the 29th September, 1307
Michaelmas
Rocamadour
Tierce

The badge seller had only a few mirror cases for sale, and they were very dear. But she had promised Goodwife Kathryn she would get one for the healing of her daughter. She opened the catch again. The mirror reflection was quite clear; not perfect but good enough. The punched decoration on the copper was even and attractive, with a crown for the Queen of Heaven around a sword. The case closed with a firm click.

But she had to keep enough coin for the return journey, and she was not permitted to beg. She could tell Kathryn that there had been no mirror cases for sale, but how could a liar expect a miracle? Ramón was good at convincing people to part with a coin. He could beg for them. But he wanted a new monkey, and that would be very costly. Where was he going to get one? And when?

"Are you taking that or not?" The stallholder waved his finger under her nose. "Buy it or move on!"

It was the right thing to do for that poor child. God would provide a way for them to get home. She placed the coins in the man's outstretched hand and slipped the mirror case into her purse.

Joyce was waiting near the gate, watching the steady line of pilgrims file along the street in their strange costumes. She fiddled with the new badge of the Virgin sewn to her cape. Christopher stood next to her, his arm in a sling, his expression wary. He was always uncomfortable in a crowd. Above them, the looming grey cliff with its tall buildings reverberated with sound. It was time to ascend the stair and begin their proper penitence.

"Where are Ramón and Richard Orosius?"

"They went ahead. Ramón said he would help him up the stairs."

They'd been thick as thieves since Cadouin. It was not clear what they spoke of as, more often than not, it was in whispers. Christopher, who'd been eager to befriend Sir John at first, seemed put out by Ramón's attachment to Richard Orosius – if you could have a friendship with such a changeable character.

"I'll be slow going on my knees. You two go ahead of me, and Christopher stay with Joyce. Don't let her out of your sight. I've heard what can happen in these crowds."

They all looked up towards the towers of the sanctuary, blazing in a rare patch of sunshine.

"Meet me at the entrance to the Virgin's shrine, Joyce. We should go in together. Remember your prayer beads as you mount the stairs. Each one a word, each word a prayer."

Joyce looked nervously at the flights of steps swarming with people and felt for the beads on her belt.

"I don't think Father would want you to go up alone." Christopher looked around. "Find a group of nuns," he concluded, gesturing at the array of pilgrims, and led Joyce away.

Illesa followed them and saw Christopher bend his head so Joyce could whisper something in his ear. Illesa had spent hours tending him when he was ill at home, but his resentment of her authority and the difficult voyage had pushed them apart. Meanwhile Joyce had a dwindling chance of any kind of future, except in a silent order of nuns, to which the old argumentative Joyce would have been entirely unsuited. It seemed that all the effort she and Richard had put into their lives had come to little.

Two Poor Clares, barefoot, in rough wool habits and veils, heads bowed, passed her as she hesitated. Surely they had little enough to repent of. Over two hundred stone steps had to be climbed on bare knees. Christopher and Joyce were climbing quickly, weaving through the crawling pilgrims. Someone was chanting a penitential psalm. Illesa reached for her beads. She would follow the sisters, with their bare pale legs, scabbed and scratched already.

The stairs were cold. It was hard to pray, climb and not get tangled in her skirts. She was falling behind the sisters – who'd obviously done this before and knew the way to move. On her right a very crippled man was pulling himself up each step with his hands, his useless legs dragging behind him. She must concentrate on the reason she was here or it would all be worthless. Illesa felt for the largest bead, began the prayer and then fell forward and had to stop climbing. She looked behind her. Perhaps she had gone thirty steps, no more.

Start again. Think of your sins, beg forgiveness for your lack of faith. If Reginald had lived, she would not be here doing this. Perhaps if she had not killed him, she and Joyce would be dead. Perhaps if she had gone straight to the innkeeper, and he'd called the watch and the Sheriff they would have been released. Perhaps they would have been convicted of his murder and hanged; certainly that would have been the case if the Prince had heard what'd happened.

She gripped her beads tightly. Those men didn't care how many children Reginald hurt. There was no real justice in this world. But Heaven's justice must be perfect, as Christ was perfect. The Virgin would know why she'd had to hide his body. It was the Devil making her doubt God's mercy. This was not her sin, it was Reginald's sin, and he had smeared her with it, daubed it on her, like shit or blood.

She did not need to perform more penitence. Christ the Lord looked down on all the world, and would judge it rightly, as He did in the great map. The creatures and misguided races, the great cities and hidden caverns were all part of His plan. And she needed to find her way through it, listening for God's voice, like Christopher underground, finding his way back from the deep darkness of the cave. If she didn't listen, she might be lost for ever, believing Satan's lies.

Illesa stood up. There were perhaps fifty more steps. She walked up them, her knees aching and stinging, and ignored the pitying look of the monk blessing the pilgrims at the top of the stairs. She was not going to allow the Devil to humiliate her.

It was a marvellous courtyard, painted and bright, with the sacred buildings hanging from the cliff rocks as if they'd floated there from another land. She crossed herself. Painted on the largest wall was the imposing figure of Saint Christopher bearing the Christ child. So far he had blessed their journey and brought them safely here, despite her own Christopher's drunkenness and injuries. He was young and used to a soldier's life. Maybe, at this shrine, he would find purpose.

A throng of people had gathered in a circle opposite Saint Christopher. She could not see what was happening, but from the ribald shouting it was not a holy ceremony.

"Here you are." Christopher took her elbow. "The Chapel of the Virgin is there." He pointed.

"What's happening?" Illesa wrinkled her nose as the chanting of the raucous group got louder. Joyce was trying to see over the crowd, on tip-toe.

"You don't want to know. Some kind of fertility dance in front of the Sword of Roland. Keep Joyce well away from it." Illesa pulled her until they had their backs to the balustrade. "They will be processing into Saint Michael's chapel very soon, the Cistercian Brother told me," Christopher nodded at a monk who was trying to break up the crowd with a flail. The pilgrims scattered reluctantly, and Illesa could see an iron sword stuck in the stones of the upper chapel. Below it a large chest was covered with flowers.

It seemed that Ramón had been standing on it. The monk flicked the rope at him, and he jumped nimbly down and out of reach.

"For the love of Christ," Illesa groaned. "What's he been doing?"

"Just joining in," Ramón said, running to hide behind them. "A poor young woman could not conceive and wanted help from the spirit of Roland. I hope to remember the words of the song; they were most amusing and unusual."

The monk with the flail stared round the dispersed revellers like a basilisk.

"Don't draw attention to us," Illesa hissed at Ramón. "We don't want to be thrown out before we've even entered the shrine."

"I'm going into the Chapel of Saint John. Are you coming, Ramón?" Christopher headed for the quieter chapel on their left with no one waiting at the door.

"Wait, where is Richard Orosius?" Illesa called after him.

"Moaning in the sepulchre Chapel of Saint Amadour." Ramón pointed to a stair that seemed to disappear off the edge of the cliff and skipped after Christopher.

"Come, Joyce," Illesa said. She must keep her close with everyone else scattered. There were so many different chapels, so much to see. But it was to Our Lady of Roc, Virgin Mother of Christ, that she must present Joyce. She would understand that Joyce did not deserve to be blighted by a man's sinful urges.

They mounted the blood-stained steps. The Poor Clares had already arrived inside the chapel and were kneeling at the back of the dense crowd. Candle smoke and incense wafted out into the sunshine of the courtyard.

At the front, in the shadow behind hundreds of candles, a man was intoning prayers in heavily accented Latin. Hard to understand. The people were shuffling forward on their knees as those at the front came before the shrine and then were guided out. Illesa put her arm around Joyce's shoulders and spoke into her ear over the noise.

"When we reach the front, pray for healing. Pray for deliverance from evil. The Virgin is Empress of Hell, she can defeat all demons, even the Prince of lies himself. Ask for her help and healing. We will only have a brief moment, and I must say prayers for William and Goodwife Kathryn. Bend your whole mind to the Virgin Mother and her mercy." She took both of Joyce's hands with her prayer beads, and kissed them. Joyce's eyes were wide, excited.

The crowd of kneeling penitents bowed their heads for the moment of confession. When she looked up at the end of the prayer, she and Joyce were almost at the front. Between the heads of the Poor Clares and a short man wearing a hair shirt, the shrine of the Virgin Mary in silver and gold was just visible, painted in blue, red and gold, surrounded by tall white candles. Illesa fumbled to take the mirror out of her purse, felt one of the coins fall to the floor. She could not afford to lose any. She searched around with her fingertips, but the crowd was pushing her forward, and, suddenly they were at the front. The coin was lost to her, perhaps a payment for her prayer. She opened the mirror, held it above her head pointing at the shrine, and prayed, picturing the daughter of Kathryn walking. At her side, Joyce's face was hidden by her clasped hands.

A loud clang startled her.

A bell hanging from the beam above their heads was reverberating. She could see the clapper still swinging. But there was no rope attached to the bell. All had fallen silent in the chapel so that the noise from outside, the Feast of the

Archangel procession and its military chant, sounded unseemly and loud. Joyce gripped Illesa's arm.

"Bow down, penitents of the Virgin, for she has performed a miracle! Bring me the book!" The priest beckoned one of the monks guarding the shrine.

"What's happening?" Joyce was staring around, frightened.

Illesa turned to the nun at her side. She was looking ecstatic, her arms raised.

"Do you know the meaning of the bell?"

Someone in the crowd began to sing – *Ave Maris Stella*.

"A sailor has appealed to the Virgin for aid, promising to visit the shrine, and she has heard and helped! The monk will write the date and time in the book, and when the sailor comes to the shrine, this miracle will be recorded. What a blessing we were here on such a day!"

Illesa could barely hear her, now that the crowd was singing. A person behind pushed her shoulder hard, trying to get near the shrine.

"Bless us too, O Holy Mother," someone called.

Joyce was knocked sideways, lost her balance. Everyone was on their feet, arms outstretched. Illesa grabbed Joyce's arm and pulled her up onto the first step before the shrine. Monks were streaming in from the back of the sanctuary.

There was space between the crowd and the north door. Illesa put her arm tight around Joyce and pushed between the pulpit and a woman in penitential rags. The woman fell back against the next line of the pulsing crowd. They dodged through the people running into the chapel, past the ranks of candles and out of the door into the bright sunshine.

Illesa led Joyce to the wall below Saint Christopher. All the pilgrims except for a handful of cripples had gone into the chapels. She peeled Joyce's hands away from her face.

"Are you hurt? Did the crowd crush you?"

Joyce shook her head. Tears had made trails in the dust down her cheeks.

She grabbed Illesa's hand and held it to her throat. And sang.

Chapter XXXVII

Hospitalet Saint Jean
Rocamadour
Sext

"You should think very carefully before you do that. I've seen what happens after a miracle has been claimed, and here it is even more frenzied."

"But we can't leave a miracle unrecorded. That would be ungrateful and disrespectful to Our Lady."

Richard Orosius brushed the little fallen leaves off the bench.

"They will take her away and question her. She will have to go alone. They may examine her to make sure she is a virgin. Is this what you want?"

Illesa looked over at Joyce, who was sitting with Ramón and Christopher under a walnut tree, laughing and playing some kind of game involving pebbles. She couldn't have heard what Richard Orosius had said.

"But it has nothing to do with that! It's her voice which has come back."

"They will claim they must be sure she is of good conduct, not consumed by sin. And you will have to reveal when, why and how her voice left her. It will be difficult for you to explain without giving away the secret you guard so carefully."

She shot him a sideways look. He noticed more than she'd thought.

"Then there will have to be witnesses to her muteness to give statements."

"Why would we lie?"

"You wouldn't, but there are plenty who do to get the attention of the crowd and the excitement. So they take pains to record only the legitimate miracles. Or so they say. The inspectors sent by the Pope to look into the claims about Thomas Cantilupe wanted witness statements, reports, details. If you want to claim this as a miracle, be prepared to be disbelieved. That will not do Joyce any good."

Richard Orosius was more measured and calm than she'd ever seen him. There were dark circles under his eyes, which were bloodshot and rather empty, but his speech was well reasoned.

"But if we don't acknowledge it, don't we risk losing the blessing – or something worse?"

"You can give thanksgiving in your heart. In fact we will all go and make thanksgiving in the chapel for this great healing, but we need not involve the monks. Make a donation, pray to the Virgin privately. She will understand the reasons for the secrecy, as she understood the need for the healing."

Joyce was walking towards them, leaving Christopher and Ramón talking intently about something, their heads close together, Ramón gesturing delicately with his fingers.

"What should we do now?" She sat down on the stone bench next to Illesa and slumped against her side. Illesa kissed her forehead.

"I've been speaking to Father Richard Orosius. He has much experience of the administration of miracles and believes it would be best for us to make private thanksgiving."

"The monks can be overzealous in their investigation of miracles," the priest said folding his arms in his lap. "It can be frightening."

Joyce's eyes widened.

"We don't have to," Illesa reassured. "The main procession and Mass will have finished by now, so we can go and make an offering in peace." Illesa stroked Joyce's shoulder.

"We should thank Our Lady for healing Father Richard Orosius too, shouldn't we? You are better aren't you?"

The priest looked at Joyce, half a smile on his lips.

"We will give thanks, indeed, for her help, because your healing has lightened my soul, given me hope. But no, I'm afraid this is just part of my suffering. I will feel flat and full of reason for a while, and then I will become enlivened, unreasonable, then maybe months later I will be filled with melancholy. It happens over and over, like one of the tortures of Saint Katherine who was broken on a wheel. Round and round this goes and each time I am more exhausted by it. I can only perceive it in these days, in between. There will be some days, maybe some weeks, when my mind will be clear, and I'm glad it happens now, when the leaves are turning, and there is so much beauty to appreciate in this vast Kingdom of God."

Joyce stared at him. Then realised she shouldn't.

"Maybe this time it will stop. Maybe she's healed you too."

Richard Orosius shook his head, frowning.

"There is too much yet to suffer. The forty years of wandering is not done. I must travel many more miles before I find my heart again."

He was looking inward – had stopped seeing them.

"Our Lady is full of mercy," Illesa said. "Let's go and give thanks. Then I think we should find a good room in one of the inns. We can celebrate tonight before we begin our journey home again." She would worry about their coin tomorrow.

"Can we eat meat? Please?"

"Yes, my darling. Roasted meat!"

Joyce jumped up and ran over to Christopher, shouting out the news in her strong voice.

Christopher got up, smiling, and walked quickly over to them. Behind him, Ramón looked as if he might start tumbling and turning cartwheels.

"I wish your father was here to share this. I wish angels could bring him to us." She looked at Christopher, who had Richard's eyes and nose, who could be mistaken for him in profile.

"Archangels are here today." Ramón pointed to the sky where large birds, certainly eagles, were circling in the warm air.

Joyce clapped her hands.

"Let's go now!"

She started skipping along the path that left the hospital grounds and led down the hill to the town.

"Joyce! You must walk properly. This is not an excuse to behave like an infant."

Joyce stopped and began to pull a face before remembering that she had been blessed by the Queen of Heaven. Christopher caught up with her and they began down the path together.

Richard Orosius didn't follow.

"I will explain that we no longer require the care of the hospital. Ramón!" he called. "Come with me to help carry the packs. We'll meet you by the chapel."

It was strange for Richard Orosius to be alert to the needs of the company, thinking of practical matters. For so long he'd been a grave concern, a wildly wandering planet. Now he was planning in the worldly as well as the spiritual sphere. Illesa nodded, temporarily speechless, and followed Christopher and Joyce down the hill.

"In all of Aquitaine, this must be the best wine, anywhere," Christopher remarked loudly, draining his cup again.

"More wine," Richard Orosius ordered. The innkeeper's son nodded and climbed down into the basement with the ewer.

"Should we?" Illesa spoke into Richard Orosius's ear. "Christopher has had too much already." She too was feeling loose and lightheaded. It had been so long since they'd celebrated with a feast.

"He's a knight. Let him drink. He has things he wants to forget. Pass the bread."

They had all eaten like starving peasants in June. There had never been a capon so well-seasoned. Nor a stew of goat meat that was as tender. Joyce had eaten well, although she struggled with the larger pieces of meat which she'd not had for so long.

Ramón had already treated them to a tale about the Virgin Mary outwitting Satan when he tried to steal a soul dedicated to her. Now he was sitting quietly, looking out of the window at the square. Soon it would be dark and they would close the shutters against the night air. He looked lonely.

"Are you missing your Mullida?" Illesa asked quietly.

He turned and smiled sadly.

"You notice many things. Yes, I miss her very much. She was intelligent and loving. Not a mixture we find in many people." He shook his head. "She was the kindest to me in all my life."

It was galling to be outdone by an ape – a mere animal and a sinful one at that.

"You don't believe me, but it's true. All the people I met since I was taken as a slave, they have used me or mistrusted me. All of them." He looked up. "You too." His large, brown eyes held her gaze. She had to glance down at the table.

"I'm sorry, Ramón. It was because of Reginald's attack," Illesa whispered. "I thought you would do us harm. I see now

256

that I was wrong. You've been a good friend to Christopher –" she petered out. Tried a new tack. "I didn't know you were enslaved. How did you escape?"

"Muslim traders in the middle sea. They took me from the port of Cartagena when I was only seven. A year later they bartered me for a woman. And I escaped from the house where the Christian kept me, hid in a ship. Landed in England." He rocked his cup to and fro between his hands. "London. I was so starved I could barely walk. Reginald found me on the street, just off the quay. Took me to the tent where the players stayed. It was this time of year, this Feast of the Archangels." Ramón looked up at the sky where the evening star had appeared. "He fed me and gave me a place to sleep."

Illesa did not want to imagine the unmentioned things he'd done to Ramón.

"After all that I'd suffered, I was grateful. He said he'd teach me to be a player myself. Looked after me. I was grateful," he repeated. "Later he showed me the magical secrets of his powers on the stage. The parchments. Made me swear never to reveal them to anyone else. He told me I was very special."

Illesa stared at her hands.

"But he used you ill."

Ramón said nothing for a while. Christopher was telling Joyce unsuitable tales he'd heard on campaign.

"He did. Then when I grew into manhood, he stopped. There have been other street boys since then. Would they have been better off starving? Reginald saved my little life."

"Isn't there Christian charity, alms that could be given to these children? It should not happen," Illesa said, too loudly. "I'm sorry. I can't forgive what he tried to do to Joyce."

Ramón drank from his cup and put on his animated, tale-telling expression.

"I am going to get a new monkey and train it so that it can do cartwheels with me. We will be in much demand everywhere. We will do Arthurian tales, not just from the Bible. We will meet dukes and earls who find life tiresome and make them laugh."

He put one ragged finger on her clenched hand. The first time he'd touched her.

"You must laugh. Life is not just work and prayer. Not only bad things."

She turned away and wiped her cheek.

"Can't you return to your company of players? The Prince, I mean the King, will be missing your entertainment."

Ramón shook his head sadly.

"No, our new King Edward is more fickle, more changeable now that he has power. The company called 'The Knights of the Round Table' have become his favourites, and they will be performing at all his tournaments. I saw him in Scotland, but he was not interested in my ideas." Ramón half-heartedly imitated the new King's expression of boredom. "You see, Reginald was the leader of our company, and he led us hard. With him gone, the players all went away. There are some sad costumes in a barn in St Albans, but that is all that remains of Daniel and the Lions."

"But how will you find a new patron?"

"I will get a new monkey. That is what makes my plays better than all the others. That is what makes my life happy. I know how to train them; they were in Cartagena when I was a child. They remind me of the good days with my sisters and my mother."

"You can stay with us for a while," Illesa ventured. Richard would be angry, but if she explained perhaps he would come round.

Ramón looked away.

"That's a kindness. But you have little need of players in Langley." He mimicked a villein drinking ale. "And there's a world of towns, ripe for entertaining, no? Richard Orosius will tell me which are the best."

"Ramón," Christopher shouted, although he was only a few feet away. "Come with me. I have something to discuss with you."

Ramón got to his feet, his hand resting lightly, briefly, on Illesa's shoulder.

"I go to bed after. Rest my heavy limbs. Sleep well."

He and Christopher went out of the door into the inn yard. Planning something unholy. Joyce was gazing around the hall with heavy eyes. Richard Orosius was resting his head on the table.

"Father, will you accompany us to the dormitory?" she asked, prodding his shoulder.

He looked up, blearily.

"Certainly."

They pushed the benches back and got up carefully. The wine rushed to Illesa's head, and she steadied herself on Joyce's shoulder. They went out into the cobbled yard. The sky was clear, starlit, and the cool air cleared her head a little.

"What coin do you have left, Father? Have you enough to get to Poitiers and back to Hereford still?"

"Don't tell everyone, but I have plenty." He looked at her hopeful expression. "If the cost concerns you, I can pay for the meal for everyone to thank you for your care of me when I was ill."

It felt like another answered prayer. They'd paid for his way from Bordeaux, as he'd been unaware of the demands of the journey. Now he was seeing it clearly.

"That would be a great blessing."

"You helped me in my time of need." He had stopped at the steps to the gallery. "In ways I cannot remember. I intended to be your guide, but instead I've been your burden. May God reward you for your charity to a sick and sinful man."

"God save you, Father. You have given us good guidance today. Tomorrow we may speak of the journey to come."

Richard Orosius did not reply. He gestured them ahead of him up the stairs and paused in the deep shadow under the upper gallery as they opened the door.

"I must speak to Ramón before I retire. May the angels guard you." He bowed and turned away, taking the steps quickly.

In the morning, she would bring up the subject of the jennet. If he was able to walk, they could sell it and get enough to pay for at least the journey to Bordeaux. Or he should pay them for it. He was in the right state of mind for realising his obligations.

There would be sufficient coin. Not for comfort, but to get them home. There would be no need to beg.

Chapter XXXVIII

Saturday the 30th September, 1307
Rocamadour
Prime

Illesa felt Joyce turn over next to her. She freed her trapped arm and shook it to get the blood flowing again. On the other side of Joyce, Christopher was on his back, his bandaged arm on his chest, mouth open, snoring. Sunlight was coming in at the edge of the shutter above their bed. On the other side of the dormitory, an open window showed bright blue sky. It was late. She sat up on the lumpy mattress, her mouth dry and foul. There was no sign of Ramón or Richard Orosius in the room. They must be up and preparing for the journey.

Illesa swung her legs over the bed frame and stood tentatively. Foolish of her to drink so much. Her head ached. Joyce was hiding her face under the blanket. She could sleep a bit longer, but Illesa needed Christopher's help to speak to Richard Orosius about the jennet. Today they must go back towards the Dordogne, a night in the Abbey Church in Souillac dedicated to the Virgin, for more thanksgiving, and then maybe they would have enough coin to take a river barge as far as Sergeac, which would significantly quicken their journey.

She went to the table by the door and poured water into the bowl to wash her face. She plunged her hands in, only then seeing it. A flash of silver on her left thumb. Reginald's ring, shining with drops of light. She brushed her hands dry on the cloth and pulled it off, holding it tight in her fist, a sinking feeling in her stomach. She ran back to the bed.

"Christopher, get up." She prodded his shoulder. He stopped snoring with a grunt. Turned onto his side but felt pain from his wrist and rolled back again. Eyes still shut. "Christopher!"

His eyes opened this time, blearily, and blinked.

"What?" he raised his head a little and thought better of it, lying back. Joyce sat up, her sleeping-cap askew.

"You need to get up. It's Ramón. I'm worried he's gone."

260

"Where have you looked for him?" Christopher muttered, closing his eyes again.

"No going back to sleep!" She shook his shoulder. "Get up and meet me in the courtyard."

Illesa adjusted her veil and helped Joyce get dressed.

The calls of early traders appealing to pilgrims rose up from the street.

"Are you well, Joyce?" She had not spoken yet. Perhaps she couldn't, and the miracle had been a dream.

Joyce rubbed her eyes.

"I'm very thirsty. Why would Ramón leave?"

Illesa patted her shoulder. At least that blessing was intact.

"Put your boots on and come with me." Illesa pushed the ring back onto her thumb where it wouldn't fall off and gathered their things into the pack.

"Quick, quick!" Perhaps he hadn't left yet. Maybe it was the putting on of the ring that had wakened her, and she could still stop him.

She went out onto the gallery overlooking the courtyard and peered over the railing. A man wearing a pilgrim's wide-brimmed hat was leaning against a wall while a farrier examined the hooves of a small pony. There was banging coming from the oven shelter. The innkeeper's wife emptied a bucket into the drain.

Illesa raced down the stairs, Joyce just behind her.

"Madame, excuse me."

The innkeeper's wife straightened up and wiped her hands on her apron.

"Yes?"

"The Castilian of our party – have you seen him?"

"Yes." She was a large woman of few words.

"When?"

The woman grimaced. She shook out her stained apron.

"A while ago. At first light."

"What was he doing? Where is he now?"

"His companion, the tall priest, paid for everything and they left together."

"Both of them?" Illesa looked around the courtyard. "Did they take the jennet?"

The woman looked at her as if she were touched in the head.

"Of course they took it. It's the priest's horse."

She picked up the bucket and turned to go.

"Wait, you said they'd paid. What did they pay for?"

"Everything. I told you. The beds and the food and drink. You still drunk?"

Illesa shook her head. Joyce was about to cry.

"Did they say where they were going?"

The woman kept walking away.

"Why would they tell me?" She trundled into the hall.

Illesa took Joyce by the hand.

"Run and make Christopher get up! Tell him they've gone."

Illesa went to the gate and let herself out of the inner door. The street was busy with pilgrims and traders. It was almost a Michaelmas Fair, with so many small stalls selling trinkets and food. It was probably useless to try to catch them when she didn't even know what direction they'd taken.

She pushed through the crowded square and onto the less busy street that led to the Porte Figuier and the road south. Ramón had said he was going to buy a monkey in one of the southern ports. She couldn't remember which. But surely Richard Orosius wouldn't go that way. He was supposed to be heading to Poitiers. He had letters for the Pope. They'd been planning something together that she knew nothing about.

The guard at the Porte Figuier was yawning. He leant on his pike and eyed her suspiciously.

"Good morrow, master. I seek two men who left early this morning. One a priest, in a black cappa clausa, on a bay jennet. The other a Castilian, short, with a green tunic and brown cape."

"What do you want with them?" The guard looked her over. "Did they rob you? We've had some men here pretending to be clergy, make off with all sorts." He started listing them on his fingers. "Crucifixes covered in jewels, candle holders, goblets."

"No, he didn't steal anything." The jennet perhaps, but not intentionally. She could not send the hue and cry after him for that. "Have you seen them?"

The guard licked his lips and shook his head. His cap fell a bit lower over his eyes.

"I've only just got here. No one like that's gone out yet. Plenty have come in though. Here, you'll have to move. There's

262

a party just coming now." It was a mixed group of pilgrims, all barefoot and singing.

"Can you ask the guard who was here before you?" Illesa shouted over the din.

"The night watchman will be asleep. You'd have to pay me plenty to risk waking *him*, I tell you. Here, present your seals and documents," the guard said, stopping the group.

She would get nothing more. Illesa walked as quickly as possible back to the inn.

In the courtyard Christopher was talking to the stable boy, a tankard of ale in his good hand. Joyce stood at his elbow, arms crossed on her chest, the trace of tears on her cheeks.

"They woke him up at matins." Christopher tilted his head at the stable boy. "Got him to open the gate. Didn't say anything of where they were going."

"And the jennet is gone?"

In reply Christopher swore under his breath.

"We must talk in private." She turned to the stable boy. "Is there a room we may use?"

"Madame!" the boy shouted.

The innkeeper's wife came out of the hall and incuriously led them to a chamber off the hall.

"Bring small ale and bread, if it please you," Illesa said. Joyce looked up. "And milk."

"That will cost extra."

Illesa waved her away. She felt like cursing her unhelpful back, front and sides.

"Have you got your purse, Christopher?" He nodded. "And everything in your pack?"

"I know better than to let it out of my sight." He sat down on the stool and rested his head on his good hand. They waited until the innkeeper's wife had returned with a tray and gone again.

"Open it. And your purse," Illesa said. "I need to know if he left any coin for the horse."

Illesa tipped the contents of her own purse out and spread their combined coins on the table.

Joyce was staring at Illesa's hand, her mouth slightly open.

"Don't worry, Joyce." She pulled the ring off her thumb quickly. "I'm going to put it away. When we get to Sergeac, I will give it to Gaspar. You'll never need to see it again."

"Why do you have it?" Joyce whispered.

"Ramón took it from me last year. He'd threatened to use it to accuse us of Reginald's murder if we didn't give him coin. But he must have put it on my hand while I slept last night and —" They might never see him again. He'd disappeared just when she'd begun to understand. Illesa's eyes filled with tears. "Where do you think he's gone, Christopher?"

He looked down at the small pile of coins on the table and swore again.

"Gone to get a new monkey. Gone south."

"But why would Richard Orosius have gone with him?"

He shook his head.

"Christ knows."

"Didn't he say he had more miles to go?" Joyce looked at Illesa. "Yesterday, in the hospital garden, he said he had to travel in the world God had made, to find his heart or something like that."

"Maybe he never intended to return to Hereford. He seemed eager enough to leave. And they certainly wanted to see the back of him." Christopher took a long gulp of his ale.

"I asked for them at the south gate, but the guard had just arrived and knew nothing. Can we catch them up, do you think, Christopher?"

He laughed and spread the coins across the board with the palm of his hand.

"If we had ten times as much and could buy two swift rounceys, maybe. But on foot, hours behind, without knowing where they go? No." He pushed the hair out of his eyes. "And what would we do when we caught them? They've decided to go another road. Ramón has chosen a new friend. We can't force them to come with us. The fact that this leaves us poor and exposed to the dangers of the road will not have occurred to them."

"I should have mentioned the jennet last night when Richard Orosius said he would pay for the inn." Illesa put her tight fists side by side on the table, remembering. "Then he left to speak to Ramón. Actually you were speaking to Ramón for a long time last night, Christopher. What was that about? Did you know he planned this?"

"Don't be foolish!" Christopher looked up from his contemplation of the coins. "We were discussing other matters."

"What other matters?"

"It is not your business!"

"Don't start to quarrel!" Joyce banged her hand on the table. "It was so lovely last night; we were so happy. Don't ruin the miracle by being horrible to one another."

Illesa took a deep breath.

"I am just trying to work out what we're going to do. If Christopher knows more about it, then he should tell us."

He sat down on a stool, arms folded, mouth firmly shut.

"Very well." She stared at the sparse display of silver on the table. "Is this all the coin you have? But two shillings? Where has it all gone?"

"It's my coin. I can do what I wish with it."

Illesa opened her mouth, but saw Joyce's expression and closed it.

She counted her coin twice. With the coin she'd lost in the chapel yesterday, and all the extra expense of the horse, she had only four shillings and five pence herself. That would barely pay for their sea passage home. She'd been relying on selling the horse to retrieve enough to ease their journey.

"Check your packs."

They all looked, taking all their belongings out and laying them on the table. No extra coins had been stowed inside by Ramón's deft fingers.

"Richard Orosius has certainly taken the jennet without paying for it."

"But Ramón gave you the ring. We can sell that," Joyce said.

"No," Illesa said quickly. "I must return it to Gaspar. And in any event, it would not fetch nearly as much as the horse."

"Father Richard paid for the lodging and food. He must have thought that was his share."

"He has little experience of the cost of things, then," Illesa grumbled.

"So, as you are the leader of our diminished company, I expect you have a plan," Christopher said bitterly. He drained the rest of the ale and poured some more.

"Don't be nasty, Christopher," Joyce said. "Just because you've drunk too much and have a sore head. We're all sad because we've lost a friend. Don't make it worse." She sniffed and looked away towards the window where the grey cliff of Rocamadour was shining in the sunlight.

He took her rebuke silently as he never would from Illesa.

"We can't afford river passage from Souillac to Sergeac, so we will have to walk. Once we get to the Templar house, they will lend us the coin we need to go on to Bordeaux. We must save as much as possible of what we have left, stay in the abbeys and hospitals along the way. Find a group leaving today and join them."

Christopher groaned.

"All these groups are full of dull, tiresome –"

"Shut up," Joyce told him. "If you'd kept more of your money we would be able to take a river boat."

Illesa looked at her children. They were a very long way from home. The thought of how far made her shiver. Richard would be horrified by their situation, if he knew. It was up to her to beat back despair and get them home.

"There is an Abbey Church in Souillac dedicated to Our Lady. And I hear there is also church to Saint Martin, so you both will be blessed and kept safe. Pack all the bread. We will not eat again until this evening."

Illesa swept the coins into her hand, poured them, with the ring, into her purse, and went to find the innkeeper.

Chapter XXXIX

Monday the 9th October, 1307
Templar Preceptory
Sergeac
Nones

They limped into Sergeac like stray dogs. The Templar preceptory seemed well maintained, with a good wall, a tall painted church tower, and what looked like a substantial hall. Christopher knocked on the gate door. No answer. He knocked again. An inner door squealed on its hinges. A Templar sergeant stood in the doorway. His eyes took in their road weariness, and he relaxed his sword arm.

"In the name of the Lord, what's your business?"

"Sir Christopher Burnel and Lady Burnel to see Father Raymond, we pray," Christopher said. He cleared his throat. "And this is Lady Joyce Burnel," indicating Joyce, standing miserably in her wet cape.

"Good God, we thought you were dead!" The sergeant moved aside. "Come in, you're welcome in God's name. Tell the Father!" he shouted behind him. "The English have arrived!"

They stepped through into the porch.

"Come this way. I will take you to the parlour and arrange for your lodging. Father Raymond will come soon. He's with the cellarer, but won't be long. Ah, here is Brother John. He's had his eye out for you the past week!"

Sir John stood awkwardly grinning in the middle of the courtyard, frozen. Joyce started to hobble towards him.

"If the women could stay at the back please, Sir Burnel. You understand it is part of The Rule. We must not touch them – and should look on them as little as possible." He frowned at Sir John. Christopher grabbed Joyce's arm. The sergeant herded the small company towards a low building with the Templar cross painted on the door to the north side of the yard. "Right, in you go. Sir John, I'd be obliged if you would go to find the guestmaster," he said tersely.

The room was dark, despite the open shutters. The sergeant rushed about lighting lamps. Joyce was shivering. There'd been a shower of rain at tierce, and she'd never dried out. Their slow pace meant she'd never warmed up either and had spent hours sneezing and coughing.

Illesa whispered in Christopher's ear. He nodded and turned to the sergeant.

"Good Master, we are so grateful for your help. My sister is very tired and cold. May she be given some warm wine, please, to fend off the cold?"

"But of course!" he said, not looking at Joyce. "You all need refreshment. I will arrange matters. Wait here, and it will be brought."

Illesa sat down beside Joyce and put an arm around her. She needed a warm meal and a good bed. And not to have to walk for a few days. The past two days Joyce had only managed short distances, saying that she ached all over. Perhaps it was a fever coming.

Father Raymond arrived as they were just drinking their first cup of steaming wine.

He came in and raised his hands to bless them. They all bowed their heads. When they looked up, he'd sat down on the chair at the end of the room.

"Welcome! I only recognise one of you – the Lady Burnel."

"My son, Sir Christopher Burnel, and my daughter, Joyce. We are grateful for your hospitality, Father. It's been a long and painful journey."

"But a necessary one, I believe. I have heard the tale from Sir John. He is new to our Order and perhaps became too involved in your company. As did I – during your last visit to Gascony." Father Raymond met Illesa's gaze and crossed himself. "God forgives such innocent mistakes."

Father Raymond was grey haired, and thinner, but neither his voice nor his authority had weakened.

"Sir John behaved well," Christopher said gravely. "I did not. But Our Lady of Rocamadour has been merciful and gracious to us."

Father Raymond raised his eyebrows.

"Thanks be to God. And you were not attacked on the road?"

268

The priest and Christopher spoke for a while about the journey. Father Raymond seemed entirely indifferent to Illesa, as if she were a stranger. But she couldn't summon up any anger at the Templar. Her eyes were heavy. It was the knowledge that they were safe. Perhaps she could rest properly for the first time since leaving home. Joyce's eyelids were already drooping.

"This is enough for today. You must eat and sleep, and I will meet you after the Office of Tierce tomorrow for a longer talk, Sir Burnel."

"Father," Illesa got to her feet. "First please tell me if the player, Gaspar, lives and if he's here? I was told he'd followed you from Bordeaux."

"Sir John told me that you seek him. He is in a Lazar house nearby. Now that you have arrived, we will have him brought here. Even he is better able to make that journey than you women are in your weakened state."

He got up.

"Here is the guestmaster to see to your needs," he gestured at a man waiting outside the door. "May you rest well in the care of Saint Pantaléon, our Holy Helper, and our gracious Lord."

The servant showed them to the guest hall stair and went no further.

"Come to the refectory when you've washed and changed." He looked only at Christopher. "The sustenance for the women will be left here on a tray."

He pointed to the bottom step.

Illesa pulled herself up the stairs behind Joyce.

The room held six wide beds, all empty. Two had been made up with sheets, pillows and blankets. A trestle table and two benches were pushed against the wall next to a low door. At the far end was a stone hearth with a small fire.

Joyce sank onto a bed and lay back, groaning.

"Here, I'll help you with your boots." Illesa knelt down next to her and began to unknot the leather thongs.

"God bless these men who know the value of a good bed," Christopher said, feeling his mattress. He dropped his pack next to it and went to wash his face in the basin of water. Illesa peeled the wet hose off Joyce's legs.

"Oh Joyce." Illesa examined her bare feet sadly. They were white, wrinkled, the skin blistered and peeling. The little toe was purple under the waterlogged skin. "We must let them dry out, and then I'll put some ointment and bandages on them." Joyce tried to swing her legs onto the bed, but Illesa pulled her up. "No you don't. Get changed out of those wet things first or you'll make the whole bed damp."

The tunics in their packs were barely drier. They put them on and dragged the bench to the hearth, raising their feet towards it.

"Your food has arrived. I'll bring it up and go," Christopher said from the doorway.

Illesa followed and took the tray from him at the top of the stairs.

"It is important that you don't talk about the attack on Joyce, Christopher, even if you've had some wine. It may make them reluctant to help us," she whispered.

"You think I don't know that, Mother?" He went down the steps. "Here you are not the one making the rules, and you are certainly not the leader of our company. I am." He crossed the courtyard making for the open door to the glowing refectory.

Joyce ate quickly, and Illesa tucked her into the bed nearest the fire. She lay like the dead, immobile, so exhausted that even in sleep she barely moved.

Illesa dozed by the fire for a while, adding sticks to keep the blaze going.

Christopher came in as the compline bell rang. He'd obviously been excused from going to the Office. He avoided her glance, probably wishing she was already asleep. It was so frustrating to be blocked out of conversations with Templars. They would of course be very strict here, in one of their main houses, even though Illesa and Joyce were no threat to them. She kept her eyes on the fire.

"You stayed long. Were you speaking to Sir John?"

Christopher sat down on the bench as far from her as possible and began removing his own boots.

"He asked about the journey, the shrine, the miracle," Christopher said wearily, still not looking at her. "He was delighted that Joyce can speak, although she obviously can't speak to him. He's going to collect Gaspar tomorrow. It isn't far. He should arrive the day after, he said."

It was strange that she'd been looking forward to seeing Gaspar so much when she would have to tell him such upsetting things. It would be a terrible meeting for him. She was regretting insisting on it.

Perhaps after all their struggle to get here, he would be too ill to meet them.

"Did he say anything of Gaspar's condition? Is he able to walk?"

"I asked Father Raymond. He's still walking – it's his fingers that have suffered most." Christopher sank onto the bed. He stretched out his bad arm and wiggled his own fingers. "They have a Brother who is a skilled doctor, called Pantaléon in honour of his healing work. He'll examine me tomorrow."

Illesa's stomach lurched. He might not approve of the way she'd treated Christopher's wrist. But it was good to have a leech nearby. Perhaps he would be willing to look at Joyce's feet. Joyce had woken and was sitting up. The food and warmth had done her good.

"What did Sir John say about the miracle? Was he amazed?"

Christopher gave her a sceptical look.

"He said what everyone says: Praise Our Lady, give thanks for her great mercy. You don't expect him to say it's because you are so very holy do you?"

Joyce turned red, threw her pillow at him and sulked for a minute.

"Did you tell him about Ramón and Father Richard?"

"Of course. I had to explain why they're no longer with us. He was disappointed not to hear more of Ramón's tales. But he also called him strange and ungodly."

That was not so, Illesa thought vaguely, her eyes heavy with fatigue. Ramón was strange, but there was something pure about him, despite his untruths. Something that was stronger than piety. That was what they missed so much.

Chapter XL

Wednesday the 11th October, 1307
Nones

The Templar servants had set up two benches some distance apart outside the west door of the church, as lepers were not allowed into the preceptory and certainly not allowed to use the same goblets or beds. So Gaspar was still in the wagon in which they had brought him. Hidden inside. It was like the players' wagons, except it was covered in black cloth not bright colours – more like a funeral bier. The mules had been taken to the stable and the shafts were propped up on a barrel.

"Sit down, all of you," Sir John said. Did he want to reveal Gaspar in a dramatic gesture of some kind? She couldn't speak to him in front of the Templars. What she had to say was private.

"Can you ask Sir John to allow us to be alone with Gaspar?" she whispered in Christopher's ear.

He looked uncomfortable, but got up and spoke closely with Sir John near the wagon. The Templar nodded slowly and beckoned the servants.

The Lazar servant looked dubious, turned to the Burnels and cleared his throat.

"Touching is forbidden. You are allowed only the time between now and vespers, which Gaspar will attend through the church squint. He must sit opposite you here," he pointed to the empty bench, "These are the rules of the Lazarite Order. Gaspar of St Albans understands them very well. Do you?"

They all nodded, admonished by his solemnity.

The servant went to the back of the wagon and unknotted the canvas. A head emerged and the Lazar servant held Gaspar's arm as he climbed onto the step, and then to the ground. His face wasn't covered, which was a mercy, and it looked almost normal, although much aged, and the skin around his nose and lips had thickened. His hands were bandaged and held at an odd angle. But his feet were steady. He didn't look up at them until he was safely seated on the bench, and then he treated them to one of his old smiles. Illesa felt the tears start in her eyes.

"Gaspar!"

"It is indeed I. Dutifully present at your side as ever, although you would not want me there." His voice lisped on some sounds.

"It's so good to see you alive! I thought you'd died without telling me. This is Joyce, you last saw as an infant, and you remember Christopher, don't you?"

"I have lasting memories of you riding me like a horse," Gaspar said, bowing his head. "And now I hear you have become a knight, one that has been to war with the King." The old Gaspar would have mimed some jest at the King's expense. "It is actually the *King* who has died without permission. And what do we think of the new one?"

Illesa put her hand on Christopher's arm as he launched into a description.

"Gaspar, we have so little time with you. Let's not talk of kings."

"Very well, very well." His hands moved briefly in the way they used to when he would gesture his meaning, subverting his words. He tried to lick his lips, but he ended up drooling and didn't wipe his mouth. "You wished to see me and you have come a long way to do so. I'm grateful, but ashamed at the state you find me in. It is not easy to sit here with people who knew me before. And Joyce is rudely staring." He made a scary grimace, like a demon, and Joyce giggled. "I can still do it, but only once a day. Don't ask me for more." Gaspar looked around. "No food or drink. Perhaps we can request some? I have my own cup, and the Lazar servant may pour for me?"

Christopher got up.

"I will ask for some ale. Or would you prefer wine?"

"I am not asked my preferences any more but instructed to be grateful for whatever I am given," Gaspar said meekly. "Wine, if you please."

Christopher gave him a crooked smile and disappeared round the other side of the church.

"Gaspar, why didn't you tell me that you left Bordeaux? Richard and I were so worried about you when there was no word."

"How gratifying. I did it just so you would feel that way." He tried to wink. "Stop looking so horrified. I paid a monk to write to you and the lazy sod didn't do it. Instead they kept taking your coin in my upkeep, I gather. I thought you'd given up on me, but it was just the corrupt clergy as usual. Oh I shouldn't say that out loud, someone might be offended."

Christopher was back, and sat down a little further away.

"They are going to bring wine and bread."

"Excellent. I can't tell you how tedious the diet is in the Lazar house. No one gives money to lepers these days, it's all to the Hospitallers and the Franciscans, while we live on peas and maslin."

"I will make arrangements," Illesa began.

"Marvellous," Gaspar said. Again his bandaged hands rose and then subsided. Illesa leant forward.

"I must tell you of why we are here – why we came to Gascony, before we're interrupted."

"I thought you looked jumpy. What have you done now?"

Illesa opened her mouth and closed it. She'd rehearsed what she would say, but with Gaspar in front of her, vulnerable and hoping for good news, it was impossible. Joyce shifted beside her.

"We met your twin brother," Joyce said, glancing at Gaspar, then at her feet. "He called himself Reginald. Reginald the Liar."

Gaspar's expression froze, then he nodded slowly, waiting.

"He was at the feast when I was knighted last May," Christopher said, looking only at Joyce. "Daniel and the Lions were entertaining Prince Edward."

Gaspar dropped his head, looking at his useless bandaged hands in his lap.

"I thought he was you," Illesa whispered. "But then we spoke to him. He came to our lodging. We asked him about you."

Gaspar's head snapped up.

"What did he say?"

"That he didn't know where you were. That he'd last seen you many years before. That you'd given him this."

Illesa opened her sweaty palm and held out the silver ring.

Gaspar was frozen again, staring at her hand. After a long moment he spoke:

"Did he give you that to return to me?"

"No." Her voice was hoarse. A Templar servant was walking towards them from the preceptory gate, carrying a tray. She hid the ring in her fist.

They sat in silence watching him approach, lay the tray on the ground at a distance and leave. Illesa's heart was pounding.

"You'll have to call the Lazar servant to get my cup and pour it for me," Gaspar said.

Christopher looked around. There wasn't another soul in sight.

"Use this one." He took his own tankard from his belt, poured the red wine carefully in, and placed it between Gaspar's outstretched hands.

Gaspar bowed his head.

"I thank you for that kind gesture. Your mother will know how to wash this thoroughly afterwards." He raised the tankard in both hands. "Let us drink together and give thanks that we all still have a stomach."

Joyce sipped at the strong wine. Christopher emptied his cup with one gulp. A bird chirruped on a nearby tree.

"Gaspar," Joyce said, not looking at him, "your brother tried to rape me. Mother had to kill him."

Gaspar stared at her, mouth open. He turned to Illesa, then covered his face with his bandaged hands.

"I shouldn't have been so friendly to him," Joyce was saying. "But he was so funny. And he was always saying nice things to me." Illesa touched her hand, but she carried on, tears starting down her cheeks. "He fooled me into trusting him. What he did to me made me lose my voice."

"The truth of the matter is he wanted revenge on William," Christopher interrupted. "William had tried to help an apprentice that Reginald was using."

Gaspar still hadn't moved or looked up.

"I want to know why he was so bad!" Joyce cried. "Gaspar was always a good and trusted friend, Father said. And yet his brother was a devil. Why? It doesn't make sense!"

Gaspar raised his wet eyes and stared at Joyce.

"That is the question. You have it. That is the question."

"We didn't want to kill him, but he was trying to kill us! Mother had to. William had to hide the body in the river. It was horrible for them too."

"But the Virgin of Rocamadour has helped. We asked her for mercy and she helped Joyce to recover her voice." Illesa wiped her cheeks. "I'm sorry Gaspar. I'm sorry to bring you this news."

Gaspar shut his eyes, sniffed, then met Illesa's gaze.

"Let us drink to Joyce, who is alive and well." Gaspar picked up the tankard, tilted it into his mouth, put it down carefully and wiped away the drips from his chin with his sleeve. "Do you know what they told me when I joined this Lazar house? They said that I should pray that there would be another crusade so I could go and fight the infidel, and that would wipe away the sin that I had committed which had caused me to have leprosy. I should pray that I could die in the Holy Land killing Saracens, so that I could reduce my suffering in purgatory." He lifted the tankard again, drank deeply, then lowered it to his lap. "I do not pray for this. More death, more death!" He raised his arms in the air and the tankard fell onto the ground, spilling purple onto the sandy soil. "That's what they call for." He looked sadly at the disappearing wine. "As if there wasn't enough already in this fallen world where young boys are tortured and ruined and turned into devils by their fellow Christians."

He looked up to the sky. A few leaves were falling from the walnut trees, drifting in the light breeze.

"My brother protected me. He pretended to be me. It stopped the master player raping *me* every other night – after our mother abandoned us into his care. Pollux said it was his duty to protect me, as he was the eldest. He kept me safe from that monster. But he couldn't stop it eating away at his soul. The sin was sown so early. The cruelty he was shown grew huge inside him."

Tears were falling onto his numb cheeks. He looked at all of them silently for a moment as they sat rigid on the bench.

"Forgive him what he did to you, what he tried to do. For my sake. Forgive him. He was ruined by another. That man should be in Hell, not my brother, please. He was protecting me."

He held out his bandaged, stunted hands in supplication. Illesa couldn't watch. She looked down at her lap.

"I will forgive him, Gaspar," Joyce said. "Although he hurt me, and pulled my hair out, and betrayed me. I will forgive him, because you've asked me to." She clutched her prayer beads and began to mouth the Pater Noster.

"You are an angel. The forgiveness of a child is the most powerful." Gaspar tried to get to his feet, perhaps wanting to embrace her, but he weakened suddenly, seeing the alarm in Illesa's face and sank back onto the bench. "I'm sorry for this spectacle, but I have no pride left, no pain either except loneliness. One day soon I will join my brother in death, and I would like to meet him as a child, innocent, before he was corrupted." He began to weep again.

Illesa glanced at Christopher. He looked embarrassed, sitting on the edge of the bench as if he were about to bolt. This was not the Gaspar he remembered.

"Christopher, please get my pack from the guest hall."

He got up and went quickly without argument.

Joyce had stopped praying and was looking helplessly on as Gaspar wept.

"Gaspar —" Illesa went towards him and knelt down on the ground in front of him. "I will forgive your brother his sins against us, if you forgive me for killing him and hiding his body."

She raised her clasped hands and shut her eyes.

At first there was only the sound of Gaspar's sobbing.

"I forgive you, Illesa Burnel," he said, his voice thick, "for killing my brother."

"And I forgive your brother, Pollux, for his sins against my family, now and forever. Amen."

There was a floating sensation in the empty space before her closed eyes. When she opened them, leaves were falling around her, coming to rest on her cloak. She looked at Gaspar. He was wiping his nose with his sleeve. She placed the ring on the rough wool of his tunic and backed away.

"This needs to return to you. It's yours now."

He looked at her and nodded, taking a deep shuddering breath.

"I cannot wear it on my hand, but if you would be so kind as to ask the Lazar servant to string it on a leather thong, I will wear it around my neck and pray for him and you each day." He patted his chest. "The servant will not believe me if I tell him you gave it to me. They think we are all sinful liars, not to be trusted, especially me and my tales." He smiled his old smile.

"Come back with us, Gaspar," Illesa said getting to her feet. "Come and live near us! We'll look after you. I've told you often enough over the years. Then you will get good food and not be lonely."

"Yes, Gaspar! Come back with us," Joyce cried, jumping up and down on the bench.

Christopher was returning with the pack, his expression apprehensive.

"The journey would kill me, and then you'd be responsible for the deaths of both brothers," Gaspar said lightly. "You wouldn't want that."

"We could get a cart," Illesa began. "And besides it will all be by river or sea until we get to England."

Gaspar cocked his close-cropped head in his old way.

"Illesa, we have little time together, let's not spend it arguing," he said in a faultless imitation of her voice.

Christopher handed her the pack and poured more wine into his cup. Noticing the upended tankard, he gestured at Gaspar with the flagon.

"No more for me; it is stronger than I'm used to now. Just some bread to take with me. You would be disgusted to watch me try to eat it."

Illesa felt around in the bottom of the pack.

"Here, I nearly forgot. Richard sent it for you. He had it refilled with holy oil, blessed at Canterbury." She held out the battered lead ampulla threaded on a length of black leather, the grooves of the bowl smooth with much touching. Remembering he couldn't reach out to take it, she placed it on his lap next to the ring.

"It helped me when I went to war," Christopher added, his voice catching. He cleared his throat. "I was able to anoint a fellow knight before he died. It gave him comfort."

Gaspar nodded and patted it with his lumpy hand.

"Just like Sir Richard to send an old bit of rubbish, not useful coin," he said in his mocking stage voice. "Joyce, you have nimble fingers. Thread this ring onto the leather for me."

"Perhaps it's best if I do it," Illesa said, and gathered them from his lap.

Joyce frowned at her.

"Of course." Gaspar tried to make the face of a fool. "I'm unclean. How could I forget?"

The Lazar servant was approaching from the gate. Above him was a crescent moon the colour of a sunset.

"Here comes the keeper of time. We must say farewell."

"Will we not see you tomorrow?"

Gaspar made an exaggerated disapproving expression.

"We leave at prime. I have already cost too much time and effort for the Lazar knights. We must return to the Lazar house by sext," he said imitating his keeper. "But answer this one thing before you go."

"What is it?" Illesa put the loop of leather over Gaspar's head and stepped back. The servant waiting by the wagon frowned at her.

"What happened to your weasel? You aren't carrying a pouch full of wild, snapping teeth any more."

"It's so unfair," Joyce said. "Christopher had one when he was younger than I am. All I'm allowed is a little dog."

Another figure had appeared near the church. The tall and unmistakable Father Raymond.

"My weasel, Eve, drowned soon after you last saw her. And Christopher's bit Cecily, which took ages to heal. That was the last weasel we had." Illesa nodded at Father Raymond. He'd stopped by the bench, his hands hidden in the white sleeves of his habit.

"You don't want to hurt Cecily, Joyce," Gaspar said, standing up awkwardly. "That would lead to starvation. Find a new pet without teeth, like a talking parrot. Then it can insult her instead."

Joyce shook her head, laughing. She glanced at Illesa mischievously.

"I want a monkey."

"One should not consort with creatures even more fallen than we are ourselves." Father Raymond's voice was mild, but his eyes fixed on Joyce before he raised a hand in the air and made the sign of the cross. "May you be blessed in your journeys, arrive safe in the hands of Our Lord through the mercy of the Mother of Heaven." They all looked up again at him. "You have said your peace and your farewells. Now to Vespers."

Chapter XLI

Friday the 13th October, 1307
Matins

"Get up! Quickly!"

Illesa jerked awake and sat up.

"What? What's happening?" The only light was a guttering lamp in the hand of the old Templar servant.

"The soldiers of the King are at the gate; they have orders to arrest everyone. I must get you out now." He pulled the blanket off the bed. "We go through the store rooms, this way." He pointed at the small locked door at the far end of the guest dormitory. Behind him, Christopher was already gathering his things.

Illesa shook Joyce's shoulder, putting a hand over her mouth.

"Get up! We have to go right now."

Joyce gasped out of sleep and sat up staring wide-eyed at Illesa.

"Hurry! Get out of bed."

She pulled the boots from under the bed – began to put Joyce's on.

"No time!" The old man hissed. "They are coming! Bloody King Philip's men. Carry it all and follow me."

Illesa stuffed their boots into her pack, grabbed Joyce with the other hand and stumbled after him. The servant stopped at the door, licked his fingers and snuffed out the lamp.

"Don't make a sound." In the sudden darkness they heard the door creak open. "Shut it behind you."

Christopher, who was last, closed it carefully. There was no light. Behind her, Illesa could hear Joyce's breath coming in frightened little gasps. She was only in her shift and coif and would soon be cold. In front of her, the old man stood completely still, listening.

"Hold onto my tunic," the servant whispered. "Walk behind me." Her eyes strained to see. On either side were even darker shapes – perhaps bales and barrels under the steep sloping roof.

The air was stale and close. Behind her, clinging to her tunic, Joyce tripped and nearly pulled her over. The servant stopped short. They had reached the other end of the attic.

The servant turned around, his pale face just a smudge in the darkness.

"Shhhh."

They all listened.

A door slammed below them. Someone shouted, but it was too muffled to hear what was said. The soldiers were below them, searching the storehouse where barrels of wine were kept. The servant ran his hands over the wall, found a handle and pulled, letting in a crack of dim light.

"Put on your dark cloaks. You will be seen in those tunics," the man whispered in her face, his breath foul with decay. "This is the hayloft. Hide there until another takes you further. Don't come out, no matter what you hear." He shuffled past them, back the way they'd come.

They fumbled with their belongings, trying not to drop anything on the floor. Illesa bent over and crawled into the lesser darkness of the barn. Joyce was just behind, getting caught up on her trailing cloak. There was almost no room in the loft, it was so crammed with bales. Below, the cows were lowing, waiting to be milked. There was hay dust in her nose, and she had to stifle a sneeze. She pulled Joyce into a small gap between a stack of bales and the slope of the roof.

Christopher was closing the door, on his knees, listening. He squeezed into their hiding place.

A man was shouting in the yard.

"Where's your priest? We have the sergeants and the servants, the preceptor, and two knights. We know your priest is here. He was seen yesterday. Bring him out now!"

"What on earth is going on?" Christopher breathed.

"The priest went to the Lazar house yesterday. He is due back today." It was the voice of the guestmaster.

"And where are your guests?"

"We have none, master."

"But guests were seen here. I have a statement from the Bailiff."

"They left by river yesterday, when Father Raymond went. They'd come to see him."

282

A door slammed followed by clattering on wooden steps.

"Anyone in the guest quarters?"

"No one there. But the beds look slept in."

"So the guests did not leave yesterday. Tell me now and escape a beating."

"They left, I tell you. The servant has failed to clean the room, as we were not expecting anyone else. Especially not a company of King's soldiers," the guestmaster said, sounding aggrieved.

"The charges against you are serious. Be glad you are not already in chains. Search him for weapons and take him to the chapter house with the others. You four search the church again."

The lowing of the cows became so loud that they could hear little else.

Christopher crept out to look over the edge of the hayloft. After a few moments, he reappeared in the gap where they hid.

"There's a ladder. The barn door is open. The river is just on the other side of the wall. No one would hear us over the clamour of the cows."

"No, we must wait." Illesa whispered, taking their boots out of her pack. "Joyce, here are yours. Someone is coming to help us. Father Raymond will have arranged it." She bent over and tried to pull them on in the small space. Christopher did not reply. Maybe even he didn't want another argument about the leadership of their company in these circumstances. They were in no position to take matters into their own hands, not knowing the escape routes out of the preceptory. Christopher's sword had been relinquished to the guestmaster when they arrived. They were without defence against a large company of soldiers who'd taken even the Templars by surprise – at the instigation of the King of France. If they didn't have help, they'd be taken prisoner and might never be freed.

Joyce was trying to do up her boots underneath her cloak, breathing raggedly.

"God will guard us, my darling."

Joyce looked at her mutely. Then a sound made them all start. The low door was opening. Christopher scrambled away from it.

A man's head peered out.

It was Sir John, dressed in an ordinary dark brown tunic, a wide hat in one hand, Christopher's sword in its scabbard in the other. His lips were firmly pressed together to signal silence. He proffered the sword to Christopher.

"Two soldiers," he mouthed, pointing to the yard. "We wait for them to pass."

They nodded at him, held their breath. The voices of the soldiers came and went between the lowing of cows.

"They are going to the stables," Sir John breathed. "Stay behind me." He crawled to the edge of the loft and looked down. They crouched behind him, waiting. Straw was falling through the wide gaps between the floorboards. It would give them away if anyone noticed. Suddenly, Sir John swung his legs over the edge and started down the ladder.

Joyce went after him, her long cloak gathered over her arm. Illesa threw her pack over her shoulder and clambered down next. They joined Sir John crouching by a cow pen.

Christopher, with his broken wrist, was clumsy and much slower. They watched him, holding their breath.

"Let me strap this on properly."

They waited by the warm, pungent cows while he adjusted his sword.

"I'll take that for you," Sir John whispered, and shouldered Christopher's pack. He looked round the frame of the barn door. The sky was the grey of predawn. "We go to the dovecote and stop there. Now."

He dashed across the empty space of the yard, and they followed, Illesa holding Joyce's hand. They all shrank into the shadow. The sound of iron crashing on wood came from the direction of the church. The doves rustled and cooed between the blows.

"God preserve us," Sir John whispered. He looked both ways. They couldn't see any soldiers, but the angle of the building walls meant that they would be exposed as soon as they left the west side of the dovecote. "Father Raymond has told me how to get out of the drain. It won't be guarded. Wait here until I signal."

He went a few paces, looking left and right, then dashed towards the high stone wall. At its base was a shadow that might be an arch. For a moment, he crouched down into it, then turned and beckoned. When they reached him they all huddled against the cold stones. The archway was blocked by a double gate. Sir John pulled back the bolt and opened one side. A stone-lined channel of murky water flowed under it, down to the Vézère beyond.

Sir John dropped into the channel and reached up his hands to help Joyce. They ducked under the arch, walking through the dirty water.

"You can't with your wrist. I'll help you, then close the gate," Illesa whispered in Christopher's ear. She gave him her arm. Christopher gripped it and leapt down, splashing up dirty water. He waded after the others. She held the top of the gate and pulled it closed as she lowered herself into the stinking drain.

"Hold onto me," Christopher whispered. He'd waited for her. "You don't want to fall in this filth." They waded on – into the river mist until Sir John stopped suddenly. He pointed to the east.

"Two more guards at the gate," he mouthed. He crouched down and went on very slowly.

Illesa allowed herself a quick glance. The main watergate was only thirty paces away. The guards stood facing the preceptory, to prevent the Templars escaping. A wooden walkway led from the gate to a river jetty. A small fishing boat was moored on their side of it.

That was where Sir John was taking them. They would have to wade through the rest of the drain, the edge of the river and get into the boat without being heard.

Illesa felt very cold. She held on to Joyce's cloak in front of her. God would not have brought them safe all this way, blessed them with a miracle only for them to drown or become prisoners. She moved her feet slowly in time with the others, her back bent, her heart banging against her ribs. If anyone happened to look, they would resemble some kind of humped river monster.

The flow of the drain became slower and then the stone ran out. They were in the river and there was mud underfoot. It was harder to go quietly. The boat was still twenty paces away when someone spoke on her right-hand side. Illesa froze.

"How long before they've searched it all and we can get some ale? I've been up all night with nothing to eat or drink."

The guards' voices had carried as if they were only a few paces away.

"You think you're the only one? Shut up in the meantime, I'm trying to sleep."

"Sleep standing up, eh? If the Sheriff catches you, he'll lock you up with them." The guard stamped his feet. "It's fucking cold. I need a piss."

Sir John sank onto his knees, now waist-deep in the water. They all slowly followed. Joyce gripped Illesa's cloak with one hand, the other covered her mouth. Something brushed against Illesa's ankle underwater. She bit her lip. A fish or eel – or just river weed. It was all swirling around them, mist and water and mud. They could not stay like this for long. Joyce was shivering and her wide eyes were terrified.

But on they had to go until they came into the shadow of the jetty, and they could stand up against the timbers. Sir John signalled for them to wait and pushed out towards the boat, the water now up to his chest. He placed Christopher's pack inside and began to untie the rope from the jetty pillar. The moments stretched. The river was a mirror of the dawn sky.

Eventually Sir John pushed the boat within their reach and stood up, streaming water. He took Joyce first and lowered her in. She crouched down by the thwart. The boards of the walkway thudded and groaned. The guard had finished his piss and was stamping his boots on the wooden planks as he went back to the gate, trying to get the blood moving.

Disturbed by the noise, a family of ducks raced past the boat into the deeper river, complaining loudly. Illesa got half her body over the side, Joyce pulled her arms, and she knocked her head against the thwart as she slid in.

Christopher hauled the upper half of his body onto the boat, and Sir John pushed his legs in. The boat swung out. Illesa and Joyce peered over the stern, but Sir John did not jump in. He started pushing the boat further out into the river, his head above the water. He looked like a swimming dog.

When they were in the main current, out of the view of the guards, he pulled himself up a little.

"Help me in," he gasped. Joyce and Illesa pulled one of his arms, Christopher the other, and they managed to get his chest over the gunnel, then heaved the rest of him in, sodden and heavy. He lay for a moment, curled up on the bottom of the boat, making a great puddle of water.

"We need to get him warm," Illesa said. "Put this cloak on him, I'll share yours, Joyce." They sat in the boat, huddled together, shivering. The rising sun glowed on the water as they drifted downriver like a fallen leaf.

"What is happening, Sir John?" Christopher asked. "Why is the King arresting the Sergeac Templars?"

"I don't know." Sir John could barely speak through his chattering teeth. "Father Raymond found me before the soldiers did. He said I was new to the Order and not of their preceptory and should flee with you."

Father Raymond bore no love for King Philip – had denied him Richard as a prisoner all those years before. But this time, King Philip had come for the Templar priest, contrary to Papal protection.

"We thank God for his care. Did he escape?"

Sir John shook his head.

"He distracted the soldiers while we got away by hiding in the crypt."

Christopher shook his head.

"God preserve him. They'll all be thrown in gaol, while bloody King Philip confiscates their land to pay off his debts."

"Trumped up charges of heresy." Sir John clutched the cloak closer around his body. "That's what Father Raymond said."

"But it can't be *all* the Templar holdings. He wouldn't dare." Christopher picked up the oar in his good hand, peered into the forest on the west bank of the river. "He couldn't do that, could he?"

Chapter XLII

Prime had long since been rung from a church somewhere along the river, and the sun had risen above the trees, but they remained unwarmed. There was a stiff breeze and clouds were gathering. Joyce shook beneath her cloak. Christopher, trying to steer with his one arm, was a good colour, but Sir John was pale, nearly blue, and could not hold his oar. He desperately needed shelter and warmth.

"We must put into shore and get help," Illesa said.

No one replied. None of them knew the area – which towns were safe.

The river drifted on, going slowly around wide bends. They passed other fishing boats, but Illesa didn't dare call out to them. They didn't know why the Templars had been arrested. A war might have begun. Which side would claim them, and which kill them?

As the river began to straighten, a high, rugged promontory appeared on the left bank. There was a crenelated tower at its peak. More fortress buildings emerged behind the promontory. The whole of the tall cliff was studded with dwellings.

"Troglodytes," Joyce cried.

The boat rounded the base of the tower in front of a broad port with several jetties overlooked by a timber guardroom on a high platform.

"We must stop here and beg for help. Please God and Saint Christopher they are good Christians." Illesa bent over the Templar. "Sir John, can you speak?"

"Yes," he stuttered.

"You must say that you're a pilgrim like us; we are part of the same company. Our boat capsized." He still had his thick beard, which could make them suspicious.

She and Christopher managed to row the boat out of the current, closer to the jetty. A helmeted guard was watching them, his crossbow on his shoulder. They attempted to throw him the rope. The guard did not pick it up. Christopher stood up and tried to grab hold of the jetty pillar.

"Master! This man is ill. We need warmth and food. May we beg help from the lord of this place?"

"You can beg. Doesn't mean you'll receive," the guard said, putting his crossbow down beside him. "But you don't look capable of harming a mouse." He held out his hand and Christopher threw the rope again. "Eh, Milos. Come and help me with these drowned rats, you lazy sod."

Another guard peered down at them.

"God, where were they spewed up from? Drag that boat round to the low jetty. They look too weak to climb. Pilgrims eh? Out of their depth."

"We'll put them in the guard room. Stoke the fire. No one else is due to arrive until the afternoon."

The men pulled the boat along to a low jetty and slung the rope around a post.

"Are you a knight?" the first guard pointed a finger at Christopher. "Before you get out, hand over that sword."

Above the port, an array of lodgings were crammed on terraces in the cliff. People were climbing impossible steps carved into the rock. Smoke rose from the thin fringes of thatch. Somewhere a smith hammered on an anvil. Wheeled pulleys drew loads up in large baskets. Five levels of buildings, one on top of the other nestled in the narrow ledges. Joyce stared at it, open-mouthed. It seemed to float above them like a vision of an angel-lifted city.

"Do you want to stay in that boat staring, or are you getting out to see La Roque Saint-Christophe?" The guard looked amused. Christopher had already disembarked and was helping to heave out Sir John.

"Saint Christopher's Rock?" Illesa got up and steadied herself against the wooden planks of the jetty before climbing out. "Praise him for saving us by your kindness." She offered her hand to Joyce, who stepped out as gracefully as she could in her heavy, wet clothes, conscious of all the male eyes upon her.

They trailed along the gangway after the first guard, holding Sir John up under his shoulders, and came to a stop at the base of the lookout platform. The second guard was at the rear, examining Christopher's sword. They'd not yet noticed Sir John's. He was barely conscious, leaving heavily on her shoulder.

"Can he climb the ladder?" The second guard prodded Sir John with the scabbard.

They heaved him up between them somehow. The guardroom was scarcely furnished – only a rough table, two stools and pile of blankets. But there was a brazier, and it was lit. They lowered the knight down next to it.

"Strip off all those clothes. We'll give him an old tunic to save his modesty," the first guard said. They soon found his sword.

"You a Templar?" the first guard asked, poking Sir John's shoulder.

"No. A knight. He grew his beard as part of his pilgrimage, to shave it off when he arrives at the shrine," Illesa said quickly. "We had an accident, and you are the first town we came to. We owe you thanks for saving us from the cold."

"This isn't cold! You should be here in January when the wind blows upriver. Freezes in places, it does." The first guard was pulling the hose off Sir John's long legs. "But what did you want to swim in it for? Is it your first time in a boat?" He smirked at them, subsiding when no one smiled back. "Here, fetch me those blankets and the tunic over there, and then you get back out on guard duty, Milos. I should stay here. Don't like the look of this one."

Sir John had closed his eyes and flopped forwards. They put a blanket down and laid him flat, covering him until all that could be seen were his blue, slack lips. The first guard stopped Milos at the top of the ladder.

"Quick, get Mother Sarah. Send up the call. We can't have a pilgrim dying without offering up such a fine beard."

Milos nodded and went to the ladder in the corner of the room, pushing open the trapdoor onto the upper platform. He disappeared and a moment later a bell clanged four times, deep and loud.

The first guard joined them all kneeling around the knight. He put his hand near Sir John's mouth.

"He's still breathing. Do you want us to summon a priest as well?

Illesa felt his skin.

"I'll heat some wine – if you have some?" Illesa said. "I think he'll revive if we warm him up."

"Mother Sarah has remedies for everything. He'll soon be on his feet." The guard got up and looked in the jug on the small table. "They've drunk it all, the greedy swine." He turned to Christopher. "Where's this knight from, then?"

"Chartres, I believe. We were just travelling together. We don't know him well," Christopher said, rubbing his hands in front of the small fire.

"Do you live in the cliff?" Joyce pointed as if the walls of the tower weren't there.

"In the fortress? No. I stay down here by the port. My wife lives up there. She prefers it that way. But today I've got to climb up because I need the blacksmith to fix my dagger. The rivets came out. Quick job for such a long climb. And Sundays I go to church."

"There's a church?" Joyce looked delighted. "In the cliff?"

"It's quite wide up there. Plenty of room for churches and the Augustinian Priory. That's where Mother Sarah is. She'll be along soon, flying down in a basket."

Joyce's eyes were shining.

"Can I watch?"

There was a rapping on the ceiling.

"Soldiers coming downriver!" Milos shouted. The bell started to ring again, this time it went on and on. The first guard was out and down the ladder. For a large man he moved very quickly.

Illesa went to the arrowslit in the wall, Christopher just behind her. The angle was unhelpful, but eventually a boat came into view – a large low-slung barge. There were about twelve soldiers, armed with bows and pikes, four of them pulling the long oars.

The door opened behind them, and Illesa swung round, her heart thumping. A nun was standing in the doorway, surveying the room. She was slight, her expression intelligent, curious. Mother Sarah was an Augustinian canoness, by her habit. She placed a basket and ewer on the table, went back to slide the bolt across the door and turned to them, smiling.

"Welcome, pilgrims, in the Lord's name. Now let's see, let's see." She knelt down next to Sir John and drew the blankets down, feeling the skin of his neck with the back of her hand. It was hard to tell how old she was. Her face was young and lively, but her hands spoke of many year's work. "What is this poor soul's name?"

"John," Illesa said quickly, "John of Primey."

"The soldiers are landing at the port," Christopher said in her ear.

Mother Sarah pulled the blankets back up to his chin and went to the table with her basket, beckoning Illesa.

"Are you familiar with making syrups?" Illesa nodded. The nun began to unpack the basket. "We pour in the ingredients and you stir it continuously until it begins to thicken, while I pray for the knight."

She took out a copper pot, a fabric pouch, a cerecloth packet and a stoppered bottle.

"Do not worry about the soldiers." Mother Sarah began to squeeze the packet and honey dripped out into the pot. "We are a fortress with many crossbowmen. A few of the King's forces will not worry them. All those on the lowest level of the cliff will have their arrows aimed at the barge. Now, come away from the window, young knight."

Christopher backed away reluctantly, feeling for his sword which wasn't there.

The nun poured sweet-smelling wine over the honey, broke a piece of brown bark in two and dropped it in. "Add these herbs only when the syrup is thickening," she said, giving Illesa a small fabric bag. "Now, I need your help, young lady." The nun smiled at Joyce and made a place for her beside Sir John. "We will say many prayers and also many blessings. This man is not ready to die, so we will call his soul back to his body. Listen to my words and repeat them."

Illesa tried not to turn away from the syrup that was bubbling in the fire to watch Joyce and the nun. When it was a good pouring consistency, she added the herbs, crushing them between her fingers. Motherwort, pennyroyal, vervain. She stirred it as the scent filled the room. Mother Sarah was reciting an unfamiliar rhyme, her hands on Sir John's chest. Joyce was mouthing along, but her eyes were on Christopher by the window.

"A party is arriving from the fortress. Maybe the Steward? They are marching to meet the soldiers on the jetty," Christopher reported.

"The Steward will tell them to leave in no uncertain terms." Mother Sarah got to her feet. She looked at the pot that Illesa had taken off the fire, picked it up in her hands without noticing the heat and placed it next to Joyce. "Spoon the mixture onto his tongue. One spoon and then a Hail Mary, then another. Can you do that, girl?"

Joyce nodded, took the thin wooden spoon from the nun's hand and dipped it into the syrup, tipping it into the knight's open mouth.

"If he doesn't swallow, stroke his throat." Joyce looked surprised, then nodded.

Mother Sarah drew Illesa towards the door.

"I have some influence here, but you must tell me the truth, or I cannot help you. The arrival of the soldiers after you is not a coincidence."

Illesa shook her head and pressed her hands together.

"By Saint Christopher, please help us. We are just pilgrims."

Mother Sarah looked pointedly at the man lying on the floor.

"I said that you must tell the truth. I believe that of you and your daughter. But the knights?"

"Christopher is my son," Illesa whispered. "Injured in the war in Scotland. This man —" she hesitated. Sir John had saved them from imprisonment, and now he lay at the mercy of strangers, vulnerable to whatever the soldiers would do to an escapee. The canoness was a woman of God; surely she would not allow a Templar Brother to be arrested. "He is a Templar Knight, only recently joined the Order. The soldiers raided the preceptory where we were staying, accusing the Order of heresy, all kinds of nonsense, and imprisoning everyone. He helped us escape in the boat."

She felt breathless, dizzy. What would be happening to Father Raymond now? And all the other Templars who'd looked after them?

"The preceptory at Sergeac?" The nun had gripped her hands – was looking straight into her eyes.

"Yes, soldiers of the King came before dawn. We were all asleep." Illesa glanced at Christopher, cradling his broken wrist. Joyce would not be safe in any gaol. "Please protect us." She looked into the nun's dark blue eyes. "We have been to Rocamadour. The Virgin blessed us with a miracle. Please don't let us be captured by these men! They will use us ill. We may never get home."

The nun nodded. She squeezed Illesa's arm.

"Yes, of course. I saw it before. After what happened to Pope Boniface, it was inevitable. The Order of the Temple was too much in the thrall of Mammon, and now the King of this World will take it from them, and break and burn them, as he did to the Cathars. But that does not mean that the innocent should be swept away with the sinful." She squeezed Illesa's hands. "We will get you to safety. Pray that silly guard doesn't tell of your arrival." She went over to Christopher at the window. "What have you heard?"

Christopher was ashen.

"The King's sergeant said they tortured one of the Templar servants, and he admitted there had been a visiting Templar knight and guests in the preceptory. They found footprints on the river bank. They know we've come this way, and another barge of soldiers has just arrived."

Chapter XLIII

Friday the 13th October, 1307
The Fortress of La Roque Saint-Christophe

Illesa watched Joyce spooning the syrup attentively into Sir John. It was pointless, as they would all soon be taken away in chains, and he would probably die on the barge. While in the preceptory, Father Raymond would be manacled and humiliated. She'd not had the chance to speak to him properly since they'd walked all those miles to Sergeac. There'd always been the Rule of the Order between them. His wisdom barricaded from her. Now he'd given them a chance to go free, while he was taken away to be tortured. They would never see him again.

Mother Sarah was at the window, listening. She turned suddenly, looking around the room.

"The Steward has invited the soldiers to search the port, but no further. We have little time. They are already tethering the boats. Come. Look." She beckoned Illesa to the door and unbolted it, opening it a crack. At the base of the cliff there was a shed covered with drying, filleted fish and, next to it, the basket the nun had presumably descended in, attached by a rope to a pulley far above. "It can take three," she said. "You two carry Sir John, and get in alongside him. The girl will stay here with me, and no one will question her devotion. A new postulant for the Augustinian Priory." She looked approvingly at Joyce.

"Can't she fit in too?" Illesa put her arm out to her daughter. Joyce got up from where she'd been sitting, looking from one to the other.

"No. The rope will break if we overload it. No time to argue. Go now. You won't be seen if they're still on the jetty."

Christopher ran to the arrowslit.

"They're still there, just mustering and dividing the search."

"Can you carry him?"

Illesa looked at Christopher with his bandaged wrist.

"Yes, if necessary we will drag him," he said, bending down. Illesa picked up Sir John under his arms.

"Just hold his legs off the ground, Christopher."

The nun shook her head

"You won't manage him like that on the ladder. I'll help you."

Despite her slight frame, Mother Sarah went down the ladder first, holding Sir John's feet on her shoulders and bearing most of his weight. Illesa and Christopher lowered him by the shoulders of his tunic, one rung at a time, until he lay on the ground like a corpse.

Joyce was standing at the top of the ladder, her face tight with fear.

"Don't let them take her," Illesa whispered to the nun. "Keep her safe."

The canoness patted her shoulder and climbed back up the ladder, as one used to doing so a hundred times a day. The people of St Christopher's Rock lived steep lives. The echo of boots on the gangway got louder. Illesa heaved Sir John up under his shoulders and started stumbling backwards, Christopher lifting his legs with one arm and following. It felt as if her arms would be wrenched out of their sockets before they finally reached the base of the cliff.

The basket was narrower at the bottom, high on the sides, tied on three sides with thick ropes. They tipped him in. He slumped to the bottom, and they climbed over him, breathing hard. A bell started ringing. The canoness was on top of the guard room pulling the bell rope. Five peals.

The basket lurched, hung suspended for a moment a foot above the ground, and then moved upwards again, swinging wildly. Illesa was pressed against the side by the weight of Sir John, Christopher balancing it opposite. The wheel of the pulley squealed with the weight. Illesa shut her eyes, her head spinning. Were they rising – or falling in empty space?

The basket halted, jerked a little and dropped down suddenly before it stopped again. It spun and swayed in the cold wind.

Illesa looked up along the rope. The top of the pulley was not far away, but the turn-wheel had stopped. Christopher got up to look out, and the basket rocked even more violently.

"Sit down," Illesa said, her eyes shut.

"The soldiers are on the roof of the watchtower," he said. "They are swarming all over the port like ants."

"Can you see Joyce?"

"No. The nun will have her safe. She seemed capable of leading a battalion, never mind fooling one."

"Can you see why we aren't moving?"

Illesa felt cold sweat creeping down her temples. She gripped the side of the basket.

"Someone is going into the wheelhouse. It should start moving soon." Christopher sat down, making the basket sway again.

She prayed all the rest of the way as the basket lurched upwards and finally came to a stop. They were next to a platform extending out of the cliff on timber struts.

"This is a strange load. A half-naked man and his wet companions," a man said, looking over the side of the basket. "What happened to Mother Sarah? Have those soldiers taken her hostage?"

His smile belied his words.

"I'd like to see them try," Christopher grunted.

"Why am I nearly naked in a basket?" Sir John asked in a hoarse, uncertain voice. "Am I in Hell?"

"Not yet," the pulley man said. "But if I drop you, you'd be there soon enough, so stay still!" He reached out and grabbed one of the ropes, pulling the basket over to the platform. "Now you can get out. Mind you don't pull too hard, or you'll push the basket away and fall into the gap."

Christopher clambered out first and held one of the other ropes steady so that Illesa could climb onto the platform.

"You hold this rope; don't let go whatever you do." The pulley man put her hands around the basket rope. He turned to Christopher. "You, take his other arm." They leant into the basket to grab John's outstretched hand.

She pulled on the rope feeling her feet sliding on the slippery wood of the platform, trying not to look down. They brought his torso up and slid him onto the planks. He seemed as weak as a baby. The other man who worked the wheel leant against the brake and stared at them in amusement.

"What happened to him?" the pulley man asked. "Looks healthy and fit enough, but he's as weak as a lamb." Sir John was pushing himself up to sit, his legs hanging over the end of the platform. One of his hands was trying ineffectually to cover himself with the tunic.

"He fell in the river and got very cold." Illesa knelt down next to him and pulled the tunic over his braies.

"He'll be even colder in a minute. The wind blows like the bellows of Hell up here. Get off the edge now, and go and wait in that barn until someone can come and sort you out. You'll need to explain yourselves to the leader of the hundred on this side of the wall."

The sound of ringing rose up from the port.

"That's the bell. I've got to put the basket down again. Those bloody soldiers have caused all this extra work. Come on Savi, back to it." He climbed into the wheel and started it rolling, then slid out as the rope unwound quickly. The pulley man took hold of the brake. "Nice and easy when there's no cargo."

Illesa pulled Sir John's arm, trying to help him to his feet.

"Can you stand?"

He made an effort, and she and Christopher got him to his knees.

"Where are my clothes, my sword?" he asked, looking from one to another. "Where are we?"

They half-guided, half-dragged him away from the platform to the barn and sat him down with his back to a bale of straw. A goat was tethered nearby. Sir John shivered in the thin tunic, looking up at them like a child. All his things were still in the guard house, where the soldiers had no doubt already found them.

Illesa put her cloak over the knight and went back to the wheel platform. From this height, the people looked tiny, like the creatures on the great map. A large group of soldiers had gathered on the path next to the guardroom, and others were scattered around the port, checking in boats, knocking on large barrels.

On the level below them, the gatehouse drawbridge cranked up noisily. Joyce and Mother Sarah would have to come up by basket or not at all. It was still swinging between them and the ground.

"What's happening? Why haven't you sent it down?"

The wheel man gestured towards the tower.

"Waiting for the signal. They haven't confirmed the drop. I don't want to send it down and bring up an enemy."

"Why haven't they come up yet?" She peered out again, but her eyes weren't good enough. "Christopher!" He was still in the barn, examining the way it was attached to the cliff. "Come and tell me what's happening."

He walked to the edge and stood next to her.

"Do you really think they will take a nun hostage?"

"If they are arresting Templars, they're willing to do anything."

"Sir John left them at just the right time to avoid being tortured."

"That's not why he left! He wants to return to his own commandery near Chartres. Father Raymond made him leave to guide us. We never would have escaped without him." She looked up at her son severely. "Christopher, you won't tell him about the torture, will you?"

"He will find out."

"But don't tell him until he's had a chance to recover. He doesn't need more cold humours now."

Christopher smiled disbelievingly and shook his head.

"You are so naïve. Do you think the Seneschal of Périgord is going to walk away and leave his escaped prisoner to sport himself with Troglodytes?" He waved his hand at the soldiers lining up on the jetty. "He will just keep torturing them until we give ourselves up."

"No. He's not a demon. These are men of God. They can't treat them that way." Illesa squeezed her damp skirts in her fists.

Christopher leant further over the edge of the platform.

"I think that's them." He pointed at a figure in black on a walkway just below them skirting the lowest level of the fortress. A smaller figure was following, carrying a basket.

"Yes, that could be them. But they have to go through the fort entrance and the drawbridge is up."

"They aren't heading that way. Look. The walkway loops round the rock to the other side of that outcrop."

They were already out of sight.

"What's happening down there?" She pointed to the port.

"The men are just standing around. I imagine the Steward and the leader of the company are negotiating."

"What if they found his clothing in the guardroom?"

"I think we should find a safer place to hide." Christopher took her by the arm and they went back to Sir John. The goat was chewing on his tunic, but he hadn't noticed because his head was cradled in his arms. "Can you stand now?" Christopher asked impatiently. "We need to move."

Sir John looked dazed. He was still shaking with cold. At any other time, Illesa would be tending him. But Joyce was in danger.

"I'll try."

"Good." Christopher took his arm. "Let's see where that walkway goes."

They had to go very slowly, but in any case they were stopped and questioned by everyone they came across. Strangers in this enclosed town were unusual. After trying to go through an old woman's shelter to get to the other side of the outcrop, they were told to wait there or be taken to the gaol. A guard was put outside the door. They sat in the small room on stools while she stared at them.

"Please, Goodwife, will you find Mother Sarah and tell her where we are?"

"Mother Sarah is it?" She stuck her head out of the window and bellowed upwards.

The call was passed on and on, from person to person, echoing around the rock walls and ledges.

"She will find you," the woman said. "You all look like drowned cats. Stay here out of the wind." She riddled the fire on the hearth and turned back to the dough she'd been kneading.

"Who is the lord of this place?"

"Bérialle." She gave Christopher a hard look. "He has no love for the King of France nor the King of England. This is his own independent kingdom."

"Except anyone could come down from the land at the top of the cliff, couldn't they?" Christopher said, running his hand over the holes drilled through the rock to hang things from.

The old woman shook her head at him.

"We have lived here for many generations. We have our ways, our defences. It isn't easy coming off the cliff, a thousand

300

paces up. Why risk all your soldiers in our rabbit warren? Most people decide to leave us alone. You might wish you had too." She picked something out of her few remaining teeth and slapped a piece of dough onto the stone.

Despite her words, she made them small flat cakes on her fire stone, flavoured with anise. And despite the fear for Joyce, even Illesa felt sleepy.

She knelt next to Sir John.

"How do you feel now?" She picked up his wrist and felt the beat of his heart. His fingers were still white and very cold.

Sir John shook his head.

"I don't understand where I am."

"Do you remember leaving the preceptory?"

The door opened as he looked at her quizzically. Mother Sarah stood there, her hand on Joyce's shoulder. Illesa bolted towards her – but stopped when Joyce did not move.

"Your daughter is quite well. An accomplished player of parts. Most impressive."

Joyce smiled happily.

"I got them to believe I'm a postulant, even though my clothes were so wet. Mother Sarah arranged a veil over my head!"

"Yes, we've had some fun at their expense, but there are serious matters to discuss now. I must see your pilgrim seals. Things must be done in accordance with the decrees of the Church even in these confusing times." She held out her hand.

Illesa and Christopher opened their packs. Illesa took the testimonials in their cerecloth wrapping out of the special pocket she'd made and handed them to Mother Sarah. She glanced over them, examined the seal, did the same to Christopher's and handed them back. Christopher was still going through his pack, looking worried.

"Thank you, that all seems in order. And blessings be upon you, Petronilla." She made the sign of the cross in the air above the old woman. "Your cakes are still the best in all of Roque. Follow me, English."

Christopher stuffed everything back in his pack and got Sir John to his feet. They struggled to keep up with the nun as she adroitly turned in and out of passages and up steps until they came to a higher, wider part of the town. At the end of its long passage was an arched door under a painted cross. She led them in.

"You are allowed in this room only," she said, indicating that they should sit on the wooden benches.

Sir John slumped down, his head cradled in his hands. She reached into a niche carved in the stone and rang a bell. Joyce was following Mother Sarah's movements much as she had followed Sir John's when they were travelling to Rocamadour. A journey that seemed months and months ago.

Another nun came through a side door. Mother Sarah nodded at Sir John.

"Sister Helena, this man has been in the water too long and needs care. God will reward you if you take him to the infirmary."

The young nun looked around the room, sniffed and smiled widely.

"You all smell like the river, bless you! Come with me," she said, pulling Sir John up and holding his torso. "We will cover you in fleeces and feed you nectar." She chuckled joyfully. Sir John looked at her as though she were an angel and stumbled through the door by her side.

Mother Sarah closed it behind them. When she turned back to them, her expression was sombre.

"You three deserve to know what is happening. I'm fortunate that the Steward is my kin and takes my advice from time to time, so I was there, with my new postulant, when the Seneschal, Gaillard Daundos, was speaking to him at the port."

She went to another niche in the corner of the room where a jug and four cups were set out. She poured out the liquid and gave a cup to each of them. Christopher took a sip. Then a long drink. Mother Sarah sat down and held her cup out reverently.

"This is our mead. Our bees live at the top of the town and fly out all over the valley. And God fills our cups with flowers." She gave thanks and drank. "You will need this for my news." She looked from Christopher to Illesa and back. "The Knights of the Temple are being arrested across all of Aquitaine, across all of France. Every place had orders from Philip the Fair to imprison them and confiscate their property. The charges are heresy, spitting on the cross, fornication, denying God, worshipping idols. All the usual slanders he employs. So your

302

friend, the young knight, cannot go safely back to his commandery. Where was it?"

"Chartres," Illesa whispered.

The canoness nodded.

"If he returns, he will be arrested there, taken to Paris, held in the dungeon under the palais. The Templars from Sergeac are being marched to the tower at Domme."

Christopher got up and paced the width of the room.

"How can he do this? The Templars are under the protection of the Pope!"

"Pope Clement," Mother Sarah sighed. "He is one of our own, but not. A Gascon, but truly under the thumb of the King. High Priest ordained by God, but afraid of worldly power. I fear the King shows his contempt by not even consulting him. Sit down, young knight. You must try to control your anger. We live on top of one another here. There is nowhere to go if you are always annoyed, so we practise thought, not wrath."

Christopher sat down, looking like thunder. He gulped the rest of the mead and had to control a coughing fit. Joyce thought it very funny.

Mother Sarah placed her cup beside her and folded her hands in her lap.

"It is time to decide what you will do – what your family will do now. Here you must choose." The nun fixed each one of them in turn with her bright gaze. "The soldiers will surround our town, as much as they can. They know the knight is here, or they strongly suspect. They have threatened to burn the town – and we would go up like a candle. But it is not you they want. They will take you if they find you, but it is the Templar knight they are charged to arrest."

They all stared at the door through which Sir John had disappeared, then Mother Sarah crossed herself.

"What he chooses to do is up to him. When he is better, he will decide. We have strong defences, but the Seneschal knows we are vulnerable to fire. Will you leave him and go now, before the soldiers have surrounded us, or will you stay with him?"

Chapter XLIV

Illesa and Christopher stared wordlessly at each other.

"I want to stay here!" Joyce cried. "We've only just arrived, and Sir John needs us. It wouldn't be right to leave him. I haven't seen half of the caves yet – or the workshops. You got to go up in the basket, but I didn't."

"Child," Mother Sarah said. "Come and sit with me. This is a decision that you do not fully understand, wise as you are."

Joyce slid up next to the nun, looking chastened. She seemed to be devoted to the canoness already, and not to have suffered from the terrifying flight from Sergeac. Illesa took a gulp of the mead to settle the trembling in her chest. More decisions, with a young man's life at stake. What would have happened if they hadn't been there in the Templar guesthouse that night? If they had never come to Gascony? Sir John wouldn't have been at Sergeac, but he would have been captured at another Templar house. Was God trying to save him from this torture by putting him in their company?

"What are your dealings with the Templars at Sergeac?" Christopher asked.

"Sometimes they buy our honey," Mother Sarah shrugged. "Other than that, little enough, but we admire their work protecting the vulnerable. Without the Templars, many pilgrims would have died, their vows unfulfiled." Mother Sarah took Joyce's hand in hers. "We cannot see what the purpose of this deed is yet, for good or evil. Is it to stop an excess of greed in the Templar Order? Will it purify it? Will it destroy it for ever? Is God or the Devil prompting the King? We cannot say. But I doubt they will find any evidence of malefaction, idolatry or worship of ungodly spirits among the Templars. These accusations are malicious. I'm sure you agree."

She was looking straight at Christopher. He turned to the small window.

"How long will the Steward protect Sir John? Does he know that you have hidden him?" he asked gruffly.

"No. It seemed better for him to speak to the Seneschal in honest ignorance. And I have tied the tongues of the guards. However, the Steward will know by now. He has returned to the fort, and the news will reach him swiftly. He will come here wanting answers, demanding to see the knight." She smiled at Joyce, who was looking up at her in alarm. "He doesn't frighten me. I used to wipe his bottom when he was a babe."

The canoness turned her hands upwards in her lap, as if receiving a gift.

"It will be better if you make your choice before he comes here with his shouts and threats. I see how much you long for honour, Sir Christopher. I see that you have not found it where you thought it could be found. You will find it, for it is already within you, no one need confer it."

Christopher stared at her for a moment, then closed his eyes. When he opened them, he looked chastened.

"I fear I may have besmirched not only my honour, but those of the Templars of Sergeac as well." He looked up at the ceiling. "I made the grave error of acquiring some parchments of Hermetic magic, from the court of Alphonso the Wise, directed at the planetary angels. This was foolish enough, but in our haste to leave the preceptory, they have fallen from my pack. They will be lying on the floor, waiting to be found and used as evidence that the Templars are incantators and heretics."

Illesa rose from her seat in anger, but Mother Sarah put a hand out to stop her.

"Tell me exactly what these texts contained. It is very important, whether they are of natural magic or demonology."

"I don't know. I'd only had them for a few days with no time to study them. But I know there was a magical Mercury square, from the Book of the Seven Figures of the Seven Planets, which in certain rituals could help acquire knowledge or harm an enemy." He kept his eyes on his hands as he counted off the parchments. "And there was a list of the uses and powers of stones and herbs. Details for how to use lunatica to predict the time of death. To invoke the angel of Mars, Ascymor." His voice petered out.

Mother Sarah had closed her eyes.

"The last is the most damaging. They may use it for their accusations, but these works of wisdom from the ancients are part of the soul's search for God, search for understanding of the world and the celestial heavens. Those manuscripts, the good and the evil, have left you of their own accord." She opened her eyes. "You have played your part in their travels, now you are free of them."

"And of the coin I paid for them," Christopher muttered.

Illesa gave him a stern look. Imagine buying magical spells while on pilgrimage, putting them all at risk of censure. But Ramón could be very persuasive, and Christopher was vulnerable to the promise of power.

Mother Sarah had turned her gaze on Illesa.

"And I see how much you long to return to your home. To your husband. How you try through your own effort to make everything better. Your soul is tired of its travels and toil. It has been to the gates of Hell and all around the world, slipping the grip of Death. Let God do his work now.

"And you, most beautiful Joyce, I see how much you long for company, for mutual affection, for things to do that stretch your mind. How much there is to explore in this fallen world. You walk on the rim – between not enough and too much."

Her arms fell down to her sides. She closed her eyes.

"God blesses me with visions," she muttered.

They watched her in stunned silence. Her eyes opened and she smiled at them.

"Now you know God sees your inner minds, knows your desires and still loves you. Choose your way. Both are in his gift."

Illesa looked at her staring children, then at the canoness, calmly waiting.

"Will you care for Sir John as long as he is here?" Illesa asked. "Will you tell him the full circumstances of our decision? He saved us from being arrested –" She stopped and took a deep breath. "It feels cowardly to leave him!"

"If you go, he only has himself and his duty to his Order and God to worry about, not his obligation to you. If he remembers it. Cold water often wipes away the memory."

"I thought of becoming a Templar Knight," Christopher said, looking into his empty cup. "Now I haven't even a sword to wear at my side." He glanced up, a twisted smile on his lips. "I suppose this is God's answer as to whether I should join the Order?"

"You would look silly with such a beard," Joyce said. "And you couldn't play with me any more. I'm glad you can't join now."

Christopher smiled sadly.

"You have a way of making a compliment bite."

"Your family need you more than the Knights of the Temple do," Mother Sarah said. "But your sword will be found. You may require it on the journey home." She stood up and drained her cup. "Sister Favia will go to the bees this afternoon, up the ladders to the highest terrace. If you follow her, she will show you the tunnel. It will take you to the clifftop so you don't have to climb the overhang. A broken wrist is not useful in such circumstances. You are firm in this decision?"

"No!" Joyce cried. "I want to stay. Please, Mother!" She gave Illesa her most entreating look. "I haven't seen anything yet. And these Troglodytes were drawn on the world map."

Mother Sarah pulled Joyce to stand next to her.

"Joyce, you must be sure that you listen to the voice inside you that whispers softly, when you are looking and seeing all the different paths, some wide and inviting, some narrow and dark, and it tells you which one is the right one. That is God's voice. It isn't loud, but it speaks if we listen, a light in the darkness, a thread to follow when we are lost and afraid."

Joyce pressed her lips together, trying to keep her frustration inside.

"I want to stay longer with you, Mother Sarah."

"Maybe our paths will cross again, maybe they will weave together in a beautiful cloth one day in the future, my pretty hen." She kissed Joyce on the forehead, then turned and traced her finger in a cross incised and painted in the wall.

"May God protect and defend all those here against the spears of the Devil and the temptations of this world."

She faced them, her eyes gleaming.

"Now, let us prepare."

Sir John had fallen into a deep sleep under several layers of thick fleece blankets. They were instructed to tell the Sister what they wanted to say to him and bid him farewell without waking him.

"He will be full of health tomorrow," the cheerful nun assured them.

"Just in time to be sent to a dungeon," Christopher muttered.

Sister Helena had sharp ears.

"It may happen differently. There is much in God's plan that is mysterious, but our own stratagems might play their part."

Mother Sarah was waiting at the door, Christopher's sheathed sword in one hand.

"I must stay here to forestall the soldiers and placate the Steward. You will be safe in the hands of Sister Favia." She held the sword out to Christopher, who bowed and received it. Mother Sarah embraced Joyce and whispered something in her ear that delighted the girl.

"You'll be safe and well, pretty hen, Saint Cyricus preserve you. Don't forget us here; keep us in your prayers in your cold northern climes." She laughed, blessed them, and was gone.

To get to the upper levels of the town, they had to go through the chapel. From its tall windows, there were views over the broad, wooded valley. Then they squeezed through the workshops and past the smithy to a long thin ladder tied to stone outcrops, stretching up twenty paces or more to the next terrace.

Sister Favia led the way with a pack of equipment tied to her back. She was older than Illesa and said very little. Her wiry arms were bared to the elbow, and she climbed the ladder quick as a mountain goat. Illesa went up behind Joyce, one rung below, to steady her if needed. Christopher was last and slowest, one-armed and with a sword that kept getting caught in the rungs of the ladder.

That was not the only ladder they had to climb; the next was completely vertical, and Joyce froze half-way. She only managed it by looking up at the nun's skinny ankles for the remaining steps.

This brought them to an overgrown terrace covered in scrub. An array of skeps were lined up in the shelter of a slight overhang. The buzzing was content, not angry. Illesa looked down to the port, but the small black figures crawling around meant nothing to her. Perhaps this was how the angels felt looking down from the circle of Heaven. Clear, cold air. The urge to descend and make men understand the foolishness of those bound to earth.

"Come away from there." Sister Favia beckoned her to the safety of the cliff face. She led them to the western end where the stone floor began to break up into rubble. The nun stopped abruptly.

"Here." She pointed to a narrow cleft in the rock, behind a slight outcrop. "No one outside the town knows of this escape route. It goes to the fields above." She pointed needlessly. "You will reach a cap stone. It's not heavy." She wagged her finger at them. "Make sure no one is nearby before you emerge. It's our secret. Go south-west to Saint Cyprien, head for the tower of Saint Martin – you will see it from a distance. There you can board a boat on the Dordogne. The soldiers will not find you." She made a peremptory cross in the air and went back to her bees.

They looked at the dark, narrow passage into the cliff.

"What if it's blocked?" Joyce asked. No one made an answer.

"I'll go first," Christopher said. "I have some experience of caves and their hazards." He unbelted his scabbard and held it out in front of him. "Joyce, you follow me."

They squeezed through the gap at the entrance. The tunnel was not high enough to walk normally; they had to bend almost double in parts. Christopher cursed freely as he became snagged on protruding rocks. The light had receded behind them, and they could see almost nothing, only hear the unnaturally loud sound of their breathing, their muttered curses and prayers. Christopher was using the scabbard as a feeling stick, calling back when there were obstacles. It was airless. There was a loud singing in Illesa's ears, and her breath rasped in her tight chest.

Some space had opened between them. Illesa was going slowly, feeling the weight of the earth pressing down on her – the despair of being trapped.

"Are you well, Joyce?" she called.

"I've got soil in my eyes and my hair," Joyce complained, not far ahead. "The roof is falling on me."

The stone above them did seem to be more friable and loose.

"Maybe we are getting near."

There was a definite change in the feeling of the tunnel. They shuffled on a few more steps. The scabbard was tapping against something with a different, hollow sound.

"The tunnel ends here. The cap stone is above us," Christopher said softly. "Quiet and listen."

They waited for what seemed a long time as their breath came and went. The narrow passage was beginning to feel like a grave.

"There are goats," Joyce said finally. "I can hear them bleating."

"But will there be a goatherd?"

"I don't care, I want to get out," she said. There were tears in her voice.

"I'll open it a crack."

The sudden shaft of light blinded them all for some moments.

"I can't see anyone," Christopher said. "Help me with this stone, I can't move it away one-handed."

When they'd shifted it aside, Joyce was the first to pull herself out.

"Oh," she cried.

Christopher threw the sword up and climbed out. Illesa followed, grazing her knees against the rocks on the way. She had clambered onto a shelf of stone that gave way to a long, sloping meadow. Her children were lying on the tufty grass, framed by purple and yellow flowers, staring at the bright, cloud-strewn sky above, goats chewing curiously around them.

She put her pack on the grass and sat down next to them.

"Isn't this the most beautiful place you've ever seen?" Joyce said waving her arms at the freedom, the flying bees, the flowering meadow.

"It's just because you were trapped underground for so long," Christopher said happily.

"It is." Illesa brushed her palms over the tips of the grass. "It is. But before I die, I want to see the grass of Langley again. Can anyone see the tower of Saint Martin? We need to get there before the sun sets."

Chapter XLV

Saturday the 11th November, 1307
The Feast of Saint Martin of Tours
Langley

Light was coming in through the cracks in the shutters. Motes of dust floated in the cold air. Illesa lay, warm under the blanket, watching them rise and fall with her rapid breaths. Richard Orosius had been in her dream – riding, but not the docile jennet from Aquitaine. It was the dappled stallion from the map, with its beautiful, incised saddle and curling mane. The globe on the elaborate crupper shone. The bells on the breeching straps rang, but Richard Orosius sat immobile, eyes shut, as the horse cantered away, reins hanging loose on its flanks, towards some distant hill. She'd called after him, started to shout, and that had woken her.

There seemed no sense in his suffering, no saint who might aid his contradictions. Only his work, with its loathsome beasts and exquisite beauty, plotted in eternal time on the boundaries of earth, could explain the man.

Wherever he was, she could no longer help him.

Even if he were here, at their gate, she would not have the strength. She felt as weak as a newborn kitten. Perhaps today she would be able to stay up longer. She should check the stores of simples and salves for the winter. Mend Joyce's surcote. Put a stop to Phylis' demands – make things right with William. But the thought of it all made her shut her eyes again.

When she woke later, Richard was sitting on a chair by the bed. He bent over her.

"How is my lady? Shall I call Cecily?"

Illesa lifted her head and put her hand out to him.

"No, don't. I can't bear the fuss."

He took her hand, rubbed it and brought it to his lips.

"Very well. I won't tell her you're awake, but I warn you she has been planning a course of nourishment for you that you will not escape."

"I don't need possets, just sleep." Illesa yawned and tugged the pillow so that she could sit up a bit.

"You will have both. There is no way of stopping her. How is your leg?"

Illesa pulled aside the blanket, and Richard prodded her swollen ankle. She'd managed to injure it stepping off the ship in Bristol harbour.

"A little better," she said. Although it looked the same.

He raised his eyebrow at her.

"It needs rest, and now that I am home, it will improve." She put her hand on his arm and pulled him closer. His forehead was lined with pain and worry, but his mouth was quick and ready when she kissed him. In the end he crawled onto the bed beside her, and then she had to take off his boots.

"Cecily will knock on the door now," Illesa said. "It always happens."

He put his hand on her cheek. His thumb brushed her lips.

"Do you remember when we first loved each other? When I was newly injured and couldn't leave my bed, and you tended me – here in this chamber?" He put his lips to her ear. "My uncle would be downstairs in the hall and you would torture me with your beauty. The places you touched me." He moved down to her neck and began to kiss the line of her shoulder. "Now the shoe is on the other foot – and an injured one at that. I have waited a long time for this."

"You're a patient man," Illesa pulled his head up and held it in both hands, "but I didn't torture you for long, as far as I remember. And I was only concerned for your leg, as I hope you are for my poor ankle."

"I am concerned for all of you." He ran his hand from her neck to her knee, and she had to push him away, smiling.

Richard rolled onto his back.

"Tell me the news of the manor, husband, while we wait for night."

He turned his head to look at her.

"No disasters – and even some good fortune. Phylis has agreed to release William from the imagined engagement. I shall not discuss the cost. He's free of the threat of court and can return to worrying about the horses instead. Strange man, but I'm glad he is. I can't imagine a better constable."

A weight on her heart lifted. William would not suffer any more from her foolish attempt to marry him off. That terrible desire had passed, like smoke in the wind, and all could return to the way it had been. If the ordeal had not burnt up his trust in her.

"Good news indeed." She stroked Richard's hair. He pushed himself up on his elbow.

"We opened a new barrel of wine after we heard the decision. First time I've ever seen him weep. He thought he'd lose everything if he had to marry. Told me that ever since we took him in, he'd felt safe here. Spoke of how his family had all died, or been killed, one by one – and how Joyce reminds him of his sister. Wants nothing more than to live with us and look after the horses. It's clear he has no desire for another family."

Illesa lay back on the pillow and looked up at the ceiling. The ones who seemed strong were often the most vulnerable. Her attempt to save herself from sin had felt like a terrifying betrayal to William.

She turned to Richard and took his hand.

"We *are* his family, although we couldn't explain why to anyone else."

There was a knock on the door, and Joyce ran in before they could stop her. She saw them both in bed and came to a halt, her long grey cloak whirling around her ankles.

"What do you want, Joyce?" Richard said, sitting up.

"To see Mother! You're awake! I'll tell Cecily."

"No don't. Not yet. Come and sit down. You are dressed for outdoors. Where are you going?"

Joyce stayed where she was, fingering the toggle at her neck.

"I'm going to the mill with Alfred. The miller's wife always has news or a story, and this is the right time to catch her, after most of the women have gone."

"It gets dark very early, and the mill is further away than you think with a heavy sack," Illesa said.

Pearl came scampering into the room and fawned on Joyce's skirts.

"Take Ajax with you too," Richard said. "And don't stay long."

"I have been all the way to Rocamadour and back, pursued by soldiers. I think I can go to the watermill and return safely,"

Joyce huffed and called Pearl out of the room, not quite slamming the door.

They looked at each other, smiling.

"Another returned to her old self. As you have returned to me," Richard said, pulling her towards him.

In the end, Illesa managed to go downstairs after sext and ate a good amount of all the fortifying things Cecily had prepared. She bade Christopher farewell as he set off to visit the Templars in Enchmarsh and Cardington. Unlike her, he'd been full of purpose and vigour since their return and believed the Templars deserved to hear about the arrests from a witness. Those in the Order should have plenty of warning and time to make their plans, as the King of France would be looking for allies in his campaign against them.

William rode beside him. He and Christopher seemed closer since they'd returned, meeting in the straightforward and important matters of horses and iron.

"Come on." Richard touched her shoulder gently. "There's no point staring after him all day. I want to show you the orchard." Richard walked off across the courtyard, leaning heavily on his stick. She followed, leaning heavily on hers. The manor was quiet without Joyce and her near-constant singing. She obviously missed Ramón's tales of the road and his songs. The miller's wife would be a poor substitute.

Richard was waiting for her at the orchard gate. She should speak to him about inviting some players for the Christmas feast, to celebrate despite everything – because of everything. To make Joyce smile.

The last of the apples had been gathered and the leaves had fallen except a few on the tips of the branches. Illesa pulled her cloak tight around her. The wind was bitter. She longed to go in and warm herself by the fire. Some part of her had been spent, emptied out in the caves and roads of Aquitaine. And there was the throbbing pain in her right leg. She was dragging her body around by the sheer force of her will.

"This is the spur we should cut and graft onto that tree." He was explaining the plans he had for the improvement of their fruit stock, hoping to see enthusiasm for his ideas.

"It will be very good," Illesa said, making an effort to put a cheerful tone in her voice. "Next year we will have plenty."

"Yes, or the year after. It takes time for this method to yield the best crop." He put his hand on her shoulder. "It's something to look forward to."

"We are blessed with this land and these trees." Illesa gazed along the valley. "I will help you do it."

"You are too tired to do anything," Richard said, turning her to look at him. "I can see the exhaustion in your eyes. You look like soldiers do after a battle. Do you want me to call that woman from Pitchford to come and see to you? Cecily is far too absorbed in Joyce to notice that you need constant attention."

Illesa shook her head.

"Don't bother her. I just need sleep." And an unbidden yawn overtook her. "Don't worry. I'm like a bird after a long flight. I must put my head under my wing for a while. Let my soul catch up with my body."

He put his arm around her shoulder.

"Thank God this sparrow did not fall. Let's go inside. There are plenty of matters that require my attention there."

He opened the wicket gate, and they limped towards the hall, hand in hand.

A figure was standing by the door, holding a basket, a strange lump on its back. The thought that it was Ramón and his monkey made Illesa nearly cry out. But she recognised the woman when she turned to face them.

It was Kathryn and her daughter. They'd come for their mirror.

"My Lady! God be praised that you are safe and well! Your daughter and son too."

Illesa kissed her on both cheeks and looked under the blanket at her daughter, asleep, resting on the safe warmth of her mother's back.

"Come inside, Goodwife. Let's warm ourselves. I have your mirror."

"I'll tell Alfred to attend you and leave you to your conversation," Richard said. Not one for visitors.

Illesa led Kathryn to one of the seats by the fire, where she untied the blanket and, in an expert movement, pulled the sleeping girl off her back and around to sit on her lap. The girl opened her eyes, which were of the brightest blue under her vivid red hair. She reached up and pulled her mother's veil.

"Here we are," she murmured. "Soon you will have the blessing of the Virgin."

"I'll fetch the mirror. You've had a long wait for it."

"I was praying for you every day. You are brave to have gone so far! But you have an injury?"

Illesa shook her head.

"A silly mishap. I turned my ankle coming off the ship. It's nothing."

She hobbled into the buttery and found the mirror wrapped in cerecloth still in her pack. It had come safely through river, earth and sea and was cold in the palm of her hand. She pulled a blue silk ribbon from her veil and pushed it through the loop, tying a knot. The colour of Heaven was right for it.

When Illesa returned to the hall, there was warm spiced wine and sweet bread on the sideboard. But Kathryn's alert eyes followed Illesa and what was in her hand.

"We were there at Michaelmas, at the Feast of the Archangel. It was a powerful time to see the Virgin. She healed Joyce's tongue." Illesa placed the mirror in Kathryn's open palm.

"May the Queen of Heaven be praised," Kathryn said. She held it up to the light. Her other arm braced the girl against her chest. "Tell me what you saw there."

"The mirror has seen the image of the Black Virgin and Child, adorned in silver and gold, in the moment when she performed a miracle of healing and the great bell of the chapel pealed. I haven't opened it since. The face of the Virgin is still smiling on you. Put it round your girl's neck, close to her heart. May it give her strength."

Kathryn looked at her and nodded.

"Thank you for bringing it safely here."

Illesa pushed herself up and went to fill two cups. When she came back, Kathryn was turning the mirror case over and over in her palm.

"Do you believe it will do her good, this mirror?"

Illesa sat opposite her and put down the cups. Juliana's lips were tinged with blue. She breathed quickly, her head resting on her mother's chest. Kathryn was waiting for her answer.

"I don't know." Illesa took a sip from her cup. "I *do* know that Joyce was helped – that the Virgin in her mercy has power to save, but whether this mirror will bring her power to you –" Illesa looked down into the deep red wine. "I pray it is so."

"It might be a way of men making profit from the desperation of parents who will try anything to help their children."

Illesa met Kathryn's shrewd gaze.

"Yes, it might be. But we *will* try anything to save our children. Have faith and pray." She reached out and touched the child's soft hair. "She deserves to be helped."

Kathryn nodded. She held up the mirror by the silk ribbon and put it over her daughter's neck.

"Juliana, may this holy relic help and heal," she whispered in the child's ear.

The girl looked down at the dull copper lozenge, picked it up in both hands and clicked it open.

Illesa reached forward to stop her, but it was too late. The child was gazing at her reflection, pointing to it, and looking up at her mother.

Tears fell from Kathryn's eyes.

"Mother of God," she whispered. The child closed the mirror case, turned it over and opened it again. "In any event, it makes much amusement," Kathryn said, half-sob half-laugh.

"May it do her good. I prayed for her at each shrine along the way."

"I thank you, lady. I've begun moving her legs and using the salve in the way you suggested. She seems a little better." She wiped her wet cheeks with the palm of her hand. "There is much to be thankful for." She wiped them again, as the tears kept welling and falling.

"The Virgin understands our ordeals. I know she does. But I am tired of this fallen world," Illesa said, looking down at her swollen hands.

Kathryn sniffed and took a deep breath.

"Yes. Too much suffering. Sometimes I wish I could have been there at the beginning." She ran the blue ribbon between her fingers. "If I'd been consulted about the Garden of Eden, there would have been fewer tempting, yet fatal, fruit trees planted. But our lives are gifts. We must accept them and be grateful."

Kathryn glanced at Illesa out of the corner of her eye, to see if she was shocked. There was a moment of silence between them, filled with the distant bleating of sheep in the winter fold.

"Why create the serpent at all?" Illesa whispered.

Kathryn looked down at Juliana. The child was holding the mirror to her cheek, crooning softly.

"I can't believe she is sinful, no matter what the priest says. She has no whit of malice, yet she has to suffer so much."

Illesa reached forward and took Kathryn's hand.

"I will prepare a syrup that might help. Come back with her soon. I'd like to talk about these things with you again."

Chapter XLVI

Saturday the 25th November, 1307
Toledo
Castile

I'm an old man now, at not yet forty years. The road, the thieves, the lice, the dogs and wolves have aged me. I can see my reflection in the river, in this still pool under the trees by the bridge. There is no point in trying to smooth my hair or wipe the dust from my face. It is wild and ingrained. Inside the city, I will have my answer. I've been pushed on from place to place while people shouted 'None of that sort here. They wouldn't dare settle here. They aren't welcome here. Why do you want to know?'

Tarragona, Tortosa – no sign. Just the bright blue sea, the sun that burnt my eyes, the earth so dry it sticks in the lungs. More bare stone mountains and scrub. But here – this city, these towers will be the end. Whether or not she is here, I will go no further. I have seen enough. Enough to know how little I grasped of this terrible earth, this vast creation. I should never have dared to compass it, as if I were some angel that could see its extent or plumb its depths. Orosius! I'm a mere flea on his dog.

Look here, by this river, there is a modest plant bending in the wind, its leaves small and yet perfectly beautiful, one after another. Below it an ant goes about, looking for food, and above me a bird waits for me to leave so it can land and take the ant in its beak. Are not these the proper subjects of an artist and a scribe? The things that follow the paths laid out for them by the Lord of all Creation? And did I in my madness think I could map all of it when each pace, each length of a foot or a finger contains multitudes of beings, all getting and begetting. Even this river is the Tagus not the Ebro. In this way I have always been misled.

One more sluice of my feet, and I will try the city gate. They may not question my papers, may believe that I am still on my way to the Pope – that a strong subsolanus wind blowing from

319

behind the Garden of Eden has pushed me far off course. My wanderings will cease here if she accepts me or not. The river is deep enough.

Look at my swollen feet and tell me I have not suffered for my love. But I may disgust her, and her father may stand, as before, with the flaming sword at the gates of Paradise, to eject me from her presence. Surely the old man is dead by now. God, let there be no other man standing in my way.

The guard has believed my tale, and, even more, he has believed the silver of my last coin. I need only follow the city wall to find the Jewish Quarter, and then only find one Jew on the street who understands Latin or French.

The people are like a nest of wasps, buzzing in their strange, slurring language. And there, in black, wearing a pointed Jewish hat, is a man who might know. He is on the other side of the market, walking past the stench of the tannery, down the shaded alleys, under the arches. He knows I am following him, stops by an ornate doorway of a house of worship, fear in his eyes. Pride too. He is a learned Jew.

Perhaps he was frightened by the desperation in my face. He shook his head as if he didn't understand, and I was about to grab his gown, but I remembered in time. If I do that, I will be arrested again, beaten and thrown out of the city. I begged instead. I begged him to tell me where she lived.

And now I'm outside the closed door. If Chera lives inside there is no sign of her on the wood, the paint or the brass of its decoration. There is nothing that reminds me of her first home in Lincoln – sombre grey stone, the dark rooms where we first touched.

I am knocking on this door and all the doors I have ever passed. This door is all the doors of the world. Let me in and embrace me, let me find home.

The door has opened; the smell of bread and cardamom greets me – and a young boy of ten years. He is not impressed by what he sees. So I say her name, and he shuts the door.

I am waiting here, counting in my head, the way I used to count the doors to her house on the hill. When I have reached twenty-four the door opens again. An old woman stands there, a black veil over her head, dark eyes staring at me. She looks even older than I am. Her eyes are more full of tears. Her hands are strands of rope. Her feet are invisible in a pair of woven slippers. Her throat makes a sound that might be my name.

Is it Chera or her mother, widowed and old? She holds the door open, and I enter.

Chapter XLVII

Saturday the 28th December, 1307
Feast of the Holy Innocents
Acton Burnel
Nones

In the fleece-lined bag on my back, little Genet is warm enough. There are two layers to protect her, because I have also given her my blanket, and no doubt she has pissed on it. There is enough air for her, because I have not tightened the cord at the top too much. I can hear her calling me when she wakes up, and I tell her, it isn't far, no está lejos. But I know it is. A few miles, over the hill, through the wood, and if I don't hurry the dark will overtake me.

And they won't let me in.

They will let me in.

My legs will go a little further. It has not snowed, and that is something to be grateful for, because my feet are colder than they were in Scotland. My hands have no feeling. But Genet still calls; she is still alive and well. This is the top of the hill. This is surely the right track, and now the moon has come up.

I cannot see the manor, but it is there in the valley. And it will surely be there when I find my way through the wood into the field. Was that a flash of fire on the edge of the wood? My eyes are willing it to be. No, it was my desperation, wanting fire. Conjuring it. But here is the field gate. The sheep are in their fold elsewhere, huddled and warm together. The land is as empty as the vast sea.

Perhaps they are not at home for the Feast of the Nativity. They may have gone to another lord's manor. It is common. Even so I will find a barn, somewhere out of the wind, and give Genet the last of the dried figs, broken into tiny pieces, and she will take them in her small adept hands and stare at me, telling me that I am certainly still here when I might not have been.

I must not think of the many times my life might have been snuffed out before I was even as high as my knee. It will not happen now, cold as I am. I won't let myself die today when there is Genet to care for.

There are the rooftops of the hall. I can smell smoke, and what joy it brings. The fire is lit in the kitchen, and there may be meat on the spit. Wood and meat, I need the warmth of both.

The drawbridge is up. The moat is frozen. If they don't hear me I might risk sliding across, but perhaps the ice is not thick enough, and to drown Genet when she is so young is not right. I am her father and mother now.

Let me shout a little louder. Someone will hear and come. My voice is hoarse with cold.

Let me sing instead, it will keep me warm as I wait for someone to leave the hall and hear me, here in the dark.

Let me try another song, one of the lullabies my mother sang before they took me from her.

Someone is there in the yard. They are coming to see who I am.

It is Christopher, my friend, and William, my once enemy.

They are lowering the bridge.

I have to take Genet off my back before Christopher embraces me. I am shaking with cold. It is bright in the courtyard now; the door to the hall is open, and Christopher is leading me inside, putting me by the fire. Joyce is kissing me. Illesa and Richard are staring at me as if I am the angel Gabriel.

Illesa covers me with a blanket, she wipes something off my cheek and puts her hand to my forehead. Cecily has brought some wine and bread. Joyce is staring at the bag.

My hands are still shaking, but I untie the top and let Genet run out.

She sits on my shoulder and screams at them all.

And they begin to laugh.

Notes

The Mappa Mundi – or Cloth of the World – owned by Hereford Cathedral is estimated to have been created somewhere between 1290 and 1310. The master mapmaker left an inscription on the map: 'All those who possess this work – or hear, read or see it – pray to Jesus in his godhead to have pity on Richard of Haldingham or of Sleaford who made it and set it out, that he may be granted bliss in heaven.'

This Richard was evidently from Lincolnshire but the map was made in Hereford, as the discovery of its original wooden backboard and frame shows, through its central compass point and tree-ring analysis. On the bottom right of the map, a young man on a richly ornamented horse rides away from the world. Looking back, he takes a bearing down the angle of his hand. Nearby is the text: 'Description of the World by Orosius.'

Paulus Orosius was a contemporary of Saint Augustine of Hippo, born circa AD385. He was from a wealthy family on the Iberian peninsula and still quite young when he was commissioned by Augustine to write his *Seven Books of History against the Pagans,* which includes a description of the main parts of the world as understood at the time. His work was extremely popular in the medieval period and was used in the design of maps. Although I have yet to come across any other scholarship that attributes the figure on horseback to Orosius, through my research I have become convinced that this is the most likely identity of the mysterious figure. The dappled horse may indicate an Andalusian bloodline, and its trappings are rich – appropriate for a well-born man. Orosius likens himself to Augustine's obedient dog in the introduction to the History, and Augustine describes Orosius as a 'hound of the Lord'. On the map, near the horseman there is a huntsman accompanied by dogs and text in French *passe avant* – which can be translated as go forward, go ahead, or go beyond. (It was also used as a horse's name in medieval times.) It seems to me that the mapmaker has illustrated Orosius beginning his commission by Augustine in this section of the border. He may also have used this image to conflate his own task with that of Orosius. It may

325

even have been a self-portrait. I have taken these few facts and conjectures and constructed the character of the mapmaker in this novel.

Medieval Lincoln had a considerable and prosperous Jewish population, until they were accused of the murder of a young boy, Little Saint Hugh of Lincoln, and the blood libel caused the community to both shrink and retreat. Henry III intervened which led to the incarceration of over seventy Jews in the Tower of London. Several converted to Christianity to avoid death (rabbis allowed conversion if lives were at risk), but eighteen were hanged. Henry III benefitted from their deaths as he was entitled to their expropriated property. Many converts ended up in the *Domus Conversorum* in London, a community of converts, but few successfully integrated into Christian society due to continuing intolerance and prejudice. Little Hugh was never canonised, and Lincoln Cathedral now displays a detailed explanation of the prejudice and injustice surrounding the establishment of his cult. Jewish communities in England were forced to listen to Dominican sermons on the necessity of conversion. Royal officials were entitled to use any force necessary to ensure they attended.

Edward I expelled all of the Jews from England in 1290, except converts, in order to confiscate their property. They were subsequently also expelled from Aquitaine and France, leading to many ending up in Castile, particularly Toledo, which had a reputation for religious cooperation since the time of Alphonso X the Wise (1221-1284). Alphonso chose to explore rather than destroy the learning of people of other faiths and encouraged translation of academic texts, including what we would now consider magical and astrological texts. It is interesting to note that after the expulsion of the Jews from England, William Burnel, provost of Wells and nephew of Chancellor and Bishop Robert Burnel, was granted all the Jewish property in Oxford by the King, including the synagogue. With the money, he built a University assembly hall (aula), and at his death left all his property to Balliol College.

At Whitsuntide of 1306, 267 men were knighted at Westminster Abbey, including the then Prince of Wales, having spent the previous night supposedly solemnly preparing in the New Temple church. In fact with trumpet blasts and shouting, there seems to have been a party atmosphere. The crowd in Westminster Abbey for the knighting ceremony was so large that war horses were brought in to disperse it, and at least two people died in the crush. Roger Mortimer of Chirk, who appeared in *The Errant Hours*, was finally knighted at the considerable age of fifty. He was well known as a lecherous and violent man. Also knighted that day were Piers Gaveston and Hugh Despenser, who would both have disastrous influence on the reign of Edward II.

During the feast afterwards Edward I swore on two gilded swans (it is not said if they were alive) to avenge the murder of John Comyn, Lord of Badenoch, by Robert Bruce, which had occurred in February 1306. The new knights were also sworn to retake Scotland. 'The Feast of the Swans' took place in Westminster Hall and it was said that Edward I hired eighty minstrels to entertain the guests, including 'Reginald the Liar' and 'Matilda Makejoy', a famous acrobat. Just over a year later, on the 7th July, 1307, Edward I died in Burgh By Sands, suffering from dysentery as he continued his determined quest to defeat Comyn and regain control of Scotland. He was buried in Westminster Abbey on the 27th October, 1307.

The silver ring worn by Reginald the Liar is based on actual medieval amulet rings, some of which can be found in the British Museum, inscribed with the names of the Magi/Three Wise Men and the enigmatic magical word, *ananyzapata* or *ananyzapta*.

Much has been written and invented about the Knights Templar, and for those interested in knowing more, there are several good historical accounts listed in **Selected Resources**. What is clear is that this very wealthy and powerful military order was targeted by King Philip IV of France, who was in dire financial straits and wanted to confiscate their property. On Friday the 13th October, 1307, officers of the King, acting on orders received previously, swept down simultaneously on all the Templar communities, arresting the knights, sergeants and servants. The accusations levelled against the Templars, including worshipping idols, denying Christ, and unnatural sexual relations, had been used against other groups, and other rulers, including Pope Boniface VIII, in the past. Because they were accused of sacrilege and heresy, their Papal protection was no longer valid. They were tortured, and some confessed as a result. The trial documents still exist. In one of these accounts, John of Primey, a knight from Chartres, is mentioned. He had only joined the Order five months before the arrest of the Templars. When asked to defend the Order in court, he instead requested permission to leave the Order. I was unable to discover what happened to him.

Labyrinths fascinated medieval architects and scribes. As well as their quality and purpose of disorientation (e.g. the original Cretan labyrinth made by Daedalus to house the Minotaur) many labyrinths were used as a physical representation of a spiritual journey. The labyrinth in the nave of Chartres Cathedral is one such. Worshippers would make the journey through its coils and turns, coming eventually to the middle, which, in the past, displayed a bronze plaque representing Theseus and the Minotaur. It is not possible to become lost in this labyrinth, rather it seems to represent the journey of a soul through adversity on an invisible divine path – intentionally losing oneself to achieve a spiritual goal. Anyone with an interest in architectural use of labyrinths should read the fascinating work of John James in *The Traveller's Key to Medieval France*, listed in **Selected Resources**.

Rocamadour is an extraordinary shrine, home of the Black Virgin statue, the age of which has not been determined with any certainty. A bell still hangs from the roof of the Chapel of the Virgin, and the records show the occasions when it has rung and what miracles at sea it announced. As well as the sacred space, Rocamadour is also home to one of many 'Swords of Roland'. The huge wooden chest in the shrine's courtyard and the sword were said to have been used in fertility rites in medieval times. Starting from the lower town, worshippers were encouraged to mount the 216 steps on their knees, rising up towards the sanctuary.

The troglodytic settlement of La Roque Saint-Christophe was inhabited for thousands of years and is open to the public. One can see a reconstructed pulley as well as the remains of the cliff dwellings above the Vézère River.

The borders of the medieval kingdoms of the Iberian peninsula changed frequently. In the late 13th century when Ramón was born, Cartagena on the south coast (now in the Murcia region) was in the Kingdom of Castile.

The distinction was not always made between apes and monkeys in medieval times, so each might equally be called by either name. They were taken from their mothers to be turned into pets, as, sadly, still happens all too often today. The monkey 'Mullida' was based on the Sykes' monkey. Their range is from Ethiopia to South Africa. I was influenced by the work of the Liberia Chimpanzee Rescue whilst plotting this book. They care and advocate for orphaned and rescued young chimpanzees. Many thanks to my dear friend, Kathryn, who made a donation to this charity to be included as a character in this book.

Text References

The Dedication quote is from *The Farthest Shore* (1972) the third book in 'The Earthsea Trilogy' by Ursula K. LeGuin

The Epigraph is from 'The Tale of Ariadne' from *The Legend of Good Women* – Geoffrey Chaucer
This translation by A.S. Kline is quoted with kind permission of *Poetry in Translation*,
https://www.poetryintranslation.com/PITBR/English/Good Women

In Chapter I – the extract is Psalm 61: 1-2, 4-8

In Chapters IV and XXVI the songs are adapted from translations of medieval songs found in the British Library manuscript of the Harley Lyrics translated by Brian Stone in *Medieval English Verse*, 1964, Penguin Books – permission sought.

In Chapter XVIII the extracts from the Bestiary are reprinted by permission of Boydell & Brewer Ltd from *Bestiary*, Richard Barber, Boydell Press, 1992, 9780851153292 pp.47-49

Glossary

alms – charity for the poor

ananyzapata – a charm of disputed meaning 'Cursed be the devil by the baptism of Saint John' or 'May the antidote of Jesus avert death by poisoning and the Holy Spirit sanctify my food and drink'

Aquitaine – the Duchy of Gascony, including the further region of Dordogne held by the King of England as a vassal of the King of France 1152–1453

Armarius – keeper of a monastic library – provider of inks and parchments to scribes

Bailiff – justice officer under the Sheriff who would collect rents

breeching straps – straps around the haunches of a draft or riding animal to aid in braking

cantor – leader of chants in a choir

cappa clausa – a closed cape, usually black, worn by the medieval clergy

carole – secular medieval circle dance

cerecloth – cloth coated in wax

chrismatory – a receptacle for the oil used in church ceremonies

citole – a stringed musical instrument similar to the medieval fiddle

clarea water – spiced, honeyed water

coif – a close-fitting cap that covers the top, back and sides of the head

constable – the senior officer in a stable – later referring to the chief officer of a royal household

crumphorn – a capped reed instrument – similar in construction to the chanter of a bagpipe

crupper – piece of tack for horses and other equids to keep a saddle, harness or other equipment from sliding forward. Usually attached around the tail

crwth – bowed Welsh lyre, about the size of a violin

demesne – manorial land retained for the private use of a feudal lord

dorter – the dormitory in a monastery

ewer – jug, usually of metal

fabulatori – Italian word for court storytellers/actors

frumenty – porridge made of wheat or barley, savoury or sweet, cooked in milk, sometimes with dried fruit and spices added

gambeson – tunic of heavy cloth or hardened leather worn as protection

Gascony – Duchy including the area south of Bordeaux, bordered by the Atlantic ocean to the west, the Pyrenees to the south, and the Garonne river to the north and east

Hermetic – a philosophical system primarily based on the purported teaching of Hermes Trismegistus – a legendary Hellenistic combination of Greek god, Hermes, and the Egyptian god, Thoth

hose – tight-fitting clothing for the lower body, usually worn by men

jennet – Spanish horse, bred to be small, calm and agile

jerkin – overjacket

joculator – a showman or a joker who performed at court

jongleur – courtly singer/entertainer

kirtle – woman's loose gown

Lazar house – place to quarantine people with leprosy managed by the Lazarite Order of monks

lunatica – medieval Latin name for the annual herb Honesty – *Lunaria annua* meaning moon-shaped

maleficium – a magical act intended to cause harm

maslin – bread made from mix of rye and wheat

mither – to make an unnecessary fuss, to bother or irritate

nones – referring to the part of the month rather than the hour: 5th of June in the Roman Calendar

Outremer – overseas – usually referring to the Holy Land in the time of the Crusades

palfrey – small horse, often used by women

paternoster beads – rosary

Poor Clares – Order of Poor Ladies – founded by Saints Clare of Assisi and Francis of Assisi in 1212. The second branch of the Franciscan order to be established

pottage – stew usually of vegetables, sometimes mixed with grain

prie-dieu – literally 'pray god', a stand for a book which has a ledge for kneeling for private devotions

rouncey – good riding horse/charger for men-at-arms in battle

scrip – a satchel or pack carried by pilgrims

Sheriff – chief officer in a shire. Responsible for investigating allegations of crime and trying minor offences

shrive/shriven – forgive/forgiven

simples – herbal remedies made of one ingredient

solar – private chamber, often an upper room designed to catch the sun

squire – a young man, usually noble, training for knighthood

subsolanus wind – lying beneath the sun i.e. the east wind

supertunic – tunic worn over other clothing

surcote – sleeved or sleeveless outer garment worn by men and women – sometimes made of rich materials

testimonial – documents from the clergy giving a pilgrim leave to travel

thwart – bench seat across width of an open boat

triforium – a gallery or arcade above the arches of the nave, choir and transepts of a church

veil/wimple – headdress worn by women from the 12th to the 14th century

villein – peasant occupying land subject to a lord

weeds – garments or clothing

woodwose – a wild man of the woods in Medieval legend

Acknowledgements

My gratitude to:

Sarah Lamsdale – who pointed me in the right direction and provided a map.

Sarah Arrowsmith – formerly the Education Officer at Hereford Cathedral, for her generous assistance in understanding the scholarship and history of the Mappa Mundi.

Ann Mason – without whom I would be embarrassed to share my writing. Thank you for the time and insight you lavished on a very imperfect typescript

James Wade – a very amiable and talented mapmaker! https://www.stclairwade.com

Mike Ashton of MA Creative – for his innovative and eye-catching cover design

Alison Lester, Ted Eames, Sarah Ibberson, Karen Robinson and Honor Bleackley – for reading and responding with insight and generosity to an early draft

Manda Scott, Karen Maitland and Henrietta Leyser – for their continuing support of my work

Susan, Dinah, Stanton, Roz and Anna – Indie bookshop heroes

Jonathan Davidson, the Writing West Midlands Team and all my friends in the Room 204 Writers Development Programme.

The Gladstone Library whose collection of esoteric lore informed the pilgrimage to the shrine of Rocamadour.

All those who share their research freely on line.

Carrie Bennett, Claire Coventry, Susie Stapleton, Lucy Armstrong-Blair, Christine Jolly, Anne Marie Lagram, Sebastién & Virginie Slisse, Ruthie Starling, Kathryn Weaver, Rachel Freeth, Debs Jackson, Rae Binning, Lou and Dave Bleackley, Bob and Bonnie Havery, Peter Reavill, Stuart Davies, Liz Hyder, Liz Lefroy, Deborah Alma, Kate and Phil Smith, Katriona Wade, Heather and Mike Streetly, Catherine and Stephen Nelson – for their support and enthusiasm.

My family – old, young and in between – I am grateful for all you've taught me, and all your love, care and support for my eccentric projects.

Michael – for your love and all the ways you show it.

Selected Resources

A Dictionary of Medieval Terms & Phrases, Christopher Corèdon with Ann Williams, 2004, D.S Brewer

Bestiary, Richard Barber, 1992, The Boydell Press

Edward I, Michael Prestwich, 1988, Methuen

Edward II – The Unconventional King, Kathryn Warner, 2014, Amberley

Everyday Life in Medieval Shrewsbury, Dorothy Cromarty, 1991, Shropshire Books

Exploring Lincoln Cathedral, Joy Richardson, 2003, Lincoln Cathedral

Gesture in Medieval Drama and Art, Clifford Davidson (ed.), 2001, Board of the Medieval Institute

Guide du Bordeaux médiéval, Annick Bruder, 2005, Éditions Sud-Ouest

Hereford Cathedral, The Very Reverend Michael Tavinor, Hereford Cathedral

Kingdom, Power and Glory, a Historical Guide to Westminster Abbey, John Field, 1996, James & James Ltd

La Roque St Christophe – fort & cité troglodytiques, Vidal, Brunet and Roussot Larroque, Editions La Roque Saint-Christophe

Ledbury – A Medieval Borough, Joe Hillaby, 2005, Logaston Press

Leper Knights, David Marcombe, 2003, The Boydell Press

Life in a Medieval Village, Frances and Joseph Gies, 1990, Harper Perennial

Mappa Mundi – Hereford's Curious Map, Sarah Arrowsmith, 2015, Logaston Press

Mazes and Labyrinths in Great Britain, John Martineau, 1996, Wooden Books Ltd

Medieval Comic Tales, Derek Brewer, 2008, Boydell & Brewer Ltd

Medieval English Verse, Brian Stone, 1964, Penguin Books

Medieval Pets, Kathleen Walker-Meikle, 2012, The Boydell Press

Medieval Tales and Stories, Stanley Applebaum (ed.), 2000, Dover Publications

Medieval Women, Henrietta Leyser, 1995, Phoenix

Orosius – Seven Books of History against the Pagans, A.T. Fear, 2010, Liverpool University Press

Pilgrimage in Medieval England, Diana Webb, 2000, Hambledon and London

Red Thread – on Mazes & Labyrinths, Charlotte Higgins, 2018, Jonathan Cape

Robert Grosseteste – Bishop of Lincoln, 1235 – 1253, Rev. James McEvoy, 2003, Lincoln Cathedral Publications

Rocamadour – Great Pilgrimage Centre, Didier Poux, 2006, APA-POUX Editions

St Thomas of Hereford, Gabriel Alington, 2001, Gracewing

Saints and their Badges, Michael Lewis and Greg Payne, 2014, Greenlight Publishing

The Great Crown Jewels Robbery of 1303, Paul Doherty, 2005, Carroll and Graf

The Greatest Traitor, Ian Mortimer, 2003, Pimlico

The Hanged Man, Robert Bartlett, 2004, Princeton University Press

The Hereford Mappa Mundi, Gabriel Alington,1996, Gracewing

The Heroides of Ovid, Harold Isbell, 1990, Penguin Classics

The Knights Templar, Helen Nicholson, 2001, Running Press

The Knights Templar in Britain, Evelyn Lord, 2002, Pearson Education Ltd

The Medieval Traveller, Norbert Ohler, 1989, The Boydell Press

The Pilgrimage to Compostella in the Middle Ages, Maryjane Dunn and Linda Kay Davidson (eds.), 1996, Routledge

The Temple Church – A History in Pictures, Robin Griffith-Jones, 2011, Pitkin Publishing

The Thirteenth Century, Sir Maurice Powicke, 1962, Oxford University Press

Thomas de Cantilupe – 700 Years a Saint, Michael Tavinor and Ian Bass, 2020, Logaston Press
The Time Traveller's Guide to Medieval England, Ian Mortimer, 2009, Vintage
The Traveller's Key to Medieval France, John James, 1987, Harrap Columbus
The Trial of the Templars (2nd ed.), Malcolm Barber, 2006, Cambridge University Press

1284 AD – The uprising in Wales is over, the leader gruesomely executed, but for Illesa Arrowsmith the war's aftermath is just as brutal. When her brother is thrown into prison on false charges, she is left impoverished and alone. All Illesa has is the secret manuscript entrusted to her – a book so powerful it can save lives, a book so valuable that its discovery could lead to her death.

When the bailiff's daughter finds it, Illesa decides to run – and break her brother out of jail by whatever means. But the powerful Lord Forester tracks them down, and Illesa must put herself and the book at the mercy of an unscrupulous knight who threatens to reveal all their secrets, one by one.

Inspired by the seductive art of illuminated manuscripts, *The Errant Hours* draws from the deep well of medieval legend to weave a story of survival and courage, trickery and love.

All the Winding World - Arrowsmith Trilogy Book Two

1294 AD – Sir Richard Burnel has been forcibly recruited to lead a division into France to regain control of the Duchy of Gascony. But his commanders prove to be incompetent, and Richard is taken hostage along with many of King Edward's most trusted knights.

Meanwhile, in the Welsh Marches, resentment boils over into rebellion against crippling taxes and conscription. Lady Illesa Burnel, determined to protect her family and home, must find an ingenious way to free her husband, before Fortune's Wheel tips them all into death and ruin.

Set during the disastrous Anglo-French War, one of Edward I's rare military defeats, this gripping sequel to *The Errant Hours* interweaves old and new characters in a moving tale of the savagery of war, the insistence of love, and the power of illusion.